APPLESAUCE
AND
MOONBEAMS

Carol A. Strickland

Other novels by Carol A. Strickland

Burgundy and Lies, a sweet historical romance

Touch of Danger, vol. 1 of the Three Worlds superhero saga

Lost in the Stars, vol. 2 of the Three Worlds saga

Stalemate, vol. 3 of the Three Worlds saga

Worlds Apart, vol. 4 of the Three Worlds saga

Nothing Personal, wacky soft sci fi

www.CarolAStrickland.com

Book Layout © 2017 BookDesignTemplates.com
Front cover illustration by Chris Jay.

Applesauce and Moonbeams / Carol A. Strickland -- 1st ed.
Ebook ISBN 978-1-941318-07-2
Print ISBN 978-1-941318-09-6
IngramSpark ebook ISBN 978-1-941318-29-4
IngramSpark print ISBN 978-1-941318-35-5

With thanks…

…To my crit partners from waaay back, who checked an early (like 2009) draft of this: Tish Shaffer and Marcia Collette

…To David M. Williamson, who beta read the almost-final first edition.

…To Sarra Cannon, for convincing me that manuscripts that are too niche-y for publishers deserve their chance to find that niche-y audience. Niches rule!

…To Robert Heinlein (despite everything that has come out about him. Sigh.) and his harsh mistress, the latter of which I grew up with and loved.

…To my beloved herd (RIP), who taught me about the alternate dimension that is Cat World. Jonathan may be based on an amalgam of Morgan, Obi and Bran-Bran, but they all had paws in Jonny's creation.

…To Tang, the drink of the astronauts! (Btw, Tang is a registered trademark of Kraft Foods. Grandma Tang has great respect for Kraft's lawyers.)

1

No other site in this world could rival Sin City's seductions. Along the Strip, evening disguised itself as a false dawn. Ribbons of colorful LED and neo-neon hellfire directed the eye this way and that, inviting ordinary tourists to indulge in extraordinary debauchery. Gambling? That was the merest tip of Perdition's iceberg.

David Lumen couldn't hide his delight in watching the city's visitors hurry to their doom. Even in this new century, Vegas still advertised that what happened here stayed here. Whatever flashy personas tourists chose to adopt they could leave behind when they returned to their normal lives.

But David knew that was a lie.

He could pick out the ones who were ending their stay. With their inhibitions still loosed, they headed back to the ordered lives that society required. For many of them that reentry could turn into frustration or rebellion.

What a heaven-sent opportunity for healing breakthroughs!

"My card," he offered one man. "I can help." The man paused to read it and then nodded, offering his wrist and its info-band. David tapped it with his card, bowed his head in thanks, and moved on.

It was an unorthodox way of getting patients. David abhorred the unorthodox, but he had an unorthodox talent. In his life he allowed this one exception to conformity. The ends justified the means.

Dr. David Lumen, psychotherapist, his card read. *Licensed telepath. Helping you fit comfortably into your world.*

Out here in the crowd he could catch the ones who might otherwise slip off to wither away their lives, not knowing that another path was available to lead them to suitable contentment.

"I can help," he told another, and another info-band registered his name.

Far beyond the fakery and razzle-dazzle, the gibbous disk of Luna hovered halfway above the horizon. In a time before West Coast smog had spread in earnest to this desert city, perhaps its glow had matched that of Vegas. Now it hung muted behind a thick, sour curtain of dusty red. Still, David found it comforting to see the familiar face in the sky.

He squinted to make sure it was unchanged. Someone was building one of those Lunar complexes up there, up on the Man in the Moon's left cheek. Of course the law forbad marring the side of Luna that forever faced Earth. The might-have-been mole on the Man's face was neatly camouflaged, hidden even from a low-power telescope.

Luna was David's private joke. Humanity needed its heavens pristine and beautiful. To fulfill that purpose, Luna hid its true self like everyone else. Even the Man in the Moon had to conform to the Fashion Police's rules.

A crowd of young rowdies with alcohol breaths hustled by him on the way to an inhibition-free night. David smiled at them. They were still so malleable. In his heart of hearts he fancied himself a sculptor. He could form well-adjusted adults out of them.

Two Fashion Police officers in full, sequined Vegas display patrolled on foot just ahead. The drunks paused to video the spectacular duo. Both women were top-make Oughts: willow-slender builds with faces (and other features) cosmetically enhanced. They looked alike enough to be twins. The air-filtered warmth of the walkways had the FeePs in minimal uniform– and Vegas "minimal" was very minimal indeed. They wore their identification pins as necklace pendants.

Having Oughts on fashion duty was a spark of city marketing genius. They contrasted so well to all the voluptuous Sixty-makes who were usually employed in the Strip's entertainment venues. When more tourists gathered to admire, one of the FeePs wrote up a drooling teenager for having an untreated zit. The kid didn't seem to mind his ticket. He continued to grin stupidly at the pastied officer even as she turned away.

David couldn't blame him. The FeePs looked spectacular coming and going. Beauty might be only scalpel-deep, but they'd obviously benefited from some truly fine modern medicine.

One tipped her brimmed hat to David. "Evening, Dr. Lumen."

"Evening, Officer Dora," he returned, then nodded to the other. "Officer Elise. You're both on top of your form tonight. Officer Dora, the surgery looks great."

She pirouetted for him and he tried not to ogle. After all, he was a professional. He had an image to maintain, despite what his instincts told him to do.

"Doesn't it? I'm a perfect Ought now. Applied for my perfection pin this morning. Thanks for the recommendation, Doc."

"Dr. Haggerty's method of shaving bones is legendary. Glad I could help. But that wouldn't have gotten you perfection if you hadn't–"

Dora grinned at him. "Focused on my goals," she said, parroting her mantra. "Diet, exercise and resolve."

"That's the ticket."

Dora wiggled her now-svelte butt at him. "I not only fit into my world, but into size double-zero über-fashion. I'm recommending you to all my friends."

David laughed. "Then I'll have to see about giving you a cut of my business, won't I?" He shook his head at the FeePs. "You two should be on Vegas's advertising. Magnificent!"

They beamed at the compliment and continued on their way, scanning the crowds to maintain beauty and conformity.

David had nothing to fear from their judgment. He might be an ordinary mid-make Thirty, neither burly nor skinny, but he was a conscientious one. He kept his outrageous red hair muted under brown dye and owned this season's complete line of Jakob Gallindor superior-grade suits. Not the perfection-grade, of course. He purposefully positioned himself only in the upper-eightieth percentile of the population when it came to fashion.

Sure, he could have hit mid- or even upper nineties if he'd wanted. He could afford the surgeries to up his make as well, but being more impressive might intimidate his patients. He'd splurged on a top-line chin implant when he was sixteen. Before that he'd had only a trainer chin to disguise his weak real one. A few nips and tucks beside that were all he had needed to produce a pleasant but average appearance for his inborn body type: a mid-make.

David passed a woman whose shoulders hunched ever so slightly, which caused her chest to concave. The posture unflatteringly exaggerated her pear-shaped Eighty body make. She never looked up to meet another human being in the face. Body language told him she was protecting her core being, and her thoughts skittered scared in typical victim mode. David didn't search deeper; people deserved their privacy. Instead he pressed a hard copy of his business card into her hand and then continued on his way.

Her thoughts broadcast her rebellion at the thought of therapy. Of course she'd react that way. Many did at first. But as David continued his brisk walk toward his office building, he felt confident that she'd be calling for an appointment within the next few days. Excellent!

The warm flush of success snapped cold as that *something* brushed him again. In the warm Vegas night it felt as if someone swept an arctic fan across him, just enough to bring every hair on his skin to shocked awareness. Then it was gone.

Twice this week he'd felt that icy darkness, a sharp taste in his mind. It was so quick he would normally have dismissed it as a wild thought from the crowd, but this third time was too often to be random.

Was this someone new to the neighborhood? Las Vegas still thrived on thrill-seeking tourists, but its permanent population grew faster than most cities in North America. The city drew all types. Baser personalities in particular seemed to target the area as they responded to the historic Vegas reputation.

He threw up a simple thought-deflection shield to protect himself from another intrusion. If it happened again, he'd try to pinpoint it so he could report the culprit. Rogue telepaths could be dangerous.

When David arrived at his office building he waited patiently for one for the public vanity stations in the lobby. Mustn't run the chance of a client seeing him in slight disarray from the street. They must always know that David was in control of his world.

Everyone should fit into their role in society as well as he. How glad he was to have the skills and abilities to accomplish what he loved most: helping people. If he swaggered as he walked because of his accomplishments, it was only just enough to let people see his self-confidence so they might emulate it.

The work he did upstairs literally saved lives. He taught his clients how to live with society's rules. As the cosmetic surgeons shaped them physically, he shaped them psychically, blunting their square pegs to fit into the round holes that the world demanded of them.

Unyielding egos clashing with conformity pressures were his specialty. David reached the mirror and adjusted his clothing. His tie was the tiniest bit wider than fashion norm this month, a hint to his clients that they could still push the envelope of life's constrictions and not feel claustrophobic. Then again, that tie was ever so slightly longer than normal too. That was to remind his clients about who was in charge.

He adjusted with planned irony two small, color-coordinated, triangular snake bites to bring out the barest beginnings of friendly smile creases at the edges of his brown eyes. As usual, they stung for a half-second as they released a dose of tox over the newly-covered skin before that skin went pleasantly numb. They cemented his image as an average, friendly joe.

When he was alone at home he placed the snake bites correctly so they'd do their job and reduce the signs of aging. Out here in the world, though, he was ever conscious of the image he made.

Appearance was everything.

Now he was ready to smooth some more of the world's rough edges and face the day... or night, as it were, as his office hours were Vegas ones. A final glance at the moon outside the lobby windows: *Don't ever change, Old Man,* and he went upstairs.

David's "morning" passed quickly as he dealt by direct video with clients who were close to completing their therapy. The satisfaction of a job well done returned to him. Instead of futilely straining at society's bindings, he'd shown them how they could reshape themselves, their goals and the things they thought important, to be what the world needed them to be.

Trenton Thomas was a shining example. He was more than halfway through his make, a Seventies as compared to David's mid-Thirty, which meant he had the lean, angular features over a solid body that should signify the ideal aggressive executive. When he'd first come to David– the first cycle of sessions were conducted in person as much as possible– he'd kept twisting in his seat, and he'd had a habit of rapping his fingertips against any surface he could reach. He would screw his mouth around as if he'd just sucked on a lemon when he didn't think he was giving the answer that David wanted to hear.

Now he sat up straight. His arms lay loose on his chair, and he even crossed his legs occasionally, as David had taught him, to include the person to whom he was speaking into a more direct connection.

His expression was calm, though David thought there was a blank look to his features as well as his mind. Well, that was a final step to work on at the next appointment. David made a note to that effect after Trenton signed off. Trenton had managed to snag a prime job at NaniTech in northern Bostington. It wouldn't be long before the crisply-attired Seventy rose in their ranks.

If Trenton was a success story, Ragnar was another matter entirely.

"Good morning, Ragnar," David greeted the last patient before midnight "lunch," Ragnar Sveinsson. Because he was just beginning therapy, Ragnar came in person. He could afford the weekly trips from Reykjavik, and arranged his business so that he could accomplish other things while in the Vegas/San-San area.

It was a mark of distinction to David to have such a famous name on his list of clientele, even if the man were the *capo* of *l'Ögre*, the notorious international crime syndicate. David tried to repeat that accolade to himself every time he met with Ragnar, but the truth of the matter was that Ragnar bothered him.

Ragnar had been coming to him for a month now. He was a referral, and again David tried to keep in mind that this was a reflection on his own good name. Two very respected European therapists had thought enough of his work to send Ragnar to him.

Ragnar greeted David with a sullen nod. David returned it with a professional smile. Ragnar liked a businesslike demeanor. He required strict obedience in all his underlings, which his previous therapist hadn't been able to provide.

Here was another Seventy, but Ragnar placed at the top of the make. Perhaps his surgeons had gone too far. Perhaps Ragnar had planned to create the unnerving effect. The same facial angles that had given Trenton executive appeal seemed feral and wolfish on this man.

His large hands clenched on his chair arms. As he crossed his legs, one impeccably-shined shoe bobbed up and down at a heartbeat pace. Obviously he had no time to be sitting idle for so long. His keen eyes switched this way and that, taking in everything– or keeping watch out for danger that could come from any direction.

Two hulking Ninety-make bodyguards waited in the lobby.

David knew precisely how far he could push Ragnar. He'd studied the man and his infamous career carefully. He'd consulted with Ragnar's three former therapists.

That, and David considered himself a good telepath. Normally he allowed mental impressions to come to him without seeking them out, but Ragnar kept his mind clenched closed. David had had to delve into Ragnar's mind to lead the therapy and ease Ragnar's barriers.

But those barriers were thick. Ragnar had unconsciously kept them strong for years, over a century if the impressions David got were correct. *L'Ögre*'s history went back almost that far. It was likely that Ragnar started with the bloody business as it was born.

In David's opinion Ragnar was one of those people– too many in the world– who had no conscience. He truly had no sense of right or wrong, but was only interested in what he could get away with. He distrusted the entire world and every living soul within it. David wondered just how much Ragnar distrusted himself.

David settled deeper in his chair and hoped that Ragnar hadn't noticed that he'd angled his "Comfort in Conformity" motto plaque so that his client could see it more easily from his favorite position on the couch.

Ragnar was going to be a tough nut to crack. Already David dreaded the job ahead, and yet they had barely begun these sessions. Usually the beginnings of molding a new, acceptable personality excited David. This time he wasn't sure he could accomplish the task.

Ragnar didn't want to change. He wasn't under any kind of pressure from the law (a situation David didn't want to question closely), life was comfortable, and Ragnar saw no reason not to continue doing what he'd always done. It was only Ragnar's wife of three years who had hounded him into therapy. She was a full-make Sixty and Ragnar worshipped her. Otherwise, Ragnar wasn't ready to make the commitment.

They began as usual by discussing Ragnar's week and the situations that had set him over the edge of rage. There was always something. Ragnar knew he had a problem with anger management. That plus guns, plus the ability to hire other unscrupulous men with guns, made for the occasional body popping up here and there.

David had to consciously unclench his jaw at the revelations. He knew that even with this much, Ragnar was holding back. He reminded Ragnar of the sanctity of patient-therapist conversations. After pausing to acknowledge that, Ragnar tried to excuse his anger over a cousin who'd botched bribing a pair of customs inspectors.

A sudden picture came very clear in Ragnar's mind, his barriers cracking enough to let David see. Usually the most David sensed at such a basic level was emotions, perhaps a quick visual impression, but this time he got full color and complete sensory surround-sound. The blood was real enough to smell.

"Your punishment was excessive," he commented in the flattest, most unjudgmental voice he could summon. "Your anger went off the scale. Can you tell me why?"

Ragnar talked his way around it. How typical of him to avoid responsibility. The cousin was a good-for-nothing, a pain to have around. Another wastrel eating up the organization's money without good result. It was best that he not take up space in this world.

"Come on, Ragnar," David urged. "Trust me."

The man squirmed in his seat. Another might have sweated profusely in his position; his face was red enough. Instead he sat there smelling faintly of MaxCompoz body bar and not a sweat gland rose to the occasion.

"He was scum," Ragnar finally confessed. "He said some very nasty things about my late father." He clasped his hands tightly in his lap. First he stared at them, and then glanced quickly about the room, as if some invisible demon might be recording. "And my mother." The hands became fists. He began to slam them against his thighs. "Nobody says anything about my mother! I'll kill 'em! Kill 'em!"

David had triggered an undetectable dose of tranqui-spray when he sensed Ragnar about to erupt. By the time he got to his third "Kill 'em!" Ragnar was winding down, sinking back into the couch.

"Insulting parents is a terrible thing," David purred. "It hits us all hard, but you especially. You had such a difficult childhood."

"My mother was a saint," Ragnar whispered, a wild glaze on his eyes even as his pupils dilated.

"People know they can get you angry by disparaging your mother," David said. "It's predictable. Your reason stops and raw emotion takes over. They can slip things by you then. They think this gives them power over you."

"Power? Over me." Ragnar considered it. He shook his head almost as if trying to throw off the trank. "No one has power over me."

"Exactly. Let's see if we can lessen the negative emotional grip your childhood has on you," David suggested. He swiveled to check his neuro-hypnotics. "I'd like to try acupuncture along with directed subliminals. I think you'll find the rest of this session a relaxing one."

"Can you feel it, David?" Ragnar asked. "You're a teep. Can you feel what I'm feeling? See what I've seen?"

David looked up from his control board with its muted displays. "Sometimes I can," he said. "It's part of my job to pinpoint sessions by focusing your thoughts precisely where you'll get the most benefit."

"Do your patients' problems ever bother you?" Ragnar asked. "Since you get–" He tapped on the side of his skull.

David smiled at the familiar question. "Of course they do," he said. "Some of my patients are quite troubled. But telepathy is an invaluable tool in my work. I went through a lot of training to learn to use– as well as not to misuse– it."

Ragnar grunted.

"The privacy of the mind is a sacred thing," David said with a firmness he rarely used. For some reason Ragnar's comfort level had plummeted. Suspicion rose to take its place. "So are doctor/patient confidences," he repeated.

"Sometimes I think I tell you too much."

"My notes are triple-secured behind logarithmic password encoding," David reassured him. "Even if the police should seize my records, there's no way that they could ever access these private conversations."

Another grunt.

"I'm going to adjust your meds, Ragnar," David said as he crosschecked his patient's records. "The anxiocedin might be interacting with your omega-3 supplements." A paper fed out of the slot in David's desk. He glanced at it before handing it to Ragnar, who frowned as he read it.

"This will still keep me in clear mind?"

"Of course. I don't believe in fuzzing up people's heads," David said. "You will still be able to think clearly. That's what these sessions are all about, to help you recognize when and why you make poor decisions, and to give yourself the tools to make good ones."

The left side of Ragnar's mouth turned up. "And a little telepathic push always helps."

David let him see his recoil. "That hurt. I've never used telepathy to manipulate anyone. It's unethical. And just to set your mind at ease, I'd have no idea how to begin to do it."

Ragnar nodded. "Good," he said, and then more definitely, "Good."

David rose to get his equipment. "Glad you agree. Let me explain the acupuncture procedure as I set up."

David wasn't the kind of man to rely solely on flexochairs for good muscle tone. After midnight lunch he liked to power-walk the air-filtered streets of

Vegas, taking in the dazzle that still made downtown a world landmark. Fresh air– well, as fresh as air ever got these days– he sucked it in and exhaled his troubles. No thoughts about work now. He tried to be one with the world and regain his control upon it at the same time as his power-walk controlled his body.

Sometimes when he got tired outside thoughts scratched at the boundaries of his mind. It had been a problem in his youth as his telepathic ability had sharpened, but now he could keep the thoughts at bay as long as he allowed himself to rest after tough telepathic sessions.

Tonight he couldn't retrieve a calm meditative state. He pushed away his problems once more, but some nagging distress remained.

For a few moments it disappeared as he admired another set of Fashion Police patrolling the Strip, these two coed. Impeccable. Sexy. Stylish. Vegas had the best FeePs in the world. It was comforting to see people fitting into their niche and enjoying it.

Just as he was turning back to his meditation, the thought came: *Somebody's watching you.*

Everyone had a little voice, sometimes a whole slew of voices, in their heads. David's voices usually gave him good advice, but they rarely interrupted his meditations.

The realization shocked him out of his after-lunch haze. Who would be watching him? Not the Fashion Police. He was perfectly within bounds. But there– he could feel it now. That now-familiar icy darkness was nearby, for it had a Vegas feel to it. Strobing lights seemed to echo around it, just like the ones that surrounded him.

Maybe Ragnar's paranoia was rubbing off?

No, there was a focus to this that pulled back as soon as David reached for it. A dark mind with violence rippling behind it.

A laughing couple passed him and made him realize he had frozen on the sidewalk. What to do? His mind seemed paralyzed as well, his control over the world shattered.

He fought himself into rationality. He couldn't call the police. What would he tell them? He couldn't pinpoint this when it deliberately hid. Maybe this was just a telepathic punk out for a joy ride.

Maybe it was something more.

He made sure he kept to the crowded sections of the Strip as he strode the midnight bustle. He knew where all the civil police call-points were, where the officers usually posted themselves, and he adjusted his return route from post to post.

Every time he searched, he could sense it. It fell back before his seeking mind, but still it focused on not just any mind, but him: Dr. David Lumen.

This wasn't right. Life wasn't supposed to be interrupted by the unexpected. David returned to his office, determined to reestablish his rhythm, but he merely half-listened to his first after-midnight patient. He would have apologized, but the presence– or was it merely the memory of that presence?– obsessed him.

The situation finally forced him to admit that tonight he was doing his patients no good. He canceled the rest of his appointments. He gave his auto-receptionist a hazy apology to transmit with a request to reschedule, and then on a whim used a public, anonymous phone in the lobby to call a taxi.

The familiarity of his condo should have reassured him, but he paced the spacious apartment. A wall of windows overlooked downtown and its never-ending festival. Somewhere out there someone was tracking him.

It had to concern Ragnar Sveinsson. Only he was still in the entry-level process of a major social rehab. Only he would have the motivation to send someone out to get David.

David mulled their session. Then he checked his previous notes. Yes, Ragnar had voiced consistent concern over David's telepathy. David now possessed knowledge about ghastly crimes that Ragnar had never admitted out loud. But David would never betray the doctor-patient confidence.

Didn't Ragnar realize that?

In the east, the sky lightened. Still David paced. How many murders could he himself trace to Ragnar? How many could he guess at? And how many more would he never know about, murders ordered through layers of *l'Ögre*'s organization and never directly touched by the *capo* himself?

He replayed memories of that icy mental touch. How much of it had he exaggerated through his own fear? Not much. It was real. The mind behind it was a cruel one, clearly capable of murder or worse.

Who would hire a rogue telepath? David kept coming up with one answer. That naturally led to the big question:

Had Ragnar ordered David's murder because of what he knew?

Though such betrayal went against all codes of ethics, David finally admitted to himself that Ragnar would not trust him. Ragnar was riddled with trust issues that stemmed from his dysfunctional childhood.

And Ragnar had vast international criminal resources at his command: ordinary citizens kept on the payroll just in case. Politicians. Police. Hit men. Rogue telepaths.

With a start, David realized that he'd begun gathering clothing in a pile on his bed. He stared at it and then retrieved his suitcase from the closet. No, make it a gym duffel. Mustn't look like he was doing anything odd. He could arrange– somehow– for his possessions to follow him later.

Carefully he arranged his clothing into the rounded pack so as to avoid wrinkling. Only minimal moisturizers, snake bites and toiletries made the cut. His passport card was the single thing he took from his small safe. The hard copy of his will he left inside.

As a final step, he checked his financial passcodes. Good, they hadn't been tampered with. Yet. He triple-sealed them with new passwords, and on a whim added a retinal scan requirement with EEG. Letting out a vindictive chuckle as a thought came to him, he then sent a request to Identity Theft Central, indicating that he had suspicions that someone was tapping into his accounts, and could they keep an eye on them for–

How long? How long would he run from this? He needed to check into police protection on an international scale. He set his jaw, considered the worst scenario, and gave it a three-month window. If the situation turned out not to be what he suspected, or if Ragnar called off his telepathic dog, he could always rescind the request.

Then he placed an "In case of my untimely death" code over his notes, to be routed to authorities if and when. It was a bit unethical, but if Ragnar were the one to so grievously disregard the doctor-patient relationship, then by God he'd pay for it.

After David died.

David snatched up his bag, checked that his hair was presentable and his tie straight, and then slipped out of his apartment.

2

It was a good thing David wasn't used to seeing the sun during his "days," for he stayed far out of its sight as he ran low through the transport tubes that crisscrossed the continent. If there was a shadow to be had, he found it. If there was a crowd to get lost in, he was there.

He told himself that he had his situation under control, but he knew he lied. David Lumen was no runner.

The most excitement he'd had in the past six months was purchasing that state-of-the-art vid system, the one that came with its own senso-lounge for two. Even the cosmetic dentist from four floors down had showed up to see that. Though he'd been coming on to her for weeks with little to show for it, the setup impressed her enough that she'd stayed the night. Or rather, day. They'd alternated sex with vids, right up to the time when he had to leave for his first appointment.

An excellent investment. He could see why men got caught up with full Sixties.

Two days later he'd watched the final boxes for her own vid system disappearing with a squad of delivery men behind the utility lift doors. That was the last he saw of her.

God, he missed that system.

It and everything else he owned now sat unappreciated back home. David learned to live in a world of filthy trans stations, watching vid through shop windows and in waiting rooms, on hard plastic chairs. He couldn't use personal devices because those kept track of his location.

It was difficult to plan on hard plastic, but it did keep him focused. How could he find out which police could be trusted? Headlines wherever he went obsessed with investigations of big-city departmental corruption. Whom could he turn to for help and not put in similar danger?

More than once he paused outside a gun store to stare at the displays. Should he buy one? Guns were evil. They were an unhealthy non-solution to unreasoning fear. They were only used by people who could think of nothing besides violence as a means to control their world.

Still, this was an emergency. His fear was justified.

Oh hell, he had no idea how to use one. If it came down to it, he'd accidentally shoot himself. Or worse, he'd freeze and his stalker could then turn his own weapon against him. No, no gun.

At least while he was on the run he could still stay abreast of his favorite vid program, *Stormy Heights*. Even though its characters suffered through every trauma that humankind could imagine, its predictable daily problems were the stability David needed to remain recognizable to himself and not dissipate into shards of fear.

Its cast became his support group: The Gambino brothers, Bruce and Steele, demonstrated two entirely different flavors of ambition run amok and against each other. Helen's life was strewn with disasters resulting from her classic enabler co-dependency. Talia was a pathological narcissist with a great ass. The program provided a spectrum of escapism that would never change as long as its ratings held. Even seedy bars streamed it in the back rooms, away from the sports stations up front.

David himself became seedy. He didn't shave and his beard grew in uneven and reddish brown. Far from the filtered streets of Vegas, it didn't take long for soot and smog to settle on him. He scratched the detestable stuff off as best he could and wore a used air mask he'd picked out of a trash can until he could buy a new one. He dodged a FeeP patrol so he could get the dye stripped from his hair, revealing the copper underneath. Yes, it made him stand out against the brown hair of other men, but it made him *non-David Lumen* odd.

Sometimes the whole situation seemed a dream and he thought he might float away from this body. He was a stranger even to himself. He wasn't under his own control anymore, any more than the world was.

A few measures of *Stormy Heights*'s familiar theme brought him back to rights. There was Talia, plotting her revenge against the Gambinos. He could catch his breath as she did so. He tried to make reasonable plans and follow them as far as he could. But before long fear grabbed him again and beat him down with chaos.

He traded his fashionable clothes for worn items: plaids and polyesters. Sneakers that were far from new and had never been top-brand. He slunk through the lower-class neighborhoods where the FeePs rarely traveled, and when a patrol ventured in, he avoided them by sensing their presence first.

It was that other Presence that concerned him.

David crisscrossed the San-San network and then enlarged that to circle the entire western half of North America. Then the Presence neared in his mind, hinting of what must be physical proximity.

Should he venture into unknown territory? David checked that his passport was still valid. The picture on it no longer looked much like him now, but whose old ident photos did?

His stalker mustn't yet know that he was trailing an A-1 level trained teep. David took advantage of that tiny bit of good fortune and stretched his psyche to target him, daring to creep close. That one? That one?

No— him. The tall, dark-haired man in the black faux-leather jacket, gloves and mirrored sunglasses. A Fifties make, hard-built with a square chin and looking ready for anything. He was straight out of a crime vid: the hood who was too cool to get caught, the guy more likely to get the girl than was the cop who was after him.

Would the civil police believe David if he pointed him out? Would this guy have been careless enough to leave a record in his wake? David couldn't turn to anyone who wasn't affiliated with the cops. Civilized people believed in the mob every bit as much as they believed in fairies.

David ducked back into hiding within the trans crowd. He tended to panic in life-and-death situations. He needed calm. He needed control to think straight.

The man's name was Kane. Ethan Kane.

Now David ran across to Europe and back, accepting the hard truth about himself that he was a coward. He'd had zero self-defense training. Why, he'd never encountered so much as a bully past elementary school to force him to stand his ground.

Now was not the time to confront an armed stalker. Kane was a profession-al, top of his trade. David would only wind up another name on a long list of the murdered… or the permanently missing.

So David hid. He slept in corners, able to dodge authorities only because he was a teep. Forever looking over his shoulder and wondering why others couldn't hear his heart about to explode.

One day he exited a long-range trans tube, searched and could not feel the Presence. A momentary wave of security washed over him and then trickled away. He'd outrun Kane– for now. How to take advantage of the situation?

An ad on the near wall of the trans station caught his eye. VISIT LUNA, it said.

They might use his passport to track him. Perhaps they were already tracing his econocard use. Who could tell what kind of information people could get off the Nets these days? Sure, the UN Privacy Amendment protected people in most countries, but that only punished if you got caught.

Smart hackers didn't get caught.

Where was he? David stood at the area map and scratched his unwashed head. London. The nearest spaceport was only twenty minutes away.

Forty minutes later David crouched in a corner of the spaceport terminal, prepared to experiment with his telepathy. He'd never had to rely on it as much as he had these past three weeks. He felt over-sensitized to the world. It prick-led him unbearably as he found himself unbalanced and unable to tune out the rest of humanity.

Now he used his new range to get specific hard information. Always before he had merely tapped into the emotions of his patients to retrieve a memory that might lead them to a more direct confrontation with their problem. What he needed now was different:

When the guard would turn his back. *What* door would slip him past security checks. *Which* entrance would put him on board just after the last of the cleaning and supply crews had gone.

He slipped aboard the Lunar express and hid in a bathroom, checking his watch against terminal information. Almost time for liftoff. There had to be some spare sleep chambers on board. The spacelines were always complaining that they needed to adjust their prices because tourism had fallen off.

The tiny service pantry outside the bathroom was dark. Everyone had been sealed in already. He crept past coffin-like sleep chambers one by one. Their shiny acrylics were secured, their occupants prepped and asleep for the strenuous trip. Occupied. Occupied. Occupied.

The floor lurched underneath. David grabbed for support, but he heard no roar of engines, felt no gravity thrust. The vertigo was all in his mind. Fighting for control, he pulled himself upright.

Again the world distorted like pulled taffy. Its vortex sucked him in. David's knees buckled as his brain tried to fold in two. He let out a gasp, and then couldn't catch his breath as it happened again.

Someone was trying to take over his mind!

They wanted to kick him out of his own body. Leave him brain-dead. Kane! His smothering presence surrounded David, looming as if the teep were onboard and clearly able to see him.

A non-physical rush of wind howled at David's mind. He felt himself torn apart, looking down at his own body for an unimaginable second before he fought his way back. He staggered as his mind crumpled.

No! No!

Clawing the smooth surface in front of him, he tried to center himself with its solidity. Instead, the capsule opened. He heaved himself into it, on top of the sleeping woman already there, and fumbled to pull the lid closed. Maybe if the teep couldn't see him, he couldn't–

His skull seemed to crack, his brain crumbling like ash inside it.

The weeks of hiding had spent all his fear. From reserves he'd never guessed he had, David steeled himself inside his mind. *Out!* He shoved at that cold power with power of his own. It hesitated in surprise at the response.

When it stepped back for precious moments, the world around David suddenly seemed clearer than he'd ever perceived it. He could feel the mind of the woman beneath him as she slumbered. A mind to either side of him, Kane's mind somewhere near–

He gathered his injured mental faculties and rose up within his mind, bracing as strongly as he could against that foul Presence out there. This was David's only chance. He was a tank. His skin was armor that would not be penetrated! He raised his mental arms in a defensive block.

Last stand, he told himself. *Now or never!*

He didn't have to wait. The attack blasted in, pummeling his mind from every direction. Where to strike back? David punched in one direction, only to be blindsided from behind. He fought in an unlit cavern, flailing while trying to keep his balance. Don't expose a weak side. Twice when he struck he knew he'd hurt Kane.

I am! he shouted when Kane attacked his essence. *You can never have me!*

Long moments he hung there, deep within his mind. That Other couldn't drive it out of this body. His body. He clung to it.

He strained his senses into the lull, trying to discover from where the next attack would strike.

When it came, it rolled in from just one direction, a tsunami of horrific proportions. It bowled him over and over, sucking him down with its might until he sank beneath it.

His world went black.

3

How odd. Pippin had expected to wake up brimming with unbounded zest, free from the crushing gravity that had been Earth for the past six weeks. She should be home: back on Luna.

This trip had left the rest of her life hanging and her nerves shattered. They had already been stretched thin as a plastic sheet. During the past six weeks that plastic had been pulled and distorted, finally snapping into shreds by a lack of time and more gravity than a human body was ever meant to bear.

What she needed was a long vacation. What she faced was the most important deadline of her life.

Now at last she could pick up where she'd left and get on with everything. She'd have to do so at a dead run; her schedule was squeezed unbearably tight. Instead, she found she literally couldn't move. Was some fear of failure immobilizing her? Or worse: artist's block?

I should have refused to go to Earth, she reminded herself as she put up faint struggle to open her eyes. She thought she'd left Earth behind four years ago. But poor Jonathan. He couldn't have lasted much longer without Terran help. And of course, poor old Aunt Evie anxiously waited for him at home.

Evie certainly couldn't have survived the trip, so Pippin had put her dream on hold for six weeks. Forty-two irreplaceable days. She'd accompanied Jonathan throughout his ordeal, and had now brought him back home. She hoped he appreciated her sacrifice. She knew Aunt Evie didn't.

Her time was her own again, but time now ran oddly. It was dark. Oh yeah, she had her eyes closed, but there didn't seem to be any light on the other side of her lids. *Open, open, open,* her mind commanded, but her mistreated body groaned, *Five more minutes.*

She still felt heavy, though maybe half or a third as bad as the horror Mama Terra had been. Not only heavy but a tad claustrophobic. She squeegeed the sleep-slime in her mouth with her teeth, trying to taste what the problem was as her senses slowly awoke. Ew, got some hair in her mouth. She spat it out.

It was really quiet in here. Funny odor; guess that was the plastic sleep suit they made her wear, with its plumbing and sensors and everything. It really smelled icky. More than ripe; kind of rotten, like when they brought in a big batch of manure from the Luna C waste facility to receive its final rounds of sterilization. That couldn't be her, could it? Ew, ew. Never!

She must be still in the sleep pod. Cocooned to withstand the hard acceleration that powered the Express, it fed her enough drugs to keep her unaware of the day-and-a-half ride. The faint sounds she made as she squirmed echoed back to her, reminding her of how tiny it was.

People weren't supposed to wake up in their pods, were they? Had something catastrophic happened? She started throwing off the drug effects at that thought. Was there something wrong with the ship, that the sleepers had been awakened prematurely so they could deal manually with the emergency– or at least say their final prayers?

Meteoroid collision? Crew decompression? Was no one left at the controls?

Maybe some glitch had cut off her nutrients or, God help her, her air, and some keen animal instinct had snapped herself alert so she could jump up and–

Not bloody likely, with this weight pinning her down.

Funny, it didn't extend to her arms or hands. Her left foot also seemed to be free of it. Still, it was… well, something. An object of some kind, a smushing load, a–

"Wooo-AAAAHHH!" she shrieked. "Dead body! Dead body!"

She scrabbled her free fingers, searching for some kind of help button to alert the staff. There must be a help button. And a staff that was awake. Please,

God, a– "HAAAAAALLP!" She ended it in a pure, unadulterated screech guaranteed to penetrate six inches of solid steel if need be.

Suddenly it occurred to her that her screams might use up all available oxygen.

Oxygen or zombie initiation? "YAAAAAAAAHHHHHH! EEEEEEEEE!"

Excited voices penetrated from the other side of the pod. She shrieked as loudly as she could: "Dead! BODIEEE! Lemme out! Lemme OUUUUT!!!"

For the first time in her life, Pippin Applegate fainted.

Slowly the world swirled around David, as if he were still in his strange dream. A faraway scream echoed through the haze. He felt dislocated, out of touch with himself. Alien.

He clamped his eyes shut and smacked his lips, trying to make the funny taste go away. Furry. Must have been asleep for a month. Had he had a chance to brush his teeth this morning? What was that smell? His nose wouldn't wrinkle as much as he wanted. Stiff. Instead he opened his mouth slightly and inhaled to let the odor rise to the top of his palate. Smelled like… like musk, with a touch of urine attached. Not entirely unpleasant.

He stretched only to find his hands and back were butting up against something solid. Oh right– he'd jumped into that capsule. A woman was already in it.

He'd been hiding from something. Someone. Someone had been chasing him.

His breath caught as full consciousness crashed upon him. Kane– that telepath– had tried to take over his mind!

The memories of battle returned to him. He hadn't really expected to wake up, but here he was again. *I think; therefore, I am.*

I'm alive. I did it!

But something was wrong. He felt all wrong. Had he given himself a stroke? Surely someone would come along and take him to the hospital. Even with a major stroke he could be himself again in a week or two.

That faraway sound of screaming came again. His right ear swiveled to seek the source.

More movement, somewhere outside wherever he was. Now it was his left ear that twitched and rotated.

He dared open his eyes. This didn't look like what he'd pictured the inside of a sleep chamber. He hadn't noticed the rows of eye-big circles cut into it, revealing bright light and shadows in the room beyond.

Whatever it was, that terrible Kane presence wasn't near. These people had different vibes.

"Hey," he wanted to say, but his voice was a dry croak, a tenor "Eh."

He tried clearing his throat. He gave his head a shake. There was something furry in here with him. When he reached out to touch it, it moved.

Wait a minute.

He stretched his hand out, flexing his fingers. In front of his eyes, an orangey-yellow paw fitted with a medical tube stretched and flexed. Claws extended slightly, then retracted back.

Oh.

My.

God.

"meeOOOWWWWW!" he cried. "Yoww! Yioww! Mioww! Yoww! Moww!"

"Looks like someone's awake here too," a female voice from outside said. A large eye peered in through one of the holes. "Hello there, boy. Welcome to Luna. Bet you're hungry."

"Moww! Moww! Moww!"

"A real talker. My granny has a talker. Siamese, I think. Is this a Siamese, Pete?"

"You don't know nothing about cats. That's a plain ginger cat in there."

David might have heard the reply if he weren't heaving against his restraints, shouting as loudly as he could.

"Whups. Kitty doesn't like his cage. Why can't they learn to trank these animals enough? What do we got on hand?"

"Oh, just let him have his fit. He'll calm down eventu–"

"This is the Applegate cat, Pete. Even you've heard of Evie Applegate."

"Whoa. Okay, lemme see what I can find."

"I'm a man! I don't belong in a cage!" David yelled, but all that came out was cat yowling.

Out out out! Something agreed with him. He glanced behind to see who else was in here with him. Lord, don't let it be a female. They didn't expect him to mate with a cat, did they?

But no one was there.

Out out out! it insisted. It wasn't in his capsule; it was in his mind!

He wasn't alone in this brain! Whoever it was pushed and shoved him, but he held his ground. He knew how, now.

Was that really a cat mind? It spat at him in black fury. He was trespassing on the cat's most personal territory, but the cat was confused as well and didn't know how to fight back. How much damage could a cat mind do to his own?

He'd never heard of anything like this happening. What to do? Could he hang on forever here?

Where was his own body?

A familiar sweetish smell wafted into the carrier. David recognized it: tran-qui-mood. Fast-working. He toppled onto his side and could only blink. At least they hadn't knocked him out. *Breathe,* he told himself.

Against his will the world began to ease into a peaceful place. Damn that tranqui-mood anyway.

Out! that other voice commanded, though less forcefully this time.

Calm down, cat. I don't want to be here either, but I'm not going anywhere until I figure out what's what.

In that floating daze he listened to the world outside. Two attendants bustled about, with a third one coming and going. First they dealt with an emergency passenger– lots of concern that she was an Applegate, whatever that was. Then they seemed to go into a familiar routine. Passengers were being revived on schedule to disembark.

He'd made it to Luna, David realized. He hadn't noticed the gravity change. That was a minor afterthought to becoming a cat.

He heard gossip about the woman who was found with a man atop her. A couple of lewd jokes masked worry. Would they get sued? Applegate this and Applegate that. Who'd get the axe for letting it happen? Puter records would prove that the section had been completely secured; it would have been the man's deliberate actions that had caused the mix-up. Applegate could sue him instead of the spaceline.

He strained as much as his tranqui-doze would allow to discover what had been done with his body. Swarms of police were already on the scene, invoked by the magical name of Applegate. Good. He could go to them, track himself down.

As a cat?

Ordinarily he'd pace, but the trank left him limp and despondent. Wait. That wasn't just the trank; it was the cat.

He was temporarily roommates with a cat. Cats' brains were too small to share, especially when something was wrong other than the obvious.

David asked, *What's the matter?*

I want my maaama! Misery washed through the two of them. Utter hopelessness.

There, there. Poor little guy, Your mama is probably on this shuttle. You just wait a while and she'll pick you up.

No... and the cat rambled off into images of loss, of terrible pain. Of gravity too heavy to bear and no Mama to soothe him. Mama was gone. Mama was never coming back.

Jesus, what had happened? David wondered if some rich biddy cat-lover had died, and her will had shipped the cat off to a relative on Luna. But why would the cat think Earth was "heavy" if that were the case?

Wait, David said. *Who's that?* The cat remembered a friendly face amid the pain. Hands that rubbed him almost as well as Mama.

Pip.

Good, Pip. You focus on her. Tell me about Pip. David didn't like the depth of misery this cat had faced so recently. Cats weren't supposed to feel like that. This guy– if he was a guy– was wallowing as much in grief and loss as any human David had ever faced.

David didn't have his drugs and equipment to snap this cat out of deep depression. Depression skewed rational thinking, and David needed to be thinking as rationally as possible so he could grab what control he could of the situation. Time for some old-fashioned psychology. Treat the cat as if it were a young child.

The cat's images were confusing, but they seemed to make sense to the cat. Tactile and kinetic memories– touch and movement– and smells punctuated the cat's recollection of his story.

Mama was gone. One day she was there, and then she wasn't. Things went crushingly, confusingly heavy; nightmares held him in terror. He awoke in agony. It lasted for what felt like months or years… a lifetime. Only Pip's hands and warm, familiar Mama-like voice could make the fear go away.

Pip wasn't Mama, but Pip was familiar.

David asked him to recall Pip's voice again. Her soothing touch. He sighed. Right now he could use a little of that. It was better than tranks.

Do you think Pip is here? he asked the cat.

It didn't know. It wasn't sure of anything anymore. All it knew for certain was that Mama was gone forever. It whined softly in grief.

This time when she awoke, Pippin did so carefully. Low grav– check. Fresh mouth– check. No corpse– check. She peeled open one eyelid, then the other.

Definitely no body on top. Whew.

"Ms. Applegate, Ms. Applegate!" A Spacelines Suit wrung his hands over her, looking every bit as distressed as he should.

They'd hauled her out of her capsule and into the Travelers' First Aid Lounge area of Port Reception. It was just large enough for two reclining med couches with accompanying equipment, a couple of medics and maybe a visitor or two. Quiet music played to soothe her.

A soft crinkling sound when she moved told her they hadn't taken her out of that yellow plastic SleepSuit. Pippin checked out the room by just rolling her eyes around before her nerves allowed her to sit up. She still trembled.

"Take it easy," Suit said. He motioned to some doctor-types, who helped her up from either side.

"Your stats are fine," the one assured her.

"Can we get you a drink?" the other asked. She pushed a paper cup at Pippin.

"Sign here, please." The Suit-man directed her at a clipscreen.

Pippin didn't take the proffered pen. The cup was only apple juice. At this point she'd have much preferred some hard cider. "What's going on?" she asked. Dead bodies and now a Suit. "Are you people in the habit of–"

"We have no idea how it happened," Suit-man told her quickly. "Never in the history of Selene SpaceLines has anything remotely like this–"

"A *corpse* gets stowed in my capsule and you don't know how it happened?"

"Wasn't a corpse," Doc-One, the man, said. He checked the readings on screen next to Pippin's couch, never looking Pippin's way. "Now easy. You just got in from Earth. You've strained all your body systems."

Doc-Two said, "He's in a coma. We don't know if he was like that before or got that way during. Sometimes the trip…" She shrugged her shoulders and looked Heavenward.

Pippin knew well enough that some people went a bit nuts during space travel. She'd always attributed it to the boredom of cramped traveling through nothing, with no view to speak of and rapid death waiting on the other side of a thin hull. That's why ships had sleep capsules. Well, that and it saved air and having to hire extra human-service stewards. Plus it kept the passengers unaware of the high accelerations involved.

An atypical anger born of the aftermath of fear shook her. "I want half off my fare for sharing the space," she commanded the Suit, "and the other half for the twenty years that corpsicle took off my life." She wondered if she'd wet herself during the event, but she was still wearing her SleepSuit, so that wouldn't have mattered. Still, she could remember the smell of urine.

"Ohmigod, he peed on me," she whimpered.

"It never touched you," Doc-Two said. "You were in your suit. All clean now."

"Right. Good."

Suit-man brandished that clip-screen at her. "Of course we will cheerfully refund your full fare," he told her as he pushed the pen into her curled fingers, "plus we have arranged a day's worth of free meals and one night's stay in the

Imperial Suite at the Hotel Celestial of Luna City. It's the best in town. All I need you to do is sign right here."

"Sleepers have to be awake an hour before their signatures are legal," a familiar voice snapped from across the room.

Pippin sank back against her couch in relief. At last the dragon had arrived to save the innocent maiden.

Aunt Evie stood in the doorway, followed by an anxious crowd. She was still tall, though most people at 160-plus years began to neglect their height correction and give up the fight. Evie never surrendered to anything. She might have a few wrinkles showing around her snakebites, and her chin and eyelids had begun to sag a bit, but otherwise one would be hard-put to guess her age.

The only hint of disordered appearance was her usually crisp blonde pageboy, which now looked ever so slightly frazzled. That touched Pippin. Aunt Evie must be truly worried about her to let her appearance go– though her business suit as usual was the epitome of chic.

Still Suit-man waved the clipscreen in front of Pippin.

"One hour," she said and pushed it away. She sat and considered her situation. Dead man– gone. Earth– forever gone. Finally she focused on Aunt Evie.

Before Pippin could say anything, Evie said, "Leave it to you to create a commotion."

"I didn't–"

"We heard that something had happened on the shuttle, and even before the comm rang, I said, 'It's got to be Pippin in trouble again.'" Evie turned to the man in the green Applegate Organics jumpsuit beside her. "Didn't I say that, Sam?"

He squeezed by her at the door to take Pippin's hand. "Don't let her fool you, kid," he said. Sam Greenwood always wore minimal snakebites, so she could clearly see the laugh lines at the corners of his eyes as well as a wrinkle of concern creasing the center of his forehead. "She's been worried sick about you. How you holdin' up?"

Pippin gave him a wan smile. "Okay, I suppose. Ask me tomorrow when my brain starts to function."

"I will. I think there's a party in honor of your return then. Wouldn't want to miss ice cream and cake." He winked at her. "We Loonies know how to party."

"You mean a party for Jonathan."

Sam didn't comment, and in fact glanced away from her. Pippin knew he couldn't lie well, not even for Aunt Evie. "Thank you, Sam," she told the older man.

Her comment was drowned out by Evie's loud demands. "What the hell happened? Someone get me the latest police report. How could it have happened? Who was that man? I want him hauled before the nearest judge!"

She whirled on the Suit. "And don't think that lets Selene SpaceLines off the hook! Where the hell was your security? How many days was the flight, and you tell me no one discovered a stowaway in that time? When they're supposed to be monitoring the sleep capsules 24/7? No one even noticed the extra kilos of mass?"

Sam nudged Pippin. "See? That means that she cares."

"Only you can see her good side." She turned to the medic beside her. From his nameplate he was a full doctor: Dr. G. Lennon. Guess an Applegate wouldn't get some lowly medtech. Maybe there was a redeeming factor to The Name after all.

"That guy," she said. "You say he's comatose? Drugs?"

"Natural coma," Lennon told her. "Not medically induced. Quite strange. He must have had an accomplice bring him aboard." He still didn't look at her, but Pippin couldn't blame him. Evie's threats were spectacular when she got revved up. Pippin was just thankful that most of them weren't aimed at herself.

"Get Jonathan," Pippin whispered to the doctor.

He actually spared her a glance. "Who?"

"Her cat. He was on the ship with me. Get him and she'll shut up." He just sat there as if he didn't get the connection.

Sam must have heard, because he snapped to the doctor, "Do it!"

Eight minutes later Evie hadn't lost any steam despite Sam's subtle attempts to notch the situation down. Suit Guy actually cowered from her, and people outside the public door seemed to be shifting, as if others were pushing their way to the front. Lawyers, probably. Evie had summoned a squadron of them.

But from the "Authorized Personnel Only" door trotted a skinny Teen-make in a Selene SpaceLines coverall. In his right hand he carried a familiar blue Interplanetary Luxo Cat Carrier.

"Aunt Evie!" Pippin cried above the din. Evie didn't stop, so Pippin shouted. "Evie! Jonathan's here!"

Evie whirled, her last threat hanging half-finished in the air. As soon as she spotted the box, she clutched herself for a moment, then spread her arms wide. "Jonathan!" she called. "Is he all right?"

She almost threw herself upon the carrier and the kid holding it. Evie raised the door to her eye level and peered in.

"Jonathan! Oh, Jonathan! There you are. Did you miss me? I missed you!

"What's the matter with him?" she barked at the kid.

"He's, ah, still a little sedated, ma'am."

Evie looked closer. "He sounds sick. Is he sick? Pippin, is he–"

"Doctors said he came through a little trooper," Pippin told her. She swung around on the couch to prepare to stand. The room spun just a tad so she remained where she was. "They triple-checked him before liftoff and said he was A-OK, all systems go. He's ready for another twenty years."

"Sedated, hm?" Evie considered her cat. "Look at me, baby. Look at Mama."

The woman stood there, eye-to-eye with her sleepy cat who kept raising his paw against the bars of the carrier door only to drop it.

"His pupils are different sizes," Evie announced to the room. She glared at the kid. "That's not tranks, that's shock or worse. What the hell kind of space-line are you people running?"

"Don't worry about this here, Evie," Sam assured her. "I've got it."

She gave him a quick nod, turned on her heel and strode toward the door, the carrier in her right hand. "We're going to the vet right now. Pippin, come along."

"I don't have my bags yet and–"

"Very well," Evie said without looking back. The crowd parted ahead of her, acknowledging her as their Moses. "Meet us there quickly. And don't sign anything without me reading it first!"

"Yes, ma'am," Pippin sighed, but her great-times-whatever aunt was already out of earshot.

4

Pippin pushed her blonde hair back even though nerves and exhaustion almost sapped the energy that it took to do that much. All she wanted was her own bed and about twelve hours of undrugged sleep. She trudged down the narrow, bare Customs hallway, dragging her huge haversack behind her. Thank goodness she was back in Luna's low-grav, or she couldn't have managed that much.

She bumped into something. Someone.

"And where do you think you're going looking like that?" an imperious voice asked.

Pippin looked up. Oh no. Just what she didn't need.

Two Fashion Police officers blocked her way. Of course they looked perfect– FeePs had to be near the top of their makes– and no one could find anything but compliments to pay on their uniforms. Some corner of Pippin's brain where the lights were still working noted that Loonie uniforms had changed: more exposed belly; pointed, open collars; higher hemlines on both his shorts and her skirt. Dark blue had become royal purple.

"I had an accident," Pippin blurted as she straightened. She fished in her pocket. "See? Doctor's note."

The male FeeP's pin said "Gregory Divine." Gregory frowned a moment as he attempted to read the scratchy excuse. With a quick glance at her and his female companion, whose pin Pippin couldn't see, he let his features return to their everyday smooth emotionlessness. No, Pippin supposed, you didn't want to encourage wrinkles.

"If you were in an accident, where's your next-of-kin to escort you?"

"I had a cat." Pippin tried not to watch the female FeeP as she knelt next to the rucksack, scribbling notes on her palm screen. "My aunt had to rush him to the vet. He was involved too."

"Hmm." Officer Greg gave her a piercing study, rocking side to side to take her all in.

Gawd. She'd brushed her hair before leaving the infirmary, but of course she'd pushed and pulled at it all the way through the process of following the SpaceLines employees to retrieve her bag. Her clothes were things she'd mindlessly grabbed out of her bag– crumpled and definitely parts of different ensembles. And judging from people's reactions, her face must reveal how many traumas she'd been through today.

Pippin fumbled for her house keys, her identicard, and–

"Here," she said triumphantly as she produced her prize.

Again came the scrutinous stare. "An artistic license?" Gregory asked. He was a Seventy-make. Pippin wasn't fond of Seventies as they usually looked too corporate for her tastes. Fifties were very nice, as were the new Teens, the ones that didn't look so gangly. In her experience, men who wanted to impress without having to work for it seemed to go for the Seventy road.

It took him a while to get to her identicard. He ran it through his palm screen. "Applegate?" That got her a closer perusal. "One of THE Applegates?"

"There's only two of us on Luna. Of The Applegates, that is." Maybe that would impress a Seventy enough not to ticket her.

"A shame that one of you would besmirch the family name," he said instead. "Applegate Organics has a reputation to maintain. They're one of the major drawing cards for Luna. Don't want outsiders to get the wrong impression of us."

Female FeeP was a Sixty-nine, top of the Sixties make. For a moment Pippin had hoped she was Sugar, but up-close examination proved that false, and the different name on the woman's pin confirmed it. Damn. Sugar would lecture her, but she'd let her off.

Gregory didn't like that license. "I've never seen one of these before." He motioned for his partner to join him. She didn't deign to squint at it.

"Artists contribute to community culture," Pippin recited. "An artistic license grants them some slack in fashion code, for they must be allowed to be creative."

The woman turned the license over, as if Pippin might have photocopied one and forgotten to add the second side. The hologram and metallic watermark were in their correct place.

"Artistic hooey," she concluded. "You aren't being creative; you're just a mess."

"But my license," Pippin protested. "And a doctor's excuse."

"You've got three priors in the past six months and you're on probation. Tell it to the judge. My god, woman, your roots are showing!"

"I've been on Earth!" Pippin wailed. "For six weeks! You can't expect me to have gone to a freaking hair salon when gravity was trying to kill me!"

"Lady, I don't care if you were shipwrecked on Jupiter. No excuse." With a flourish she ripped off the extensive ticket as it printed and shoved it and the license at Pippin.

Gregory reached into his utility bag with impassive regard. It was faux reptilian skin, just three shades lighter purple than his uniform. From it he produced a folded piece of black paper, flicked it open into a bag and pulled it over Pippin's head.

"Oh, JeeZUS!" Pippin groaned from within.

He adjusted it so that the eyeholes lined up properly, per safety regs. Together the FeePs turned as if they'd choreographed the move (Sugar said some did) and instantly became smiley-faced greeters to Lunar newcomers.

As Pippin returned to her path to Customs, the not-so-low curses she huffed in righteous anger made the bag over her head pulsate.

The things she suffered for Aunt Evie.

When she got to Customs she couldn't even remove her bag for the retinal scan. Damned embarrassing.

"Anything to declare?" The Customs lady never twitched a hair when she saw the bag. Instead she went through the whole official routine line by line.

Good thing Pippin had sent the majority of her parcels back to Luna through the catapult, so she didn't have to wade through all that right now.

"Anything to report?" the Customs official asked in a dull voice.

Pippin was about to say no, but then she remembered that word that hadn't shown up on the screens she'd watched the day before departure. Sugar lectured her to being studious about such things now: fifteen minutes every morning (before she could make excuses to forget) studying the latest words coming into the language, today's number-one song, what the most recent major fashion shows predicted for the coming season.

That word she'd heard hadn't been on any of that. At the time she'd dismissed extensive research. What was linguistic evolution to her? Especially since it seemed derogatory. Why put someone down because of the way they looked?

Two staffers at the Terran clinic had called some people "hoopers" while she was there. It was an obvious-enough derision: all the hoopers had been abnormally tall. "It's like they think they should be playing pro basketball," an intern had explained to her. "You know, hooper and basketball?"

An obscure Terran sport.

"I know a word," Pippin said. Maybe this would count in her fashion favor, to contribute to the latest way to speak.

The Customs woman perked up at that. She swung her screen around to face Pippin.

"Hooper," Pippin said clearly through her bag. "It means… It means a person deserving of sympathy because they've received incorrect makeover care. As in, oh that poor hooper, I hope he sued his doctor for everything he had."

There. Much better definition, and the bag hid the smugness of her expression.

Customs lady swung the screen back, nodding. "Hooper," she said. "Probably for putting his surgeon through legal hoops. We don't have that one on file yet. Very good, uh, Ms. Applegate."

Pippin received her honor chit– a rare thing, those– for the valuable cultural input and shoved it into her pocket next to her ticket.

"Hooper. Hooper," Customs lady practiced behind her.

"Maa…" The cat's yowl came out a cross between a yawn and a snore. *That was Mama!…Wasn't it?*

It's only a dream, buddy, David told him as the world left multicolored trails in its wake. *Just like that hippopotopotabus standing behind her. I think she's a vet.*

Jonathan.

Mm. Eh… What?

Not "Buddy." I'm Jonathan.

Oh. Hullo, Jonny. 'M David. Nice ride.

With all this sideways and up-and-down motion, you'd think he'd get seasick. Those tranks must have an additive to handle space sickness too.

He was a cat now. Funny how horror no longer tinged that thought. Cat. Okaaay.

That vet-woman held the carrier high against herself. An arm crossed over the doorway cut off most of the view outside. She talked incessantly in varying pitches that wouldn't let him tune her out but he couldn't focus on what she was saying. Short, staccato threats were interspersed with sing-song cadences. Baby this and Jonathan that.

Each stride reiterated that he wasn't on Earth anymore. A jarring step raised him momentarily, but the slump afterward was easy and drawn-out. It recalled a childhood of jumping on beds, and the gentle roller coasters of elementary school. He'd forgotten the wonder of freefall.

A change in exterior lighting made it feel like they'd gone inside somewhere. But everywhere on Luna was inside, wasn't it? The cat sniffed the air and flinched. It smelled of animals and fear.

Oh that was right, he was the cat.

Multiple voices accompanied them to a back room. The carrier came to rest with a bump on top of a stainless table.

"The doctor will be with you shortly," someone said. The vet-woman released the latches of the carrier door.

"Jonathan?" A woman's voice asked.

Surprise raked through him. *MAMA!*

Before David even realized it, Jonathan hurled himself with automatic reflexes out of the carrier, skidding on the slick, cold surface. Hands snatched him before he could fall.

"Oh, Jonathan!" that voice cried, and the arms wrapped around the two of them, David and Jonathan. "At last. At last!"

Inexplicable relief and excitement washed through David. Something inside him recognized that slightly raspy voice like no other. The hard nubs of the woman's knuckles rubbed his shoulders in a mockery of shiatsu. Long nails scratched his chin. For a moment, David thought he'd swoon from sheer happiness.

How he adored that face! It was beyond the aid of snake bites, to judge from more-than-slight wrinkles. Sharp blue eyes captured his soul. They were the eyes of the ancient Mother Goddess, all-wise and all-loving.

"JONNNNathan!"

David trembled in ecstasy from the music in the voice.

A part of him managed to stand apart from these strange emotions. This woman was old, so old she'd let her blonde hair go silvery. So old he could see the faint line of contacts– contacts!– in her eyes. Her skin revealed that even Luna's gravity had an effect on the human body. She must be over 100, possibly well over that mark since they were on Luna.

But something not that deep within himself shouted with joy: *Mama! Mama!* David desperately rubbed his head against her, alternately trying to get her scent on him and urging her to pet him harder.

She obliged him. David closed his eyes to savor the unfamiliar feeling of tensionless repose. His endless run was over now. He had no schedules, no demanding patients calling him to complain about their latest panic attack.

Someone came into the small room and Mama set David down. The stainless counter was cool beneath his paws and butt. He lay down upon it and sighed. A bright sun shone first in his left eye and then his right. Maybe that sun stuck something in his ears and mouth, and maybe not. Someone far away stroked him, long and languorous, from just underneath his ears all the way down his sides. Mama's voice sang a lullaby.

He'd always imagined Hawaii would be like this. Some bikinied girl would kneel beside him in the cool shade of a palm tree to rub lotion over him. He'd be pleasantly drunk, just like this, with not a worry in the world.

"That's a good Jonathan," the woman's voice cooed.

David rolled over on his back to offer her his chest to rub, and she did.

Yeah. Hawaiian vacation. Safe. Warm. Fed. All he needed was the sound of the surf.

He didn't notice the conversation going on around him. Barely took note of someone lifting him up and putting him back in the carrier. In there, it felt more like a big, soft bed. He was tucked away safe from the world. Mama would take care of him.

For the first time in years, David slept soundly.

"Fumming!" a muffled voice shouted from inside.

Pippin tapped her foot against the step to work off negative energy that otherwise would have propelled her fist through the door.

At last the apartment opened to reveal a woman who of course was of a height with Pippin, since Pippin was of standardized height, and who was blonde since of course she was a straight woman and all straight women were blondes.

But this woman was a full-make Sixty, a primo Sixty-Nine, pinned with a 24K gold name tag that said "Sugar Morales." She'd reached such a state of perfection that she had to be tagged to be differentiated from other such perfect specimens.

But Sugar's face was outlined with gauze. Sugar being Sugar had styled her hair into sleek sweeps that incorporated the bandage– designer, of course; the embroidered blood-red "Gretchen Kahn" signature stood out– into its overall coiffure. More bandage filled in a braid in the back, its gold trim adding sparkle to her shining blondeness. It was a magnificent bandage.

Pippin paused to take in the full picture. Under the perfectly-applied makeup was the faintest trace of bluish purple. The sculpted cheeks seemed a little puffy today. Had Sugar really dared to perfect perfection?

For a moment Pippin again wondered how old her friend was. Twenty-five? Sixty?

In that moment of silence and confusion Sugar checked out the woman with the bag over her head and then, with a disapproving frown that only a Fashion Cop could make look sweeping, announced, "Bibbin."

Pippin groaned that her name would be Sugar's first guess.

"You'be been bagk for how lon'?" Sugar asked. "An' alweady you'be been baggedt."

"It wasn't my fault."

Sugar sighed. "Id never is." She reached out and grabbed Pippin by the collar to drag her into her place. Pippin held on to her luggage and let herself be manipulated. "Don't wan' de neighbors to see you," Sugar said, and Pippin could understand her point of view.

"What the hell's with you?" Pippin countered. "You didn't say anything about surgery. You're talking funny."

"Nod fudny. Hell. C'bon." Sugar led her deeper into the apartment and sat her down for some hot cider, which Pippin accepted gratefully. As usual in Sugar's apartment, a police scanner muttered unintelligibly in the background. With a flick of Sugar's hand to signal her home systems, the sound turned off so they could talk.

"You would not believe the day I've had," Pippin began.

"How long?"

"Have I been back? Just a couple hours."

Sugar rolled her eyes, but the movement looked painful to Pippin. She told Sugar of her emotional travails and the added humiliation of the bagging.

"…And I was hoping you could get this nipped in the bud," Pippin urged. "I was in the right, all the way. None of this was my fault."

Sugar nodded as she poured more steaming cider. Her kitchen was large enough to have a cozy breakfast nook adjoining it. A large windeo displayed a view of New York City's Central Park. A tour bus trundled by with accompanying soft rumble. Like any standard Lunar windeo, the speed of the scene was slowed to cater to residents who might find jerky high-grav movement upsetting.

Even with post-surgery bruising, Sugar's oval face had an almost-natural peaches-and-cream complexion. Her blue eyes nearly glowed, though perhaps that was the brand of mascara doing that. Her clothes were always the latest fashion, chosen to show off her fabulous figure and taste. Sugar made even the other Fashion Police smile in admiration whenever she passed.

It was those very Fashion Police that had brought them together. As had happened far too often since, Pippin had been stopped by two officers shortly after she'd first moved to Luna.

"Artist," she'd reported to them as she tried to tuck her hair back into place. She'd had to present her license as proof, and still the police gave her a stern warning. They advised her to buy a designer backpack to hide her real *plein air* pack in, so as not to cause public upset.

"This isn't Outer Mongolia," they told her. "Here we show we're civilized."

"Yes sir. I'll get that pack right away."

When she'd turned around, there had stood Sugar.

"Are you really an artist?" perfect Sugar had asked. She cocked her head to give Pippin a thorough check. Clearly, Pippin was a new kind of raw material just waiting for a maestra to shape her into proper form.

They'd been friends ever since.

"Sounds like you got hold of a couple of neos," (Pippin translated the statement from Sugar-speak.) "Neos," Sugar added in a dark undertone. "Misusing their authority. They don't understand the responsibility that comes with being a FeeP. I think I've heard of that Greg guy. He's down at the Ninth." She scrutinized Pippin's tickets. "Leave these with me for a day or two," she said. "You may be a mess, but you're my mess. Nobody tickets you but me."

Pippin thanked her parole officer, who waved it off.

"You're trying, which is more than what I usually see," Sugar told her. "Though you've got farther to go than most people. Of course, most people aren't artists." She added darkly, "Artists." She rattled her finger at Pippin, and they both chorused, "You want to be tagged, not bagged."

Sugar tried to frown at the flippancy given her lessons. "Maybe now you'll get some more work done on yourself. You could go on to 24-level. Or skip 24 and go straight to 25."

"I have much too much work to do to fuss with–"

"A professional artist presents themself professionally," Sugar recited from some article she'd read about a year ago. Pippin was sick of that article, but every now and then she admitted that parts of it might make sense. An unfortunately large part of art was its marketing. Otherwise you wound up in an asylum in southern France cutting your ear off because the pain of that was better than that of no one buying your art. Of no one appreciating it, and thus the artist.

Okay, perhaps she didn't use to pay that much attention to her own looks, but Pippin had been Sugar's student for quite a while now. She was miles ahead of where she'd been. Why, she owned deliberately matching outfits these days. She made an effort whenever she went out– unless somebody decided to up and die on her or go into a coma and scare her half to death. Really, she wasn't that bad. Why did everyone make such a fuss?

"But what's with you?" Pippin asked. "You didn't say anything about–"

Sugar shook her head. "Last-minute decision. I figured with you out of town, there went half my work load. I could take a few days off. It's the smile muscles. They started to go wobbly on me."

On-duty Fashion Police needed to smile at all times.

"Couldn't maintain the expression," Sugar continued. Just being Sugar could have charmed most people, but she knew the regs. "Thought I'd go ahead and have them worked on."

"I hadn't noticed you having problems before I left," Pippin said uncertainly. "Did it happen that fast, or–"

"It's that Shelanda bitch," Sugar growled.

"Shel– Shelanda Jones?" At least, that was the only Shelanda Pippin could think of. The only one who was over two years old, she amended to herself. These days lots of baby girls were named Shelanda.

"That's the one." Sugar switched to hard cider. "Ms. Most Perfect Woman in the World."

Pippin straightened up at that. Time to show off the work she'd put in. "As indicated by the Eurasian PopStar Interactive Index last month," she said. "And she's gotten at least two major beauty recognition awards in the past two weeks. *Paris Match* and, and…"

"And *Time*. Chosen Most Beautiful Person of the Year," Sugar said.

Pippin tapped her lower lip, trying to put the clues together. "She's a Sixties make too," was all the connection she could surmise.

"But her nose. Her nose!" Sugar turned to the wall and a vid screen swung down to come to life with the face of the beautiful Shelanda in close-up.

"Why, it's not like yours," Pippin marveled. "How can she be a Sixty-Nine and you too, and you two not have the same nose?"

"Because she's an experimental Sixty-Nine. New design. It's a return to ethnicity, don't you see? Retro chic; neo-Nefertiti."

Ah, yes, the nose was a millimeter or two longer than normal, and not nearly as perky as was Sugar's. It held the merest whisper of a convex curve to it.

"So what does Shelanda have to with Sugar?"

"It doesn't take a genius to realize that they're going to start requiring all Sixty-Nine FeePs to have a Shelanda nose," Sugar told her. She picked up a stylus and threw it at the screen. It hit dead-center, right on Shelanda's offending feature. "I don't like her nose. I like mine."

"Her nose looks all right."

"For her. Not for me." Sugar waved the screen off and it slid back into the ceiling. "The force requires a minimum of one major cosmetic surgery every two years for upkeep on top-makes. I was right on the edge of that window."

"You didn't want the nose, so you had your smile muscles done?"

"Let them try to touch my nose," Sugar warned the world. She lifted her chin so her nose had a commanding view of that world. "I'll show them. You know, I received civil police basic training when I first qualified for FeeP. I can handle myself almost as well as any cop out there."

"I'm going to sic you on Aunt Evie someday," Pippin promised.

"The old biddie has it coming to her." Sugar raised her mug of cider in a toast. "To giving people what they deserve," she said.

"But you don't deserve the nose? Don't you want to be perfect?"

"Honey, I am." Sugar tapped her tag with an immaculate fingernail. "Here's the proof, engraved in gold."

"But–"

"Listen." Sugar leaned over her drink toward Pippin. "You're a Twenty-make. What made you go for Twenties instead of Oughts or Sixties?"

"Well, ah, I guess because my family are all Twenties. For the most part."

"And why do you think that is?"

Pippin thought about something that hadn't occurred to her to think about for a decade or two. "Oughts are skin and bones, model-types," she said. "Sixties are more the, um, well, sex kitten types. Round, that's it. Sixties are round and Oughts are straight up and down."

"And twenties?"

"Twenties are a cross."

Sugar shook her head. "It's all about the bones and flesh," she confided. "The best top-makes move to their own body type. Your type is a solid Twenty. That's the make of choice for predominantly Japanese genes. It goes well with that heart-shaped doll face of yours."

"Grandma Tang would take issue with that. Not Japanese."

"Well then, it's strong East Asian ethnic. If you hadn't had your petuimones done, I bet you'd be about five feet tall. Men would be begging to bind your feet or make you wear high heels. You know some people still do that, don't you? Xtreme foot fetishists, fmeh. Well, you've got the ends blunted, but you've kept true to form. Your core is still there. That core is a Twenty."

Pippin sat back with a grunt. "Aunt Evie wants me to start up again but switch makes. Forties are executive material."

"Evie is an idiot," Sugar said. "She should stick to what she knows. Why, look at her. She's had so many surgeries she's gone generic. Mixing her make. Now she's trying to Ought-icize, have you noticed?"

"Is that what it is." Pippin paused to stir a cinnamon stick into her new cup of cider. "I thought she just hadn't been eating right, pining for Jonathan and all."

"She's been a Twentyish Forty for a long time, but since she's rich she can get away with it. I've seen it happen in older women, trying to regain their babyhood by becoming an Ought. She's getting ready for the surgery, I bet. She's due." Sugar dared to whisper, "How old is she?"

Pippin shrugged. "Old enough to be in the Lunar settlement history books. Old enough to boss everyone else in the family around."

"Including you." Now Sugar leaned back to consider Pippin. She'd taken off her head bag indoors, and the fatigue in her friend clearly showed in both paleness and blotchiness of skin. Lackluster blue eyes within that East Asian slant, a resigned slump to the mouth… "My god, what did you have to endure on Earth? All that gravity and dirt and chemicals."

"Forty-two days of high grav," Pippin moaned. "Forty-two days that I couldn't work up more than a half-hour a day's worth of energy to paint."

"I wouldn't have done it for the old girl."

"I did it for Jonathan."

"Or even for that old cat."

"Not old now. Complete rejuvenation. They practically cloned him and stuck his brain in his new body." Pippin paused over her drink and looked sharply at Sugar. "Do you think they could do that someday? How horrible!"

"How long until your show?"

"Forty-two days. I've lost half my lead time."

"You can do it."

Pippin grimaced an expression that Sugar could never pull off. "Evie's got something up her sleeve. You know her. She'll come up with some kind of trick I can't get out of. She'll need me to do something for her, as long as it keeps me away from my art."

Sugar gave her friend a fond if painful smile. "And you can never say no."

Pippin's hand closed into a fist. "I can."

"Sure you can, hon," Sugar said. "But you need to practice it a little first, just to see how it feels. Build up your strength. How are you going to be able to say no for the big stuff if you haven't strengthened your 'no' muscles with the little things?"

"She told me I was supposed to join her right away at the vet," Pippin admitted. Instead she'd come straight to Sugar.

"Good for you! There's hope yet." Sugar winced and touched her cheek muscles.

"Can I get you anything for it?"

"Don't worry about me. I've got another three days' worth of pain patches. This one's still got another hour on it."

"Good." Pippin raised her cup to Sugar. "Because whatever it was, I was going to say 'no' to it."

Sugar laughed and returned the salute. "Here's to saying no," she declared, "to new noses and to Evie Applegate."

"And saying 'yes' to ourselves," Pippin added.

5

David gradually awoke to movement on the bed. A woman's room; he could tell by the scent that lingered in the air of powder, perfume and human. A quilt's padding lay underneath him. Part of him puzzled at it being below him and not him underneath it, but it was soft and cozy, and the woman's quiet breathing hypnotizing. She had nestled him beside herself.

He stretched, and wonder at the thoroughness of it brought him out of his drowse. The first stretch would have dislocated a human's shoulders as his paws reached far out to dig before him. Then it was up and over those paws, dragging his hips and back legs in an extension akin to a yoga sun salute.

Not only he was surprised. but Jonathan was too. *How long has it been since I could do that?* Jonathan asked himself. *I think I was sick,* he confided to his brain-mate, *but I feel much better now.*

David got the impression of years, possibly, of being trapped in a body where he felt too brittle and heavy to move. Was that Earth? Or the effects of something more than just gravity?

Jonathan began a surprisingly methodical but quick inventory of each muscle. Twitch. Flex. Stretch. A few shoulder rolls and he surveyed his surroundings lustily. *Freedom!* Time to be up and about.

The room was dark, the woman asleep. David/Jonathan padded over to look at her nose-to-nose. The old lady. Mama. Asleep and oblivious to him. Jonathan drew her scent deep into his lungs.

Without her makeup she looked even older than before. She wore triple-dose Nite-Bites not only at the corner of her eyes, but next to her nostrils, above her upper lip, and in a bizarre pattern over her forehead. It made her face look like an African tribal mask carved from rough wood.

Doubled perceptions came to David as he surveyed the room. He saw small obstacles, easy to knock over: holos of the family and various bedroom knick-knacks. That thing Mama always stared at when he wanted to be petted instead: a monitor screen.

David hopped down from the bed and fell on his face. Mama's deep breathing never wavered.

Don't do that, Jonathan rebuked him.

He took a step and wobbled. Took another and fell.

Stop that! You're messing up everything!

I'm just walking, David replied. How hard was it to walk?

You call that walking? My body. Mine! Go away.

Okay, let's see you do it.

David eased back and Jonathan stood up. Before David realized, his body flashed across the room, scampering in a controlled low-grav tumble. Tippy-toe, tippy-toe, leap and rebound! It left David breathless and Jonathan, with more energy than ever.

It's been so long! the cat rejoiced. He took great hallways in three low bounds and skidded around corners familiar to him while David shouted, *Slow down!*

But Jonathan knew the territory. David tried to take it in as they raced past: large rooms that could have housed his entire apartment, deeply-upholstered furniture. Thick rugs that stopped his slides across what he thought must be a truly inspired re-creation of wood floors.

For Jonathan these were textures to be navigated and territories to be conquered.

You must be joking! David cried as Jonathan eyed a towering bookcase and leaped.

There was such power in those back legs, regardless of the gravity. Had David's body ever been so strong? Had he ever pushed it like Jonathan did?

Books slid off at their landing. Something *ping*ed as it hit the floor. Jonathan peered over into the abyss at it: a small globe of some kind done in multiple layers of brass, now twisted out of round.

It had been in Jonathan's way. Now it wasn't, and it provided amusement on its way to death. He leaped again, and David cringed with sudden vertigo as the floor came up slowly to meet them.

Touch down on both back and front toes, then propel forward from the haunches to leap again and scamper.

Tippy-toe, tippy-toe.

Let me try, and David took over. He stumbled and Jonathan gave him a sharp laugh, but he picked himself up and then took it slowly. Tippy-toe, like a ballerina. His claws made the faintest series of clicks on the hardwood. Still he was afraid to pick up any speed. This was so peculiar, walking this way, fitting into this body. Seeing the world from far too low to the ground.

He handed control back to the impatient cat. Suddenly he reared up to stretch against the arm of a chair. It wasn't wood, but it was some lovely, barkish material that seemed to beckon David to scratch it. So he did. With it he could also stretch very high to hang from his front claws.

He used his back feet to bounce against the chair just because he could. The chair lurched a few inches to the right, *bump, whump.* It brought a set of heavy curtains into view.

Ah, Jonathan muttered to himself and detached from the chair, landing only long enough to launch again. He fled across the room to leap up on the curtains, which hung from the ceiling. The very tall ceiling.

David grabbed out of sheer survival.

What are you doing? Jonathan demanded. *Let go!*

The crazy cat was going to kill them both. As David reached to dig in harder with his claws, Jonathan retracted them just enough to use them as mountaineering crampons. He scurried vertically at what seemed the speed of light. In seconds they reached the top. David bumped his head against the ceiling as Jonathan swung them up over the valance.

Jonathan surveyed his kingdom. It was so very far down to the ground! David couldn't think of it in human measurements since he was in a tiny cat's body. What was the equivalent: ten stories? Fifteen?

Jonathan rappelled down with David in tow. Down was definitely slower than up, as Jonathan actually seemed to take some care with the technique. Still too far from the floor he kicked out at the wall under the curtain and launched himself at the sofa. From there it was a hop and a race against himself back to the bedroom.

Jonathan/David took the short cut under the bed to the bathroom. David had never been under a bed. This one had old-fashioned slats and cobwebs that even the vacuum bot had missed. Two fuzzy balls were down here, plus a very interesting-smelling thing of real fur. David batted at it, fascinated by the heady aroma that whispered to him of wild prey and open spaces.

It tinkled as it skittered across the floor.

David gave it a good swipe and shot after it as it arced into the outer hallway.

How long had it been since he'd played soccer? He'd quit when he'd gotten to high school. By then it had been time to settle down and begin to learn his future profession. He'd given up team friendships and the thrill of diving for that perfect save– all to become a man.

Now David the Cat launched himself onto the shelf where the fur-thing had landed. He rolled when he hit, coming up fast, alert, and on the prowl. There it was. He fell on it and sank his teeth into it. Kicked at it with his hind paws.

Power. Strength. Superiority.

Fun!

"Jonnnathan! Go to bed!"

David froze in place. Someone else was here, calling from a nearby room.

Pip, Jonathan supplied.

The two cat presences waited to see if Pip would repeat her order. Long moments passed. Maybe she'd gone back to sleep.

Now David's war on the fur-thing (*Mow-Mouse,* Jonathan informed him) went into covert mode. He hid from it, streaking from cover at the last moment to send it shooting in high, low-grav trajectories, rebounding against cascading knickknacks and burrowing into enemy territory. This was guerrilla warfare. Jonathan knew it well, and he taught David.

"JonaTHAN!" This time the shout was closer.

David clobbered Mow-Mouse just for spite. Instead of squashing it, it spun away on the slick floor as its bell tinkled. David ran after, utilizing the surface to sliiide just by–

He missed. He fell into a floor rack, sending a half-dozen things clattering to the ground. Umbrellas– on Luna? The landslide distracted him for a strategic moment. He lost track of the mouse.

Footsteps clomped from the hallway on the left. He tried to make himself small under two interlocking umbrellas.

Hands picked him up. He dangled as she adjusted her grip. "It is two o'clock in the damned morning," that woman told him, a firm hold on the back of his neck. The other supported his butt. "People sleep at night. You sleep. Doctor says you're supposed to rest. Ditto for the rest of us."

David cringed. He was naked in front of a strange woman!

What's "naked?" Jonathan asked.

Nothing he could do about it. He twisted his neck to see her, but she shook him gently. All he got was a quick look at a face with thick night makeup and a patterning of normal-dose Nite-Bites at the outside of her eyes and between her brows.

Pip carried him across the house, oblivious to Jonathan's pitiful yowl. "You can have fun tomorrow," she commanded. "Tonight we all sleep."

This time David took closer note of the many rooms: a library, a sitting room of some kind, a spacious home office.

Pip deposited him with unnecessary lack of courtesy in the kitchen. "You stay in here until morning," she told him.

David glanced around. He wasn't tired. What could he do in here? He could smell something familiar just around the corner.

Litter box, Jonathan told him.

Good. The urge was beginning to make itself known. Another smell told him there was something good to eat somewhere– ah. A bowl of fishy food sat on a small floor mat next to a water dish. How long had it been since he'd had a decent meal?

Even so, he'd rather explore.

He turned and made to scoot between Pip's feet as she closed a pocket door. She blocked him with a foot and a hand that exhibited long practice.

"No," she told him in a firm voice as she pushed him back in. "You stay here."

As he resignedly turned to explore the kitchen, she tossed Mow-Mousie into the middle of the kitchen floor.

David leapt after it in delight. The door clicked shut behind him. He hesitated a moment and then returned to his conquest.

Pippin almost skipped into the kitchen for breakfast. "Just cidercaff and a dainut, Tiffany," she said as she reached for a Granny Smith. So good to be back on Luna, where the food was good and didn't take an Olympic effort to eat.

"You're back." Tiffany turned toward Pippin just long enough to double-check. Then with one long grunted juggle, she retrieved both pastry and drink from storage and popped them into the nuke.

Aunt Evie had once told Pippin that efficiency consultants often studied the laziest person on the job to learn the absolute essential motions it took to accomplish a task. Those experts would beg to study Tiffany.

Layers of cheap jewelry threw off the ambiance of the traditional black and white maid's outfit: four gold necklaces, dangling shimmers of earrings accented by additional ear piercings, a ring on each finger and bracelets on each arm. To Tiffany's credit, she now wore a Heelzit where various other painful-looking facial piercings had marred the skin when Pippin had last seen her.

Piercings were such an odd concept. Besides, as Sugar had mused more than once, why deliberately mutilate one's body when one should be working on perfecting that body instead? Pippin would bet money that Aunt Evie was now nagging Tiffany about her ears.

An Eighty make with a pear-shaped frame and Sophie di Roma shoes that she claimed she needed for her arches (though Pippin had never heard of a

Loonie with arch trouble), Tiffany was indentured from Earth. Terrans often brought strange habits with them. Why, some Terrans even practiced tattooing. Pippin shuddered at the thought.

It never entered her mind that four years ago she had been Terran too.

The maid didn't switch the vid volume down, and only glanced at essential equipment as she made her way around the kitchen and its housing control panels with her morning duties. Otherwise she was glued to the action.

"Glad you noticed I was gone. How've you been?" Pippin hopped from one foot to the other as she made polite small talk. She had so many things to do! Luckily, Tiffany wasn't one for conversation.

The nuke finally dinged and the maid handed her two dainuts dripping in icing. "You got skinny," Tiffany commented, and Pippin was touched that she'd notice. She slid the cup of cidercaff in Pippin's direction and then returned to her vid show.

North Americans and their vid. They couldn't live without it.

Pippin gathered the food and bounded through the back french doors of the kitchen. Two steps down and she was in her studio. A narrow path wove between a central grouping of tables and taborets, and the storage racks that lined the perimeter. Dried paint lay spattered on both vertical and horizontal surfaces. Canvases, finished and in progress, covered the walls and crammed shelves. She had enough room for a small, raised stage for still lifes and portraits, though her specialty was obviously landscape. Moonscapes, to be precise.

Unlike the rest of the house, this section was tucked into the outer rim of the crater under which Luna City sat, and thus didn't have skylights. Instead, a grid of spots shone down on her work areas. They were easier to control than outside light, anyway. North light might work fine on Earth, but here on Luna there was no atmosphere to disperse sunlight into an even, unchanging glow. Pippin adjusted the grid to a cool range and let out a happy sigh to be home and working.

Forty-one days. She might be able to do it at that.

There it was, the moonscape that Pippin had thought about for the last six weeks. She wriggled it out of its storage slot and positioned it on her easel. Yes, the value problem was so obvious now. She knew exactly how to fix it.

"Not so fast." Aunt Evie's voice came from the kitchen door.

Pippin spun. Aunt Evie rarely came into her studio. She held Jonathan close to her chest, from where he emitted a loud, continuous purr.

"I need you to help me take Jonathan to the clinic today," Evie said.

"And I need to stay here and work. I lost six weeks on Earth. There's only six left until my show."

Evie frowned. "Jonathan is sick. His pupils are uneven."

"You slept through the Normandy Invasion reenactment he put on last night. He's fine."

"I do not take chances with Jonathan." Evie licked her lips as if remembering some rule of civility. "How are you? Have you recovered from Earth? And the… incident?"

Pippin shrugged. "I have a few nerves left. I want to find out who that coma creep was. But that can wait. I need to work."

Evie stepped down into the studio and Pippin took a step back. "I haven't told you yet," Evie said. "I'm going into rejuv day after tomorrow."

"Rejuv? Day after–?"

Evie's pageboy bobbed as she nodded. "We decided last month. The doctors are giving me two days to make sure Jonathan adjusts well, and then I report in."

Pippin didn't know what to say. She knew that Aunt Evie had been unable to hide the signs of aging this past year. She'd been surprised that she hadn't gone in before this, maybe while Jonathan was in rejuv as well, but Evie'd been training a new Veep, Brock Monark.

This might be just what Pippin needed. A few days without Evie and her art criticism– paradise!

"I'll need you to look after Jonathan," Evie told her.

"Sure, I can do that." Pippin considered the amount of time it would take from her schedule. Cats were independent and didn't need much supervision. "He seems very happy to be home. How much did he break last night? If they rev you up as much as they did him, you're going to be a holy terror when you get back."

Evie's eyes crinkled as she smiled at the cat in her arms. "I haven't seen damage like that since you were a kitten." Her lips pursed and tiny vertical lines splayed from them. "His eyes are better than yesterday, but I still want him looked at. And watched."

She raised her chin to command Pippin. "I want twice-daily vids of him. I'll tape some messages for him to watch until I can have visitors, and then I expect to see him in person once a day."

"Okay, Guess I can't paint around the clock. I can handle a visit break every day. You make it sound as if recovery's going to take a while." Pippin reached for a filbert from a crowded vase of brushes.

"And I want you at the Orchards."

Pippin put it back. "I have to work. Here. That was our deal, that when I got back you wouldn't bother me about my art until after my show was over."

Evie inclined her head. "I'm not bothering you about it. Have I said the first word about the condition of this studio? No. But my rejuv is locked in. I can't postpone without half the hospital staff having to completely reschedule their time."

Evie's mouth worked the tiniest bit in consternation. "And Brock is still so green. He hasn't come along as quickly as I'd like. Odd thing; he's a Seventy and Seventies are usually quick learners. The company needs you there to make decisions. Harvest in Proclus and McNair is in another month, you know. They're still setting up the new processing units."

Pippin's hand formed a fist, but she could only press it against the top of the nearest table. Something a little more than a basic rejuv lasted how long? A week? That would be a sixth of the time she had. "You promised me–"

"I didn't foresee this. The doctors–" Evie rolled her eyes–"said I'm getting old. That I can't put a Total off."

"A Total?" Pippin couldn't help it; she gasped.

Evie shrugged. "It'll happen to you sooner or later. The doctors are telling me this will be my last one."

Good thing there was a chair behind Pippin. She sank into it. "No."

"Oh, don't go writing my epitaph yet. This'll get me another fifty years." Evie tapped thoughtfully against her ever-so-slightly sagging chin. "Unless science has advanced by then. I'm rather counting on it. They'll probably be able to squeeze out another fifty, maybe more."

"A Total." Emotions clearly warred over Pippin's face: pain at the thought of Evie's eventual death, frustration at another delay. "How long? I mean, before you can go back full-time?"

"They tell me six weeks."

Pippin bit back a curse. "My show's in six weeks!"

"I can work from home well before then. All you'll have to do is take up my slack."

"No." Pippin gathered herself and stood up. She locked her legs in an aggressive stance. "I've had to wait long enough for this. First I had to assist with the harvests in Clausius and van den Bos. Then it was help Brock get settled in. Then it was Tsu Chung-Chi and the heating snafu, and then Jonathan's Total Rejuv. On Earth. For six weeks of sheer hell."

"You have my most grateful thanks for accompanying him. I would not have survived there, dear."

Don't dear *me!* "I know that. That's why I bleeding went," Pippin spat. "But that's it. I have to pay attention to me now. My career. We made a deal."

Evie nodded. "All you had to do was get your career solidly built in three years while I supported you. You were to help out to pay your way."

"And in those three years how many times have you pulled me away from my art to work solely on the business?"

"But Pippin, if your art doesn't work out, you're going into the family business. You need to learn it completely to take over from me. You've come so far already. The family is very proud of you."

Pippin slammed her fist against the table. "But I don't want to sit chained behind a desk! I want to be an artist. I *am* an artist. And I'll be a respected one."

Again Evie shook her head. "A starving artist in some garret. What is a garret, anyway? I hope it comes with air and heat. Food would be nice as well."

Pippin whirled away from her aunt to stare at the canvas that needed work. How many more were here that could be finished as quickly? How many new canvases, new ideas would remain unrealized because of lost time? "I insist on doing my work. If you cheat and drag me away from it again, I'll never get a true chance to prove myself. Don't do this to me, Aunt Evie."

Her aunt sighed and for the first time seemed to take in the studio's atmosphere of creative work. "You have been helpful these past three years," she admitted.

"Four."

"Yes, even when you were apprenticing for your degree. I'm glad you moved to Luna. The house was rather empty before. Although it could do without some of your more colorful friends." Pippin started to retort, but Evie waved her down. "Part time. You'll look after Jonathan. Once he gets over whatever it is that's wrong with him now, he should be fairly independent. Just make sure he's amused."

Pippin nodded.

Evie met it with a single, crisp nod of her own. "And you'll work part time at the company. Five hours a day."

"Three."

"Four."

"Two. Surely Brock can do *some* work. What do you pay him for?"

Evie painfully closed her eyes. "Three it is," she said.

"Weekends off. Three-day weekends."

"And weekends off. Until I get back on my feet."

"An extension on our deal."

Evie's eyes snapped open. "No extension."

Pippin's tongue worked around her mouth. Finally she said, "Done," and reached for her brush. Evie turned on her heel and closed the doors behind her.

Pippin rapped the handle of the brush against her knuckles. "No," she practiced. "No!" It sounded good and forceful, but it was too damned late.

6

The carrier bump-bump-bumped against the old lady's hip. Without yesterday's motion drugs David felt queasy. Hell, he was queasy just from being where he was:

Inside a cat. His tail thrashed at the thought. Jonathan grumbled at his presence– or maybe his attitude.

I'm trying to keep the stay as short as possible, Jonny, David reassured him. *All I have to do is find my body.*

Street after ceilinged street passed by outside the breathing holes in the carrier. David tried to memorize his route and then gave up. When he got away from Mama, he'd strike out on his own path anyway. Find out where his body was, take possession of it again, and then get lost on Luna until he could figure a way to go home safely.

Getting lost on Luna should to be an easy thing to do. According to the tabloids and vids, abandoned tunnels and sewer societies thrived on the world. Fine with him.

It was safer than Earth right now.

Maybe he'd been reported already to Ragnar as a completed hit. David could slip back to his apartment, gather his possessions and move somewhere where Ragnar would never hear of him again. For some reason Hawaii came to mind.

He could set up shop near the beach and concentrate on tourists getting ready to return from their vacations. It would be like Vegas, but with tans. He couldn't advertise widely, so he'd have to switch to Minute Therapy. It charged less– the practitioners were invariably less qualified than he– but they got four times the appointments per day.

David's stomach sank. It wouldn't be as fulfilling as seeing someone all the way through therapy. Still, he could make a living at it. Better unhappy than dead. Maybe he should change his name. And his make.

He allowed himself to despair over his coming life until he realized that he was cleaning his face with a paw damp from his own saliva.

Cut it out, Jonny. Not when I'm trying to think.

I have to get that stupid smell off me!

The cat might be right. David caught the off-kilter scent from Jonathan. *Medicine residue,* he guessed. *You've had extensive work done. It'll wear off sooner or later.*

Now! Jonathan licked the fur on his right shoulder and then his left. He used strong downstrokes as he tried to reach the part of his chest directly under his chin. Then he licked his paw and used that as a washcloth.

Actually, that did make things a little better, David decided. He used the washcloth-paw-saliva technique to attend to his face, especially around his nose and mouth. Then his ears got attention. They were too far up on his head to David's tastes. Jonathan saw to them well enough, starting at the base in the back and pressing the ear forward with three passes each.

It felt so good to get clean! Still, if Jonny made for their nether regions again, David was going to fade out for a few minutes.

Don't worry, Jonny, he said as they bathed. *When I'm out of here the first thing I'll do is deliver you back home, safe and sound.*

Thanks, David. You're okay for a human.

David paused his wipe. *And you're okay for a cat, Jonny. Thanks for putting up with me. I promise, it won't be long.*

Mama loaded them into an individual transport, which neatly swooshed them to wherever. He couldn't catch the direction they took. There was probably nothing to see out there besides white tunnels.

He'd read about the tunnels of Luna, which networked the crust of the moon. There were so many that the authorities couldn't keep track of them all. Thus they became homes to illegals and the desperate. Vids were full of stories of the low-lifes there.

A tunnel would become his home soon. He was desperate.

He jerked awake. Had he been asleep? At a time like this? The interior cat seemed to think that this was normal, but then came the sharp smell of hospital. Astringents. Other animals. David's nose wrinkled and he hissed. His heart began to pound.

"Yes, yes, we're at the vet's," Mama's voice came from outside. "It's okay, baby."

As unfamiliar hands reached in and dragged him from the bag, David felt Jonathan shrink away. Too many doctors; too many scary things. Jonathan didn't want to face them.

Calm down, Jonny. David tried to mask his own trepidation. *They think you're sick because I'm inside you. They're trying to make you well.*

White fear answered him.

Now, Jonny-boy, don't you feel so much better since you got back from your trip? They made you well.

You're here.

Ah. That was an accident. I'm working on getting out. Don't you worry; I'll handle this. You fade out for a while, that's a good boy.

They set him down on a stainless steel table. He didn't even get a paper robe to wear. David reached out to the cold, slick surface cautiously as the doctor and Mama talked. He took a step and almost fell over. Damn! Forgot about the tippy-toes!

"Baby!" Evie cried.

"Just having a little adjustment from the carrier," the doctor said.

David owned ergonomic shoes of Italian design, and his steps had always been confident and sure. *Prove your worth to the world by how you walk in it.*

In his effort to appear confident he fell again, almost clobbering his chin before someone caught him. They held him down as they talked soothingly. *Good boy, stay still...*

They still used rectal thermometers! David had read medical history that mentioned them and of course the old jokes remained, but he'd never actually seen one– or experienced it– until now.

"He's a very tense cat, isn't he?"

"Not at all," Mama snapped. "Jonathan baby, relax for the doctor."

She rubbed his neck and ears and despite himself David leaned into it. It was so calming, it almost made him forget what was–

"There," the assistant said triumphantly. A quick beep let her extricate the thing almost immediately.

The numbers on the readout alarmed David until he realized once again that he was a cat. What was normal for a feline?

The doctor wore a tunic printed with pictures of frolicking puppies and kittens. David sat up and braced himself against the doctor's booming voice as he discussed his symptoms with Mama. What kind of vet spoke in that tone before a frightened animal? Amateur. David prayed he wouldn't prescribe anything stupid… or dangerous.

"Let's just take a look, shall we?" As the doctor leaned closer, something within Jonathan rose up and snapped at him. The doctor drew back immediately, his hands flying up to protect his chest. Fear etched his face, making his snake bites stand up and quiver.

Go back to sleep, Jonny, David commanded. *I'll keep you safe.*

The doctor approached his patient warily. He pried wide David's eye and shone a light that seemed like a supernova. It was so bright it almost felt like a physical pressure against his eyeball. David strained against the hand, but more hands in back had him blocked.

His left eye got the same treatment. Amateur!

"Hm," the doctor said. As the dots before his eyes faded, David looked around to seek a diploma of some kind. Any kind.

David distrusted physicians. These days they seemed never to share what they knew. Instead, they forced the patient to do all the research on their symptoms, and either decided that the patient was right and treated them for that, or said they were wrong, which signaled expensive tests.

David's experiences with doctors categorized them as either (1) don't-care clockwatchers, or (2) more interested in money than patients. What had happened to the ones who were conscientious about their work and patients?

David leaned toward the doctor as he was coming in for another look, and the doctor drew back again. Didn't like animals, did he?

Mama stroked reassurance into him. "He's just been Rejuvenated," Mama reminded the doctor.

"Oh yes, I can see that. Fine work, fine work." The doctor glanced at his records. "Wish we could get some of that tech up here. Won't be long, I suppose."

Warily the doctor prodded David about the midsection, peered at his teeth or gums or maybe both (the assistant handled David then), and *hmmed* a little more. David tried to act as normal as he could imagine a cat to be. He couldn't afford to be cooped up in a cat hospital. He had things to do.

"Here we go," the doctor said as his computer screen pinged with a completed download. "Edinburgh reports Jonathan was in excellent shape when he was released. It must have been the trip. Sensitive cats sometimes react to sleep transport."

"Jonathan has never been high-strung," Mama said.

"Yes, well. It's a physical reaction, not a psychological one. He's just gotten over a major medical procedure, right? How was he before?"

"Calm. Nothing fazed him."

"I mean physically."

"Oh."

David looked up at Mama. Her brows were knit in a troubled frown. "He was very weak. Couldn't get around much anymore. He had arthritis and couldn't wash himself enough. We had to give him baths every few days. You've got the records. He was going blind, he only had two teeth left, and his kidneys were failing. But he was a good old cat. The best."

Did she say I'm a good cat? the small voice inside David's head asked as it appeared the worst of the exam was over.

David felt around his mouth. It seemed to be filled with healthy, solid teeth. *Yeah, Jonny. She says you're the best cat around.*

You still don't walk right.

David sighed. *I walk perfectly fine. There's something wrong with the way this body works.*

I'm a cat. That's how I walk. Jonathan may have added a "stupid" after that, but Jonny was a nice cat and the intention may have been blunted to "silly." Still, David admitted that he had a lot of learning to do.

The doctor nodded. "And now he's young again. That's enough to strain even a human who knows what's going on. He's been away from home far too long. Remember, kitty years are longer than human ones. And he may have been bumped around by the transport crew before they stowed him."

He scribbled a note on his padd. "This seems to be a slight concussion, but I don't think it's anything to worry about. You keep an eye on him and if his pupils aren't equal in a week, bring him back and we'll run him through the full gamut of tests. I bet he just needs some rest in a familiar home with the people he loves."

What a cowardly, pat answer, David thought. Why did this guy even pretend to be a doctor? Fifties were supposed to be better than this.

"He's got that," Mama said. She rubbed his ears in precisely the perfect spot. David sighed and closed his eyes. His plans could wait a little while.

When they got home, Mama rewarded Jonathan with hugs and kisses for being "a good boy with the doctor." She clasped him to herself as she cooed in babytalk. "Oh, I missed you so, sweedie-pie! Did oo miss Mama too? Um hum!"

Jonathan almost swooned in her arms. David had to admit that though it was a bit over the top, it wasn't that bad as long as no one he knew saw him like this.

The afternoon led into a quiet party of Mama's friends. They petted Jonathan and exclaimed (softly; Mama kept shushing them for Jonathan's sake) over the change in the cat. They dangled toys for him and to their great delight, he swatted and jumped at them.

Four pots full of fragrant growing greens were placed next to Jonathan's food dish. David nibbled on them while the humans had hors d'oeuvres. Those were tasty too. A man named Sam whose shoes had a wonderful, earthy smell kept sneaking bits and pieces to David. Nice guy. Jonathan liked him as well.

Eventually the party ran down and Mama saw everyone to the front door. They wished both her and Jonathan well with their rejuvs.

Mama held Jonathan tightly as if afraid to let him go. David wondered at the love bond between pet and owner, let alone the other way around. Let them have their time together. He'd tell Jonathan about Mama going away later. This was going to take tact.

Mama's lengthy departure from the scene meant that David had to focus on that other woman. Pip.

As if she sensed his thoughts, she walked in. David took a good look at her. Underneath the mussed hair and slightly oversized coveralls, she seemed pert. Confident. Content. Here was a woman who'd never wind up in his office.

Evie accepted a thick courier packet from her. "It was just delivered," Pip said.

Evie refrained from opening it as she eyed her paint-spattered niece. "Why weren't you at the par–?"

"Working."

The older woman's lower lip pushed out. "You could at least try to clean up now and then. Once you leave your studio–"

"I thought this was my home."

"It was and it is. You are an Applegate."

"Thanks to whoever changed the name a few generations ago. Or was that you, Aunt Evie? To boost sales?"

"It was Grandmother Tang," Evie said as she set Jonathan on a desk. "There was a trademark problem or linguistic snafu or something at the time about the name 'Tang Apple Juice.' Grandmother went with the marketplace and decided on a name that would appeal to consumers."

"Applegate Organic Orchards." For some reason Pip's mouth twisted as she said the words.

Evie pulled the contents out of the envelope. It contained slices of something that didn't smell like apples, David decided. They had an overtone of orangeyness.

"Very wise woman, Grandmother Tang. It's a shame she didn't live longer. I'm sure she could have taught me a thing or two even up here." Evie passed a slice to Pippin. "Here, it's the new citrus cross. R&D's trying to convince me that crosses will be better received than designer mutations. Citrapples."

She held the slices to her nostrils and sniffed hard enough to wrinkle her nose and the snakebite upon it. "They've given up trying to convince me to plant real orange trees. Oranges are too acidic for the market. I think we'll stay on course with the mutations."

"Organic mutations." Pip gave it all the irony a person could deliver a line. As she finished chewing her sample, she slid into an overstuffed chair that was part of an intimate grouping here in the den. "People like extremes now and then. That was one of the few nice things about being back on Earth. I had lemon with my tea, and orange or grapefruit juice every morning. Very decadent." She flashed an taunting smile at her aunt.

Evie would have none of it. "It's over the top. I can see citrus for vitamin C, but nutritional supplements already provide that. Edible citrus has nostalgic value, but we shouldn't go too far with it. It's a limited, specialized market. Mutations will cover it."

"I say go for the real oranges," Pip declared. "Customers will try them because they're so different. Then they'll keep buying them because they're good."

She tapped on her chin, and David noticed a slight spot of pink paint there. "It's like using bright colors. Experts say to decorate in calm colors, but when people shop for paintings, they always stop longer at the bright ones. Good thing I like painting those."

Evie made a face. "They may stop, but they don't buy. Your paintings are much too bright, even for the most unfashionable." She shook her head. "Fuchsia and day-glow greens. Blues splattered all over!"

"That was four years ago; I was just a student then. You've seen my new work."

Evie slapped the envelope, slices and all, against her bony arm. David/Jonathan jumped at the crack. "You can't support yourself doing that," she declared. "It's nothing like they've ever seen before. It's not right."

Pip's shoulders slumped. "I don't want to argue about it anymore. I'm tired of arguing."

"It's not popular," Evie persisted. "The public won't consider it. People will look at the Applegate name and think that Applegate Organics is just as strange. I want it stopped."

Pip's chin rose the tiniest millimeter. "No."

"At least change the style. I'll give you this much; underneath all the foo-farah, you have some talent. I don't mind if you want to paint after hours. Winston Churchill painted on the weekends. No one thought ill of him for doing that, and he still managed to win a war while he did it. He knew his priorities. He knew his true talent."

"Give me time. Building an artistic reputation doesn't happen right away. Did our orchards grow overnight?"

Evie gave the remaining sample slices another measuring sniff. "No, but apples and art... well, might as well be apples and oranges. Not the same thing."

"How long did it take Applegate Orchards to catch on? Back on Earth they were just another agricultural operation, and not a very successful one."

Jonathan purred loudly as he bumped Evie's arm with his head. She obliged him with a loving scratch.

"It took the right person at the helm," Evie said. "I saw a market opening for us that no one else was using. When I noticed the abandoned surface colony on Luna, the waste processing plant that needed an outlet– It all fell together for me way back when. It took a lot of work to get Applegate Organics up, running and profitable. It took people like Sam Greenwood. Now when Terrans look to the sky, they remember that we are here, and that we are as pure as the sky itself."

"And it took you how many years to get them to that point? Give me some time, Aunt Evie."

"Apples and oranges, Pippin. You agreed on three years."

Pip's chin drooped. Her shoulders caved inward as she wrapped her arms around herself.

"This exhibit of yours will demonstrate it to you once and for all. You're going in the wrong direction. This isn't the profession you're suited for. You're an Applegate through and through, Pippin. Time you realized that."

"Then why aren't any of the rest of the family up here with our orchards?"

"Because they're cowards. Dragging themselves around down there under that atrocious gravity. Wheezing the filth that infests the air. Slithering through the chemical goop that makes up the ground."

"And yet we sell Terran apples."

"Our apples are Lunar apples, child. Organic. That is where the company's reputation sits, on the pristine conditions one can only find on Luna. Look into the sky and see purity. Taste the innocence of Luna."

"Pure hokum."

Evie allowed herself a slight smile as she regarded her great-great-grand niece. "Perhaps. But our intentions are good."

"The road to hell is paved with good intentions."

"And the field of intention shapes the universe," Evie snapped. "I want your three hours a day fully documented, along with the time you spend keeping Jonathan amused and happy. When he's napping doesn't count. I'll expect you to respond to company calls here in addition to your time in the office. After all that is done, you can play at your art."

Pip drew her knees up until she huddled in a fetal position, cradled in the chair.

"You'll learn the hard way, I suppose. Monday after your show, I expect to see you at the office, ready to work full-time."

David studied the collapsed ball of human flesh that used to be a confident human woman. Pip. She smelled like prey to be conquered. Now here was someone prime for his own business. It hadn't really struck him before that she considered herself a serious artist.

Artists! If he'd been human he would have laughed. Artists had no real role in society. People could print out the entire history of art from gallery down-loads. There was nothing new to paint. It had all been done.

When he got back in his body, he would certainly give Pip his business card. No one deserved to feel alienated from society because they thought they were a "fine" artist. He'd set her back on a better path, possibly the one Mama had in mind for her.

He'd even give her free sessions. After all, it was Pip who was going to get his body back for him.

David allowed Jonathan to have his early bed time with Mama. She'd be gone tomorrow. Jonny was such a nice little guy it would be a sin not to let him have his simple pleasures.

So Evie cooed and sang to Jonathan as she sat in bed. She explained to the cat that she was going away for a while, but she'd be back and that she'd talk to him every day while she was gone. Maybe Pippin would bring him to see her.

She never knew that Jonathan now understood her every word, thanks to David's translation.

But Evie finally lay the cat down on the spread next to herself, and snuggled under the covers to sleep. Soon her breathing settled into an on-again, off-again drone. Jonathan settled upon her pillow with a sigh.

Not so fast, big fella, David told him.

I want Mama.

Jonathan had taken the news of Mama's imminent departure well, but David thought that was because he didn't understand it, or didn't understand what "tomorrow" was. *We'll come back when I'm through, okay?*

No. Stay with Mama.

Do you want me in your head forever? I've got a plan. You need to trust me and do what I say.

No.

David argued gently but firmly with the cat, promising to return to Mama later on with translations for all her coos. Finally Jonathan agreed. They eased up in their one body and jumped lightly to the floor.

The sudden jolt set off a quiver inside them. Something was wrong. Was this a side effect from the rejuv? Maybe the rejuv had gone wrong. David's stomach clenched terribly. His body knotted into rolling cramps.

Was the cat's body rejecting him? If that happened, where would his mind go?

No one would even know he was gone.

He hacked. He was choking to death! *Hack. Hack.* A final, massive *houlk* coughed up a long tube of grayish yellow, slimy hair.

David thought he was going to pass out. He'd never thrown up before. Jonathan sat back on his haunches, then reached up to lick his front paw and clean around his mouth. Then he began grooming a spot on his side, beginning his next hairball.

How could he take it all so calmly? The hypnotizing repetition of washing made Jonathan sleepy. He got up and stretched, preparing to jump back on the bed.

But the stretch alerted David. He reminded Jonathan of their mission and turned to pad soundlessly out into the hall. A nose opened a cracked door enough to slip through. Pippin's room lay in darkness through which David could clearly discern.

Clothing was thrown this way and that, luggage lay open but wasn't entirely unpacked yet. The vanity held a swath of cosmetics.

Pippin sprawled on her back on the edge of her great bed, her arms flung out as if she'd collapsed without settling in, though a sheet covered her.

Together David and Jonathan jumped up to join her. He settled next to her head, and Jonathan tucked his front paws under his chest in patient waiting mode.

David began to construct a dream.

7

Pippin couldn't focus on her work today. Again and again, she'd had to scrape the paint off new sections of her painting. She felt schizoid.

And the darned cat got into the studio. She always made sure to close the french doors that barricaded the rest of the house from her space, but somehow that crafty Jonathan had snuck in.

He barreled around the path that circled the central worktables in the room, and then began to jump onto the ledges made by piled art books, boxes of materials, and canvases.

"Daviiid!" she shrieked, and the cat ran from her to disappear through the french doors. As she shut them securely, she wondered for a moment why she'd thought Jonathan's name was "David." She shrugged to herself. Post-Earth brain fart, probably.

After another hour she determined that nothing else was going to get done here. She'd already wasted a couple hours of the day helping Aunt Evie check into the Rejuv center and reassuring her about both Jonathan and the office.

Time for a change of scenery. She scrolled through the all-Luna Arts & Entertainment calendar in the *Luna C Magasite.* According to the listings, if she could get over to Aldrin by thirteen, she could catch a *plein vacuum* bus. That would certainly force her to focus. She grabbed her pressure suit and the pack that she kept prepared for such excursions, stuffed it into a designer bag to keep the FeePs away, and took off.

She made it with fifteen minutes to spare.

Tito Roland looked up from where he was helping an Eighty-make woman onto the bus. Terran to tell, as she couldn't quite get the knack of hauling herself into a tight double airlock while wearing a rented pressure suit. She had that wild-eyed look of a first-timer on the Lunar surface.

"Pippin Applegate!" Tito exclaimed. "I haven't seen you in ages. Joining us?"

She made a face at him. "No, I always wear a p-suit when I go strolling. I've been gone. Don't even know what phase we're in."

"Full Earth," Tito replied, giving the Eighty a surreptitious shove.

Earth would be at the zenith, its bright side toward Luna. Pippin's mood perked up. That meant a cool light upside. She needed more cool colors for her show.

"Let's go," she told Tito as she breezed by him.

"You're the only person I know who likes New Earth for the light and not the drama."

"That's because you ferry around people who never studied Monet and his hay stacks. They never learned the magic of light."

Tito sealed the hatch behind her, giving the bottom latch a kick to ensure the job. The jaunty black beret he always wore for the tourists bobbled on top of his head above the hard, high collar of his p-suit. It was his trademark as Luna's well-known "heavenly artist." "That's not today's lesson. We are here to study form and value. Full Earth's the only time we can really get in a solid value lesson, and even then…"

He grimaced and once again Pippin wondered why he'd ever come to Luna. At one time she thought he considered Luna a stepping stone to Mars and exotic pinkish butterscotch-skied Martian landscapes, but Mars was a long way from being a comfortable place to stay yet. And it could get decidedly too windy for *en plein air* painting.

"You teach; I'll paint in the back where no one can catch any of my bad ideas," Pippin assured him.

Few people had boarded the window-lined bus. Tito did have enough professional ethics to advertise the jaunt for artists and not for touring. He was probably missing out on a better income, especially during times like Full Earth. Tourists ate up that view.

Still, there were two touristy-looking types here who sorted through sample art kits that Tito provided. They were probably here to get a close-up look at gaudy Full Earth as she hung all blue and wispy white against the stars. It was the stuff of postcards.

Three artists she knew, amateurs all. They stowed their gear as they settled in and gave her a nod as she passed. Five other artist-types looked fairly new to the scene, including the Eighties woman. Pippin trundled to the rear with a skip in her step.

She squeezed by Ricardo Raj, who regarded her with a sour look on his Teen-make face. All bones and angles, he cultivated the "starving artist" look. Society's matrons couldn't get enough of him.

"Pippin," he almost spat.

"Ricardo," she deigned as she pushed past. She could hear him mutter something under his breath behind her, but she muttered something as well. Once she had told him exactly what she thought of his phony work and what kind of artist would try to pass it off as art. She'd never apologized.

The short lift to the surface and the bumpy trip from there buoyed her spirits once more. She was out and about. *Plein vacuum* painting got her to the source, the actual light and textures, the true *feel* of the unearthly Lunar surface.

They chose a good spot to stop. The bus leveled itself and slowly pushed its walls out with a hissing of extra atmosphere to create viewing bays. Pippin had her easel set up and palette deployed within two minutes. Tito continued the lecture he'd been droning since they'd taken off, but now he went around to each artist and gave them helpful suggestions, sometimes using their work to show the class– usually as an example of what not to do. All but Pippin were working on paintings of Mama Earth.

Pippin tried not to listen. Tito's admonishment to his students that *plein vacuum* painting was best to teach the new artist how *not* to paint what the landscape presented had about 10% merit to it.

Pippin hadn't always been Loonie; she'd grown up on Earth. Her first *plein air* paintings had been rough. What to paint out of everything in front of her?

How to paint without making it look like a photo? It took her years to discover that she had to leave out most of what she saw and rearrange elements to create a dynamic composition. The gist of it all was painting a dominant impression capturing the personality of the place– and the artist holding the brush.

Tito might as well have been instructing his students to paint white foam blocks in a studio. And worse, he tried to Terran-ize the moonscape.

He told them to visualize the rock formations as foliage, to add atmospheric perspective to the airless landscape in front of them. "The alienness of the moonscape will force you to reevaluate how you use shapes," he told the crowd. "Obviously, you can't paint a lunar landscape if you want to sell your work."

He paused as his tour of the easels brought him to Pippin's work. He took a look at it and then turned quickly away.

She'd sketched her design, nudging the moonscape here and there to lead the eye into the painting. She had to search for few colors, since the scene in front of her already exuded the blues and purples that she had hoped for, reflected by the friendly globe in the sky. She merely accentuated them, making subtle color notes directly on the canvas that she could erase once she got home and began working on a more complex version of this composition.

Plein air on Earth was a frantic affair. There she'd learned to slap on paint as fast as she could. Weather could come up from nowhere and dissipate just as quickly. There was always something hurrying across a landscape and refusing to stay still. A scene just didn't stay the same from one minute to the next.

Light changed so quickly as the sun sped across the Terran sky. Why, one instructor had told her that a painting that took over 25 minutes to produce was worthless because the time-variation in shadows and highlights would be noticeable.

Here on Luna it took days for the light to waver. Shadows remained just as long from morning to evening, though of course that was on Earth time, not Lunar time. A Lunar day lasted a Terran month. There were no clouds plotting against her, no rain to splatter her sketch colors, no wind to send her canvas flying. No bugs to die in her drying paint.

It was lovely to be able to come back to almost the same conditions day after day until she got things exactly right. Of course, here on the bus she only had a few hours before they returned to Aldrin.

So she painted in fast washes and daubs. She took photos for later, and stopped to add an entire three pages of written notes and scribbles to her notebook.

Tito came by again, shadowed by Ricardo. By then Pippin had three small canvases completed, with no Earth in sight.

"Keep those away from them," was all Tito muttered as he turned back to his group.

His comment couldn't burst the euphoria of a day well spent after all. As everyone packed up, Pippin covered her wet canvases in Saf-T-Seal, passed her brushes and palette through her porta-cleaner, and plopped down onto her seat with a happy sigh of exhaustion. She was ready to hit the sack and be ready for great day of work tomorrow– if she didn't have any more of those crazy dreams.

That night Jonathan wailed inside David. *Where's Mama?*

I told you, Mama's gone for a while. Just a few days, maybe a couple weeks, David tried to reassure the being inside himself, but the waves of loneliness and confusion still lapped at him.

He curled himself into a ball on Mama's bed and tried to catnap until Pip would emerge from her studio.

"Yoooowww," he finally cried, and got up to pace the house. Maybe exercise would get Jonny out of this funk. He hopped onto furniture, leaped across shelves and narrowly avoided the antiques that Eve had foolishly thought safe at high altitudes.

Wasn't that fun? he asked Jonathan even as he tried to figure another likely obstacle course. The portrait over the room's mantelpiece caught his eye.

It was of Mama, dignified and powerful, seated in the very chair upon which he now sat. The flat photo process, like all the flat photos scattered around the house, gave it an air of antiquity.

There she is.

Mama? Where?

His heart sped up from Jonathan's question, and he fought the urge to look around.

There. See, the picture?

Mama?

David concentrated on the picture. He tried to show Jonathan that this was an image of his beloved Mama. Bright spot there was actually light on her forehead and nose. There were her eyes. There was—

Comprehension sank in. Darks and lights suddenly coalesced into form. *Mama! Mama!*

Yes, Jonny, that's a picture of Mama.

Jonathan's wonder was palpable, that somehow Mama's presence was right there. He jumped onto the mantle, noisily displacing various bric-a-brac, and sniffed the portrait. It didn't smell like Mama. He pawed at the frame, but it lay flat against the wall. Mama couldn't be in there, could she?

Here, let me show you more, David told him. Now he prowled the house, hunting photographs. Each time he found one of Mama, Jonny *yowed* in delight. The cat knew this wasn't Mama, but it was close.

When they found the picture of Evie and Jonathan together, the one that sat on Mama's night table, Jonny refused to let David leave. Instead he sat and stared contentedly at it.

That's right, that's Mama and Jonathan, David told him. He reached out his front right paw and touched the button on the side of the picture frame.

"Isn't Jonathan a good boy?" the picture said in Mama's voice. "Oh yes, he's such a good widdle boy! Jonnnathan…"

Jonny went crazy even after David hurried explained the not-quite-reality of it. He showed him how to trigger the sound and even twenty-five rounds of "Isn't Jonathan a good boy?" didn't begin to sound monotonous.

They woke from a contented doze when Pip trudged to bed from her studio. David waited a half-hour before he padded into Pip's bedroom and hopped onto the bed. He snuggled next to her.

For a moment David paused to inhale the delightful musk of woman. It reassured him that he was still a man though he lay in a body that wasn't even his species. Next to him, Pip breathed heavily, and he wondered how much of that was cat hearing and how much was semi-snore.

She was warm. And soft. Without noticing he began to knead her butt. There was nothing sexual about it, but it gave him a deep feeling of satisfaction. Streeeetch and ease. Streeetch and ease. He could feel the stretch deeper when he extended his claws and–

"Jonathan!" Pip batted at him. "No claws, cat. I know she's not here, but you've got to go to sleep, poor fella." She gave him a pat on the head with an extra, quick rub around his ears, and then drew the sheet back around herself.

David clasped his hands under his chest while he sank into a focusing trance, which was almost too easy to do in this form. After he was certain she slept, he regarded the wall of the bedroom. He practiced making mental pictures against it, running them like vids. Then as Pip reached REM sleep stage, he reached for her mind.

I'm inside the cat, he told her silently. *My name is David. Learn to listen to me. Help me get out....*

"I blame it all on Earth," Pippin confided to Sugar the next evening. Sugar was talking almost normally now and her opaque post-op makeup was only thinly applied.

The bulk of Pippin's luggage had finally arrived. To save shipping charges she'd had crates catapulted in from Earth. Together the two ripped apart an outer carton in the spacious Applegate entry and plowed through all the cushioning.

"You better not expect me to clean that up!" Tiffany bellowed from the kitchen and her house monitors.

"It's given me the weirdest dreams," Pippin continued. "Dav– I mean, Jonathan claims that he's not a cat."

Sugar took a moment to regard the yellow cat helping them make their way through the spongy material. Unfortunately his way shredded it and made a worse mess. "Now you're even dreaming about him."

"And I keep calling him 'David,'" Pippin said. "I mean, even when I'm not sleeping." She lowered her voice so Tiffany's monitors wouldn't pick it up.

"Maybe it's the stress from my deadline. How much stress can someone take before they get delusional?"

Sugar managed a snort that sent the gilded edges of her bandage rippling. "Or maybe you're just crazy to begin with. You should see a shrink."

"I think I did. In my dream."

"What?"

Pippin shook her head, trying to remember. "I think there was a shrink there. Or maybe it was the dead man. Anyway, David, I mean Jonathan was yowling all through it, and I wake up and he's in the kitchen, yowling away."

"Pay dirt." Sugar reached farther in and pulled out a box emblazoned with a brand name. "Well, look at that."

Pippin watched Sugar's face for approval. "Did I do good?"

"It's the right company. Let's see what you've got."

They unpacked the one box. After they cleared an étagère of antiques– Grandma Tang's things, from the age of them– woks and pans, fans and paperweights and a small sword, they spread new jars and tubes of white, pearl and pastels across its shelves and various chairs. Pippin unearthed more boxes and sorted them into art supplies, dirty laundry and more cosmetics. The cosmetics joined the first.

Sugar closely examined each item. "This is so new I haven't seen it listed on department notices yet," she said. She thumbed the label, which projected an enlarged list of contents.

"You said I needed a good night crème," Pippin began.

Sugar waved her silent. "Polyoxy-E, hydrallurinol, crachat des larves," she read with some difficulty. "I've never heard of crachat des larves." She shrugged. "It must be okay. It's French."

"You aren't going to look it up?"

"Look, it's a legitimate maker and they say 'Increases deep derma-elasticity by normalizing alkaline/acid balance and sebaceous sebum.'"

"What's sebaceous sebum?"

"It's... well..."

"You don't have any idea."

"I'm sure it's perfectly marvelous," Sugar snapped. "And you'll get credits for being the first to register this stuff through Lunar FeeP." She set it aside for registration.

"But it's not going to eat my face off while I sleep?"

"I sincerely doubt that. What the hell's the cat doing now?"

The women watched as Jonathan nosed the cosmetics this way and that, almost as if he were rearranging them on purpose. He stood on his back feet to reach, and carefully patted each jar into place: Darling brand deep-clean cream, Aphrodite firming gellé, Vita-Retinol generic patches, Iridescence nite-bites, and Dark Druid firming lotion.

"What does he want me to do?" Pippin asked as Jonathan sat there, looking expectant.

"Maybe he wants to maintain his rejuv."

Something about it was eerie. Pippin studied the arrangement. The initial capitals of the brands began to stand out to her. D. A. V…

Sugar shrieked. "You got some hydrocollastem crème! Lady Love!" She pulled a large box with the heart-shaped logo of a cameoed Victorian woman from the carton. "A whole case! How the hell did you manage that?"

Pippin turned to see what Sugar was talking about. "They were having a sale in Paris." She batted down irritation at Sugar's approval. It had distracted her from something important–

Sugar ripped open the box. "I swear, if you don't give me just one of these, I'll… I'll… I'll rip up that credit of yours and let you go to fashion court alone!"

The almost-serious tone made Pippin laugh. "It's all for you," she said. "It's a case full of FeeP bribe. But I'm going to portion it out. You know, use it as I need it."

Sugar clutched one porcelain jar to her magnificent bosom. "Only if you promise to pull something outrageous every time I get near the last of it," she said.

"You know me."

Sugar eyed her parolee. Pippin's hair was liberally dabbed with bits and pieces of insulation and fluffed out at frightening angles due to the static electricity of the packing material. She still wore her paint-spattered smock, and her arms and chin displayed unnatural color that could only come from paint.

"I certainly do," Sugar sighed. "Here, let me help you put this up and then I'll show you what to do with it."

As they gathered their second load to take to Pippin's room, the front door buzzed.

"Tiffany!" Pippin wailed.

A faraway voice called, "My program's on!"

Pippin balanced jars and tubes as much as she could to her left side and finagled the doorknob with her right hand. It took a few balancing jumps and lucky hits to activate the thick outer airlock. Aunt Evie's place had originated in a time when accidental vacuum sometimes lurked just outside. Instead, this time it was an early-Forties woman in drab but neat jumpsuit.

"At-Home Services," she announced herself. She raised an eyebrow at Pippin's condition but didn't comment.

"Oh yes." Pippin nodded the woman and her small case in. "I almost forgot about you."

Pippin had called first thing this morning to install the handicap-accessible accessories onto Aunt Evie's puters and around the house. It had seemed a good idea at the time to go ahead and get it done, though Evie wouldn't be needing it for over a week from now. Now Pippin wondered why she'd felt the need to get it done so soon.

"Whatever," Pippin muttered to herself and, still loaded with the cosmetics, showed the tech back to Aunt Evie's home office.

David's tail thrashed as he watched the tech show Pippin what she'd done. Evie's puter had been adjusted so that she didn't need to have full use of her voice or hands to operate it. At long last, the humans left.

David jumped up on the puter desk.

When can I see Mama? Jonathan asked.

It's like I told you, Jonny. It's going to be days at least before they'll let you visit. I'll bet she'll pull strings and get you in the hospital. David pawed the sensor until the puter hummed to life. *Until then, they're going to play pictures of Mama for you that she made before she went to hospital.*

Jonathan still seemed doubtful about tapes and events that weren't happening in real time when they seemed as if they were.

Here. David turned away from the puter to point his nose at a flat picture of Mama and Jonathan. *Here's a photo you can look at.* He pawed the sensor and the picture began to move. Mama petted the photo's Jonathan, who began to purr loudly.

"Doesn't he sound nice?" Picture-Mama asked with a smile.

Jonathan's tail swished wildly.

David backed away from the puter. Mustn't interfere with the controls. Instead he took a breath, told himself to be patient, and let Jonny enjoy it for a few more repetitions.

As he pawed the frame Jonathan glowed with pleasure from the idea that Mama had pictures of him so she could look at him.

That's probably how she got along when you were away too, David explained.

David had to push several pictures next to the puter so he could glance away from the monitor every now and then and let Jonathan gaze at them. It was the only way he could get any work done.

It took a bit of doing to master the primitive way of navigating the electronics. One of the first things he did was to have the puter recognize "Mow" as "Enter," which speeded the process enormously.

Short minutes afterward David had a section set up for himself in the family's personal memory space. No one without his passcode would ever know. He began a search for one David Lumen, late of Earth, now on Luna. Lunar bureaucracy operated differently from Terran, so that had to be sorted through as well.

A popup ad for cheap people-finding services bounced around on the screen. Jonathan batted at it.

Stop it, Jonny. It's not a toy.

He tried to explain to Jonathan that he was just going to have to let David keep control right now if he wanted David out of his mind.

That popup really was colorful.

David dismissed it and searched the local newspaper for a mention of his escapade the other day. Ah– there was a short article, buried but with multiple links. Probably someone at the shuttle company didn't want bad publicity. It didn't mention where the body had gone, much less whom it had been identified as. "Unknown male stowaway," was all it said.

He swatted at a popup to make it go away.

Obviously, they'd take a comatose body to a hospital. How many of those could there be on Luna?

Jonathan took care of the next popup. How quickly Jonathan dealt with the touchscreen! David admired the cat's style and then triggered another popup just to tease him.

It was a game popup. Jonathan batted it back and forth.

To your right, David urged the cat. *That's it. Here it comes!*

Jonathan patted the screen exactly right.

They both laughed as Jonathan swatted the popup so hard that it disappeared. But he had trouble with the next. David showed him. *It'll go this way and then here and here.*

Jonathan didn't care for the logic of the movement. He saw it begin its path, and *pak!* reached to make it bounce.

They made a game of it. Jonathan would bounce it, and David would figure where it would go next. Then he'd bounce it in multiple zig-zags to test Jonny's mettle. It was all David could do to keep up with the cat. Jonny had left paw; David had right. At some point he gave up trying to teach and just played the game, internally shouting his encouragement to Jonny and exulting when he himself made a score.

Tiffany humming to herself on the other side of the bedroom door brought David's attention back. *Enough play.* He tried to sound stern, but they both knew better. *I've got work to do.*

As Jonathan pouted David discovered police reports about his body. They'd taken him to Memorial Hospital, LunaPort. David clicked a map. LunaPort was right next door to Luna City with only a safety margin for potential transport disasters separating the two. From there they'd transferred him to a local hospice.

With his doctor's credentials, he even managed to find a room number.

It was late. *Let's go to bed,* Jonathan suggested.

I have to arrange another dream first, Jonny. If you hang with me a little more, maybe by this time tomorrow you'll be sleeping alone in your own head.

David tried his best to weave a dream explaining how he'd become a cat. He showed the sleeping Pip his life in Vegas as well, and gave her the flavor of being two minds in one body. The effort of it– or maybe it was because he was a cat now– exhausted him.

He wrapped himself into a ball and fit himself into the small of her back. She smelled familiar and female. She petted him almost as well as Mama.

Pip was a nice girl. She made calls to Mama's doctor and asked good questions. She seemed to truly care that the old lady was doing well. Drowsily, David wondered what he'd have thought of Pip if she'd ever come to Vegas.

A movement who knew how long later brought him awake in an instant. As Pip bounded out of bed, David rolled to avoid the general cataclysm. Sheets and blankets flailed this way and that. She reached for her robe and then discarded it– right on top of him.

By the time he'd managed to unwind himself from its depths, she'd already run out of the bedroom. He chased after her, but she closed the door to her studio just ahead of his whiskers.

Damn! He couldn't start conscious work on her. She was primed for mind-to-mind communication, but without being able to see each other it probably wouldn't work.

8

With inspired focus that had come too little of late, Pippin grabbed the nearest toned canvas she had ready. Wrong proportions. She grabbed the next, which was much better.

A few scribbles and she had her layout. She could see it in her mind so clearly; no need for extensive pre-planning. Her palette was ready to go. All she had to do was unseal it. The two sketchbooks she'd used yesterday she now adhered to the top of her easel within view, and she clipped one of the *plein vacuum* small canvases beside her for easy reference.

She worked like lightning as she always did when her muse was visiting. If ever she doubted her talents as an artist, it was times like these that reminded her of who she truly was.

She swabbed in the value pattern– beautiful enough just by itself. With a spritz of fix, the oil paint dried and she went on to develop the color scheme. She exaggerated the lunar landscape into cascades of reds and oranges that led the eye this way and that.

Two small, suggested buses parked on the surface provided an excuse for the colors. She'd seen it before, how some rock formations came to life when the soft lights of man drove by. Now she played it up and added blue light from Earth just to make it all vibrate.

When she stepped back to look at it as a whole, it almost seemed like Las Vegas, but with realistic shapes and a subtle base that made the tight, brisk strokes of pure color all the more startling. This was a canyon that Earth could never begin to match.

Pippin propped it up high on her easel so she could step across the room and gaze at it. Such pride and satisfaction surged through her! She knew that after a few minutes more of study, she'd see the imperfections, the "why didn't I–" spots. So instead she called a break and declared to herself that she wouldn't look at it again today. Let it have twenty-four hours of being perfect. So few things in this world had that chance.

She strolled into the kitchen: bare feet and nightshirt. Tiffany looked over from the vid and took her in. "I suppose you'll be wanting dinner early," Tiffany said.

Pippin turned to the clock. It was afternoon! "My god, where has the time gone?" Pippin asked no one in particular.

"Office called," Tiffany said.

"Oh, Jesus." At least the maid hadn't interrupted her with it. Pippin had to have three hours of office time documented today, as well as time with Jonathan.

The cat lay on his side on top of the kitchen table, softly snoring.

"Just get me some breakfast," Pippin told Tiffany. "I'll eat it when I'm out of the shower. Dinner late. I've got to go to the orchards."

She wasn't sure if Tiffany even heard her over her vid. Instead, Pippin ran off to discharge her mundane duties.

David had waited all morning for Pip to return from her studio. Had he missed her leaving? Where could she be? She might have a boyfriend or lover who could keep her from returning to her bedroom tonight. He paced the front hall until Tiffany shooed him out of the way of the waxer bot.

You think too hard, Jonathan complained. *You're noisy.*

Sorry. And then David mused some more. He must get his body back. Once he found himself, how could he get his mind back inside? Would it come naturally, or would he have to perform some technique? The process of disengaging from it hadn't been easy at all.

He tried to work out the mechanics. Old telepathic theories from school flitted through his mind, but none seemed to fit.

Oh well. He'd cross that bridge when it appeared. Right now he had the beginnings of a plan. He knew where his body was. Pip would provide transportation there if he could just get at her one more night. One way or another he'd get back into himself. But after that– what?

He'd have to go somewhere. He padded into Mama's room and activated her puter. The rest of the morning he spent printing out maps of the tunnel network that linked lunar cities and suburbs. Then he ran a quick ID on that woman, that Sugar FeeP. She'd been an officer for a long time. Whew. A *long* time.

FeePs weren't real police, but they palled around with them. No one would induct a FeeP to a crime organization. After all, they were just *FeePs*. Important, but not important at all. This Sugar Morales might be able to tell him who was safe to report to.

Someone who could make sure he could go home safely.

He awoke slowly before he cursed. *Jonathan! I thought I said no naps!* He'd just come into the kitchen to grab a bite.

The cat gave him an obnoxious comment about how humans' sleep patterns were all too long, and then forgot any hard feelings. He stretched just enough to attract the maid's attention.

"Hey! How long you been on the table? Get down! Her highness ain't here now." Tiffany scooted him off just as Pip appeared from opposite the direction to her studio. She must have been here all along.

She held the cat carrier. "C'mon, Jonathan," she urged the cat. "I need double time credit today. You're coming with me."

David wanted to ask, but Pip supplied the answer without the question. Was she tuning into his brain or just talking nonsense to the cat? "We'll go to work first and then we'll play," she said.

Jonathan liked that translation. He jumped up and trotted into the carrier without putting up a fight.

"Will you look at that," Pip said, perhaps to Tiffany. She stared into the box as Jonathan settled, and then she closed the door.

Security was tight at the doors of the MacLear Crater HQ of Applegate Organic Orchards, Inc., especially after the guards recognized Pip. She was crisply greeted with "ma'am's" along her route to the back. No one questioned the cat carrier.

A handprint opened the door to a large office. She slung David's carrier onto a chair. David peeked out as Pip opened its gate.

"It's Aunt Evie's office," she said helpfully. "Window, please."

Beige paint on one wall lightened and then turned completely transparent. The office looked out over a long, dome-covered valley where rounded trees grew in neat, green rows. Pip took a seat at a desk perpendicular to the view.

David jumped up to the sill and pressed his nose against the window, trying to see it all. What a spread!

Occasionally Pip grunted or talked to herself in short phrases that David didn't understand, but mostly kept quiet as she worked. David watched the trees. Somewhere down there a breeze blew, causing the leaves to wave gently. There was no red-gray haze, no coating of dirt on the trees that he could see.

Of course, he'd noticed his cat's eyes couldn't see red that well, and not-that-distant venues were out of focus. Jonny was near-sighted. Were all cats?

The dome allowed filtered sunlight through. This could have been an idyllic Terran setting before all the smog and pollution moved in.

Craters were fairly cheap here on Luna. Who wanted craters, when people lived underground? Mama must have been the one who installed the crater domes and irrigation systems. David had heard something about the setup. Lunar farmers turned municipal waste into compost and in turn sold oxygen and freshened air back into the system. It must take a long time to make fertile dirt out of lunar soil, but then again it also took a long time for these apple trees to grow this tall.

And to think Mama had come up with all this. *Your Mama's a very smart human,* David told Jonathan. *Powerful too. Rich.*

She rubs my ears.

So Jonny wasn't impressed by anything other than Mama being Mama. Maybe he had a point.

David roamed around the office for Jonny's sake, sniffing every new smell. He paused to take a deep whiff when he caught Mama in spots, opening his mouth to let the smell slide across the top of his mouth, where smells seem to steep. It calmed Jonny and made him feel closer to his missing Mama.

A wadded sheet of paper that missed the trash can became a toy for three minutes. Then the door opened without a knock.

"Pippin? I thought that was you."

David looked up. A dark-suited man stood in the entryway, a high Seventies make. For a moment David's heart stood still: Ragnar had found him!

But this wasn't him. This guy was a 77 or 78, not yet Ragnar's 79-plus ultra-make. The angles were still slightly soft on him. His makeup was professionally applied and the suit was sharp. Looked like CEO material to David, except for the dullness to his expression– or was that in his mind?

Pip had also turned. "Brock, you surprised me. Next time, could you knock?"

He sauntered in, his upper lip curved in what might have been meant to be a smile but came out more as a simper. Did David feel a stab of jealousy? Here was a man who could deal with Pip as another human being.

"Sorry," Brock said. "So you're finally back from Earth. We've all missed you. I've missed you."

"It's good to be back, though not here. I heard you stopped by the party but didn't stay long."

"Evie didn't say that, did she?"

David examined this man's body language closely. The sudden sheen on his forehead, the tightening of his jaw…

"Sam mentioned it."

"Oh. Just Sam." Brock relaxed and David realized that he was afraid of Mama.

Brock's smile returned long and slow as he took in Pip. He twirled the seat in front of her desk so it faced him, seated himself, and swung back toward her as if he'd just performed an acrobatic trick that she should applaud. "I can understand why you don't like the company, Pippin. You don't have the same temperament as the old dragon. Whoever she leaves the company to needs to be able to command the troops. They need the dragon fire."

"And of course you've got that," Pip said. David couldn't hear the first bit of irony in her voice, clever girl. She took after her aunt in many ways.

"I live for this company." Brock tapped his chest. "You've seen that. Your aunt has too, and yet she hasn't said anything, much less put anything in writing about it. Unless she's shown you something?"

"As Veep I'd expect you to have seen everything."

"Your official title is Vice President as well, Pippin."

The shudder that came over her couldn't be hidden. "That's just an emergency contingency. As in now. You're still in training. I'm sure that in time Aunt Evie will bring you in."

Brock crossed his legs and leaned back in his seat. David aimed the paper wad at his nose: *whap!* Brock jumped at the near-miss. With a jerk, he looked around for a culprit and spotted Jonathan.

"The cat looks well," he growled.

"Doing great. Ready for another twenty years before the next one." Into Pip's pause David could have sworn he saw a devilish gleam light her eyes. "I think I heard Aunt Evie tell one of her lawyers that she was thinking of leaving the company to Jonathan if anything happened to her."

Brock didn't see the tease. "She couldn't do that, could she? A will like that would be thrown out."

With a straight face Pip replied, "I've heard of similar wills. They held up for the most part."

"You'd be executrix."

"Maybe. Maybe Sam Greenwood would. He knows the apples backward and forward. The Terran branch of the family would support him."

"No, they'd support you and then me." Brock got up and began to stroll the room. "How's your aunt doing? This rejuv is kind of chancy for her, isn't it?"

"Any Total is chancy. I don't like the idea of a person's body being spread out between three different rooms even for a few minutes, much less a few days. But the doctors keep telling me that she's coming along fine. She had a bad moment yesterday, but everything's back on track."

"Oh. Very good." Brock paused before some folders on a bookcase, lifted the cover to two of them and checked what was inside.

Pippin leaned forward. "Tell me, what do you think about the new citrus cross?"

The question clearly caught him by surprise. As David watched the emotions play across his face, he knew that Brock was not the world's fastest thinker. Or the world's best actor. Obviously he was trying to couch his answer the way it would best reflect upon him.

"What does the dragon think?" was all Brock could come up with.

"I think she's wrong," Pippin said. "And since she's gone, I'm considering doing something that she'd never do. Will you back me up?"

"Ayum… On the cross?"

"Which way do you think we should go?"

"I think… I think…" Brock licked his lips hard, his eyes darting back and forth from wall to wall as if he were trying to communicate with his brain only to get a dropped connection. Finally he came to an opinion. To emphasize it– or perhaps hide the time it took to arrive at it– he slid a stylus from his pocket and twirled it between his fingers. "Evie's only going to be gone six weeks. The experiments have waited this long. She'll be in charge of this company for a long time. I'd have to say that the prudent course is to go with her choice."

"Prudent for you or for the company?"

"Evie Applegate *is* the company, Pippin."

Pippin smiled at that, an easy grin that seemed friendly enough. "Absolutely true. And getting on Evie's bad side can only bring trouble."

Silence hung in the room as they stared at each other. Was it actual expression or a battle of mental wills that David sensed? Why did Brock seem so familiar?

Brock twirled the pen again, and the impression struck home. Steele Gambino on *Stormy Heights*, the multimillionaire who ran the big casino, did that as well. Come to think of it, he was a Seventy who also wore dark suits with striped shirts.

It was almost déjà vu as Brock sat on the edge of Pip's desk. He had all of Steele Gambino's moves down. Did he realize that Gambino was the villain of the show? Of course, he was also one of its most popular characters. People loved him for his decadence. They tuned in to see what he'd do next– and he'd do anything for money. He was also quite the ladies' man: suave. Debonair.

"Uh, still doing that art stuff, hey?"

"Yes, I'm still dabbling away," Pip replied dryly. Only David saw her right cheek twitch.

"Yeah, well. I hear that kind of thing is coming back."

"Coming back?"

He must have known he'd said something wrong because he spun the stylus some more. "You know, back into vogue. Hand-painted stuff instead of, well, posters. Photography. You might catch the popular wave if you time it right." His eyes switched to the right and then left. Shifty eyes were not a Gambino characteristic. "You could do a show or something."

"As a matter of fact, I'm working on one. But right now I'm trying to slog through all of Aunt Evie's affairs. She bribed me to do it while she was under the weather."

Brock rose and moved to her side of the desk to lean over her. "I could help–"

"No, no, thanks all the same. I know you're a busy man." Pip pushed her chair away from him and gave him a wide, empty smile. "Perhaps if I get into trouble in the coming week or so, I'll buzz."

"Don't hesitate a moment to call me." Brock was still standing expectantly, but Pip returned her attention to her monitor. "Ah," he said, "you'll be all alone in that big house while the old dragon's away. How about joining me for dinner? We could even go dancing afterward."

She looked up. "That sounds lovely, but I've got a ton of work at home. Some other time, Brock?" Again with the dismissing smile.

Brock agreed to an unspecified rain date, dropped his head in a semblance of a bow, and departed.

David let out a low growl as the door closed behind him.

"You and me both, cat," Pippin said before she heaved a sigh. She thumbed a button on her blotter. "Get me Sam Greenwood."

Pause. A beep.

"Sam?"

The speaker responded, "Pippin? You in the office today?"

"Yes."

"You should come down to van den Bos. Helluva situation with the compost. I need a witness to the condition so I can file an official complaint."

Pippin glanced at the clock on her monitor. "I can be there by three. But right now I need to talk to you about the citrus mutations."

"Evie speak to you about it? I sent her the hybrid samples."

"Oh yes, she made herself quite clear."

Somewhere in the orchards Sam groaned.

Pippin smiled at the sound. "And I'm afraid I disagree with her," she said.

"So you want the cross."

"No, I want orange trees. Real orange trees from the roots up. And lemons too. That was one of the only nice things about Earth, having a slice of lemon every now and then."

Sam laughed and Jonathan's tail twitched. "Lemons! That's one of the few things I miss from the old days. Evie's not going to like– But you don't care, do you?" Sam's voice took on a rasp.

"Of course I care, Sam. It's just that I think it's time for Applegate Organics to expand in more than just acreage. Melissa Crater– I've always liked that name. Aunt Evie was concerned that it was too far off the beaten path for us, but by the time the trees bear there'll be tunnels enough to it. It's here on the far side, so we don't even have to worry about camouflage. That will cut start-up expenses."

"Melissa. It's a bit of a commute, but that might work. It'd be out of Evie's way, that's for sure."

"We'd have to keep the temps tropical year-round, Sam."

David could hear the smile in Sam's voice. "I might add a sand beach while I'm at it. Just a little corner, with a windeo of an ocean view."

"And pipe some island music in as well. It'll make the trees feel right at home. You want to polish the details? I can link you to some preliminary stuff someone came up with years ago. Aunt Evie didn't like it then."

"And she won't like it now. She'll see the sense of this. Eventually. But if we can get most of the work done before she's up and about—"

"I like the way you think, Sam. I'll start people cooking the numbers up here."

David sat back on his haunches to consider Pip. Apparently she knew the business. Knew it better than ol' Brock Gambino. By all the evidence, Mama was a shrewd businesswoman, and Pip was her choice for successor. Mama should know.

It wouldn't be that hard to steer Pip into a useful position for which she displayed such skill. David gave his shoulder an off-handed lick. Once he got his body back, he'd repay her with the gift of conformity.

"Here we are," Pip announced as she set down the carrier.

The trip had lasted maybe an hour, with a change from public transport to a private shuttle that traveled tunnels that hugged their tram so closely they might be pneumatic, like the transoceanic tunnels on Earth. Doors opened directly upon an industrial-sized airlock with a more human-sized one embedded in it. It only took a couple minutes to cycle through.

David poked his head out when Pip released the gate to his carrier. This was one of those orchards. He couldn't tell how big the place was because of his low viewpoint and near-sightedness, but the dome certainly seemed to stretch an enormous way.

"G'wan, stretch your legs," Pip told him and gestured toward the trees. "Run. Even though it's not 2 AM and this isn't Aunt Evie's knickknack case. Work off some steam."

A tall woman came up to Pip, dressed in the same baggy coveralls as Pip wore. Badges on their left breasts labeled them as products of Applegate Organic Orchards, Inc.

"I don't know about this," the woman said as she and Jonathan/David exchanged measuring stares.

"He won't chew his way through anything," Pippin told her. "These trees need something jumping around on them. Otherwise they might as well be hydroponic fiberglass supports. It's probably healthy for them, you know, forest animals and such."

"This is an orchard, not a forest."

"Where's Sam Greenwood?"

David's neck stretched as he looked up and up to the top of the trees. He'd never seen apple trees this tall. Was it genetic enhancement, cat point of view, or the moon's low gravity that allowed them to grow so high? Still, they kept their rounded shapes and hadn't gone scraggy from overgrowth. They were lusher than any trees David had ever seen. Not a single leaf had been burned brown by acid rain. Instead, dew sparkled on the nearer leaves. A bee buzzed by his ear.

Over it all– and how many acres and acres must it be?– stretched that vast dome. Grids of lights in one section still shone brightly, but sharp-angled sunlight came in from the opposite direction from outside. Shadecloth stretched up the sides just above what must be the rim of this crater, to disappear beyond the foliage. The filtered light seemed ever so slightly dappled before it reached the trees.

Another bee buzzed by on its way to check out the thick clover that dotted the ground with purple flowers. Jonathan took off to catch it.

"Don't go too far, David," Pip called. "I mean, Jonathan," she said half to herself. "Damn, that's the darnedest thing." She straightened her shoulders and adjusted her coverall straps. "I keep forgetting his name all of a sudden," she said with a hint of apology.

The staff woman said, "Maybe you need a gingko patch."

"Maybe." As Pip stood from her crouch, she dusted dirt from her hands. "Well," she said, "he'll work off some energy and I'll get some sleep tonight. Sam said he was checking on a problem with a new load of compost?"

David trotted tippy-toe, tippy-toe along dirt pathways. It was so quiet in here, with just the occasional buzz passing by. A breeze stirred the odor of wet earth…or moon, rich with humus. Nice touch. Wonder why they'd pro-grammed one.

Excitement built in him: the magic of new territory to conquer. The lust of new textures to explore. He couldn't stand it anymore. He gave in to Jonathan, stretched up along one trunk, and sank his claws into it. Sooo good! He scratched and scratched, grinding his claws down to acceptable levels. The gritty vibration coursed through his skeleton. It was better than sex.

An easy clamber brought him to the lowest branch, and from there he climbed higher than he'd ever been. The thought of going down never entered his mind. He kept climbing, occasionally jumping to the next tree with an ease that was sheer, unadulterated freedom of movement.

His body was in prime condition. He was young and powerful. He had an entire forest to himself. No stalkers, no killers. No bills to pay, no responsibili-ties. All his needs were taken care of.

There was no reason to be human any more. Cat was all he needed.

He eyed a branch an impossible distance away. The branch he was on had a nice heft to it, a good spring as he crouched and tested.

He made it with inches to spare.

That was nothing, Jonathan told him. Jonathan ran and leaped into the air.

David gasped and scrabbled nothing but oxygen.

Be still! Jonathan ordered. He reached out an unholy distance and grabbed onto a limb. Their momentum swung them neatly about to land on it. As David caught his breath, Jonathan jumped again.

Woo hoo! David yowled. *Faster. Higher!*

Jonathan laughed and obliged. Ten trees over they found themselves falling through empty air. Now there was just "down" to go.

There was a lot of "down."

Time for the human to take over! David tried to figure Lunar gravity accel-eration versus the distance to the ground. He could see it right below, as he was falling upside-down.

As his brain shot neurons this way and that, with David offering God every bargain he could think of to get him out of this mess, Jonathan twisted in mid-air. Sideways. Other way sideways. His limbs stretched and his body yawed. Somehow he righted himself.

And neatly made a four-point landing.

Man, you have got to learn how to relax.

No, what David needed to learn was to shuck off his humanity. High atop the orchards of Luna, Jonathan taught him how to do just that.

Jonathan crept into the kitchen: tippy-toe, tippy-toe. He was Stealth Kitty. He kept to the dark edges of the room, slipping under the kitchen table with a mission to ambush Tiffany. She made such a satisfying shriek whenever he pounced.

His ears twitched to take in every sound these humans might make. Tail lowered, his body compact and ready to spring, he was Primordial Hunter Cat from a time before human domestication.

His dinner would be Tiffany's right ankle, so bare and tempting in front of him.

A familiar voice spoke from above.

"I know you killed Stephen," a woman accused.

9

"You know nothing of the sort. If you did, you'd have called the police. And I could have told them all about your stay in the mental ward last year."

David's whiskers tingled. *Stormy Heights.* In a wink, he ran out from under the table and jumped up to the surface.

"Cat!" Tiffany took a half-hearted swipe at him, but she was too interested in the television monitor.

David settled down beside her, rapt with curiosity. Had Helen finally put two and two together? Could she make a case to the police without falling to Brad's blackmail?

Thank god soap operas took so long to play out. He hadn't missed anything. In fact, things were just coming to a head– or so it seemed.

What was that gray thing Brad hid behind his back? Was it a remote? A dagger? A bottle of pills? The object was kept tantalizingly out of focus.

A lightning-quick swipe of his paw brought a pile of Tiffany's applecorn with it. David lay there munching along with the maid as they watched his favorite vid.

When the program was over he stood up and stretched in that thorough way cats had. It felt so good, but he couldn't get used to it. Today he'd almost forgotten that he was a man.

Time to get his own body back. Time to bring things to a head before he lost himself.

Sevan Branson gave Pippin's floral-print robe a quick, approving glance before he checked out the rest of the entryway. She secured the front doors behind him. "Nice place," he said. A roll of his shoulders dropped his knapsack to the ground.

Pippin watched appreciatively as he bent over to retrieve it by the handle. Oh my. And he had that sexy shoulder roll down pat. She wondered what other movements he could do well. Such a good-looking Ninety, with sharp eyes and surprisingly supple sculptor's hands.

"My studio's in the back." She directed him there, past doors whose views to Aunt Evie's luxurious rooms made him whistle appreciatively. Pippin wanted to whistle too. Sevan was a big man per his make, stuffed into a tight black tee shirt and boot jeans. That luxurious, glossy mass of umber hair on his head made her fingers itch to comb themselves through it. Forget Thirties and neo-Teens; this Ninety was just right for her.

It had been months since she'd had a really good time with a guy. Very long months. A true artist needed to refresh their fount of creativity, and a good bout of sex always seemed to do the job best.

"I must sound like a money shark," he said as they passed through the kitchen. Pippin had given Tiffany the night off. "But it doesn't really attract me that much. You know, not like some people."

"Like Tito Roland?"

"Well, yeah. Tito's had a tough life. He never made it as an accountant, even when his parents brought him into their business. And then he went into shipping, and then something else, I forget."

"I think he taught school once."

Sevan laughed. "As if there's any money in that. He told me that one day he was telling someone about all the old famous artists who starved their lives away and he figured he was at that point, so the least he could do was do something he liked."

"You're kidding. Tito actually likes to paint?" Pippin couldn't picture it. Tito and his leech-dog Ricardo were traitors to the profession. There was no way that either could have a true spark of artistic fervor in them.

"Sure he does. And he's smart. He found out what the public wanted to pay for, and he does it. Better than anyone else up here."

Pippin began to protest as she blocked the way into the studio, but Sevan held up his hand in a stopping gesture. "You can't blame him. No one likes stale oxygen and day-old bread. So he's got a cushy life now. You might think of doing the same. Spend half your time on what the public wants and the other half on what you want. That way you could support yourself." He peered beyond her into the darkened room. "You've certainly got the setup."

Pippin leaned against the doors. She rolled her head so she could gaze up at Sevan from under her eyelashes. "So you want to be rich?"

The left side of his mouth curled up as he touched the tip of his thumb to her cheek. He ran it to the edge of her mouth. "Me, I like to check out the other side just to enjoy the difference. I don't necessarily have to own it, but I like a taste every now and then."

With that he bent to kiss her.

It was a bit dry but nice and slow. They were certainly on the same wavelength. Pippin closed her eyes to savor it, like a cool drink after being in a too-heavy desert.

"You sure you want to go in my studio?" she asked in a lazy voice.

"I thought that was what I was here for. At the very least I want to see what you're up to now. I never know if I should be shocked or excited by the Pippin Applegate experience."

Pippin reached behind herself to wave at the light switch, and the room came into view with color-correct light. Under the circumstances it was a bit harsh, but Pippin would never show her work using mood lighting.

"I always aim to excite," she purred as he turned to take it all in. She watched carefully to see an honest reaction before he might cover it up.

His gaze came to rest on the nearest painting: shock. Was that a flash of wonder? His face settled into a studious regard. At least he hadn't shown repulsion.

"Now, don't take my critique as the end-all. I'm just one man."

"It's either you or Ricardo," Pippin said. Sevan continued to assess the work in the room as he moved around. He rearranged some pieces for a better view.

At least he was showing some interest. He made some positive comments about her colors, though he didn't say anything about the pieces as a whole.

Still, he was here. He felt art too. And oh my, those hands. "Looks like you've almost got enough for a good-sized show," he said. Still no mention of overall quality. Pippin pushed that thought out of her mind.

"I'm glad you're here to counsel me, and not Tito," she said.

He flashed her a disarming grin. "I hate to say it, but he'd have started painting over all of these within ten seconds. They're not his style."

"He's not my style," Pippin said.

It was all too chummy for David. He'd trotted in after them, weaving his way between Sevan's feet until the man had to stop to let Jonathan lead the way. Instead, David stopped as well, even sat to lick his shoulder, until Sevan forged ahead. Then it was back to the weaving.

"Davi– I mean, Jonathan, stop that."

"Nice cat. And this is a great space," Sevan said after an awkward pause. "Do you mind–?" He gestured at a table next to the modeling stage and she began to clear her equipment off it.

"Part of it was a farewell gift from the folks on Earth," she told him.

That got them talking about their families back home. Sevan pulled materials out of his bag: a lazy susan with a two blocks of gray Insta-Klay, a pack of armature wire, and sculpture tools whose edges looked part kindergarten and part lethal.

David didn't like this guy. He didn't like the way he moved: like a clumsy, well, human. And he smelled funny. David half-listened to Pip's story, though it should have fascinated him through enlightenment gained. Why, when Pip's family had insisted she study marketing at university, she had maneuvered them into a deal guaranteeing her a double major that included fine art. If that didn't reveal the soul of a true businesswoman, what did?

But Sevan didn't understand. He was interested in other things besides saving Pip's soul and forming her into a useful and content member of society. At the least he should reiterate what she said and restate it so that she knew he was hearing what she had to say. He needed to establish emotional feedback if he was here for what David thought he was here for.

And yet Pip seemed like she was responding to him. Worse, she smelled like a huntress.

David hated Sevan's holographic snake bites. They were too flashy and bespoke a huge ego. Well, Nineties as a rule had large egos, didn't they? The opposite of Teens, Nineties were completely sure of themselves because of their dominating size and often adopted flashy accouterments to finalize the business of attracting mates.

Snake bites should be muted so you could focus on someone's features. Pip, of course, went all the way with hers. They were skin-colored. When she smiled, you saw the smile and not the flash of silver or magenta attached to the flesh.

David blinked at her. On her it worked. Rather endearing, actually. The snakebites on that low-make face were a way of telling the world that she was not a woman to fake her way through life.

The two humans wrestled a tapestried chaise from one of the front rooms up onto the low stage. It was purple with bright daisies woven into the fabric. As Sevan rotated the stage, Pip took a seat. David jumped up onto Pip's lap and nudged her so she'd scratch his chin. He leaned into the caress. Sevan set up lights whose brightness Pip directed by vocal control.

"Good enough," they decided together. Sevan took a position by his Klay.

Pip set David down on the main floor and stood up. Then she slowly dropped her robe. Underneath it she was naked.

"How do you want me?" she asked.

"No, no, no!" David yowled.

Sevan took a step back from David. "Does he bite?"

Pip frowned at David and then turned a warm smile to Sevan. "He's just angry because I stopped petting him."

David stormed to himself as he paced back and forth. This was not going right!

Pip settled upon the chaise like the Queen of Sheba, all temptation and womanliness and control.

Sevan made some suggestions as to pose and gesture and Pip complied, snuggling back into the cushions to get comfortable. Sevan moved his primary light and stepped back, then–

Don't TOUCH her! David wanted to scream. He trembled where he stood as Sevan arranged Pip's arm so it haloed her head, thrown back against the line of the couch.

No! Pip was David's to use. She was going to learn from him when he got his body back.

He was going to shape her, not this man.

She shifted slightly and Sevan said, "That's great. Right there." He walked around her, shooting photos from different angles. Sevan returned to his work-table and quickly began to construct an armature from his wire. When he applied bits of clay to it and the form grew to that of a human woman, David seethed.

Through the blackness of his rage he wondered if he could force Sevan out of his body and jump into it himself.

"Shall I talk to myself to keep awake, then?" Pip asked.

"Sorry."

David didn't like the play in her voice. She was a lonely woman. A woman who should be well-kept. This man was not a good match for her; anyone could see that.

David growled low.

After a long while of fiddling with the clay, Sevan announced, "Break."

"Thank God." Pip reached for her robe and wrapped it around herself to check the work in progress. Sevan stood back from it, scowling at the figure.

"Ah, so sculptors feel it too," she murmured to him with a sly smile. She moved near him and stroked his arm. When she spoke, her breath must tickle his ear. "It's a very strong start. You have real talent. Can I get you a drink? Or would you like a... longer break?"

At that he turned to her. His head cocked slightly to the left as he regarded her now robed, as if he hadn't been studying every inch of her naked. His gaze darkened from angst to arousal.

"I wouldn't mind a chance to stretch," he said.

Pippin wrapped her arms around his so-talented Seventy arm. "I know a great place to do that," she whispered in his ear.

David sank his claws right into Sevan's Seventies calf.

Sevan let out a very feminine shriek. Pip jumped back until she saw what had happened.

"Da– Jonathan! Sevan, are you hurt? Jonathan– Bad cat! No! Bad cat!"

David stood up on his hind feet and used Sevan's leg as a scratching post.

"Get it off me! OFF ME!!"

"Jonathan! No! No, get down! Sevan, he's not doing it in spite. It's just a cat thing. He thinks you're a tree or something. Jonathan!"

David easily avoided Pip's swipes as she simultaneously attempted to soothe her would-be lover and capture David. He had to release, but he circled around, looking for another opening.

Sevan sank to the chaise and held his lower leg, howling at the ceiling.

Pip swung David up to her chest. She reached for Sevan's shoulder as he bent to cup his wound. Blood dripped from several deep scratches.

"Is it bad?" Pip asked. "He's never done anything like this before. Nothing at all." She hovered over him. "Should I call 911? Can I get you a pain patch? Bad cat!"

Sevan glared at David. "That cat is insane!"

David hissed at him, making sure his spittle found Sevan's eyes.

Pip fought the growling, spitting animal in her arms. "Bad Jonathan!" She ran to the french doors and tossed the cat through them, snapping them shut before he could get back inside. David threw himself against the doors, hard enough so they rattled.

"I'm so sorry!" Pip called again before she secured the front airlock. It sealed with a long hiss. She stomped back to the kitchen, where David was noshing on a well-deserved dinner. He took one look at her and fled into her studio.

"Bad cat!" she shouted as she followed. David hid under table legs, but she leaned down and pointed at him. "What the hell got into you? Am I going to have to take you to the vet? Shit, I am never going to get laid."

David crouched behind a pile of sketch pads and e-readers. Suddenly he began to claw the screen on the top one.

"Stop! Do you know how much I paid for that? Bad, Jonathan, bad!" Pip shrieked. She ran around the table to pull him off. He flailed in her arms, careful to retract his claws, and she dropped him onto the floor.

He ran through her legs to attack the screen again.

"David!"

But by the time she'd turned to him, he pushed the screen of *Basic Human Anatomy*'s cover toward her. His clawing had magnified one part of it.

"*Human*," it said.

"Bad cat." She huffed and then looked at him, puzzled, as she put what remained of the reader out of his reach on a shelf. "What's gotten into you? Devil cat. Jonathan's a devil cat. God, I hope he doesn't sue."

David jumped to the shelf and flipped the reader off. It landed on the main table. Then he leaped down next to it.

"No, I am not playing your game," she said as she began to straighten up the mess. She reached for the reader to put it back.

He jumped in front of her to protect his screen. "MOWWW!" he shouted and patted it. He pushed it toward her and patted it again.

"What? What do you want?"

He patted the screen. "MOWW!" Then he trotted two paces, turned to look at her, trotted three more, and turned.

"MOWW!"

"Rrr." She closed her eyes. "I am so not playing with you," she said, but she followed him. "Let me see your pupils in some good light."

Her covered palette sat on the far table, surrounded by brushes and sketchbooks. David jumped.

"Get down from there!" Pippin yelled as he scraped the loose lid off. He stuck his paw into the pool of Cerulean Blue.

"Get out of the paint!"

Even as her hand reached for him, David smeared a "D" on a sketchbook cover.

"Huh," she said, coming to a stop.

David made almost all of the "A" before his paw ran out of paint.

"What in… Where the hell…"

He redipped, and made a "V." An "I." A "D."

Then he turned to regard her with what he hoped she'd interpret as a "So…?" expression.

She sat hard on the floor.

10

"David," Pippin said to herself. A jar of paint dislodged by her heavy landing fell on her head, disgorging a splat of its green contents before it clattered onto the floor.

David patted the paper.

"Yes, I know it spells 'David,'" she snapped, "but the question is: do you understand that?"

She leaned forward, her eyes level with his, and peered into his uneven pupils. "Cats can't spell," she accused.

Again, David patted his name.

Pippin peeled off a snake bite from her forehead and checked it. Then she did the same with her other bites and the various medical patches that dotted her upper arms. "They look legit to me," she finally surmised. "No illegal drugs, no mind-altering substances." As she worked her way down the other patches on her body, she muttered to herself, "You don't think there might be a drug interaction?"

David's ear-splitting yowl interrupted her theories.

"Okay, okay. You're David, that's what you're trying to tell me?" She held her head. "I've had a stroke, that's it. Damned Terran gravity gave me a stroke."

David cocked his head at her. Maybe he shouldn't have picked a crazy woman to communicate with.

He turned back to the palette. A dull orange appealed to him, so he scrawled the word "YES" on the left side of the sketchpad cover, over his name. Then he used a black that turned out to be dark brown to spell "NO."

"Ah, ouija board time." Pippin rubbed her upper lip. "Look, do you mind if I get a drink? I suddenly find I need one."

David rapped his kitty knuckles on "NO" and sat back expectantly.

"Ooookay."

When she returned she held not only a small glass filled with amber liquid, but the bottle as well. Plus a damp washcloth. She dabbed her face with it after she sat down.

She took a swig. Not too deep, David noted. And she made a face when she swallowed. Not a heavy drinker then.

"Your name is David."

YES

"You're a cat."

NO

"Where's Jonathan?"

"Yow."

"Oh, sorry. Um. Is Jonathan dead?"

NO

"He's alive."

YES

"He's… on Earth?"

NO

"What, he's still here?"

YES

"Inside you?"

YES

"The two of you are inside there?"

YES

"How did this happen? I mean, um…" She took another sip. "It was part of Jonathan's rejuv?"

NO

"Not a part of the rejuv? What could have caused it? It's unnatural, right? Not normal?"

YES

"You're a teep," she said in wonder. "I bet you."

YES

"Why would you do this to a poor cat? Jonathan's a good cat."

YES

"Huh? You'd do this because– Oh. Jonathan is a good cat."

YES

"Him being a good cat had nothing to do with this."

YES

She set the glass down and pulled at her chin. "You had a reason for doing this."

NO

"An accident?"

YES

"Where's your body? You're human, right?"

YES

"Okay, where's your body?"

David smeared a large question mark on the canvas, this time in green.

"You want your body back?"

YES YES YES

"Well, good. It can't be too comfortable in there with the two of you."

NO YES NO

She chuckled at that. "Things aren't too bad, but you want your body back, right?"

YES

"How's Jonathan? Is he okay?"

YES

"Good. We won't tell Aunt Evie about this."

NO

She leaned forward, eying the kitty writing as if it were out of focus. "You were that dead guy they found on me."

YES

"Not dead after all. Did you know that? That he's not dead?"

YES

Then David pounded on the "?"

"Ah. Where is he indeed? He doesn't have your mind in his body, does he?"

NO

"Where do you store a zombie?"

NO

"Okay, not a zombie. Well, of course they'd take him to a hospital first. I can't believe I'm having this conversation."

YES

"Were you running from the law?"

NO

?

"What's that? You want me to ask another question?"

YES

"Along the same lines?"

YES

She blew air out in exasperation.

"Running. You were running from something. Someone."

YES

"Not the law."

YES

"A bad guy."

YES

"You were running from a bad guy and you had this accident, and because you were a teep, your mind just– That doesn't make sense." She raised an eyebrow as David began a flurry of writing. It was difficult because of the unnatural size of the letters he felt he had to make in order to create them clearly.

THINK

He stared at her, trying his best to use his telepathy more directly than he'd ever done before. *Bad man was a telepath. Bad man was a telepath!*

"Think about what? Teep."

YES YES YES

"Why'd I say that? The word just came to me." She sat puzzling at the cat. "Teep," she said again.

YES

"Yes, I know you're– Oh, you mean the other guy was a teep too? A bad teep? Jeez." That required a swig. "He didn't follow you here to Luna, did he?"

NO

Then: ?

"Ah, you don't know. This all happened on the flight, didn't it? Or just before?"

YES

She settled back in her chair. "So. We know that inside the freshly-rejuvenated cat that belongs to my aunt, resides not only that cat's brains, but also the mind of one teep named David. What's your last name?"

David began to work on that project.

"And that for some reason you were being chased by a bad guy– a teep– and somehow you wound up on the Luna flight and fell into my capsule while your mind wound up in Jonathan's body."

David finished spelling "LUMEN" and hit YES as well.

"Well, I'm glad that's cleared up at last. Now all we have to do– and correct me if I'm wrong– is find your body, get your mind back inside it while not disrupting poor Jonathan's mind, make sure that the evil teep guy isn't on Luna, and find some nice men in white coats to take me to a mental asylum."

YES, Jonathan tapped on the canvas.

Pippin saluted him with her glass.

It was stuffy on this lower level of the city. Pippin plucked at her collar, trying to fan her neck with it. The afternoon breeze was a long time from getting here, as was the LunaPort bullet-trans that would take them to the hospice.

They came upon a pretty cross-street made up like Old Europe with all the fake antique stonework and wrought iron framing flowerbeds. This city square was open to the levels above, from which the tiniest of welcome drafts disturbed the stale air, and a bright patch of light played upon the pavement as if it had been Terran noon. Two outdoor cafes sat catty-corner from each other. Pippin sat down at the less colorful one.

She reached in her pocket for her camera and took some shots. Intricate details got close-ups for reference. Then she sat back with her sketchbook and pen in hand to enjoy the pedestrians who seemed to travel a little slower here in response to the setting.

Twin girls, maybe twelve, merited a quick sketch as they giggled with heads together. A mother saw to correcting the smears of makeup on her toddler; that made a nice composition as well. Pippin scribbled away with different colors to get the bolder characters. A handsome man, striding purposefully. Lovers sharing a pastry at their tiny table.

It was a nice place to visit, but she wouldn't want to live here. If her FeeP tickets added up, she'd be exiled down to this level or farther, away from the warmth and fresh air the upper levels enjoyed. Crime rates crept higher in the darkness. Down here the people were less educated, less groomed to perfection.

She sighed. On that latter point, she'd certainly fit in. But people seemed unhappier down here. Without the high ceilings it felt claustrophobic. On the really low levels she'd bet money that Loonies became truly loony. Could she stave that off before she earned enough fashion credits to return to the upper world?

Pippin looked over her sketches as she saw to her own cup of apple juice. "This isn't a bad one," she said to Jonathan/David. She pulled his carrier up onto the table and showed him the page with the two girls.

A cat grunt was all she got in reply.

"Well, aren't you as useful as all the humans in my life. How about this? Or this? See anything you like?"

Suddenly he let out a shriek. Pippin dropped her sketchpad.

"Hey!" she warned the cat. "You'll get us kicked out of here. Shut up!"

"Oooowwwwwwwlllll," he replied, with an emphasis on the *oowwwwww*. *That was me! Me!*

"What? I can't make out–"

Me! That one! Where is he? Where'd I go?

"This?" Pippin went back through the pages for the solo man.

A red-haired man. His strange hair color had caught her attention. A mid-Thirty make. His hair curled to a medium length. He wore his clothes in street-tough mode: faux leather jacket. Nondescript pants that she hadn't focused on.

She'd managed one shot of him, and scrolled to find it.

He had a slight slouch, his hands jammed in his jacket pockets. His collar was bent up, covering part of his chin from her view. He had walked quickly, his eyes straight ahead as he followed a route perpendicular to her seat, which made him an easy sketch.

Me! That's me! David cried in her mind. *What are we doing sitting here? Catch him! Catch him!*

The feeling of having to rush after the man certainly came through clear enough. Pippin checked the picture again, comparing it to the streets in front of her. She turned the cat carrier so David could see:

Crowds of people coming from that direction. Some major trans must have just arrived.

"Maybe he caught the trans," she said. "Maybe he kept going. There's no way to tell. It's been a while since he passed. He could be anywhere by now."

David threw himself against the sides of the carrier, making it lurch across the table.

"Calm down," Pippin ordered. "He's gone. Maybe he wasn't you. He looked like just another Thirty to me."

Red hair! I know myself!

"Yes, red hair. But aren't you supposed to be lying in some kind of hospice?"

Go! Go!

She shook her head at the shot. "He doesn't look that much like that passport picture you showed me," she said. Still, he didn't look that much not like it, either.

She stood up and swung the carrier around to carry it by its shoulder strap. Signaling a taxi, she told it to follow the trans as closely as possible. She peered out both sides at each stop to check both directions of exit, but did not see any red-haired men. David looked with her, running from side to side of the vehicle to search. The end of the line came, and there was still no redhead.

"He could have gotten out at one of the main stops. There were a lot of people. Easy to get lost in the crowd."

David gave a soft, low moan. She patted his furry head.

"We'll go to the hospice and see if your body's still there. I bet it is. Then you can just hop into it and this will all be over."

The blonde at the information desk was a 45 make, trying to look like a 69 through camouflage and body-sculpting exo-enhancements, padded bras and girdles and such.

"Supersizing is never a good idea," Sugar had told Pippin of such tactics. "People can always see through the fakery."

"Never trust a Sixty," was what Pippin's mother had always told her. Sugar seemed the rare exception to the rule.

This one had too much boob pressed out of an unzipped neckline, a waist that seemed a few ribs short of normal, and lips poufed out to there. She wore her uniform a size too small to display her perfection far past any thinking person's desire to see it (which of course didn't include men as they didn't think with their brains). It wasn't a body, it was a trap for half of humanity.

And she wore a swarm of metallic snake bites around her eyes, most of them rendered useless by their position. What was that all about? Maybe she was going for an ancient Egyptian look, but even Pippin knew that much black around the eyes in the daytime was vulgar.

Yet David paused in his moaning to appreciate her.

Cleopatra eyed the carrier. "You can't bring animals in here."

Pippin gave her a reassuring nod. "We're only coming this far. I heard my brother was released this morning ahead of schedule, and I haven't been able to contact his doctor to confirm."

Cleo pouted as she looked up the name, and Pippin wondered if that was as close to a frown as all those snakebites could manage. Certainly there was no hint of a furrow of emotion in that perfect, angled brow. Maybe that's why she had been assigned to the information desk. Hospices dealt with a lot of emotion. No need to make matters worse by actually responding to or sympathizing with it.

It took her agonizing minutes to find a name. "David Lumen," Cleo confirmed. "Woke from coma last night. Released five hours ago."

"Five hours?" Pippin set the carrier on the counter next to the screen. "He didn't call home. He hasn't arrived."

Again Cleo perused the screen: scrolling, peering, pouting. Finally she shrugged. "The cops wanted him for some kind of questioning, it says. He was actually released first thing this morning but they kept him here for a while. Maybe he had to go to police headquarters. What'd he do?" The woman peered at the record of David's condition. "Somebody beat him up?"

Pippin wanted to slap some speed into her, but now it was time for her to think fast on her own feet. "Um. Yes. He might be in danger. Did he leave a message as to where he was going? Aunt Evie's upset already. How can I tell her he's lost?"

"I don't have any–"

"What did he put down as his address?" Pippin demanded. "He's probably run back with that slut he was living with. She's the source of all the trouble, I tell you."

"A girlfriend?" Cleo blinked at her. Slowly. "I thought redheads were…" She paused to sort it out. "If brunet men are usually [she stressed the word as if she'd been burned in the past] straight and blonds are gay, then redheads are… bi?"

"Oh. Yeah. He is, but he tends toward straight. He's still experimenting, you know how some men are. Heteroflexible. Six weeks ago he was brunet."

"Ah." The receptionist's lower lip drooped as she tried to comprehend.

"Right. But his girlfriend, she's got an ex-boyfriend who thinks he's still got possession of her." Pippin craned her neck to see the monitor, and Cleo turned it away– directly at David.

"There was a big fight," Pippin told Cleo. David's head was weaving from side to side as he worked his way through the screen info. She needed to stall. What was it Tiffany had been telling her about that vid program?

"His girlfriend got cut bad– she was released from St. Francis just last week. I heard that David messed up the other guy pretty good before the guy's buddies got him back. David's got a good right on him."

Well, that took care of the coma, Pippin thought. Judging from her wide eyes and gaping mouth, Cleo seemed to be buying it. Now how to explain why he wouldn't call his family? "He– He's also a runner. Redhead or brunet, my brother always runs when he gets into trouble. Police protection is his only hope. And they can't help him unless he can identify his attackers. I need that address! What if those men show up again?"

Damn– must have hit a situation Cleo had been trained for. She showed all the emotion she could by pushing out her chest, blinking her over-bit eyes, and pouting. "We do not give out addresses. Your brother is of age. His records are private, no exceptions. Do I need to call security?"

Pippin glowered at her. "No need." She grabbed her carrier and stomped out of the hospital.

832 Milan Street, Level 5, David told her as soon as she'd calmed herself enough to receive. They had to go through it many times before the numbers came through correctly.

"Luna City or LunaPort?"

Luna City. Let's go.

Pippin made a beeline toward the nearest trans station, but her pace slowed until she stopped. "Why are we assuming that the guy who attacked you has your body now? How do I know you're really David?"

Who else would I be? Jonathan the cat?

"Maybe this guy is on the lam from you instead of the other way around. Maybe you attacked him. Maybe he's in his proper body now."

And I took a cat body just to be efficient. Trying to get his body back instead of my own.

Pippin could hear his tail snick back and forth, brushing against the walls of his carrier. She spotted a bench and sat down. "I have to think about this."

"Nnnnoww!"

"He'll wait. If that's his real address, it will still be his address in a while." She considered the carrier for a long time and then stared off into space. Every time he said something, she brushed the thought away.

How to tell truth from lie? Some lies could be twisted so they were almost the truth. And here Pippin was, dealing with some cat guy who could mess with her mind. What kind of danger was she dealing with?

And would this count as Jonathan-time to Aunt Evie?

"What's he done with his own body, then?" she asked. "If he's taken over your body, that means that there's another body around here without a mind in it. I don't see any of those. Do you?"

Maybe it wasn't Ethan Kane. Maybe this is someone else. Maybe he was an old man dying in the hospice and my body just sucked him up or something when he went.

The more they did this telepathy stuff, the easier it was to hear the quiet voice in her mind. "In that case, there's no extra body you can inhabit."

I want my body back! This cat's making me crazy. It thinks like a cat.

"Mow!" Hey! *That wasn't nice, David.*

"Jonathan's still in there, isn't he?"

Yes, yes, he's here. It's just crowded and there's not room for the two of us. I want out!

"You should have thought of that before." Pippin stood up but had no idea what direction she was headed. Finally she chose a StarBuffs. As she sat between two pieces of unused exercise equipment and waited for her cidercaff and apple butter scone, she checked net notices from various Luna Port Hospitals.

"Three deaths this morning," she told David, whose carrier she'd stuffed next to her feet in the shadows of the table. "Two women, one man. One an accident victim, the others old age. Jesus, they were over two hundred."

If one was a teep, they'd be damned skilled by then.

"Maybe they've been pulling this for lifetimes. Live a long life and grab a young guy on your way out. Maybe they're like, a thousand years old. Say, here's something. Three people went into coldsleep."

She cross-linked. As she waited for the links to coordinate, she pulled off a bite-sized piece of scone and stuffed it into David's carrier. David sniffed at it and then ate it. "Two women and a man. The guy's not old. Doesn't look like anything's wrong with him, but you never know. Why would a young guy choose coldsleep? Trying to outlive someone?" An idea occurred to her. "Was he trying to outlive a statute of limitations? You know, a niche in time saved Stein. Isn't there a law against that now?"

A shame if this coldsleep guy were the bad guy in this. Why did so many bad men have to look so good? You'd think they'd be able to get anything or anyone they wanted on looks alone. What reason did they have to go bad?

This man could have gotten her, easy. He looked toward the tall end of accepted male height. Confidence oozed as his cool, dark eyes gazed out of his ID photo. Dark hair of course, and an expression on his mouth that seemed to ask, "Why do I have to get this photo taken?" like he'd dare to buck the system.

Non-conformist? Pippin's heart stirred within herself before she quashed it back down. This might be a bad guy. Really evil, with powers and everything. Look but do not approach.

She spotted the personal info on the photo cutline. Damn it all.

Let me see! Did he have an address?

"How about that. It's the same place that David Lumen lives," Pippin said coolly, though her heart pounded in her chest.

Surreptitiously she lifted the carrier so David/Jonathan could see her monitor but the counter help couldn't see him.

ETHAN KANE! David screamed in her mind, every syllable crystal clear. *He's here. He's got my body!*

At least this seemed to back David's story, but how? Could this be an accomplice? Could this scheme be so illegal as to be dangerous? Teeps in from Earth.

One teep was just a victim. Two teeps was a conspiracy. She set the carrier back down.

Pippin thought as she munched on her scone– StarBuffs standard, same as the ones served at any of its million other locations– while every now and then David punched her ankle from inside the bag.

Finally she got up with him and boarded a trans to the address. She should call the cops, no matter what David said. Fake some story to make it sound semi-plausible, get them out here, and stand back while they uncovered whatever there was to be uncovered.

Or she could sit here across the way from the apartment complex's main entrance and just stare at the door like a moron. After a while she dialed a few magazines for her padd and pretended to read while keeping one eye on the door.

"Ladies, increase your bustline the all-natural way," an ad buzzed at her ear She waved it off and renewed her no-spam option for another ten minutes. When her time was up and an ad told her that Christian singles in the area were interested in her, she turned off the magazine, pocketed her padd, and strolled the street.

Two old ladies chatted on the sidewalk. She could tell they were old because they'd let their height lapse and both had shrunk with age. Instead of snakebites they used bowiebands that stretched across what were probably deep wrinkles underneath. Their makeup was much too thick– Sugar would have a cow if she saw them– but their skirts were hiked schoolgirl-high underneath faded bare midriffs.

Pippin knew their type. Some ethnic pools's roots ran deep. These women came from the days when their communities stuck together against the outer world. They would be the ones who might notice their neighbors, maybe even talk to them.

"Excuse me," Pippin interrupted. They must have heard her, for the one playing the loud hat 'n beak music turned it down and both looked to her expectantly. "I'm looking for my brother. He's a Thirty and he's visiting friends somewhere around here. Have you seen him?" She flashed a picture of red-headed David.

The woman with the music spoke out of just the right side of her mouth like crazy Cousin Mutsu back on Earth. "No see, mayup."

"No flyboys roost in this burb," the other said. "But that hair slid by rikki-tikki not two hours ago."

"He's not gay," Pippin told her.

"Then why was he tracking for GayTown? He might be crownin' red, but you could tell, you know? Totally skew-troll, going red."

"Praved?" the Mutsu wannabe asked her friend with abnormal curiosity.

The other woman shrugged. "Maymay sparky time." She turned back to Pippin. "Two hours ago. Right before I went to Mars-Mart. Why he go red? You know gays like bruces, guys who make to be straight." She eyed Pippin. "He really your brother?"

"Some straight-lines like to skew." Mutsu whispered confidentially, "They say they're gates. I think them gates really open just one way. They just posture that the hinge swings both ways, but snowbird makes bad gumbo."

"Maybe his cosmedoc just made a mistake. Hooper?"

Mutsu eyed the picture again. "Nah. Too hot for hooper. He was a real pat-a-cake."

The other woman nodded sagely. "Hoopers got cold-rush."

The cat growled softly within his carrier.

"Ooh, zat a kitty?" Mutsu asked. She bent down to peer into the carrier door. "Ginger cat. Not many Loonie gingers. Now a Burmese– that's a Loonie cat."

"You can get ginger cats if you know where to go," Pippin said. "So he went to GayTown?" She regarded the direction to the suburb. It would be more difficult to track someone just by hair color if she waited. Hair was easy enough to bleach or dye.

GayTown was a good spot for a villain to lose himself, as Luna C's Gay-Town celebrated its colonial ambiance by observing law that was shadier than elsewhere. This situation was already creepy enough without going in with no plan.

"Well, that's odd," she told the women. "There's probably a story behind it. Guess he'll tell me when he decides to come home. Thank you, ladies. Have a nice day."

"Hot jets."

The women watched her walk the opposite way from GayTown before they resumed their music-backed chat, this time more animated and with frequent glances in her direction.

11

Two hours later Pip gently stuffed David into a new carrier. It was roomy, a steel gray made of sturdy ally-cloth, though the bottom and sides were stiffened so he could lie inside without fear of it collapsing around him. The sides were cleverly woven so that from the inside he had a fair view of his surroundings, though from the outside the carrier was opaque.

Pip had carefully painted, "APPLEGATE ORGANIC ORCHARDS, Official Use Only" on its sides. A fancy comm unit hung via heavy-duty double-sided tape on one side, making it look like an on-site equipment bag.

Blankie was inside, adding to Jonathan's comfort, and there was a little fountain tube for water. David wondered what would be done if he had too much water during a long trip. Maybe that's what blankie was for and it was really a super-absorbent fiber. He toyed with the tiny, tinkling mouse he found tethered to the inside. It smelled of luscious catnip, though it didn't give him the high he expected. Faux nip. Well, he needed his senses alert.

So far he seemed stable within the cat's body. He wasn't going to suddenly disengage and become a formless wraith, doomed to walk… where? Would his spirit remain on Luna? Go back to haunt his former home on Earth? Would angels appear to escort him up a long tunnel toward the light? What about that flame and fire business? Did anyone believe in that anymore?

He burrowed blankie around himself and tried not to think about it. Right now, the important thing was to stay with Jonathan here.

Jonny, you and I are buddies, aren't we?

I like you.

I like you too. Now, you know we're working on a way out of this, but until it happens, we stay together, okay? If you feel me slipping away, you hang on to me, right?

Don't worry, David. I'll protect you.

Jonathan batted the mouse around against the gentle rocking of the carrier.

The main upper tunnels of Luna were much more spacious than David had imagined. Rather than shopping-mall wide, they spread more like pedestrian malls, wide paved boulevards with frequent stands of trees and flowers. They were neither hot nor cold. What seemed like full-spectrum light filled them.

He watched the crowds, better-dressed on average than Terrans. He didn't see any bums or street people, but Pip might not have chosen to walk tunnels where those types would be welcomed.

No one ran around in the spacesuits you saw on holodramas. The only thing he saw was casual wear and upper-scale fashion. Facial bandages were the same here as on Earth, though they didn't seem as gray. Perhaps Terran bandages soaked up more air pollution than here. Was there any air pollution on Luna? David had never researched. The place looked immaculate.

Children seemed normally cheery and over-energetic. One boy who came up beside them matching his parents' quick pace was picking at a bandage from what looked like a recent nose job. His mother gently rebuked him and reminded him that he had to wear it three more days.

"I want a Spacebird bandage," the boy pouted. "This looks like dookie."

"But the Spacebird bandage makes you look like you have a bird beak for a nose."

That sent the kid into a flurry of squawks and bird cries. He had the Spacebird vid down pretty well, David thought. The boy flapped his arms with his fists tucked into his armpits, having the time of his life pretending to be something he was not.

Spacebird squawked at the carrier and Jonathan hissed. David didn't blame him. The bandage did look pretty pathetic for a kid. Kids shouldn't wear adult bandages. They should be allowed to be themselves.

"Hospital" and an arrow pointing to the left: David barely saw the sign before they turned. The felt mouse was putting up an imaginary fight, and Jonathan was showing it who was the predator in this carrier.

A new smell assaulted him, definitely medicinal. Keeping his claws sunk into the felt toy, Jonathan looked around with David as Pippin stopped at the front desk.

The vet, Jonathan guessed and tensed.

No, we're going to see Mama, David told Jonathan.

Mama? Mama!

I shouldn't have said that, David amended quickly. *Don't get your hopes up for today. Pip will see Mama. They probably won't let us sit with her. She'll be feeling pretty sick right now.*

Jonathan's shock rolled through David.

No, it's not bad. She'll feel better in a few days. You just got a rejuv too, didn't you? That's what she's getting. How did you feel after that?

What's a rejuv?

What they did to you on, on that place. That strange place.

Heavy place.

Yes. They did a rejuv on you. That's what Mama just had.

Mama?

You felt better after a little while.

So long...

I suppose it must have seemed a very long time. But you feel good now, right?

I feel great. Mama'll feel great too?

Not today. But Pip is trying to sneak you to visit her to cheer her up. Mama loves you. You're just what she needs.

Pleasure washed through David from Jonathan. *You'll have to be patient with her, though,* he told the cat.

Mama! Mama!

Talking patience with a cat was a waste of energy.

Hush, cats aren't allowed here, David admonished his host. *We have to hide. They won't let us in if they suspect.*

Jonathan lay trembling with excitement as Pip made her way up, down, and through the rejuv center. David had to keep reminding Jonathan of the need to be still, and that it could be very soon before he saw his mama. *You really are a good cat.* David was proud of his behavior. Jonathan purred quietly in response.

"Aunt Evie?" Pip called as she opened the door to the private room.

"That you… Pippin?" The old woman lay propped up at an angle upon the bed, her knees also elevated by the bed's hydraulics. Her voice was faint; breathy with a heavy rasp. The usual rejuv bandages covered her face, but her eyes wore heavy gauze as well.

Must have had a retinal transplant, David mused. *She can't see you,* he told the cat. *They worked on her eyes too.*

I couldn't see for a long time, Jonathan confided to him.

No one else is around. It's okay to make noise. Let her hear you.

"Prrt? Yow. Yow, yow, meow!"

"Brought Jonathan? Good girl! Putting you… back…in my will."

"I don't believe this. He went quiet as could be as soon as we entered the clinic. It was like he knew what was going on. C'mon Da– Jonathan." Pippin set the carrier down, reached in and handed the cat to her aunt.

Evie patted him all over to reassure herself through her thick gauze gloves of his size and texture, that it was really him. What could be seen of her face relaxed into a smile. "Jonathan," she croaked contentedly.

As she held the cat close with one bandaged arm, she lifted the other up and managed an imperious if slight crook of her index finger. "Now. Report."

David could barely hear Pip's report over Jonathan's purr. He began to knead his mama.

You'll hurt her, he warned. *Sharp claws against tender skin…*

Jonathan immediately stopped.

Try it with your claws sheathed.

Jonathan pushed out with his front right paw experimentally, then tried the same with his left.

I think that's all right.

Jonathan proceeded with deep gusto, and began to drool down the front of Evie's bed coat.

The guy knew how to have a good time.

Evie gave only the occasional grunt or one-word comment to Pip's commentary. Vocal cord replacement: a tricky business but one that healed fairly quickly. Still, David was surprised that the doctor allowed her to talk at all. Maybe the procedure had been improved since the last one he'd seen.

David fell into a slight trance. On one side Pip's melodious voice lulled him; on the other was Evie's soft if quilted chest and Jonathan's thick purr. Perhaps it was the altered state that allowed him to catch the threat:

Doctor coming, he fiercely transmitted to Pip. *Doctor!*

"How often does the doctor come around?" Pip interrupted herself to ask.

"Dunno."

"I, uh, think I heard something. Come here, Jonathan."

The cat let out a soft yowl of complaint as Pip snatched him and stuffed him into the carrier.

The room door opened.

"And how are we– A visitor," the newly-arrived doctor observed. He was a Fifty, pretty far along, with fine-sculpted jawline and matching nose, authoritative but not bushy brows.

"I just got here," Pip said. "Good to see you, Jack."

"It's a bit soon for Evie to be getting visitors," he said. "I will assume this is your first time here. You haven't been making her talk?"

"Just a word or two. No more than five, honest, all total."

"Good." He touched the computer screen next to the bed and it fired up with medical stats. "That's not a cat carrier there, is it?" he asked offhandedly.

"Oh, this?"

Be quiet! David warned the cat.

"That's just a bunch of work I'm bringing home. I decided to drop by here first."

"Uh huh." He flicked through a few screens. "How ya doin', Jonathan?" He tapped the top of the carrier. "You don't let anyone else catch a whiff of this cat, do you hear? And he stays home after this as incentive." Dr. Jack nodded at Evie. "She'll heal that much faster if she can't see him for a while."

"I can't… see him now," Evie managed to say.

"Watch it, or I'll order a deadbolt on your door, no visitors at all," Jack growled good-naturedly.

His attention returned to the screen. "You're doing very well. We may be able to take the eye bandages off late tomorrow. If you keep your mouth shut– as if you ever could– we'll allow you to talk the next day."

Evie nodded her obedience.

The doctor raised his eyebrow at Pip. "If she'd been this biddable when we were married, we still might be together."

Evie opened her mouth to retort, but closed it again.

Jack laughed. "Got her where I want her. Listen, Evie, I did some of my best work on you. When those bandages come off, you owe me a dinner. Someplace nice, and not too dark so I can admire you."

She mouthed, "And your handiwork."

"That too. Fifteen more minutes, Pippin, and then you and Jonathan have to leave. I've downloaded some audiobooks that I thought you'd enjoy, Evie. Adventure romances. You always liked romance with the adventure. Guess that's why we got along so well."

He leaned down to give a peck to the bandages over Evie's forehead. She reached to pat his hand and smile. Then he left.

Eternity, Inc. was off the beaten tunnels and a long way from the nearest trans station. If Pippin hadn't been fresh out of Earth, the miles of unexpected walking with a cat carrier in one hand and no taxi in sight would have taken a toll on her. She should have rented a gyroseat.

But she was determined. If she could get all this done in one day, she could return to her work without any further distractions. If this Kane guy was indeed here at this coldsleep company and David/Jonathan could confirm that the body had no mind, then she could turn what evidence they had so far over to the police. Let them track down David's body.

The turn-off tunnel displayed an unimaginative corporate logo and commercial holo. "It doesn't look very state-of-the-art to me," she muttered at the entrance.

A "meow" answered her from the carrier.

Inside the lobby was downright shabby. Dust coated the frames around mass-market art reproductions. Threadbare carpeting and a sofa needing new upholstery finished off the room. Perhaps they didn't have anyone to impress. People going into coldsleep usually got a personal home visit to discuss it, since homes were so much cozier than sterile offices. Especially when the offices weren't so sterile.

After being prepped in a hospital, the client would be unconscious by the time the meat wagon collected them for transferal to Eternity. Incorporated, that was.

At least that's how Sugar's third cousin had done it.

As far as Pippin knew, Sleepers had to sign the majority of their savings away to pay for perpetual coldsleep care. They left a small amount in interest-bearing accounts to build over long years so they'd have enough to live on when– or if– they woke up.

There seemed to be no receptionist, so Pippin pushed open the only interior door from the lobby. A bony Ought-make woman sat in a gray cubicle, working on a game of double-solitaire.

"Yes?" She looked up with such a startled expression that Pippin knew she had to be the first visitor in at least six months.

"There's been a terrible mistake." Pippin tried to put her heart into the rush of words to make it seem real. "My husband. You haven't frozen him yet, have you? Oh god. He was upset. We're going through a divorce, you know, messy and– He told me how desperate he was, but I never realized he was this desperate. He left a message on my machine. Said he was taking the coldsleep here. I didn't even have a chance to say goodbye. Never had a chance to say I was sorry. That I still love him. I want him back!"

Not bad. Pippin had rehearsed several times in front of a mirror.

"Name?" the woman blinked at her.

"Kane. Ethan Kane." Pippin tried to summon some tears, but they refused to come. Plan B was theatrics. She dropped the cat carrier, fell to the floor in front of the Ought's desk, got up on her knees, and clutched blindly. The receptionist squawked as styluses and screens scattered.

"Please!" Pippin bleated, sure that her performance was over the top. "He can't have gone all the way under yet. I just have to see him one more time. Just have to tell him it was a horrible mistake!"

"Kane," the woman said as she hurriedly checked her main screen. She glanced back and forth between it and Pippin, and Pippin knocked over a picture.

"Eeeethan!" Pippin crooned. She thrashed on the floor, flailing her fists and feet. "Eeeethaaaan!" She reared up in a rush, springing to her feet.

The Ought cowered.

"Ethan!" Pippin shouted. "Ethie, can you hear me? Ethie, I'm here, baby! Make a sound! I'm coming! I'm coming!" She made as if to throw herself at the doors leading to the back, but a burlish man suddenly appeared from those very doors. What make was he? Over a Ninety. Giant make. Too many growth hormones, a hooper for sure.

"You can't go in," he said, but his lips drew back from his teeth as if she frightened him.

"You've got my Ethie back there! I've got to talk to him. He won't go if he knows." She grabbed the giant's lapels. "We'll give you half of whatever he has left. You've just got to let me see him. It's a matter of life or death."

"I don't–" The giant glanced at the Ought. "Vilma?"

"Ethan Kane," she told him. "Should be in the cooler. Don't think he's gone into the booth yet."

Mr. Giant chewed his cheek.

"Half," Pippin urged. "Do you want me to sign it over for you now? We're still married; I still have access to his accounts. Did he mention that when he signed your forms? That some of the money he gave you was mine?"

The legalities of that must have decided him. With a jerk of his head, the giant let her by him. He even held the door after she snatched up the cat carrier. But he looked askance when that carrier started to make a *hool*ing sound.

"Jonathan can't live without him either," Pippin said quickly. "He must know he's here. He's devoted to his daddy."

David *hool*ed even louder as they approached a swinging door clearly labeled "Prep Room." "Don't do that, baby," Pippin told the carrier. "It makes Mama nervous. We've got to be on best behavior for Daddy so he'll take us back. Is he here?"

The giant swung the door open and stood back for her. A frosty mist spilled into the corridor. "First pallet," he said.

It was the only occupied pallet in the room. Business must not be the gangbusters thing most of the coldsleep places advertised.

Hooooooooo. Hooooooo. Hooo–

At last David shut the hell up. Pippin just wished he hadn't done it so abruptly. It gave her the creeps.

"Ethie!" she screamed, and fell at the foot of the gurney onto the icy floor. Now what?

She chose to pat the figure under the white blanket as if it were the body of a saint and she a pilgrim. That was difficult to do around all the plastic tubing that had been stuck into it.

"Oh, Ethie, I thought I'd never see you again! Ethie, speak to me. Why doesn't he answer?"

"Because he's unconscious, crazy lady," the giant said.

Though a part of her felt like slugging him for the insult, a larger percentage exulted that he had bought her performance. By God, she *was* an artist!

"Ethie, Jonathan's here too. Get up, baby. Say hello to Jonathan. Oh baby, come back to us."

The giant fiddled with the IV drips. Pippin clasped her hands together and clamped her eyes shut– most of the way– as if she were praying. He turned away, fiddled with some stuff in a drawer, then something in a refrigerated cabinet, and came back with a hypospray.

The body jerked when he administered it. Pippin actually looked at the body now, taking it in for the first time. Dark hair– well, that was normal. The identifying jawline and cheeks of the Fifty seemed off because the features had sunken, probably due to all the drugs and the coldsleep process. She eyed the sheet. Brawny, but in a nice way. Woofish. She'd always liked bad boy Fifties. And bad boy Nineties. And bad boy Thirties…

"How long does it take?" She tried to stanch the criticism in her voice. She must keep in character.

What would she do when he came back to consciousness? If he didn't have a soul, would he even open his eyes? What if this wasn't their guy, but a close lookalike? People could look remarkably similar.

If he was the right guy, would his proper soul return somehow? Would he try to hurt her? To cover her conflict, she decided to babble. "Can I take him home? He can wake up there. He'll be more comfortable at–"

"Ba– bee," the body croaked. Fingers twitched under the sheet. The eyelids strained to open. "Baby? Is that you?"

12

His eyes opened as if he were recovering from a two-week bender. "Pip?"

Pippin wanted to say something. She wanted to do something. Mostly, run screaming away from here. Some strange Fifty coldsleep loser recognized her.

It occurred to her that Jonathan was silent.

"Ethie?" she asked. "Oh, Ethie. Oh, Ethie!" She broke into tears for real now because she didn't know what was going on. Was David in there instead of inside Jonathan? Was Jonathan in there with him? What would Aunt Evie say?

His voice was deeper than she'd thought it would be. "Baby, I was afraid to talk to you. You came. Does that mean you still love me?"

She clutched his hand. "Of course I do. Come home, Ethie. Please come home. *Let's get out of here. Now.*"

He managed a faltering grin and made movements as if he were trying to sit up. "That's what I've been waiting to hear. I'm yours, sweetheart. This was all a horrible mistake. Let's go."

He glanced at the giant as if first noticing him.

"I said we'd give him half of what you had left, Ethie," Pippin said.

"Half? Oh. Sure. It's worth it. Worth it to be alive again. Human again." He blinked at the giant. "I mean, um, I didn't feel human without my woman."

"Or your cat." Pippin spared the carrier a quick check. Jonathan lay inside, staring wide-eyed at Kane. Was the cat dead and his eyes just hadn't closed? Maybe both minds had transferred to the human body.

With a quick lick of his front paw, Jonathan returned to staring quietly.

"Ethan" managed to prop himself to a sitting position before Pippin thought to help. "Good ol' Jonny. He's fine. Where are my clothes? Anybody have a cup of coffee? I feel like I can't wake up all the way. God, a hot coffee would taste great. I'm freezing!" He began to rack with genuine shivers.

"Anything you want, Ethie. I know a place where they make it," Pippin chattered as the giant started sifting slowly through files on his puter. Probably looking for release forms so David could sign Kane's fortune away. David wouldn't know this Kane guy's codes. The gig would be up.

"Here you go," Mr. Giant said, and passed David a padd. He gave him a stylus, all smiles and solicitude now as he was about to get a wad of money.

Pippin peeked at the screen. It was already cued to Ethan Kane's accounts, security passcodes plugged in and everything. For a moment she wondered at what kind of financial setup coldsleep required, but then she froze.

David was watching her, a grotesquely wobbly smile spreading across his face. Was he Kane the hit man, faking being David? David the hit man, faking being an innocent shrink? Or was this indeed only David the Cat-Man?

David gave a better grin this time. "This is worth it, to have the woman I love back. I take it this is you?" His attention returned to the man and he pointed at a link on the screen. The giant grunted. David nodded. "Gladly, gladly, take it." He waved through the amount and then did some other things.

If it were her in this situation… Pippin decided that as long as he had access, he probably was transferring the rest of Kane's money to his own accounts. It couldn't be much, just a coldsleeper's final– Wait. Think.

The puter would have automatically refunded a good deal of the money due to the client backing out. They'd have taken out what they'd already spent on him, plus probably kept a cancellation fee… But most of Ethan Kane's accounts would still be there for him. A fake coldsleeper would have more money in their savings than the average patient, not having spent it before this final act of desperation.

Would that kind of money be enough reason to stage this kind of impersonation?

It would be so much easier to think of David as an innocent victim whom she had just saved. Maybe she could live with that until she could sit down to figure it all out. Do some investigations of her own. Talk to Sugar; she'd had a little police training.

"New life, new passcodes," David said as he kept fiddling with the padd. With a flourish remarkable for its grace, considering how many drugs he must have flowing through his system, he handed the padd back to the giant. "Many thanks. You've saved us all."

He turned back to Pippin and opened his arms. "Darling!" he said. "Show me that you love me!"

Even with the giant's attention turned to the screen to admire his new balance, Pippin found such sudden public display embarrassing. Still, it had to be done.

She gave him a quick peck. He pulled her close, an uncomfortable move because he was still sitting and she standing.

This kiss was definitely not a peck. It was hot and hard and more than a little possessive. "Baby, I've been waiting too long for this. You make me feel like a real man."

Pippin hugged David tightly just to keep him on his feet if not continue their cover story, and David had the temerity to keep stealing kisses from her.

"Cut it out," she whispered around one kiss.

"Baby, I'm so glad you saved me," he said loudly. They waved goodbye to the receptionist but got nothing in return.

Once outside Eternity, Pippin disengaged. David raised up the cat carrier and looked inside. "Good ol' Jonny, how you doin', boy?" he asked. "Isn't it great to be in separate bodies?"

Jonathan turned around and pointed his butt at the window and David.

"Hey, buddy, you know I'm very thankful to you."

No sound from inside other than the cat settling. David shrugged his shoulders and overbalanced. Pippin caught him.

"Not used to this body," he said.

Pippin wished again for that gyrochair at the very least as they wobbled back toward the nearest trans station.

David kept walking on tip-toe.

"Stop that," Pippin demanded. "Bad enough that you're wearing that–" David wore clothing Eternity kept around for revived customers. Apparently they hadn't revived anyone in some years. "Do you have to draw the FeePs' attention by walking weird?"

"Sorry. I've been a cat for too long." He tugged at the neck of his sweater and twisted his chin around, as if he wanted to tug his own soul into a more comfortable position.

He was walking just fine by the time they reached the station. As a matter of fact, he was walking more than fine. He skipped; he danced. To Pippin's wonder, he performed a quick jig.

David felt liberated. Humanity was a breathless attribute to have. Jonny had given him incredible bouts of energy and a total lack of cares. With that had come dependency on others, a lack of freedom that was stifling only to David.

But this– !

This was true freedom. This was being human, being a man again.

David hadn't noticed that Jonathan was fixed. Other problems had concerned him at the time. Besides, he'd been a cat; peculiar enough condition, that.

But now human testosterone flooded him. He could feel the potent chemical compound racing through his veins. He sucked in the clean lunar air with his eyes closed, just so he could savor it, utilize the oxygen for the sudden rush of ideas that occurred to him.

His new hormones made him drunk. Dizzy. He felt like ripping off his clothing and shouting as he ran through the streets. He could run for miles and leap impossible distances. People should see what a human body was capable of.

He could certainly appreciate others' human bodies. He slid his hand down Pippin's side to rest solidly on her shapely hip. Twenties were an excellent make.

"David," she muttered. A light crowd ambled around the station waiting for the next trans.

"Sorry. Just balancing," he lied as he released. He ached to grab hold of that luscious human female ass of hers. Feel how much give it had. Imagine what he could do with it if they were, say, in Pippin's delightful bed.

He'd never had sex under low grav.

"Oh yeah," he growled, and she glanced at him. Why did she look so troubled? He was in charge now. He knew what he was doing. He was human. He flashed her a knowing grin. His eyes crinkled with the joy of possession. She was his woman to touch and mold. He caught everyone around him with that smile to make certain they knew that he had staked his territory.

Just a little while longer until they got home. Would she object if he pulled her into an alleyway here?

He ran burning hot and freezing cold. Here he was! Human! Male! Ready! The chuckle that came from his chest was a different timbre than he expected.

"Stop feeling me up." Pippin squirmed next to him as they waited.

"I'm not feeling you up," he lied again. "Though you do feel great. No, fantastic."

She raised an eyebrow at him. "High praise coming from a cat."

The smile he now gave her was conspiratorial. "One hundred percent male human animal here, baby," he assured her. "Care to make sure?" He pointed out a dark corner behind the security office ahead. "There."

"Wha– You're joking."

He turned her to face him and held her with his hands on her butt. His fingers sank in just enough. Firm but not too firm. Soft but not too soft. "Serious as a priest," he said. As he pulled her against him, she should be able to feel that much was true. "I don't think I can hold it much longer. You've got me hot and bothered."

She blinked wide-eyed at him as if no one had ever told her that. When her mouth opened in surprise, he took advantage of it.

She tasted great. Felt even better. After a second and a half, she kissed back. He pressed her to him. Hard. She, on the other hand, seemed to be turning soft under his treatment. Yeah.

She pushed away and caught her breath. "I, I don't think you are joking. You aren't?"

"Now," he whispered into her ear. "Hey, there's a hotel. Let's get a room."

"A room! It– I– How–" Those tempting lips flapped as she blinked at him. "I have a perfectly good house that– I need to get back to my st–"

"Now."

But the trans slid into the station with a soft sigh. "Okay," he told her. "Home it is." He guided her in a strong pull to the trans doors. At first she hung back, but then trotted beside him. "David, you're– Are you always like this?"

"It's like being struck by lightning. I'm human again," he told her. "We need to celebrate."

"Oh. Celebrate." She slowed down. "So it's not about me, is it? I understand, getting a body is an important step to you getting your own back."

"Here." David almost picked her up to deposit her inside he tram. He pointed to a pair of empty seats and slid in beside her. "Baby, I just got reacquainted with my hormones," he said. "Allow me to enjoy them."

"So you're running amok with it?"

He gave her a hunter's gaze, steely and tight-focused. "I promise I'll only run amok with you."

"You presume an awful lot. I am more than a prop for your hormones." She pressed the cat carrier to her chest and squeezed away from him.

He gathered her back with an arm around her shoulders. "I saw you with that loser. That Sevan. He's too lowly to unpeel your snake bites."

Pippin jerked away from him. "You saw– You were there."

David flexed his fingers in a clawing motion. "He didn't shred good. But he fell nicely."

"If I had known–!"

She was getting angry. He didn't want her angry. Hell, he was a psychiatrist. Time to think with a cool head. "What I know is that you're just barely in from Earth. Heavy old Earth, where you could hardly move, much less find some interesting exercise. That must have been difficult for a vibrant woman like yourself."

"And you're the one to give me the exercise I need? Wonderful. First I get to feed your male ego, and now I'm your handy personal gym."

"Better than a gym, baby. And I need to try out this body, see what it can do if I'm to use it to get my own back." He added a private aside to her: "Though I'm quite certain it isn't half as good as the real me."

"That ego is breathtaking in its enormity."

He chuckled. She had made her own wants so obvious in the past few days that he'd known her. Time to play to those. "And you are just plain breathtaking. Lovely Pip, the go-getter. The woman who knows what she wants and has the talent to get it, no matter who objects. I have to respect that. One day you'll be famous, perhaps even powerful. But for today, you're merely… breathtaking."

She stopped squirming under his arm. "You think I'll be famous? That people will like my work?"

"Absolutely," he lied. "It's just a matter of time. Your eyes are like a morning sky."

The gaze she gave him was measuring; the small smile, crooked. "I had them de-saturated to blue when I was eight."

"Mm. Your hair," he drew his fingers through it, "as soft as polysilk."

"Texturized when I was nine."

"Your lips…"

"Twelve."

"Your–" His eyes traveled south.

"Fifteen. I called a halt to things after that. Well, for the most part."

"Only because you were complete then. Beautiful Pippin."

Those blue eyes rolled until she looked to Heaven, calling its attention to the scene. "You really think you're getting me tonight, don't you? First night out as a human. I am not desperate. Despite what you might have seen with Sevan."

He had the audacity to lift her hair and nuzzle her under her ear. Pippin squirmed. Just a little.

"Tonight," he whispered. "Anyone would love you for your body, but I love your, ah, art as well."

"You do?"

David wanted to heave a sigh of relief. At last she looked interested. "Absolutely. Your paintings are full of, um, the mystery of eons. The cosmic dawn. The very secret of life." He remembered those phrases from an article in the NAJM, but they had been describing the origin of DNA.

She'd stopped breathing. Then she licked her lips. She turned to study his face before settling on gazing into his eyes. "Keep talking, cat-boy."

David realized that he'd never paid a bit of attention to the things littering her studio that must have been her paintings. "I've only seen them through Jonathan," he said. "I can hardly wait to see your paintings with human eyes. They're so… unconventional. Different from anything I can remember. Full of fire and life, like you."

"Fire," she whispered to him.

"I want to see the colors, to see if they're the way I saw them or more vivid. Outrageously bold." He leaned his face down to hers. "A modern-day master."

She grabbed him and pulled him to her.

"Get a room," someone behind them groaned.

They fumbled to close the massive airlock behind themselves. Pippin tried to check where Tiffany was so they wouldn't be disturbed, but instead David dragged her to the bedroom.

"Jonathan," they both said to each other.

David set down the carrier and released the gate. "Get lost, Jonny," he instructed the cat. As he rose to his feet he pulled off his shirt.

Pippin was doing the same, he was glad to see. Very, very glad.

Pippin awoke, still tangled with David. He held her tightly even in sleep. When she retrieved her left arm he stirred and she paused, waiting for his breathing to return to normal.

Whom had she given herself to: David or Ethan Kane? Who really had the piercing eyes, the captivating smile… the electric, probing touch? Was David's true skin as rough as this? From his pictures she knew he had curly hair. She stroked this straight, dark stuff, and wondered if the curls would be coarser or finer.

Dark eyes opened slowly. She stilled. His lips curled up and she relaxed.

"Good morning," he whispered before he kissed her.

It was a very good morning kiss. Hot. Moist. Full of promises and desire and–

David drew back, looking as if he'd tasted something bad. "Sorry," he said, and found his place again.

Pippin wrapped her arms around him as he rolled with her until he was on top. She caught his lower lip lightly with her teeth and he chuckled. The stubble on his cheek rasped, proof of a man who'd stayed all night.

His hands smoothed her down and squeezed. He pulled her butt toward him and eased open her legs with his thigh.

She knew from last night– several times– that this would be spectacular. She paused at his earlobe…

But he didn't proceed. In fact, it seemed as if he'd frozen in place.

"Um," he said, and it wasn't a groan.

She raised her head. "Something wrong?" she purred. "Tell me what it is. I'll make it right."

He blinked at her. They'd ripped snake bites off each other in a frenzy last night, so when the furrow appeared between his brows, it had nothing to hide it. His face spelled apologetic horror.

"I think I'm gay," he said.

13

David shook his borrowed head until his brains sloshed. "Can't be. No. No!"

Pippin pulled him closer. "You were definitely not gay last night," she said before she gave him a long lick up the side of his jaw. She seemed to have a hot breakfast in mind.

He caught his breath. He could overcome this. The body might be gay but his mind was not, and the mind was the most potent sexual organ there was. Surely he of all people could reprogram himself!

"Oh yeah," he said, trying to fall into the flow of Pippin and her wet tongue. She had marvelous, talented hands, but her tongue work was not to be taken lightly. "Yes," he groaned and squeezed her.

Female flesh. Soft. Creamy. Smooth. Musky with woman.

Doinngg! Like a spring, he sat straight up in bed.

Pippin blinked at him.

"Shit. Shit, goddam, and–" he used the f-word. About twenty times in increasing combinations. He pounded his fist in the pillows and thought up thirty more variations.

Pippin drew up the sheet to cover herself.

Pulling his hair didn't accomplish anything other than reminding David that the strange texture and length weren't his. "There's a scale," he finally said. "Everyone tracks in the middle somewhere, somewhere not 100% gay, not

100% straight. Except for some freaking, effing morons on the ends. This guy is one of them!"

"Kane did this to me," he hissed. "First he takes my body. Then he leaves me– gay!" His bared teeth flashed at Pippin. "With you in my bed." He punched the headboard and left an indentation in the wood-grained plastic.

"My bed," Pippin correctly weakly, and David nodded.

With one hand he pulled the sheet to his waist for cover. With the other, he pulled his strange chin down as far as it could go. His jaw snapped back up. "I'm sorry. Dammit! This couldn't have waited for at least a few more hours." She lay there looking confused and hurt. Her upturned blue eyes could only stare at him.

"Or days. My god, you are beautiful."

At least the look he gave Pippin was filled with longing and despair. She lay there with the sheets pulled up to her neck. She didn't get it. That body couldn't be gay. It was muscular, naturally brunet– hell, he was hairy brunet all over. He was practically a cave man. Cave men hadn't been gay, had they?

"So was the guy who made love to me Kane or David?" she asked, but he didn't answer.

She'd seen the pictures of how comatose David had arrived in LunaPort. Curly-haired, red-headed, undernourished other-David could easily be gay. Redheads were odd to begin with. They'd enjoy taking the lesser-traveled road.

"Are you sure?" she asked.

David glared at her. "If I had any doubts, your toes would be pointed at the ceiling, baby."

"You couldn't be bi, could you?"

He gritted his teeth and got a far-off look in his eyes. "I could sure as hell try," he said. Then his shoulders slumped. "But it's going to take me a while to work on it. This guy is really flying his flag full in the breeze."

He slammed a fist into the palm of his other hand. "By God, I'm the expert at teaching people how to overcome themselves. I can do this." He pointed at her. "Don't give up on me. It's just going to take–"

"Some time." She eased back on her pillow with her face carefully blank.

He clasped her hand in both of his. "I can't believe I had sex with you last night. One part of me wants to jump up and down, and the other wants to throw up."

"Gee, thanks." She considered him. "Which part wants to jump up?"

"It's not you, babe. You are…" His eyes traveled over her, covered in her sheet. "You are something I could really appreciate last night. Even now, I can appreciate you, but in an intellectual way. A creepy way. Not gay-odd, but creepy."

He gave a little gasp and held it. That far-off look came over him again. "Really creepy," he whispered. He met her gaze as horror washed his face. "I knew he was a hit man, but this– There's not just a bad attitude here, there's evil." He flung out his arms away from the both of them as if it were something he could shake off. "A black cloud masking his world. Violence."

"Violence?" Pippin reached for her robe without dropping the sheet. She didn't want to be in bed with a gay, evil man. Could this really be David?

His dark eyes held a touch of cruelty.

"Ssh, not against you. Never against you." He flexed his fingers, examining his new hand. "This body has killed many times." He gave a sharp bark of a sound. "Proving its manhood, maybe. The old phallic gun theory come to blazing life." His fists opened and closed, turning first palm toward him and then knuckles. "Guns. Lasers. Ah– personal death-dealing; strangulation. For a telepath, I think he prefers a more physical kind of violence."

"David–"

He held up a flat hand to stop her. "There's something either recent or pending here. Plots and electronic death. Let me try to get it," he said as he closed his eyes. He shook his head. "Something… Something terrible. Big. As in explosives. Military action-type guns."

"On Luna?!" Pippin pulled her robe's belt tight with a snap. "Are you sure? Or are those his memories of Earth? You said he could be on the run."

David rubbed his stubbly chin absently. The blanket dropped, but he was used to being naked in front of Pippin. "It might be. Funny how the memories take root. They're vague, but the cells still hold them." He stared at the backs of his hands as if the memories might be written there. With a grimace he added, "Might be a good doctorate in examining the situation. I'd have to study this guy to compare impressions versus experience. He's not the type I'd want to meet."

"You need to, to get your body back."

He wiped his hands down his sides, trying to scrape the negativity off. "Yeah," he said softly.

From nowhere, Jonathan jumped up on the bed. David scooped him up to rub him with his big, knobby hand. "How ya doing, Jonny?" The cat purred loudly.

"Guess he forgives me. I was okay with being with Jonny," David told Pippin. "He's a happy little guy. All he wants is his Mama and to be able to raise a little hell while he has a good time. He doesn't want to hurt anyone. But Kane…"

He licked his lips as if he tasted something sour. "Feels like big self-worth problems. In some places the old prejudices are still alive. Is it possible that because he was gay, he thought he had to prove himself to someone? Maybe a father. Maybe his mother. Maybe the friends he fell in with."

"But whatever, he's definitely bad news now, right?"

David looked up to see that Pippin had gotten dressed.

"Yeah."

She grabbed her paint smock and swung into it without checking the fit in her mirror. "Figures," she muttered. As she stormed out of the room, she called over her shoulder, "Tiffany– that's the maid–"

"I know."

"She'll get you some breakfast."

And with that she was gone. David looked down at Jonathan in his arms and said, "I'm the guy in someone else's body. What the hell's gotten into *her?*"

Jonathan was still contentedly ensconced on his arm, gnawing on his knuckles, when the front door buzzed. David set down his cup on the kitchen counter with the last swigs of cidercaff in it. Tiffany's attention hadn't strayed from the vid.

Well, it might have taken a few buzzes to catch his attention too. "Should I get that?" he asked. The buzzes shortened to a rude *bzz-bzz-bzz.*

She shrugged, which was more attention than she'd paid him since he'd come in and asked for breakfast. She'd given him a quick up-and-down, said, "Whatever," and turned her back. Somehow breakfast had arrived on the utility island anyway.

The buzzes became manual knocks. Someone was pounding hard to get the sound to travel through that thick door up front. David quickly walked to the entry while reassuring Jonny. Cats liked quiet. Their little ears were sensitive and so were their nerves.

On the doorstep stood Officer Sugar. Whoa, good make. Even his hormones could respect this handiwork.

She too, seemed taken aback by him. "You're not the maid," she accused.

David started to point with his Jonathan-free arm toward the back of the house and Pippin's studio, but Sugar pushed past him.

"Pippin!" she called. She stood in the foyer and looked in all directions, as if trying to decide where to proceed.

"Studio," he pointed again. He secured the door with some difficulty and then followed her. "I don't believe we've been formally introduced," he said.

"Pippin!" Sugar shouted.

"Hey, stop upsetting Jonny. There, there, boy, it's okay. It's just Sugar."

Sugar whirled on him and eyed the cat, who didn't seem concerned with the woman. "Who the hell are you?"

"I'm David," he said as blandly as he could. "Well, not this body, but the mind inside is. Dr. David Lumen. And you're Officer Sugar, Pip's friend. I should tell you that in my professional opinion, she's a lost fashion cause without extensive personal realignment that will require professional therapy. Although you've made a valiant effort," he quickly amended as her puzzled expression grew into suspicion.

"PipPIN!" she bellowed without turning toward the studio.

From the kitchen came the sound of Tiffany's low complaints that she couldn't hear her show.

"I need to talk with you about my own situation. It's a long story." David waved her on with one hand. Jonathan jumped down to accompany them.

With the french doors marking the entrance to the studio in sight, David told Sugar, "Don't go in. You shouldn't encourage her. Make her come out to see you."

"What?"

He cocked his head at her as if he were instructing a patient. "Professional opinion. We must begin to wean Pip away from this art fantasy. If she wants to interact with others in an acceptable manner, she needs to learn to do so in an acceptable venue."

Sugar scowled at him and entered Pippin's studio. Pippin didn't look up. She was engrossed in a huge canvas which she attacked with a large brush. Slap! A swath of black arced across the canvas.

"Crap," she said as she worked. "Sheer and utter crapola."

"Pippin! Hell, I thought you were in trouble!"

"Excuse me, Pip," David called from the kitchen, "but you have a visitor. Why don't you both talk here in the house?"

Pippin looked up at that. She stared at the french doors for a moment and then her features tightened into frustration. With a deliberate step, Pippin left her post long enough to slam her doors shut– or at least slam them as much as they let her, which wasn't much. They bounced open with the force of it. At last she spotted her other visitor. "Oh. Sugar."

"Don't 'oh, Sugar,' me," Sugar growled as Pippin returned to her canvas. "You call me up, weeping and wailing that everything's wrong and the sky has fallen and now all you can say is, 'Oh, Sugar'?"

Sugar regarded the canvas in front of her charge. "You're right. This is crap." She folded her arms in front of her. "Why are you painting crap?"

Pippin scowled at her work. "David," she said.

"I'm in the kitchen," he called from Beyond the Doors. "Come in here to talk. It's very comfortable."

Sugar turned to Pippin. "Who is this guy?"

"We have apple dainuts," David cajoled. Pippin either groaned or growled; Sugar couldn't tell.

"Maybe you could use a break," Sugar said. "C'mon."

With great reluctance Pippin followed her out of the studio. There David stood waiting, a carbohydrate reward for each of them. "Very good," he said more to Pippin than to Sugar.

Sugar snatched the pastry from him. "Okay, I'll bite," she said as she did. "Who are you?"

"Long story." Pippin grumbled.

David led them to the stools around the kitchen island and motioned the audio on the vid to lower. Tiffany arranged a private sound cone for herself.

"Not so long. I'm a friend of Jonny," he said. The cat heard his name and jumped up onto the island. David scooped him into his arms and rubbed his neck, evincing a purr of contentment.

David turned his most beatific smile on Sugar without a false thought in his heart. The world was wonderful today. God was in His Heaven, David was in a human body. Not the right body, to be sure. And damn it, it couldn't appreciate Pippin, but things were getting on the right track.

He cupped his hand to his chest, right next to Jonathan's head. "Dr. David Lumen, as I said. Psychotherapist in Las Vegas, North America, Earth. Licensed telepath. Target of a telepathic hit man. I got knocked into Jonny here, who very kindly didn't kick me out, and then Pip helped me find a body to live in. Unfortunately, the owner of this body is living in mine, and I want it back."

He held out his free arm as if to welcome applause.

Sugar sat there, staring at him. Finally she turned to Pippin as if to say something, but though her mouth opened, nothing came out.

"I said it was a long story," Pippin turned back to her studio. Anything to get away from David and the humiliation– or was it failure?– he represented.

He'd been man enough– make that straight enough, she corrected herself quickly– last night. Last night she'd been good enough for him. Better than good enough.

He'd seduced her by praising her as an artist. He'd taken her to breathless heights she'd never attained even as he'd whispered her own worthiness. And then this morning– rejection. Disapproval.

Her blatant inferiority had turned him gay. How much lower could she sink?

She picked up one of her largest flats and made another slash– this time of red paint– onto her angry canvas. She punctuated with three shots of purple splotches, wham, wham, wham, and the canvas obligingly vibrated in rage.

David handled Jonathan's carrier as they commuted to the office. Such a glorious day! David sucked the air into deep, human-sized lungs. He made his own way; no one controlled his movements except whoever designed the trans route. If he wanted to, he could hop off. If he wanted to, he needn't even accompany Pip to work.

Freedom. Humans knew it best.

David drummed his fingers (and opposable thumb!) atop Jonny's carrier as he sat next to Pip and enjoyed the view outside. So good to be of a height to see things. Good that his body didn't process the blare of life at the volume that Jonny's did. At last he wore decent clothing again– though this suit felt a little uncomfortable now. It wasn't a Jakob Gallindor, but rather a respectable Lunar knock-off. How strange that the perfectly-tailored fashion seemed not to fit.

Now it was time to repay favors, despite the grumpy mood that his seatmate was in. Pip badly needed transformative therapy. If he couldn't get her to come out of her studio willingly, then he could offer positive reinforcement to her when she attended to her proper office duties.

Today he'd point out the parts of her job that she particularly enjoyed. She might see planting that orange grove as an expression of not conforming to her aunt's wishes or a plot to get herself fired, but he would turn that around. She was obviously operating from a sound business mind and enlarging the family business in a logical manner she could ultimately enjoy.

As he sat in smug satisfaction at his mastery of the situation, the never-ending infocrawl inside the tram caught his attention. Time, headline, stock report… date.

March fifth. His birthday.

David wondered if other people got that particular ping of familiarity as their special date got mention. "Birthday" was still an everyday word, but who celebrated one? Birthdays were a signal of time gone by and an aging body left in its wake. A birthday was a reminder that it didn't belong to the body he presently occupied.

He frowned at himself. He did not believe in omens!

And then as they stopped at a station he stared in shock out the window. He blinked. His lips flapped a moment before sound came out.

"That's me!" he hissed to Pippin and pointed.

She peered out. "Which one?"

"Thirty-six. The Thirty-six!"

He shifted his weight to get up, to run out of the car and chase himself down when he realized that this fellow must be a thirty-seven, maybe an -eight. No, a nine. A pin of perfect make glinted on the man's lapel.

"False alarm." His teeth gritted around the pounding of his heart.

"Not you?" Pip asked. She too, had started to get up. Now she curiously examined the false-David outside as the tram pulled away. How disappointing; this one had conventional brown hair. David was developing the habit of letting her down.

"No. Sorry. Guess I'm jumpy." To calm himself he reached to set to order the first thing he saw: Pip's collar. He smoothed it with his thumb, the tip skimming Pip's neck. For a moment he recalled a similar gesture the previous night, and his gaze moved to her eyes.

She must be remembering the same thing. Her sullen expression turned sultry, the pursed lips relaxed into the beginnings of a smile. "Nice make, that Thirty-series," she told him.

He smiled back, but his was big and friendly. "You've caught me on a bad day. Just wait until I get back into my body. I'll be able to appreciate a Twenty make the way they're supposed to be appreciated."

She gave a slight nod at the almost-compliment, the spark in her eyes cooling.

"You'll like me," he told her. "I won't be burdened with a misaligned sexual orientation."

"You won't be gay," she translated.

"I'll be the proper orientation for my body. Straighter than–" he tried to picture the straightest thing he could and didn't come up with the first image.

"Can't you, um, rise above this?" Pippin asked. "The man I met last night–"

"That was sheer testosterone overdose," David hastened to say. "At that point it could have happened with anyone– but I'm so glad it was you," he hastened to add at her grimace. "It was magic. You know that; you were there too. It'll be better when I get my body back. I promise."

She gave a unconvinced "Mm."

David shook his head to clear it. "It's this body. It's not designed for clear communication. Maybe that's the reason he turned to crime: frustration. I'm not saying this right at all, damn it."

Jonathan said, "Mow," and David patted the carrier.

"Not much farther," he assured the cat before turning back to Pip. "Jonathan is very fond of you. You cared for him when he was lonely and in pain. I picked that up from him, but I also see that you're a good person. Someone I want to know better."

"And a genius of an artist," Pip said sourly.

She must have suspected that his compliments had been for seductive purposes only. David didn't want to upset her so he nodded his head– for now. He said, "I understand that you're committed to this art show of yours. You need to make sure that you do everything you can to do it right."

That way when it failed she could turn to the family business full-time with no regrets, no what-ifs.

Pip's mouth turned up into a small smile that bloomed wider. The woman had a wonderful smile. "Why, you meant what you said," she said in wonder.

"I always do," he lied. A couple beats later he sat amazed at himself at the ease with which he did it, but his mouth continued without his brain, "I'll even help you. Perhaps I can put in a good word with Mama– I mean, Evie, when she returns."

Pippin laughed. "That is so cute. Jonathan thinks of her as his mama?"

"Absolutely. He's really her spoiled baby." He laughed along with her and they regarded the denizen of the carrier, who stared back at them suspiciously.

"Don't worry, Jonny," David told him. "We're laughing with you, not at you."

Pip made sure security clocked her into work both automatically and manually. She left a message for Evie as further proof and then diligently worked through the day's mails and memos that the secretary had earmarked. On the other side of the office, David used the company computers to track down his body.

He looked up when Brock Monark entered. Damn, that man looked fine. Even without Ethan Kane's extra chemicals pumping through David's brain, David knew that. He was almost top of the make, a Seventy-series. Chiseled features, confident stride; a commanding smile and practiced steady gaze. Executive material all the way. David bet even his ass was CEO material.

"Oh, Brock," Pippin said, and David's tensions eased to note the slight disdain in her regard toward the intruder. "Glad you came in."

"I was wondering if you'd had lunch yet." Brock withheld some of his charm as he studied David, clearly trying to reason why the stranger was here. A glance at Jonathan's carrier made his upper lip curl just enough for David to notice.

On the windowsill overlooking the orchards, Jonathan himself also watched Brock. His tail twitched and twitched again. Brock's path curved away from the cat.

"I'll get lunch later," Pippin said. She swung her desk screen around so Brock could see. "Aunt Evie said that the consumer test panel reports about the new banapple were due in yesterday. I can't find them. Did they come to you?"

"Banapple?" Brock settled in the farthest chair from Jonathan. "I thought that was the applechik report."

"Banapple," Pippin prompted. "Complete with extra potassium and peelable, stores well for months." She turned the screen back to herself. "Looks like you were copied for the main report. Maybe with Aunt Evie in the hospital, they didn't think to send it to her office."

Brock pulled out a screen from his breast pocket. "Oh yeah," he said. A different color light playing across his face made it clear that the screen's page changed. "Here it is. It just arrived even though it's dated two days ago, of all things. Damned e-delivery. I'll read it when I get back to my office." He glanced up. "Do you want me to copy it to you?"

"Would you?" Brittleness edged Pippin's smile. "We're holding on those results."

David didn't think the need had really registered on Brock's cerebral cortex.

"When do they need it?" Brock asked.

"Yesterday. We've got Tsu Chung-Chi sitting practically empty right now since the snafu."

"Mm?"

Was the man actually daydreaming as he was talking to a superior company officer? David couldn't believe it. A Seventy's training should come automatically with the surgeries; you'd think someone would have instituted that by now. This Brock only had the superficial aspects down.

And Pippin– David hated to admit it, but though Pippin had a good grasp of the business itself, it was people she dealt with poorly. That was part of her personal presentation problem. It would be simple enough to get her up to intermediate level on that, at least, but it would take time.

Instead he prompted on her behalf, "So you'd need those reports by, what, two o'clock today? Brock?"

"Mm?" Again, Brock's meager attention swung to the stranger. "I don't believe we've met. I'm Brock Monark, veep of Applegate Organics."

"Dr. David Lumen. I'm the Applegates' houseguest."

Brock's left, perfectly groomed eyebrow jerked. "Houseguest," he echoed.

"And Ms. Applegate needs that report. By two o'clock."

Pippin watched the brief interplay. "Yes," she said, "I should have been more specific. Two o'clock. We can have a meeting with Development and the Tsu staff first thing tomorrow morning if the results are favorable. What do you think about Melissa?"

"Melissa." Brock shifted to a more comfortable position, his left leg swinging over his right knee to block David's presence.

"Melissa Crater. The citrus experiment?"

"Ah yes," Brock frowned. "I heard about that."

"I hope so. I sent you a detailed memo."

Brock shrugged. "Probably got hung up with the other memos. I'll get nIT to check for glitches."

Pippin glanced at David. He grimaced at her to show her that she wasn't alone in her estimation of Mister Brock Monark. She swung back to face the veep. "You still have no opinion?"

"I didn't say that," he replied quickly. "I just…" Now he slowed down. His gaze no longer met hers. "This is not something the dra– Evie would approve of. She specifically stated that designer mutations were the way to go."

"Not if we want to expand our market with a solid product," Pippin said. "Real citrus will be a very new, very different product for Luna. People will eat it up." She smiled at her unexpected pun. "Literally."

"Can't make a screwdriver without orange juice," David volunteered. Pippin rewarded him with a chuckle.

"But Evie won't like it," Brock declared. "Evie is Applegate Orchards."

"The market is what defines the success of Applegate Orchards," Pippin told him. "Aunt Evie will discover that there's a large market out there for citrus. She'll be very happy she has trees to supply it."

"We'll get in trouble if we do it."

"It's already done." She gave him a beat. "It's in my memo."

"Then we either have to hush it up or soften the blow. Start a campaign to convince the dr– Evie to okay it."

"I've okayed it." Pippin gave Brock a tight-lipped grin. "If she loves it, I'm her fair-haired child. If she hates it–" Her lids lowered ever so slightly as if going into a pleasant reverie–"she can fire me. I'll take all the blame. And who knows, maybe some oranges on my way out too."

As soon as Pippin said, "fire," David sensed something in Brock coming alive. Eagerness at the aspect of Pip getting out of his way. He wanted her fired, out of the picture. Instinctively David didn't pry, but he could still reason. A vice president hired because of his potential and not real worth, Brock would be looking for ways to do away with his competition. How much simpler if she herself managed that? It was easier than applying himself to the job.

David wondered how much Mama knew about Brock's character. Surely now he'd blurt the plan to her behind Pippin's back.

"The doctors won't allow M– Evie visitors yet," David announced. After a moment he knew that it must sound completely off-subject. Pippin looked at him strangely, but Brock reacted with a scowl. "Not those who aren't family," David corrected with a steady gaze that said, "I'm family."

"We'll be sure to inform you when she's up to discussing business," David added as comprehension slowly blossomed on Pippin's face.

Pippin nodded. "They told me that any shock might be very damaging to her right now. If something should happen–" she shrugged–"I guess I'd be stuck with the company myself. Hate to see that happen. Sam Greenwood's the man to convince her about the citrus." She gave Brock a warning smile, friendly with steel backing it. "He's on her 'family' list too."

"Oh. Sam Greenwood." Brock's jaw worked for a moment before he nodded. "If anyone can convince her, he can. I suppose that means the citrus orchard is a go." First his left eyebrow went up and then his right before both regained their normal position as if his thoughts shifted from one hemisphere of his brain to the other. He may have rejected one plan but maybe he'd adopted another. His shoulders straightened and a wolfish gleam appeared in his eyes. "So perhaps we should celebrate? We could go out to lunch. My treat. I know a place where–"

Pippin's smile went sour. "I need to get my hours in today before I do anything else," she hedged and then brightened. "Besides, you can't make it. Two o'clock, remember?"

"Two–"

"O'clock. Banapples." Pippin waited expectantly.

"Ah. Yes." He got up from his seat hurriedly. "I'll get that report together. Results should be interesting."

"I'll just bet," Pippin muttered as the door swung shut behind him.

14

David sat back in his chair and rubbed his chin. "Seventies aren't supposed to be like that," he said. "I've handled a lot that were unprepared for the higher points of their make, but he's definitely in the remedial class."

"No one employed in this company should be a shmuck," Pippin countered. "I didn't think Aunt Evie was so shallow that she couldn't see beneath the surface."

"But the surface is the part of us we show the world. It should always reflect our inner selves so as to keep both aligned with what society requires of us. This allows for easier self-correction."

Pippin turned to him across her desk. "You are beginning to sound ever so much like a real psychiatrist." As the pleased expression began to show on his face, she added, "Have you learned anything useful? I mean, besides listening to my business?"

David glanced at the monitors around him. Dead ends all; no David Lumen or Ethan Kane yet. "Besides hearing how well you handle all this?" David gestured to take in the office as well as the orchard outside the window. "I tried to find Kane's secondary accounts, if he has any."

"Not primary?"

He flashed her a mischievous grin that made him look so sly. Pippin fought against her instant response to a bad boy who wasn't afraid of the power he wielded. *Gay,* she reminded herself.

"I took care of those yesterday while the hospital had them open. They had passcode access to them— a dangerous way to do business for their patients, if I may say so. I don't think that was a reputable company at all."

Pippin let out a wheeze that might have been intended as a whistle. "Identity the— What did you do?"

"His accounts were much too large to keep them available to him. And he was practically asking for it. A hit man who doesn't pay attention to security?" David thought a moment. "Maybe he had a plan of possessing someone and wanted a clear shot at being able to get at his own money without going through any kind of body scan. Yes, I bet that's what he had in mind. Lucky for me."

"How lucky?"

He tilted his head at her. "He wasn't a threat to buy out your aunt, if that's what you mean, but he had enough that he probably thought it was time to retire in comfort. In my body." David made a few adjustments on one screen and saved it with a flourish. "He won't be doing that now. I locked him out of his own accounts."

"He won't like that."

"I don't like not having access to my own accounts. Which are very securely protected from him, by the way. He can't go to the authorities to claim identity theft. I know too much."

Pippin tapped her stylus against her desk. She didn't like the sound of that. She'd heard too many murder dramas that used that line.

"But you say he had a lot of money? Was anything deposited lately?"

David rechecked his screen and pointed at hers, where he'd sent a copy. She leaned over her own monitor with interest.

"Look at all the activity," she said. "Jeez, look at the amounts!"

"Much of it seems to be arrangements for the coldsleep," David assured her. "But look at line eleven. Someone on Earth made a sizable deposit into his account a week ago." He rubbed his chin. "Maybe for killing me. Maybe he pulled a double-cross and reported the job completed."

"Or maybe it's a down payment on something he'll do," Pippin said. "You've got to find out. Explosives and pressurized tunnels– they don't go well together."

David nodded as Jonathan jumped off the window sill to settle on his lap. They held a brief, silent conversation.

"Jonathan wants to know if I'm content now."

"That you're human?"

He gave her a crooked smile, apologetic but warm. "That I have you. My mate. Despite being neutered, our Jonny is very much a tom cat, don't forget that. I don't think he understands this. Hell, I don't understand this."

His gaze seemed far away as he scratched Jonathan's neck. "It seems so theoretical now: the Storms-Gray Sexuality Axis. It's programmed in through a complicated combination of genetics, histones, womb chemicals, and epigenetics. It makes it all seem so happenstance. But believe me, from in here it seems like a universal mandate."

He grimaced at her. "I'm so sorry. Last night was–"

She let the sentence hang in the air before she said, "It was."

"This morning was nothing to do with you. Nothing at all."

She sighed and he rose with the cat in his arms to walk to the small mirror that hung next to the outer door. He checked his skin tones to make sure he'd matched them with his new foundation. They were darker than he was used to, and he wasn't sure how a non-spf formula would blend. On a whim he'd chosen metallic snake bites, and he admired the subtle flash they brought to his eyes.

"It'll take me a while to get used to this body. Strange how the physical can so influence the mental. Of course, that's why we psychiatrists prescribe drugs. This body is an entire new set of chemicals and rhythms that influence my mind."

He adjusted the mirror slightly downward. "You'll get better use out of this if you can see yourself."

Jonathan regarded him through slitted eyes.

"It took Jonny a while to get used to another mind in his own body too. I know what to expect now. I should be myself soon." Shouldn't make promises… "Or a good portion of myself, at any rate."

Pippin turned her screen to business matters. "We wouldn't want David Lumen turning into a hired killer."

"Don't worry. I won't. The mind is the most powerful tool a human possesses." He sucked in his breath. "Why, I'm in a position no one in history has ever been in. I've been on both sides, straight and gay. I understand both in a way no one ever has before. Do you know what this means?"

Pippin leaned on her hand. "What?"

"What I do… I change people," David explained. "I improve on nature. I show them how to shape themselves into what they need to be. Imagine all the gay people throughout history who have hidden from themselves and society because for so long homosexuality was seen as a negative trait. It still is. People don't like to acknowledge it, but gays are still perceived as different, the Other."

A sudden shaft of light reflected off the moving shade system of the orchard outside caught the edge of David's face, illuminating it. "I remember what it was like to be fully straight. I think if I apply myself I can come up with a system that will actually allow gays to function in the world as if they were straight, and get pleasure out of it."

"Why would they want to do that?" Pippin asked.

"Why wouldn't they? People want to conform in order to fit human society. Like everyone, they want the absolute approval of their peers. I hold the answer to the gay problem… if I can just pinpoint it." He rubbed his chin. "It might take a few days. Or longer." He shook himself. "But I have other priorities. My own body."

"A hired killer in it," Pippin reminded him.

"Yes. But still–" He couldn't stop the sense of wonder at his own position. "I could change the world. Finally, there'd be a way for everyone to conform. No wild spirits, no troublemakers, no unhappiness."

"No artists," Pippin murmured as she concentrated on the work in front of her.

The gun shop almost looked like the ones on Earth, except that the warning signs that outlined the outer, barred door were more numerous and with smaller print.

Explosives in a pressure-sealed environment: not a good thing.

The woman behind the counter didn't wear any facial bandages. She should have. She had a scar high on her right cheek, and the corner of her lower lip stuck out as if she usually sucked on something that hung out of her mouth. Her expression was sullen and closed. Her mind was murky.

David was feeling the same way. Maybe it was just part of the process of settling into this new body. After teaming with Jonny for so many days, he felt very solitary in the universe. He himself was the only one he could rely on.

"I want to buy a gun," David told the woman.

"What kind?"

He hated to show a weakness. This body rebelled at it; his mouth almost refused to open. "I don't know. I need something for protection."

"'It is a felony to buy a gun for the use of committing– '" the woman began to recite.

"I may have someone after me. My friends might get in his way. I don't want my friends hurt."

That made her give him a slow once-over. Apparently he passed her inspection. She nodded. "Projectile, electric, sonic, or laser?" she asked.

What to say? "Whatever will work most efficiently." He paused. "Something that operates at a short distance."

"Killer force?"

"Yes. No! I just want to stop them, not kill them." Maybe this body had too much testosterone. He must control it and the urges it released within himself.

Most projectiles were discouraged on Luna because of pressure problems caused by the more common arms. The shop carried some uncommon ones behind the counter and out of sight. Because of the tunnels and closed areas of lunar civilization, simple sonics could accidentally amplify to mass-destructive levels without expensive frequency adapters. That left shockers and lasers for the everyday citizen.

Lasers required linking to a computerized targeting system that could be strapped to an arm or leg and hidden under long clothing. Shockers required close proximity to the victim.

David preferred to take out this killer Kane from a distance, but sometimes even he couldn't control the universe. Sometimes a man had to be a man and do what had to be done.

"Where can I get lessons?" David asked as he purchased one of each.

The woman cued his palm screen for local shooting range addresses. "You'll like Denny's," she guessed. "They specialize in instruction for beginners. They also have self-defense classes."

"Ah. Good, thanks."

David quickly left the store with his gun boxes tucked under his arms. How had Ethan Kane's ident check cleared Lunar firearms authority without raising multiple alarms?

Kane had been shaped by a lifetime of violence. Unless he had some ulterior motive– and David suspected that one could be connected with this– he would stay on David's trail until he brought his prey down. If others got in his way…

David's arms pulsed with goosebumps. If Pippin or her family should draw Kane's attention, they could find themselves expendable. If Kane felt they were impeding him from his mission, they could be in dire danger.

David should leave the Applegate house immediately. But where could he go? Anywhere habitable would be around innocent people. Conditioned space was at a premium here. He'd learned that the clean tunnels of Luna were neither heated nor pressurized where people weren't welcome. Unlike what vid melodramas liked to pretend, unheated tunnels on Luna would be at least a hundred degrees colder than the coldest unheated Terran tunnels.

Maybe Kane's ident check had alerted local police to his presence. Were they watching him right now?

He glanced at the far ceiling, past the day-spectrum lights to the security cameras. Were they focused on him?

A sudden arrest would screw things up completely. On the other hand, if the cops just kept a protective eye on him, they'd be keeping a protective eye on Pippin as well, if he were to stick to her.

He hefted the light boxes and straightened his shoulders. He had guns now. With them he felt more whole. He could handle anything Kane could bring on.

David stopped in his tracks. Pedestrian traffic paused and then flowed around him as the realization hit. Though for a moment he'd felt completely at ease with them, David Lumen knew nothing about how to handle guns. Without training, guns were merely a penile fantasy. With training…

He grinned to himself. With training, they were a penile fantasy that delivered solid results. He turned to take the left street toward the trans and a new education.

On the way back to Pippin's house with his new, now-familiar guns secured variously about his body, David strolled the pleasant upper ways of Luna City. It wasn't Vegas by any means. For one thing, it was much smaller. Some culs de sac were even on the claustrophobic side, though ceilings on this upper level were usually kept high enough in public places for the trees of numerous small parks to stretch comfortably. In many places he couldn't tell if the brightness was artificial or reflected somehow from the surface.

The city had an abundance of broad boulevards lined with tropical trees ranging from palms to who-knew-what they were, which sheltered masses of fragrant and colorful shrubs and flowers at their bases. Pressurized Luna never suffered from frost. Exotic birds squawked from the green canopy.

For a while he might even have thought he was somewhere on Earth except for everyone's walk– or slow lope. It was an easygoing stride with a distinct arc involved. The battle against gravity was won up here. Not too little; not too much.

And yet his body chafed at the ease. Something inside him kept wanting to kick it up, get going. Work off excess energy. Kane was fairly young, but more than that, his body was in top condition. These weren't artificial muscles, pumped up just for show. David could almost feel the individual sinews.

Just as there was on Earth, on the corner of any busy intersection sat a Star-Buffs. For the first time, David realized that the local gymnacaf was really that: a gym. Everyone knew that one went to StarBuffs for caffeine, nutrinosh and chat, but the cafes must have started out as gyms somewhere along the way.

StarBuffs' logo showed a flexed arm with muscles bulging, its hand grasping a steaming beverage cup. Membership came with access to the gym equipment, but of course no one actually used it. David had never given it a second thought before. All the equipment was merely decor.

He stepped into one cafe. Small tables were scattered before large windows to the outside so the noshers could see and be seen. And along the wall next to the counter–

Exercise equipment: three large pieces involving seats and handlebars, pulleys and flywheels.

He went up to one piece, a stainless steel and black flexigrip octopus with digital readout, drink and food holders, and vid screens. It wasn't an antique. He'd seen this sort of thing offered last New Year's during the annual fitness craze that went along with resolutions.

There were only six customers here, thank goodness. Few witnesses. Two minimum-wage kids stood behind the counter. One wore the surly expression that came with tooth megabracing, or maybe it was just a typical teenager snarl at the world. They awaited his order without greeting him.

After studying the menu over their heads, David said, "Cidercaff. Make that decaf."

"Latte? Double-cinnamon? Honey whip? We have fresh tarts."

"Just cider."

As he waited for the laborious production to finish dispensing plain cider from a hissing machine, he asked, "Does this stuff work?" and waved at the gym equipment.

Snarlie checked him out in a once-over. "You aren't old enough for rejuv," he finally decided.

David returned the favor. "Right," he said. "And guessing age is rude. I should report you to the manager." As the kid took a startled breath, he added, "Don't sweat it. I just want to work out."

"You going to Earth or sumpthin'?"

"Do I have to fill out a personality survey to use the gym? There's another StarBuffs next block up."

In the end, the kids had to summon the manager by vid, who crosslinked them to the company's Director of Personal Training. He went by the single name of Achilles. This guy was back on Earth. The cafe's equipment was pretty much for show except for rejuvies who were under doctor's orders to shape up to their new bodies, or for residents bound to Earth.

Thus David received personalized, if remote, training. As days passed, he became the entertainment for customers who drifted in and out of the cafe. Achilles faxed him info about the new megasteroids, legal and illegal, and also programmed a suggested dietary regimen as well as daily Luna-friendly exercise lists.

"I never get to do this much," Achilles told him with enthusiasm. "Ever since the new faux-muscle tissues dropped in price two years ago, people haven't wanted to build their bodies the old-fashioned way."

"Faux muscle doesn't work," David said.

"But it looks good."

"I need something that works as well as it looks."

Achilles gave him a nod. "You've been exercising pretty well up to now, I see."

"Needed something new to do, now that I'm on Luna," David explained as he finished this set of reps. His delts didn't seem to mind what his other body would have been screaming from.

"Ethan!" some man called from the entry of the cafe.

Something inside him perked up, some remnant of the previous occupant. His body's name was Ethan. Could someone be–? He looked away from Achilles on his monitor.

A hand gripped his shoulder. "Ethan. It *is* you!"

He turned to a man of wiry neo-Teen make. Neo-Teens were not supposed to be as bony as the old Teen class, but this one was. He had blond hair with inch-long black roots: the most blatant bi-and-looking signal there was.

"What?" David managed to ask.

Who was he? The guy definitely looked, well, not right. Maybe it was the sexual identity bit that was throwing newly-gay David off. He wore beat-up leather or a good faux imitation, with big belt buckle and flashy studs decorating his suit. His chin was bandaged, probably from a recent chin implant but maybe from a street brawl. It was a plain white bandage. The snake bites around the outside of his eyes were gold. He could have used some for the wrinkles starting at the corners of his mouth. Many people didn't like to admit their age even to themselves.

"What, you don't remember me?"

"Don't be stupid," David growled. He didn't want to reveal the weakness of ignorance. He raised his chin and narrowed his eyes into slits that he hoped look dangerous. He gestured the com line to Earth cut with a fist instead of the usual wave.

The guy took a half-step back. "Hey, I thought you said we was all fixed. No problem."

"Yeah. Right. No problem." David allowed his shoulders to relax.

The guy let out a breath. "Good. You know I'd never want to rile you. I've been up here for two years now. No buzz from the fuzz, snowbirds. And now you show up? What the hell you doing on Luna?"

David shrugged. "Things happen." When did his voice become this gravely?

"You on assignment?" The guy's smile trembled and caught. "Or is this a pleasure trip?"

"David! David!"

Female voice, not Pippin or even Mama. David turned ever so slightly, unwilling to let this unknown factor out of his sight.

"Oh no." Only one top-make Sixty FeeP knew him by name here. Though he couldn't read her tag from here, it had to be Officer Sugar, in full uniform. Damn the equipment for being in front of the street window!

Sugar waved to him brightly from the door. He gave her a nod, hoping that would be enough, but apparently she took it as a signal to come over. She wasn't alone. Her male partner accompanied her.

"Don't mention anything about… you know," David muttered to the guy.

"A little sidebar, Ethan? You jumping the fence these days? Never figured you for a gate, but she's prime."

"Business. She's peripheral to my business."

"Peripheral? What's that?" Guy asked, but Sugar was upon them. She'd ducked and dodged her way through the sudden late-afternoon caffeine line, a difficult low-grav ballet that David would have hesitated to attempt.

"David!" Sugar caught her breath. "Have you seen Pippin?" She eyed Guy and his half-black hair. "Are you in that new artist group of Pip's?" she asked.

David unwound himself from the equipment. He needed to stand, to be ready if things went sour. "This is Officer Sugar," he said, more to prompt Guy than anything else. It wouldn't hurt to reveal that much. After all, she was in full Fashion Police uniform and tagged.

Luckily for him, Guy fell into place. "Dougie Chu," he obliged and stuck out his hand. Sugar shook it warmly. "I'm a friend of… ah…"

"David, you've got friends on Luna," Sugar said. "You hadn't mentioned that." She gave a nod to her partner. "Rod Sherwood."

Officer Rod scrutinized them with a cold Nineties stare.

David said, "Pippin's working in her studio. I took off for a while."

"I suppose it's good for you to get out of the house now and, uh, looking for, you know." Sugar eyed Dougie's hair even as she talked to David. "I take it the lovers' spat is over?"

"That's not what you think," David said.

She gave him an all-knowing smirk.

How to get rid of her?

"Uh, nice skirt," he tried. As a rule FeePs loved compliments. He'd never seen any wear quite so tulipy a tulip skirt as she had on, though it was a becoming shade of blue.

But the comment didn't have its desired effect. Sugar's face turned dark. "It's a Shelanda knock-off," she snapped. "New regulation uniform."

"Shel– Shelanda Jones?" David chided himself for not checking into the tabs before venturing out. A clique of women walked past the windows, all wearing similarly-styled skirts. The famous celeb must have appeared somewhere important in such a dress and spawned an instant fashion must-have.

Still, Officer Sugar positively reeked of anger as she thought of it. David took a physical step away from her.

Officer Rod reached into his holster to produce a lasertape. Snatching the end of one of Dougie's hairs, he pulled it to its full extent. Dougie grimaced but said nothing, as if he'd been through this before. The laser flashed a reading of the length of Dougie's roots.

"Forty-two millimeters," Officer Rod snarled.

"I have a hair appointment two hours from now, Officer," Dougie declared with all sincerity.

Rod snapped the lasertape back to its place. "The law says forty millimeters max for sexual lifestyle statements."

"Two millimeters is not a prison offense," Sugar soothed as whatever it was about Shelanda Jones faded. "For all we know, it's humid in here and the hair stretched."

Officer Rod slapped his ticket pad against his hand. His mouth opened as he started to say something, but Sugar beat him to it.

"The primary role of Fashion Police is to teach, not punish," she said.

"But we can't have them inflicting their imperfections upon the rest of us," Rod replied.

"I suppose. Can't fault a man for doing his job," Sugar said with faked heartiness. "Good spot, Rod."

She turned to Dougie with her best FeeP Instruction face. "You should check your roots every three days. If you want to make a statement, make sure that statement is clear and not against the law. Remember, any more and it goes on the books as just plain bad roots. We'll let you off this time. Consider yourself officially warned. Rod?"

Officer Rod clicked a shot of Dougie's face into his palm screen. "I put a two-day call-back on you. You'd better have had your hair done when we come by again."

"Yes, Officer." Dougie ducked his head in obedience. "You can check with the salon if you want. It'll save you a call."

"We'll do that." Sugar heaved a sigh and cocked her head at David. "Teens. Their make is their age. They always think they can outsmart the system."

"Er, ah, I see you're–" not "in uniform;" apparently she had a problem with this week's dress code–"on duty," David said.

"How observant." Still, Sugar preened slightly. "I got upgraded to active status a few hours ago. I've got missed quotas to fill."

"Is that why you're looking for Pip?"

Sugar laughed and even grim Officer Rod cracked a small smile. "I wanted to warn her to keep off the streets. I might forget myself and ticket her within an inch of her life."

"I'm heading there in a while. I'll tell her."

"Good. You two made up?"

Dougie's curiosity oozed around him like a fog. "Nothing to make up about," David declared with heat. Why did everyone try to butt into his business? Why couldn't people let him be? "Everything's fine. Good to see you, Officer Sugar. Officer Rod," he hinted in dismissal.

Rod perked up as he spotted something through the windows. "Tell me that's not what it looks like," he told Sugar.

She gaped over David's shoulder even as he twisted to see as well. "Designer rickets; I'll be damned," she said in awe. "Didn't anyone tell her that retro-trends are so yesterday? Those had better be natural! Go get her, Rod. I'll be a minute here."

With a nod, Officer Rod left to do his duty outside.

Sugar turned back to David. "Pippin needs someone to make her happy. I'm glad you–" Sugar's eyes slid over to regard Dougie for a moment, "straightened everything out after the other night, eh?"

"Ah, sure," David said. Anything to get Sugar out of here. Maybe this Dougie would follow her. David wanted to be alone and… And what? Sulk. Simmer in his own juices. Something. He shifted uncomfortably.

"Excellent. I wouldn't want her to get mixed messages. She loved that you support her and her work, David. I guess that's why she adores you."

"She doesn't adore me." Go away!

"She doesn't know it yet. Give her time."

Two soft chimes sounded. People set down their cidercaffs and noshes and corrected their posture. The front entry of the store opened wide.

A breeze blew through.

David started in astonishment. A breeze– on the streets of Luna? Yet everyone closed their eyes to it, breathing deeply. It brought a moist freshness with it, as if a gentle storm had just cleaned the air.

Now people all around the room, including Sugar and Dougie, drew in deep breaths. David realized what they were doing and joined them.

He took ten breaths deep into his abdomen. Each breath he held for a count of ten, and when he exhaled, he blew out from his belly. Each time he breathed he tried to imagine white purifying light entering his body and racing to every cell. Each exhale was a chance for those cells to release toxins they'd been holding. Each exhale let some of the tenseness go.

Conversations around the store had stopped until the last person completed their ten breaths. Now everyone had pleasant smiles. David couldn't blame them. The brief meditation was invigorated by the fresh air that surrounded him. He hadn't noticed the flat air before.

Sugar nodded to him as he finished his final breath. "Guess that means that I'm running late," she said. "Hadn't noticed the time. First day back excitement, I guess. Let me go rein Rod in from ticketing every other Loonie out there. Tell Pippin I'm coming over after my shift, David."

"I will." He managed a smile.

Together the men watched the curvy blonde hurry out the door and then toward the business district. "So it's David now?" Dougie asked.

"Huh."

"Who's this Pippin?"

"Bodyguard assignment." Hired killers had those, didn't they? "The officer is misreading the situation. Anyone who comes near my client–"

Again Dougie stepped back at his hard gaze. "Wasn't even thinking about it, Ethan. I never heard of her. Never saw you, either… Unless you want to look me up off-duty."

"It's going to be a long time before I get more than an hour off. I should be getting back as it is."

Dougie nodded. "If you need help with this job," he said, "I'm in the book. And I've still got some of my equipment."

"Good to know." David gave a crisp nod as he dismounted the equipment. Then he actually turned his back on the man, probably an assassin himself, and walked casually away. *Don't run.* He tried to scan for any sign of suspicion, but Dougie kept his mind closed. Maybe that came from working with telepaths. Deadly telepaths.

15

With a start, David realized that he was heading to someplace he identified as "home": the Applegate house. It must be leftover feelings from his merger with Jonathan. Still, the door recognized him as a resident and creaked open at his approach. Inside he paused in setting the empty gun boxes on top of an antiques display and peered around instead. Something was–

Jonathan charged at him. The cat's tail curled in a shepherd's crook shape: play mode. David dropped his boxes, crouched and sprang.

Jonathan wheeled about before bounding back down the hall.

"Gonna get you, Jonny-Boy!" David yelled at the cat. Jonathan peered behind himself and David ducked into a doorway. He peeked back out long enough to make sure Jonathan saw him, and then knelt next to the doorway.

After a moment, Jonathan appeared at the doorjamb. David snatched him up. "Got you! Got you!" He rubbed the cat in a frenzy. Jonathan squirmed in David's grip and managed to jump down, only to come back to rub against David's legs. David sank onto the floor and gave his buddy a good rub-down as Jonathan pulsated with loud purrs.

Pippin found the two of them there. She heard David's voice before she came upon them: "No, buddy, I've got to go. I don't belong here."

Jonathan perched on David's shoulder so the two were eye-to-eye. "Rrt?"

"I'm sorry," David replied. "I don't want to. That's just the way things are." He looked up to find Pippin there, and his face broke into a smile.

Pippin's heart melted at the sight. David's dark good looks, his open happiness to see her, and the sweet cat conversation– why the hell did the guy have to be gay?

"You've got green on your nose," he told her.

"And you're leaving," she said. "Why?"

He gave a good-natured shrug at that. "Name's not Applegate, either in this body or my own." He settled Jonathan on the floor and stood up in one liquid movement that reminded Pippin of a more lateral one he'd made the other night. "Thank you for all your help, but I need to get a room and start a serious search. I just came back for–" He looked blank for a moment, as if he didn't know. "To tell Jonny. And to thank you."

"There's no need for you to go." She gave him her sultriest voice.

David's eyes sharpened on her. "I would love to stay and give you anything you wanted, Pip, but you and I both know that biology is not working in our favor."

"Have you tried your psycho techniques on yourself today?"

"Well… no. Haven't had time."

She leaned against the wingback chair. "Maybe proximity might help."

He scrunched his nose in the most endearing way. "Don't think so, babe."

"Still, you need a place to crash. Might as well be here."

His brows furrowed in puzzlement. "There's no guest room."

"My room is the guest room."

David crouched to rub Jonathan as the cat walked back and forth between his legs. "I don't think you're facing reality, Pip. Now, once I get my body back–"

"Maybe that will be tomorrow. And by then you'll be comfortable in my room." She trailed her fingers across the back of the chair and David knew what it felt like. "You need a place to sleep. And you get along so well with Jonathan– could you take over babysitting duties for him? It would help me."

David eased back down to the floor just so he could look at her. What was it about her that was so compelling? She was entirely typical, just another square peg needing his help to round the edges to fit into society. Yet there was something unique about her too. Special.

Her appeal, despite the fact that she was female, was obvious enough. "You've helped Mam— I mean, your aunt a lot with the company, haven't you?" he asked and then continued before she could reply, "And you went all the way to Earth to stay with Jonny. You don't know how much he appreciated that, Pip. You may have saved his life. He might have died from loneliness and fear otherwise. And you're good to your aunt, even though you and she have completely different goals for you."

Pip obviously didn't know how to answer. She wouldn't. She was a good woman, David decided. Warm and protective, someone who truly cared about others to the exclusion of her own needs. That should be balanced and he could help her with that, but it was also something you didn't find every day.

David felt as if he'd been searching his entire life for that. He needed some place to call home, someone who would provide that sense of safety and relief from the world's troubles.

Where had that come from? The only true danger David had ever encountered had come from Ethan Kane. Yes, when Mother had died it had cut him off some from the yin of the world, but many people went through that trauma and survived.

Maybe it was this body that craved safety. As a hit man, Ethan Kane lived within a maelstrom of violence. He wouldn't be allowed to demonstrate any feelings he had about his job, so he had to be repressed. As a telepath, he'd have to work doubly hard to shield himself from his victims' fears and innocence. Maybe… Maybe all Ethan Kane really wanted was safety.

Pip wasn't just survival. Somehow with that big heart of hers she was life.

Again David promised himself that when this was all through, he'd help her with her own problem.

"I'll stay," he said.

"Good."

That night she snuggled into bed next to him. "Still nothing?" she asked in a small voice that seemed to want to sound unaffected.

"It's not you," David replied. "I'll work on myself tonight."

"I'd rather you worked on me," she said with a hopeful lilt.

"You know what I mean."

That evinced a sigh. "I suppose it's all for the good. One night of sex with you and my art left me flat. You've heard of chakras?"

"How esoteric. They're mystic energy centers within the body, yes."

"They say the sex chakra is the creative chakra as well. If you blow it out with sex, there's no energy left for creativity. So if I want to get some real work done tomorrow–" She pushed him playfully– "Keep away from me."

He chuckled to support the rationalization. "I can always sleep on the couch."

"No. Stay." She held her breath for a second and then said, "Did you really mean it when you said you liked my work?"

"Of course," he lied. Damn. He would have to remember to check out the pieces in her studio sometime soon. She might ask him for details. "It's very unique." It seemed right to lie to her about this now. It would be a sin to hurt Pip.

He hesitated, but placed his hand lightly on her bare arm. "Would you like me to hold you?" Maybe that would make the loneliness in both of them go away.

Jonathan jumped up on the bed and walked over David as if he were a rocky ridge, just to settle between the two of them.

"I think that's a 'no,'" Pippin said. "Everyone go to sleep."

Sugar had to strain to keep up with Pippin as they practically jogged in lunar slo-mo through the mid-level streets of Luna City. Other people walked sedately to accompany their companions who were often in after-surgery wheelchairs or medi-scooters.

"I'm sorry," Pippin said. "You know I had to exercise a lot to get ready for Earth. I just feel peppy."

"But you were there for weeks," Sugar protested. "Surely all that energy wore off."

"Now that I'm back, I feel like I could run a million miles. And besides, this is faster than the trans."

Sugar signaled a stop and Pippin obliged. "Gasping is not fashionable," Sugar told Pippin. "We stop before I make a fool of myself." Still she was out of breath.

Pippin let her rest a moment. "I've got to do something about my FeeP tickets. You know all the ins and outs. You tell me what my options are."

Sugar shrugged and then corrected herself to a polite nod. As long as they were stopped, she attended to sopping up some slight sweat on her face. "Individually, you could get out of any of them easily," she said. "You just cross-reference between the faux pas and the police reports. Temporary dishabille is legitimate in times of extreme stress or accident, as long as it's another's fault."

"Whew. All right."

"But," Sugar continued, "the sheer volume of your tickets is enough to make a judge stop to take a second look. You have a pattern of accidents."

"Not my fault!"

Sugar waved that off. "If you get the wrong judge, they're not going to care. Habitual scofflaw, they'll say."

"Unfair!"

Sugar checked her teeth for lipstick. "You can appeal, but the process might take a while. As in a year or so."

Pippin let out a cross between a squeak and a moan.

Sugar put away her touchup kit and pointed at Pip. "Of course, if the defendant has just had a very successful, avant-garde art show, the judge will be likely to rule in her favor. He might give bonus points as well."

Pippin considered that. She puffed her cheeks in consternation, then blew out her frustration. "Just what I needed, more stress," she said.

"Stress is good. It keeps us on our toes."

"Yeah, and it keeps the trank manufacturers rich." Pippin eyed her friend. "You rested? I have a gallery to measure."

Sugar checked her pocketpack to see that all was secured, and then smoothed out the two wrinkles of her skirt. "After you," she said.

"Waitaminnit," David said. "When did Lorne's baby become a teenager?"

Tiffany slapped a wave in his direction. "Shh!"

David shut up and tried to catch up with the goings-on on *Stormy Heights*. During a party scene, which was filled with mid-week small talk that wouldn't affect the plot one way or another, Tiffany finally broke the silence.

"Lorne is such a hunk. I had me a man, and he looked just like him."

"Brad's hotter."

"You just say that because you're gay. Lorne is hotter for straights."

"I'm just as straight as I am gay. Brad's the one. Hell, even when I'm full straight, I'd tap that Brad."

Speak of the devil, Brad and Sheila were sneaking upstairs to have a torrid rendezvous in their host's bedroom.

"Mm mm-mm mm," Tiffany said as the explicit scene got underway.

David had to agree. Every inch of the actors' bodies was perfection, even if some of it had to be computer-generated, and they were certainly up on their sexual positions.

For a moment, David wondered how much a sex consultant for one of these shows got paid. How did they choose someone for that? And what did the job entail? A lot of research?

David thought of Pippin. Unfortunately, he couldn't build up a lot of lust for her. Pure and innocent devotion, yes, like a sister to come home to.

But that Brad was a hottie.

Damn this body anyway. He pushed away from the table.

"I'm going out," he said, though Tiffany was too engrossed in the pornography to hear him. He had to continue searching. Find his body. Get himself straight again, and then set some things straight with Pippin too.

Pippin squelched more sunlight by adjusting the polarization of the bus windows. This hadn't been a good day for her to go to the Far Side for a group *plein vacuum* outing. She wasn't in the mood for angled sunlight. The shadows were wretched. The light didn't reflect her dark mood.

She'd gotten up extra early to attend to the office, precious hours away from the studio. Even so, David had been gone, leaving only Jonathan to snore softly on the bed. Then Brock had shown up to their breakfast meeting late, squandering her time. Worse, he hadn't been prepared. Again. She'd yelled at him– how could he be so unprofessional?

Wasted, wasted time. She laid in her values upon the canvas board in long, frustrated swipes that left almost liquid paint in its wake. Outside the bus the lunar landscape lay in eternal silence. The low sun still drenched the rocky ridge in brightest, colorless white. Incredibly long shadows wrapped themselves around everything, turning black and white order into an insolvable puzzle. Stupid, stupid shadows.

They looked like the shadows underneath that front lock of David's hair, the one that fell over his forehead. Sultry dark eyes under darker eyebrows would peer at her from those shadows as if he could unmask her every secret.

And she wanted him to. She wanted him to throw every civilized convention away and take her. But every night when they went to bed he just rolled away from her like a gentleman– a gentleman who was rejecting her. Damned genes. Damned psychiatrists who said that they could change themselves if given enough time.

She knew about time. There was never enough of it. First it never came at all and then it passed too quickly.

She squashed her brush against her canvas, right up to the ferrule so the hairs spread out in a feathered circle. Killing her brush slowly, she scribbled in the black sky.

Pippin didn't know the class instructor well. She'd only managed a last-minute, spare seat. This bus was chartered by Luna C University and the instructor was a professor of art there, Abigail Vootan-McCully or Wotan-O'Sully or something like that. She was a Forty who acted like she wanted to be a commanding Eighty, and thus tended toward more heaviness than she should have carried. She wore a bored expression as the students scratched their heads at the moonscape and tried to put something on the canvases in front of them. Mostly she worked on her own private screen.

After they'd been there an hour the instructor's screen dinged. Vootan-Wotan eased up out of her seat, stretched her back with a great groan, and then wearily made her way down the bus aisle to examine the students' progress.

No one had produced anything that particularly impressed her, but then no one had done anything for her to particularly dislike. She seemed to think that art must take the middle road.

"Good brushwork there," she told one and almost immediately went on to the next. "Watch your value patterns." Then, "Remember the law of sameness." "Out of medium? Use your thinner. So it's not archival; it's not like you're painting a masterpiece." From one to another she strolled, never varying the tone of her voice, never truly paying attention.

The professor stretched some more, which required another grunt, just before reaching Pippin's station. V-W chewed on the inside of her cheek as she considered the canvas. Her eyes remained at half-staff.

"Needs more color," V-W announced.

Before Pippin could react, V-W seized one of her good brushes, jabbed it into first a blob of vermilion and then lemon yellow, and struck bold if unevenly-colored dashes across Pippin's harsh moonscape.

"Hey!" Pippin yelled, but V-W had three more dashes to make. Pippin grabbed the brush from her. "What the hell! You've ruined it!" She wanted to throttle the vandal. Her right hand actually reached out in a fury colder than the lunar morning outside, fingers flexed for death, before it froze in mid-air.

The professor never noticed. "Honey, it was ruined long before I got here." V-W slunk on to murder the muse of the next person in line.

Pippin could only make inarticulate noises as she stared in frustration and fury at the rubine and yellow stripes that transformed into a plastic red where they met. Trashed. The entire thing was crap. She could scrape off the offending paint but the paint underneath hadn't been set.

She held the red brush in front of her. "Traitor," she accused, and threw it across the bus. It arced slowly and then settled to an easy roll across the floor, not even sending up a satisfying clatter.

Pippin hoped V-W rotted in hell. And the worst part was, she couldn't yell at her. She couldn't create the righteous scene V-W deserved, to show these beginner students that they were being led down a sinister path if they followed this woman.

V-W was right; the painting stunk before she got to it. Still, that was no excuse to make it worse.

Pippin cleaned and packed up her supplies and then sat glowering with her arms crossed in front of her for the rest of the trip. Wasted, wasted time!

The mood stuck with her even as she disembarked.

"What's this?"

Vootan-Wotan picked at the back of Pippin's p-suit collar as they stood on the air side of the airlock. "Nasty bit here," she said. "Good thing we didn't have to go out."

Pippin screwed her head as far as she could trying to see, but the woman didn't elucidate and instead wandered off to infect another part of the world with her presence. Pippin stripped off the suit and then held it up for examination.

The back of her collar was chipped, deep enough to be exposed where the helmet would clamp on if she had to put it on in an emergency. Pippin's air would have rushed out of her suit, leaving her in cold vacuum. She couldn't imagine what would have done this kind of damage.

Damn. If it wasn't one thing, it was another. Fixing this would take up another hour, maybe an hour and a half of time she couldn't afford to lose. Pippin dragged the suit behind her as she hiked her fashionable canvas tote up to her armpit and set off in search of a repair shop.

David chose the closest StarBuffs to Pippin's place. One StarBuffs was the same as any other StarBuffs: industrial chic, industrial food, presented in identical ways. Even the exercise machinery seemed to have the same layer of dust from store to store.

He could swear that the very placement of the first fern on the left was the same as the StarBuffs on the corner from his apartment back in Vegas. "Excuse me," he prompted the employee behind the counter. The lanky kid looked somewhere around the very beginning of his make, a little too thin for a realistic fifty. Well, a lot of kids wanted to look instant-tough without really thinking it through. Some FeeP should explain things to this one.

"Sir?"

"I need some of the gym equipment unlocked."

"The gym?" The kid looked around as if it was the first he'd noticed the rows of machines and video screens. "Oh. I– I'll call the manager."

"If you would," David nodded. The kid disappeared behind a faux-wood door.

"Ethan Kane is really working out at StarBuffs?" a familiar voice said from behind him. "You must be kidding me. I thought the first time was just a fluke."

David turned slowly. It was Dougie Chu. Dougie was dressed in Morning Exercise Casual and had a tiny spot of whipped cream on his chin. "Dougie. Where would you suggest I go?"

"I know a doctor in Old Town who does great muscles."

"Artificial muscle-pumping only gives the illusion–"

"–Of muscles, not the fact," Dougie finished for him as if he'd heard this before. "I know. Ethan Kane needs real muscle to get his job done. Still such a macho flambé."

When had the wiryness of Dougie become sinister? Real or imagined? David said, "Yeah. I need real workouts. Luna grav's been too easy on me."

"And you have your job."

"Yeah." David straightened and jerked his collar to order. He'd never worn faux leather in his old life, but here on Luna it felt right, even if the material tended to slump in places. His new preference to the informal must be the Jonathan influence.

He squared his shoulders and took a stance that if he'd noticed, he would have labeled "tough guy." "Time to get back on track," he said in a growly timbre that wasn't his own.

"I was beginning to wonder about you." Dougie clapped him on the shoulder and let his hand lie there. "Dorn's Gym; it's got the best ring on Luna. You knew that Luna authorizes old-timey boxing matches, didn't you? This is where they train."

Vids were the closest David had ever gotten to fighting, burly actors punching each other with cheating camera angles, fake blood and sound effects to make it all seem real. But Ethan Kane wasn't imaginary. Eventually Kane would be looking him up. The former inhabitant of this body wasn't the type to wait long for vengeance.

"You through?" he asked Dougie of his latte.

"Guess so."

David nodded. "Lead the way."

These days on Luna quickly formed habits for David. He'd rise up early to jog the neighborhood just to get his blood flowing, to remind himself that he was alive and human. Then he'd circle around to Dougie's gym or a StarBuffs, ending his route at Denny's Shooting Range for practice. After that it was home to play with Jonathan. He kept copious notes for Mama not only of the time involved, but the particular tactics Jonathan used each play period.

"Mow-Mouse almost got the upper hand," he recorded, "but Jonny spotted him laying his ambush and counter-attacked. Victory!" "Served Jonny the tuna flavor with egg, but he turned up his nose at it. He much prefers the salmon, even though it may smell the same to humans. It's more piquant, in an aged-kill kind of way."

When Jonny took his naps, which was often, David searched the Lunar nets and *The Daily Lunatic* for any sign of Ethan Kane in David Lumen's body. If Sugar called Pip, he buzzed in to ask if her resources had turned up anything.

Sugar avoided answering those questions. Though he knew she'd followed through in reporting his situation to the civil police, he didn't think that they'd given the story much credence. He didn't blame them. But he could also feel Sugar's embarrassment that her report wasn't enough to warrant further investigation. He felt a deep need in her to be considered the equal of a civil cop.

Afternoons David attended martial arts class and got in a few more sessions with Jonny between his naps. He caught *Stormy Heights* with Tiffany in its first airing of the day right before dinner, at which time Pip sometimes joined them as she returned from office, hospital visit, and/or studio.

At night she snuggled up to his back as she slept. David truly did try to analyze the differences in sexual orientation. Was what he felt real? At which point did the body supersede the needs of the mind, and vice versa? How could he approach his own perceptions of the world? They seemed insurmountable. They just *were*.

His world was as it was: homosexual, and the longer he was in this body the more difficult it was for him to remember what it was to crave a female. They were merely a part of the landscape. Sisters, mothers, aunts and cousins who bore nothing to do with his sex drive. Breasts were interesting but not lust-worthy. Truth to tell, if he thought about women below the waist it was more than a little repellent.

He tried to work up some desire. Tried to remember how he'd been when he'd first landed into this body. It could be stirred by a woman. No, it could be stirred by his mind, and the mind was the most powerful sex organ of all.

So he used his mind to imagine wild and frantic sex, rolling around under the covers with Pip or any woman, laughing and panting. Single-minded in reaching a climax.

Meh.

Maybe he was going about this the wrong way. Pip had to be psychological-ly reshaped to secure her future and redefine her own terms of contentment. Her aunt wanted her to switch to a more corporate make.

Along the way, would Pip consider a gender change?

Behind him Pip stirred in her sleep and burrowed deeper into the back of his neck. No, she probably wouldn't.

What are we going to do about Pip? David asked the cat who shared his pil-low.

Pip is Pip.

Somehow that was the entire problem. There was something about her that had to be precisely the way she was. It supplied the basis on which her entire personality had formed. She was so sure of her so-called talent that a remodifi-cation would require the most subtle therapy he had ever performed. Above all, he mustn't hurt the trusting, earnest Pip. He mustn't betray her heart.

16

"Heeey, Ethan! Ethan!"

David turned to see Dougie, arm raised in greeting, trotting his way. Damn, he appreciated Dougie's good looks. Except for beginner lines next to his improperly-placed snake bites he looked young, but that could just be sub-cutaneous sculpting or the abundant energy he exuded. Everything else was quite adult. Wiry. Chiseled.

A body like that had to be great action in bed, didn't it?

David's shoulders clenched and he forced himself to give a quick, friendly nod. "Dougie," he said. Not an invitation!

"Yo, man, you didn't say you were staying so long," Dougie told him as he fell into step beside David. "You gotta watch that. Lunar grav's rikki-tikki addictive. It got me. You wouldn't catch me thinking of going back to Earth."

"Might be staying," David said.

"Job or pleasure?"

"A little of both." David didn't like the hopeful gleam in Dougie's eyes, so he added, "Maybe I'm settling down," with an emphasis on the final word.

Dougie looked puzzled. "Not on the make any more?"

"And legit," David said.

Dougie laughed sharply. "And I don't believe that for a second. C'mon with me, down to GayTown. You think the Latin Sector's wild, you should see GayTown. Anything goes, if you know where to go. And I know where to go." He slipped his arm around David's shoulder.

David didn't flinch. The contact felt inviting. "I'm serious. Ah, maybe someday I might check it out. But not anytime soon." Would this guy get the hint?

"Not even with me?" Dougie sidled closer. They walked hip to hip.

David stepped away. "Sorry, Dougie. I've met someone and it's solid. You can respect that, can't you?"

"Respect it, yes. Believe it, no. Not for Ethan Kane."

The air grew warmer as they drew into a bowl-shaped amphitheater. Grasses and paths crisscrossed the outer perimeter, but the center featured a small stage.

Dougie nodded at it. "The *Renzao Meinu,*" he said as a group in robes approached the stage. "Seems we're in time for the latest show. Could be fun."

His hand still guided David's shoulder, and they stopped at a concession stand. Most of the liquid menu consisted of Luna C Mead. David read the label on the beer-shaped bottle: "The only mead for true Lunatics. Made by happy bees." The bottom displayed the Applegate Organic Orchards logo. David took a hesitant swig. Definitely not beer, though it was beer-ish. He shrugged– a buzz was a buzz– and wandered toward the stage.

Makeover graduates, those who'd reached the nine-point-nine level of their makes, often came out at such events to show the world that they were ready for anything. These were the *renzao meinu,* the manmade human masterpieces.

The first grad, a woman of the 60's make– now a fully-healed 69– was first to drop her robe and slowly walk around the stage. She stopped, posed, then turned and posed again. Those who'd gathered applauded appreciatively. Her skin glittered, wet and inviting.

"Nice body lotion," David noted. How would he look in something like that? How would Pippin?

"She's all right," Dougie said. Together they waited for the first man, who was number three in line, to show his body.

They were rewarded when he handed his robe to his doctor and assumed the stage.

"Oh yeah," Dougie growled just before he let out two enthusiastic whoops amid the applause. The man spotted him and nodded before proceeding to strike his poses for the other side of the crowd.

"He's a professional model," David surmised. And Dougie skewed far more gay than his hair advertised.

"Professional something," Dougie said.

His hand had dropped from David's shoulder to applaud. As he walked toward the exit stairs from the stage, he paused long enough to turn to say, "Call me when you get back in the swing."

David nodded and then went to seek out the graduate's doctor. He'd done a splendid job of bodywork, truly art-worthy. A crowd surrounded the doctor as he examined some potential clients, tilting their heads this way and that with a thoughtful expression on his face and then stepping back to look at the rest of them. They'd point to their noses, their chins, their bellies.

David exchanged a few words among the other congratulators. Dr. Reep frowned at David. "Who supervised your make?" he asked, and before David could reply he said, "Should have gone with a Thirty, not a Fifty." He frowned again and twisted David's head back and forth. "Bone structure for a Fifty," he finally admitted, "but for some reason I want to run you down a Thirty track."

Dr. Reep gave him his business chip and urged him to make an appointment. David tucked it into his pocket. If things didn't turn out right… Well, maybe he could get his own body back through surgical means.

He hoped it wouldn't come to that. He didn't want the ghost of Ethan Kane inhabiting his body for the rest of his life.

"Lean on me," Pippin instructed Aunt Evie as David pulled the gyrochair up to Evie's bed.

"I'll get her. You take the chair," he commanded.

"She'll do no such thing," Evie snapped in a grizzly voice. She winced as Pippin steadied her. "Where's that nurse I ordered? I'm not sure who you are, young man, but you're no nurse. Explain him to me again, Pippin."

"Your nurse will be here in an hour, and he's my guest. He's staying in the stud—"

"In her room," David corrected. "A very special guest. I'm the one who's been sending you Jonathan's reports."

Evie grunted from within her bandages, either from pain or acknowledgement as they pivoted her into bed. Pippin stacked more pillows behind her so she could sit up comfortably. Evie took the bed controls in her gauzed hands and made the final angle adjustments.

David hovered around her. He felt oversensitive these days. Her pain was like pinpricks all over his skin. "Is that better? Do you want some more pillows? I could get you some tea."

Mama Evie was still swathed in bandages, the unfashionable, serviceable kind. What skin showed through was bluish, or greenish-yellow from where bruises were healing.

When had he come to regard cosmetic surgery as something to be done every year or six months? Granted, total rejuvs were major, but even minor procedures held their own dangers. David's mother had died from a simple chin-lift.

Evie grumbled, "A gigolo, out to take Pippin for all she's worth."

"Aunt Evie–"

"I bet he told you it was love at first sight, something silly like that. You can be too sentimental, Pippin."

"Actually, I'm gay right now," David said as he took a chair within reach of the bed, "I'm here because of Jonathan, not Pippin. Are you sure you don't want some tea? I could slice up a lemon. I bought one today, fresh from Earth." He caught Pippin's eye and smiled. She gave him a surprised one in return.

"Jonathan?"

The cat jumped up to the bed and nearly bowled Evie over in her cocoon of pillows. "Jonathan!" The woman's face stretched dangerously against her bandages as she broke into a smile. "How are you, boy? Now we have all the time in the world together."

Jonathan insisted on getting his ears rubbed. He licked what he could find of Evie's hands with his rough tongue between mighty purrs.

"Jonny," David said. Jonathan's ears twitched his way but did not move his adoring gaze from Evie's face.

"Jonny." This time David snapped his fingers, and Jonathan turned. "What did we practice? Say 'Mama.'"

Pippin laughed. "You're kidding."

"'Mama,' Jonathan," David urged.

Jonathan turned to Evie. "Myamya," he said clearly. "Myamya."

"He thinks of you as his mama," David said as Evie's jaw dropped.

"It can't be real. He's not really saying–"

"Myamya."

"Oooh…" Evie's bruised eyes started to squint in suspicion, but then widened again. "I don't care if it doesn't make sense. He said 'Mama.' Jonathan said, 'Mama!'" She lifted him and deposited kisses all over his forehead, and then rubbed her own against him. "What a smart kitty you are, Jonathan!"

"Myamya!"

Evie sniffed her tears back and pressed the cat to her breast as she rocked back and forth. She scratched his chin and then massaged his shoulder and neck. He leaned upright against her and closed his eyes.

David swiped at his upper cheeks. Weren't they sweet together!

When the first waves of wonder had exhausted her, Evie raised her gaze to David, then to Pippin. "Maybe we'll keep him around for a few more days."

David cleared his throat. "I hopscotched in here with Jonathan. And now I've hopscotched again. It wasn't my plan to impose upon you. I had no plan at all. It was an accident, but a fortuitous one."

"Fortuitous?" Evie examined him sharply. "You're no tunnel worm."

"Psychiatrist, although I'm between jobs. Between homes."

"Between bodies," Pippin put in. "This isn't his; it's a borrower."

"Um hm," Evie said, stroking the cat.

Together they told the story. Each time Evie's disbelief clearly and vociferously raised, Jonathan said, "Myamya," and then they could advance to another level.

"Back when I was a girl, teeps were the enemy."

"Bad publicity," David reassured her. "Nowadays with all the telepathic training, we have to be fully licensed and passed by psychiatric councils. Any telepath you find is going to be someone you can trust. If we don't pass, we don't continue the training."

Evie pursed her lips as much as she could. "This Kane fellow is a fine, upstanding citizen, eh?" she said.

"Ah." David looked to Pip, whose expression was just as questioning.

"I don't know," David finally admitted. "It's like guns. Guns have to be licensed, but some people always manage to sneak around the system. I don't think Kane ever went before a teep council. He could be a wild card, a teep whose abilities manifested too strong and too early. Uncontrolled." That might account for how Kane became so dark, as he had never fit in anywhere. Maybe he'd never learned to tune people out.

"And maybe he's been trained to do the things he does by people who have nothing to do with legitimate channels," Evie said. "I've seen the dark side of Earth. That was a big reason why I left. That and all the grime. Organized crime has taken over in some areas, no matter what kind of pie-in-the-sky twaddle they tell you on the newsvids."

David bit his lip and then nodded. "You may be right. Kane's not a good man. He's overly needy resulting from deep psychological problems. He'd likely have been the type to be attracted to *l'Ôgre* because they promised him rewards he couldn't achieve otherwise. They probably encouraged him, ego-stroked him, as he sank in deeper with them."

"*L'Ôgre* has teeps working for them…" Evie mused. "Is *l'Ôgre* here on Luna?"

David shook his head. "I've met one of Kane's friends, but I don't think he was *l'Ôgre*. He didn't mention any kind of organizational schedule. And Kane getting here was just a fluke, following me."

Evie's bruised eyes were still sharp on him. "The moment something suspicious happens here is the moment you get an eviction notice. Effective immediately."

"Don't worry, M– Evie," David reassured her. "I'll see that nothing gets near you or Pippin… or Jonny. I'm a good teep. I'll be able to sense danger."

Maybe.

The doorbell rang and a subscreen popped up on the main security screen to show Sugar waiting outside. Tiffany never moved from her stool as *Stormy Heights* sped to its daily climax.

"Just a minute," David intercommed.

Onscreen Talia inched toward Bruce. She was hidden in shadow and brandishing a knife as he bent over the corpse of the Mysterious Man who'd arrived in town just three weeks ago.

Bruce prodded the body. "Are you all right?" he asked in vain.

A harsh ribbon of light caught Talia's cruel profile as she sneered.

The doorbell rang again.

"We're in the kitchen!" David snapped as he released the front door lock.

The final shot was of Bruce suddenly turning as he heard Talia's harsh breaths, his face lifting in question.

The picture faded to black.

"She'll kill him!" Tiffany shrieked. "Carter won't get there in time."

"If she kills him she'll never convince a jury the first murder was an accident," David countered. "Bruce is a trained arbitrator. He'll talk her out of it. Or stall her until Carter arrives."

Tiffany rocked sideways on her stool. "What will his baby think when she finds out her daddy's dead? Poor little girl! And the hospital fund– what'll happen to that? Everyone's been working so hard for it! They should kill that Talia bitch instead. Kill her! Kill her! Ah, poor baby!"

Sugar entered the kitchen to find the maid in hysterics and show credits crawling up the vid screen. "Good episode," David told her as explanation.

"Where's Pippin?"

David inclined his head toward the studio. The french doors held a large, hand-printed sign: "DO NOT DISTURB ON PAIN OF DEATH!!!"

"I've got to get a drink," Tiffany announced. She made a quick check of herself and must have decided she didn't look too frazzled for public display. She dropped her apron on the way out.

"Did someone move the booze?" Sugar checked to see that the small liquor cabinet was still in place.

"Corner bar," David replied. "Sometimes life gets too rough for Tiffany to handle."

Sugar took the maid's place at the kitchen island. "I know how she feels sometimes." She reached for a couple of dried apples slices and popped them into her mouth. "I guess Pippin forgot about our appointment."

David stood up. "I'll get her."

"You planning to die today?" Sugar crooked one eyebrow at him.

"It's important. You're teaching Pip about appearance. I understand that she's in a bit of legal hot water."

"More than a bit." Sugar used another slice to indicate David's general deportment. "Is that how a Vegas shrink dresses these days?"

David glanced down. He'd bought this outfit just yesterday, along with a few others of similar make. It was all dark colors, faux leathers and tough, no-nonsense fibers. Instead of a tight collar and tie, he wore his collar open. His cuffs were rolled back. He needed freedom of movement in case of emergency.

"I haven't figured out who I am yet," he said, and then wondered at his words. "Switching bodies has turned out to make more of a difference than I would have expected."

Sugar held up a hand for silence and checked her personal police scanner unit. It babbled at her in cop-talk as she listened intently.

But David listened to his body. Who was he? He'd changed in these past weeks, and not just in bodily form. His physical circumstances were affecting him far more than he should allow. He had to knuckle down and get back to being David Lumen, world-class psychiatrist, even if he was in a hit man's body.

When had he decided to go into psychiatry? Dad had been a psychiatrist, true, but Dad hadn't bullied him into the profession. Mother hadn't chosen his college with psychiatry in mind.

He smiled to himself. Mother had sat down with him once when he was in high school and pointedly extolled the life of the professional medium. "You're a telepath, David," she'd told him. "You could do that. I saw a vid special about mediums. There's a lot of money in that, a good future."

He'd had to tell her that telepathy and mediumship were quite different animals. She'd never broached the subject again.

That had been soon after Aunt Rachel had died. Mom was probably trying to find a way to communicate with the sister who had always been so close to her. *Well, Mom,* David thought, *you can speak to her all you want to now. I hope you two are happy wherever you are.*

Death and life. Choices made. David counseled his patients every day to assess their decisions and to make a plan to bring them in line with what they knew their place in society was. Conform and fit. If you followed your true self you'd be cursed to be a loner.

Sugar turned down the sound of her scanner. "That 10-460 is too far from here," she muttered and realized that David was listening. "If it were closer, I could go watch," she explained. "You have your little soap opera, but police work– that's the real excitement in life."

David gave her a weak smile, encouraging the harmless fantasy. Imaginary goals were what kept many people happy while maintaining conformity in the real world.

Sugar sighed and shifted back to the world of the kitchen. "I wanted to tell Pippin that according to the telemetry, she finally made her one-four-five this morning."

"One-four-five?"

She held her palm screen out to him. "A woman's hip measurement should be precisely 145 percent of her waist. I've had Pippin on an extra daily dainut these past two weeks, and it finally did the trick. Good thing. In another week I was going to order a bustle for her."

David eyed the data. "She hasn't gone running for a week," he said. "She needs it to clear her mind. Improve circulation, all that."

"Nonsense. She's got a butt now; that's what's important."

Sugar had a point. And soon there'd come a time when David would be able to admire that butt the way it should be.

Sugar holstered her screen as she rose from her seat. "See if you can't get her to dress that butt in something that looks nice, won't you?" She gave him an eagle look. "Or should you be undressing that butt?"

He spread his hands. "Still gay. Tell you what, Officer Sugar. You take care of Pip on the outside and I will take care of her–" he tapped his skull–"on the inside. We'll make a successful executive out of her yet."

She gave a laugh at that as she turned to the door. "Executive? Pippin will never stand for that. I'm not setting that unrealistic a goal for her. I just want her to be able to walk down the street without disregarding half of the fashion rule book. If we let her get away with it, soon everyone will be dressing the way they want to."

"We'll see." He turned back to the vid, clearing the screen to go to puter mode to begin another search.

"By the way," Sugar called from behind him, "I didn't know you had a Loonie brother."

Insane brother–? For a moment the meaning eluded him. Oh, a brother who resided on Luna. "I don't have a brother," David said. He turned toward the doorway, where Sugar had paused.

"That's funny," she said. "I ran into that Dougie guy, that friend of yours. He said to tell you that your brother was doing fine up here. If you don't have a bro–" Her eyes widened just before she tightened her jaw.

"Ethan Kane," David said in a hollow voice.

17

"Pippin!"

She turned at the call and waved. A man in an Applegate green jumpsuit jogged up the track between trees. Lean and limber, Sam Greenwood was an old hand at treading these orchards. His face was broad, friendly, and glowed with a depth of healthy color that pasty Lunar residents seldom developed without cosmetics.

"Pippin!" He said, not a whit out of breath. "I haven't seen you in a week. Good to see you getting out of the office."

He nodded at Pippin's accouterments: her beat-up backpack with the folded easel hanging off. Her old clothes and sunglasses.

"I put in my minimum, Sam," she said.

"Minimum?" His eyes were sharp on her.

She shrugged. "Okay, maybe a little more than minimum. Can't have Brock screwing up things while Aunt Evie's out."

"She claims she's doing well. Is she?"

Pippin gave him a coquettish smile. "Why don't you come by and see? You know you don't need an engraved invitation to visit. She loved your flowers."

He wrung his gloves as his mouth worked, fishing for a clever comeback. Sam might be a smart man but that intelligence didn't stir when he was embarrassed. Instead he said, "I never got a chance to ask before: how was Earth?"

"Heavy."

He grunted with a nod. "Nice place to be born at, but after that–" He shrugged. "Give me Luna anytime."

"Amen." Pippin shifted the pack that would have weighed her down if she'd been on the mother planet. "I'm looking for springtime today, Sam," she said. "The board said this would be it." This orchard was filled with deep green, with matching apples dotting the branches.

"Those idiots in nIT were working on the schedules," Sam gave as explanation. "I'll knock a few heads together up there and get it corrected."

"So where's spring this week? Lalande?"

"Lalande's waking up real well," he said with enthusiasm. "But I bet you're more for Pytheas. Pretty as a little girl in her Sunday best. Blossoms everywhere you look. Come on."

The two loped companionably to the orchard airlock, from where they caught a company bullet tram south.

Sam had the faintest hint of gray near his ears, something he'd probably take care of in the next few days. He wasn't the height of fashion, but he took care that he looked respectable in the Applegate organization. He was, after all, manager of orchard operations.

"How many years have you been here, Sam?"

"Let's just say that when Evie planted her first apple seed in MacLear, the soil she put it in was the stuff I had tilled and composted."

"That would make you…" Pippin teased.

"Are you being rude, young lady?" His brown eyes twinkled at her and they both laughed. "I could ask you when you're going to quit that folderol and come work for the company."

She hit him playfully. "You know the answer to that. Besides, Aunt Evie's got Brock to take–"

Sam snorted.

"Oh? Brock not working out?"

Sam glanced around to make sure no one in the tram behind them was near enough to hear. "That phony's got everyone bamboozled. If Evie lets him run the company, that'll be the end of us."

"Aunt Evie thinks he'll be great once he's fully trained. Maybe she's right. She's got an eye for these things. He certainly seems…" Pippin searched for the right world. Commanding? Knowledgeable? "Executive," she finally decided.

Sam snorted again. "He may look the part, but it's all surface. Dumb as an earthworm under it all, and not nearly half as useful. Evie should find herself another veep."

"Not me," Pippin said immediately.

Sam chuckled. "Sometimes I think Evie hired Brock to fire you up, make you take your place in the company."

Pippin reared back and stared at him. "You're kidding."

He shrugged.

"She'd never stoop to putting her own company in danger from a man like that just in hopes of snagging me. She should make the obvious choice, and choose you."

Now it was Sam's turn to gape. "I'm hands-on, not office material. Why, every time I have to attend a meeting I get hives."

"Ditto."

"Not so one would notice." They rode companionably in silence for a while before he said, "Nah, not you, Pip. Waste of good talent, that. You've got the smarts to take over, but it'd be a shame not to see you coming through with your paints and brushes all the time. You've got something in here," and he tapped his forehead, "that shouldn't be bottled up behind a desk."

"I always knew there must be a good reason to like you, Sam Greenwood. I couldn't get you to repeat that to Evie, could I?"

"Not until she finds a good veep. Someone besides ol' Brockie."

Pippin pressed her lips together at the problem. "You'd think she'd take your opinions of Brock into account. She thinks so highly of you."

"She does?"

Pippin couldn't be sure, but it seemed that Sam's face brightened more than a complimented employee's face should. "She's always telling people what you're doing in the orchards. Says you're the finest agrarian in the history of the solar system."

Sam sat silently, gazing at the backs of his hands.

"You should step up to the plate," Pippin urged. "Maybe she could arrange a co-vice-presidency or something. You deserve the formal recognition, if nothing else. You keep this company in line, Sam. Aunt Evie can find someone to do the bean counting while you to do the real work." She smiled warmly at him. "You do love your apples."

He sighed. "That I do. And I love these orchards. We put 'em together, Evie and me and a few other people, way back when. MacLear Crater– now there never was such a place coddled and coaxed by man. For a long while there– you know how many failures we had– we didn't think it would happen. And now look at us."

The tram slowed down. "Here we are," he said, and when it stopped they both hopped off. Through an airlock they entered Pytheas Crater Orchard.

Blossoms of purest white filled the orchard, lacing the rows of trees that stretched farther than they could see. The entire valley and then some almost glowed in the low, morning light.

"Yes," Pippin breathed. "This is what I want to paint."

Sam chuckled. "You like it during spring and autumn cycles. I like it during every cycle. These trees will last long after I'm gone, and they'll feed more people than I can imagine. As long as I look after 'em, they won't have a care in the world. They can just grow and talk amongst themselves."

"Talk?" Pippin asked as they headed east, so as to catch the best light.

"Come in here during the night, Pippin, and if you're real quiet, you can hear them rustle."

"Breeze generators."

"Even without the fans. They whisper to themselves. They speak of things that their great-great grandfather trees back on Earth used to do."

"Sam Greenwood, you're a romantic. You're worse than me."

"Oi yes, Pippin, I'll vouch for that. You play with your paints, and I'll play with my trees. I'll work for them and I'll see that they're fed and watered, warm or cool as they want, and then I'll enjoy a nice pint of hard cider every evening as I watch my orchards grow."

"What you need is to get laid."

He gave a faraway, faint smile at that. "I'm afraid I'm much too picky for that."

"Lunar population is rising all the time, Sam. You should go down to the clubs and check out the new immigrants. A guy like you shouldn't have any problem. Quite a catch." She tried not to look amused as she needled him in the direction she wanted him to go.

He grinned. "You watch those compliments or I'll be coming after you, though you could be my granddaughter or worse."

"Play your cards right and I could be your grand-niece."

"Ah-hrum!" Sam checked out the bark on a nearby tree.

Pippin didn't dare laugh as she released her pack. Together they got her set up in only a few minutes: easel, table to mix her paints, even a small stool.

"You'll be all right?"

"I will, Sam. Thanks." She squinted at the scene in front of her and flipped her sketchbook to the first available blank page. "You should talk to Aunt Evie about the veep position. Tell her there are other ways of running the company. I'm sure she'd appreciate hearing it from you. She really would love it if you'd visit."

"I might, Pippin." Sam gave the gaudy valley one more fond look before he turned to go.

David checked the inside of the StarBuffs before entering, searching for a head of red hair. Was this new instincts, or old habits of his borrowed body?

As he got a to-go cinnamon wassail venti, he decided there was nothing out of the ordinary in the area. It was as plain as any StarBuffs. The old punchline came to him: "That's what's wrong with Lunar bars: they have no atmosphere."

He ambled outside. Again David reveled in the calm and relative quiet of Luna City's streets. No one would ever have guessed that the plain brown box under David's arm hid an addition to his growing weapon collection.

How idiotic it was that Ethan Kane could legally buy a gun so easily! How could a hit man with so many notches on his gun belt not have racked up a record that would alert the weapons control system? All David had to do was pass a test showing that he understood the restrictions that pressurized lunar passages required of firearms.

This gun did not have an explosive at its heart, but rather a laser-precise shot of air that propelled its bullet. The bullet itself was hard rubber: soft enough not to harm the walls of a lunar tunnel, but hard enough to penetrate human flesh.

Even with the ambulatory arsenal he already owned, David felt better with the new gun under his arm. Different conditions called for different tactics.

If people were going to threaten the security of him and his, they would pay dearly. Sometimes a good example was all it took to warn everyone else off.

"David!" a male voice called from behind.

David clutched his box tighter and clenched his teeth. Dougie Chu– calling him "David" instead of "Ethan." He ignored him and kept walking.

"David, wait up." Dougie jogged up to him in that slow lunar way that didn't require adrenaline. "You've been avoiding me."

"I'm on a job. And besides, you didn't give me your address."

"Since when does Ethan Kane need an exact address? Looking good... David."

"I go by David here. Remember that." David's eyes slid to Dougie and then casually glanced around to see if someone else was watching. A couple of Thirties passed by, but one was a lower make, one a higher, than David Lumen.

"Sure," Dougie said as he fell into step beside him. He craned his neck at David's box. "Good model," he concluded from the tiny label. "Been wanting one of those myself. Pricey."

David tried to sort through Dougie's thoughts. He was treading lightly; feeling David out. But was he setting him up for a trap? "You do jobs on Luna?" David asked. From some cellular memory he didn't realize he had, he added, "I thought you got out of the business years ago."

That certainly triggered a pang of uncertainty from Dougie. David almost gloated with the doubt he'd managed to raise.

"Yeah," Dougie said, "but there's not much call for it up here to begin with. This is a good place to get away and stay away from the business."

"That's good advice. You should take it."

Dougie looked at him sharply. "What advice?"

"Stay away from the business. It's dirtier than ever."

Dougie chewed on the inside of his cheek, his nose crinkled as he thought specific things that David couldn't catch.

Finally Dougie asked, "Going home after the job's done?"

"Don't know how long this job'll run. Maybe I'll stay if it's as clean as you say here. It might be time to retire."

Dougie nodded and they walked a block in silence. Still no sign of redheads, but David could sense the image of his true physical self in Dougie's mind. He'd seen Kane. Recently.

"You should go back soon," Dougie finally said. "After a while, the gravity lag'll get you if you put it off."

"I've got my job to finish. You can tell the impostor that too. I don't like amateurs messing up my business."

That brought Dougie to a halt. Not too sharp, Dougie. It took him a half minute to put things fully together the way David wanted him to see them.

"Are you saying–?"

"Don't let people talk you into believing the ridiculous," David said. "He's just a teep who's trying to mess with your mind. And my business. I don't appreciate it." David hiked the gun box under his arm. "And I don't tolerate it. I'll get my business done, and if he tries to interfere it'll be the last thing he does."

The snakebites on Dougie's forehead crinkled as he tried to digest it.

"Tell him," David said. He turned his back as if to take in the new home surgery kits display in the window of a Go-Go-Lipo parlor. He felt strangely calm, though knife-edges of potential lined that smooth veneer. He could feel the moments passing, feel the minds around him. If anything came at him, he was more than ready to handle it.

He was more than David Lumen now; he was David Lumen with Ethan Kane's killer instincts. He took note of the direction of Dougie's retreat. He'd check it out later through Officer Sugar and her access to security cameras. Right now it was time to train for the inevitable showdown.

He put in ninety sweaty minutes at the gym, then another hour at the shooting range. Returning home, he'd left a message for Sugar, and noted that the "keep out" note to Pip's studio that had been there for days was gone. He really should check in there, just to glance at whatever it was she did so he could lie convincingly about her work, but David had more important things to do.

David snacked on applecorn, hot and buttery with a hint of cinnamon, as he and Tiffany watched *Stormy Heights* in the kitchen. Pieces of one of his guns lay spread out across the island worktop along with a rag and cleaning solvent. Jonathan snored very softly next to that rag, one paw on a printout of Luna City's lowest pressurized level. Evie was also asleep, although in her own room.

Tiffany made no pretense at work. This hour was sacred to her.

"Don't do it, Sapphire!" she instructed the vid woman.

But on screen, Sapphire hesitated and then blurted to Raoul that the baby was his.

"I knew it," David muttered. "Idiot. Bet you she's wrong, though."

"Wrong about her own baby?" Tiffany never tore her eyes from the scene before her.

"Sapphire was sleeping with three men last fall, remember? Bet you that none of them were on birth control. People on soaps never are. Idiots."

Tiffany paused the broadcast. "Three? There was James."

"Roberto."

"Roberto? I don't remember him."

David did a quick search and directed the glamour shot to the TV screen. "The pool boy," he said. "They did it in the backyard waterfall."

"Ack! The waterfall!" Tiffany pointed at the screen-in-screen shot. "I remember now. That guy was *hawt*."

Unfortunately, David now remembered him with a great deal more interest than he'd had when he first watched the show. Damn body chemicals and genes anyway!

Tiffany linked from the s-in-s to check the actor's credits.

"That explains that." David read the screen along with her. "He got a better job on *That Tender Summer.*"

"Crappy show," Tiffany restarted the action as David took the miniscreen to search mode. Even so, the plot of the soap stalled of its own accord. Instead the camera panned over drink and clothing labels and the actors kept up mindless, filling dialogue: product placement time.

"I never saw *That Tender Summer.* Look, it was just canceled." David highlighted an entertainment headline. "He's free to come back and be the baby's father."

"Or say he is," Tiffany considered. "Ooh, he could fight Raoul. I'd love to see him fight. He'd take his shirt off, wouldn't he? Isn't this the yummiest show?"

Ordinarily David would tell her that it was the clever plot twists and believable if aberrant characterization that kept him glued to the program. Instead he said, "Hon, it just drips yum."

They both looked up as Pippin entered the kitchen, swearing. The left side of her hair stood straight out, as if she'd been electrocuted. A smear of something brown and powdery marred the cheek on that side. She dropped two shopping bags onto the floor.

"Honestly!" she said as she grabbed a bottle of Granny T's Best Apple Beer from the fridge. "It's getting so you can't walk the streets of Luna C without some freak trying to run you down!"

"What?" David jumped from his stool to check her condition. He dabbed at the spot on her cheek: just dirt.

"Some idiot in a high-velo scooter," Pippin growled. "All wrapped up in layers as if he were freezing to death. Maybe his foot was frozen to the accelerator, I don't know. But– zoom! Whump!–" She flailed her arms in a great conflagration. "He busts into me without even trying to swerve. I could have been killed! Well, if he hadn't hit the curb sideways."

"You've been to the hospital?" David licked his fingers to wipe down her cheek.

"I've seen enough of hospitals lately." She pulled his hand away. "I'm okay, David. Just bumps and bruises. The cop who responded said that her grandpa always swore by plain aspirin. I think we've got some patches around here somewhere."

Now that nothing was an emergency, Tiffany's attention returned to the television. David rummaged through cabinets until he found a patch drawer.

"I'm a doctor. I can prescribe something stronger if you need it," he told Pippin and then paused. "Of course, convincing people that I'm who I say I am could be a problem. Here. Aspirin." He passed the unlovely patch to Pippin who looked at it warily.

"Under the upper arm," he suggested. She was wearing a shirt with sleeves that would cover it.

With a nod that brought a grimace, she stuffed the patch up her sleeve and smoothed it against her skin.

"Good enough," she declared after a few seconds. "I suppose I can work now. It'll take my mind off things."

"You should take a hot bath and relax. You sure you're okay?" David wanted to know. He held her head gently between his hands and took stock of her. "Are you hurt anywhere else?"

"Nowhere you'd get a kick out of looking," she said ruefully. Without warning her face twisted, her lower lip trembled. "Oh, David!"

She reached for him and he enclosed her in his arms.

"I was so scared. It was so sudden. I was fine for a few minutes and then I just started shaking. Don't know what came over me. I mean, nothing really bad hap–" She snuffled and buried her face into David's shirt.

"Perfectly natural," David soothed. He muttered calming noises and rubbed her back. She didn't ever achieve a full crying state, he noted. Strong woman. Very strong in the way she clutched him.

"Did the cops get an ID?"

She shook her head against him. Her clutch turned into fists that pulled in small jerks against his shirt.

"To make things worse," she growled, "I got a ticket."

"A ticket? You were the injured party!"

She leaned back from him and then reached into her pocket to slap a lavender chit down on the table. "The fashion police!"

David snatched up the slip. Rumpled appearance in public, it accused, and gave as evidence a still picture of Pippin in her injured state.

"It's my fourth since I got back," Pippin moaned.

"We'll contest them all," David promised. "You've been caught in situations beyond your control."

"The judge will never believe it." She moaned again. "I'll be forced to live down-levels."

"No you won't. The evidence on all these tickets– well, the ones I've seen– is clear. Not your fault. Wait until I get my body back and respected Doctor David Lumen will just have to snap his fingers to get the fashion police of this city to cancel these charges."

Pippin's eyes were large with hope.

He gave her his most reassuring smile. "I promise," he said.

The doorbell rang for the third time. "Tiffany, can you get that, please?" Pippin called from the studio.

Tiffany's voice was distant. "I'm a housekeeper, not a maid. Get it yourself!"

David was gone again, his face unnaturally grim before he left, so Pippin put down her palette, wiped the swipe of alizarin that had somehow scrawled itself across her thumb, and made for the front door. "Housekeeper. Maid. Must remember to check my dictionary," she muttered.

She checked the doorscreen. "Good god." The heavy door whooshed open slowly, pivoting on its axis and obviously reluctant to let its seals open. They had to get this thing replaced. It wouldn't do at all for Aunt Evie in her condition. Pippin needed to call a–

"Good afternoon, Brock," Pippin tried to sound pleasant.

18

Brock stood in front of her with his usual dark suit and imposingly executive presence. Damn that he was so much taller than her, anyway. She'd be willing to bet that in addition to human growth hormone, he wore shoe lifts. Despite official fashion prop to keep everyone on the same level, it was too true that height equaled power.

One of the few things Pippin didn't regret about any of her cosmetic procedures was her parents' insistence that she receive petuimones. Her gene pool ran to the short side.

"Pippin. You look wonderful." Right eyebrow carefully pulled up, accompanied by an appreciative half-smile. "I caught you painting."

"Yes. Aunt Evie's resting right now. I'd really prefer she weren't bothered unless it's an out-and-out emergency."

"No emergency at all. I came to see you."

"Me?" And here she'd left the bug and pest spray back on Earth.

"It occurred to me that I've never seen more than one or two pieces of your work. I was wondering if I could take a peek. To see it's as beautiful as the *auteur.*"

"Artist." She found herself smiling at him and wiped it off immediately. Heinous, power-hungry clown, to try to get at her through her one weakness! She searched for any excuse. "I have a friend coming in a little while," she said. "She's sitting for a portrait. A private portrait."

"Ah. A quick tour, perhaps? I'd love to see your studio. The dragon talks about it all the time."

Pippin wondered if she should switch on a recording device so that Aunt Evie could get an earful later.

"So what do they call *you* at work?" Pippin said as she reluctantly led him through the halls.

He peered into each room. Avidly. Hungrily. "I may have heard 'young lion,' but perhaps they weren't speaking of me."

Pippin thought that "lyin'" may indeed have been part of the phrase. Was there any way to get Tiffany to watch over these rooms in their wake? From the way he was drinking everything in, he might have a vacuum concealed on his person. Sucking up knickknacks, spoons and antique letter openers…

Into her silence, he said, "Evie certainly has collected a lot of antiques."

Was he telepathic too? "Some of this stuff she brought with her when she immigrated. Some she snuck in along with the company's equipment. But she does like to collect still. You'd be surprised what you can find in a Lunar yard sale."

"It must remind her of home. Does she want to return to Earth when she retires?"

Good lord, what made him think that anyone would want to– "I don't think she plans on retiring. This is a one-profession life for her."

"Really. How quaint."

"How long will it be for you, do you suppose? Are you a twenty-year guy? Or ten?"

"I've been with the corporation for ten years already. I transferred over from the mead division. I'm the one who came up with the 'happy bees of Applegate Orchards' idea for our honey," he said proudly. He fluttered his fingers through the air in decidedly butterfly-like and not bee-like motion. "Depending on what the company does with me, I could go for life as well."

"How nice."

They stepped down to the cool tile floor of her studio. "Whoa," escaped him before he could calculate a response.

Pippin looked around proudly. It was a "whoa" kind of place at that, a monument to art and its creation. To the far left was a cubicle where she could do her office work, then a clean space for packing and protecting, matting and framing. A door led to a storage room dug into the lunar bedrock.

The rest was studio, full of paint-spattered taborets and tables spread with tubes of various media. Vases scattered through the room overflowed with brushes: that one for acrylics, that one for soluoils, that one for aquarelles. Paint sticks, waxes and nouveau-pastels had their own niches. Stacks of canvases and prepared boards awaited their turn at becoming Art. The one clear area was the small stage.

"I feel like I've been transported to the, oh, Seventeenth Century," Brock said in proper tones of reverence. "This must have been how Rembrandt worked."

Oooh, he'd actually had her for a moment and then blew it by thinking too big. "I doubt he'd even recognize some of the media I work in," Pippin said. "And of course nowadays he'd probably have had his eyes rejuved. Did you know that he toned his works much darker the older he grew? Probably vision problems, though he was just as brilliant. I wonder what Matisse would have turned out if they could have fixed his eyes. Or Renoir and his arthritic hands; Cassatt and her cataracts.

"A lot of artists don't really understand their art until later in life, you know?" she continued. "It would have been interesting to see how the real geniuses would have evolved if they'd had a chance at more years and better health. And heat and air, of course. It would have been nice to know that vanGogh could have sold more than one painting in his lifetime. He would have enjoyed that. Sometimes I want to use a time machine to go back and buy one, right in front of him, just to see his face."

Brock's perfectly-plucked and coiffed right eyebrow now went up. "There are time machines?" he asked.

Pip's eye roll just could *not* be avoided. "In my imagination."

"Ah. I knew that." He fiddled with some tubes of paint to cover his faux pas. "Your things are selling well?"

"Meh." Pippin shrugged. "I haven't put many out on the market yet. I've been testing with a few juried shows, but mostly saving to target a solo exhibit. We'll see."

He walked around the office part of the studio, hands clasped behind his suited back, as he examined the paintings that hung from wires suspended from the ceiling's edge.

"Hm," he said. "Hm." Step back to ponder from a distance, then move to the left for the next one. "Hm."

That's what vid people did as they walked around museums. Pippin wondered if he had a clue what he was "hm"ing at.

"Interesting," he improvised. Now a silent stroll took him into the studio itself. Pippin kept an eye on him and his oily fingers. He might be a Toucher. Doofoids liked to go up to paintings and touch them, spreading their acidic personal body oils on objects that didn't appreciate that.

With one sudden movement, he spun around and Pippin jumped. "I might want to buy one of these."

"Oh? You really don't have to." As God as her witness, no canvas of hers was going home with this man! He'd just throw it in some corner or worse, some recycling bin, and let it rot away unloved. "Well," she hedged, "keep that in mind, but I need all the paintings I can to make up my show."

His face brightened. "You must be excited about that. Am I invited?"

No way to get out of it. "Of course."

"Good." He settled on the chair on the modeling stand. "Perhaps I could commission you for a portrait?"

"Perhaps." *When Luna births a blue sky.*

"I could take you out for dinner. We could talk about it. I'm sure that all this work, plus caring for your aunt, must be wearing on you. You need a night out with excitement… and perhaps, romance?"

She didn't like the way his gaze slid over her. It was too hot to be a polite invitation for a first date.

"Things are quite exciting enough here," she said. "And really–"

"Here? You don't get claustrophobia?"

She raised her arms to take in the room. "This studio doesn't confine me. It sets me free. I do go on the occasional *plein air* trip– I mean, *plein vacuum*– so I do get out. And Aunt Evie isn't much trouble with the nurse we hired. Tiffany's here too, and so are David and Jonathan. We all take care of her. She's not that bad at all, most of the time."

"The dragon?"

"Guess I'm a dragonet. It runs in the family."

They matched frowns for a moment. His was confused but demanding; hers was uninterested and resolved.

"Pippin, I'm here!"

She turned to see Sugar standing in the doorway, taking stock of Brock. Sugar wore a confection of pink and frills, with just a touch of maribou to tickle her ears. Her golden hair had been arranged in loops anchored by jeweled pins. No trace remained of her recent operation.

A police scanner murmured static on her fashionable belt.

"Sugar. Brock, I told you I had a friend coming by."

"Ah yes." Brock stood up from his model's chair.

"Oh, don't go!" Sugar protested. "Pippin could paint you instead. I see you as dark and sinister, like that Steele Gambino on the vid." She made a frame around her view of him with her hands, as she'd seen Pippin do so many times. "*Chiaroscuro,* isn't that the term, Pippin?"

"Yes it is. Dramatic lighting."

Brock stepped down from his pedestal. "Thank you for the offer, but I do have some business to attend to."

"Do I need to introduce you two?" Pippin asked.

Sugar replied, "No need. I know his type well enough."

Brock obviously didn't know how to take that, but he did respond with a dark look in Sugar's direction. As he passed, he took Pippin's hand and pressed it into his.

"Perhaps dinner some other day? When you aren't so busy?"

"Maybe," she hedged. She hoped she hadn't gotten all the paint off that hand. "Can you see yourself out?"

"Of course." He gave a little bow to both of them and left.

After a moment to let him clear the kitchen, Pippin hit he intercom button. "Tiffany, keep an eye on him. I don't want any of our silver missing."

"Do I have to?"

"Any missing items come out of your paycheck."

"I'm on it, boss!"

Sugar shook her head at Pippin. "So you do know what he was after all. But my God, Pip, you've barely got any makeup on."

"Love me, love my real face."

Sugar gave her an exhausted sigh. "What are we going to do with you?"

"And what are we going to do with you, Sugar?" Pippin flashed her friend a smile. "You sized him up instantly. How do you do that? You must teach me."

"It's all observation." Sugar lifted her chin as she unconsciously fell into an "at rest" stance. "You know, I took police training. Observation, detection, protection and offense. I scored highest in my fashion police academy tests."

"Something's different about you these days." Pippin peered at her friend. "You aren't smiling as much."

"Doctor said to lay off smiling except when I'm on duty."

Pippin motioned Sugar to the stage. "You live in a different world than I do. I smile when I'm happy. It doesn't matter if I'm getting paid to do it or not. Of course, I'm not a FeeP."

"And you never will be." The look Sugar gave her was a pitying one. "I don't know why that doesn't bother me more. Maybe it's because–" she glanced around the studio– "you're doing what you're supposed to be doing. Strange how that crazy aunt of yours can't see it."

"She's not crazy, and she's just protecting her interests." Pippin paused as she spread her thickeners and accelerants and brushes over the table next to her largest easel. "Maybe she thinks she's protecting her family. Apples equal family, you know."

"And you're the bad apple?"

That made Pippin chuckle. "Rotten to the core, I suppose."

"Nah, you're not, even if you got another ticket. Yes, I know about that– idiot FeePs. Anyone could see the circumstances. What do I do here?"

Pippin dragged a deep-upholstered chair over to the stage. "I think I want to paint you unsmiling," Pippin said. "I mean, who ever heard of a top make who didn't smile?"

"Not even a Mona Lisa smile?"

Pippin sniffed. "The system's most overrated painting. Who wants her? I need a few portraits to round out my show, and an ordinary, 'my, aren't I lovely' portrait won't go with anything."

Sugar twisted her mouth more than Pippin thought she could. "I shall endeavor to coordinate with your odd lunarscapes," she said.

Sugar settled her exquisite self in the chair, bouncing and readjusting to make sure she could hold a pose for a while. "You sure I don't have to smile?"

"Whatever you do– don't."

"Good. I don't feel like smiling these days."

"Don't settle in yet. Let me mix some paint so you won't have to wait around while you're posing. You want to pick some music?"

As Pippin covered her large palette with ranges of warm colors and cool, all centered around flesh tones, Sugar scrolled through music choices.

"At least I can't fault you for not having the latest," she said. "Red Corner Square– they just released this yesterday, didn't they?"

"Last week," Pippin replied automatically.

"Very good. Who polled top of the East-Asian pop-vid list?"

"Ah… Oh. Your favorite. Shelanda Jones."

"Ugh. Okay, what company just released Hoppin' Berry perma-stick?"

The quiz went on for the while it took Pippin to set up. "Very good," Sugar finally said. "I'll count you as a superior pass for today."

"Would you put on the top five songs for today? I haven't listened to them yet." Pippin added quickly, "But I do know the titles."

Sugar frowned at the computer screen and deleted a track. "You don't want to listen to that. It's crap." She scrolled down. "All of these are crap. Crap." Delete. "Crap." Delete. "Crap."

"What the hell are you doing? You'll get me in trouble."

"By the time anyone finds out, if they ever do, these will be last year's news. You can't play old stuff. Gotta think young. Keep on the cutting edge. Otherwise everyone will think you're old, and old is bad."

Sugar cross-referenced and downloaded a range of songs. Music began to play softly. It was slower stuff, less strident than the current hat 'n beak vogue. This was music of a generation before Pippin– at least.

"Ahh," Sugar sighed and closed her eyes as she savored the song.

Pippin regarded her friend. It was impolite to ask age, but she'd always wondered… "You're having a mid-life crisis," she accused.

Sugar opened one eye and then the other to coolly take Pippin in. "And how should anyone know how long they'll live to call anything 'mid-life?' she asked.

Good question. Pippin didn't know the answer.

Sugar said, "Do you realize that there was a time– a long time, millions of years ago, when age was respected? The wisdom of elders was sought and revered. Youth was crap. I know– I looked it up as part of my final FeeP Academy project. How have we gotten this way?"

"What way?"

"The way we are." Again, Sugar settled in the portrait chair, as it seemed that Pippin had filled up most of her palette space. "Worshippers of youth. Have you ever had to talk to a kid of twenty? Idiots, all of them. Pandered and spoiled. They'll never grow out of their stupidity. That's something to look forward to: from now on we'll have generations of idiots surrounding us."

"Hold that expression," Pippin ordered. "It's perfect. 'Sugar Considering the Future Generations.' Let me get the lights right." Quickly Pippin had the puter swing the lights around so that deep shadows swept Sugar's face.

"This'll knock their boots off," Pippin muttered to herself as she feverishly slashed the first lines of her portrait onto the canvas. "That's it, Sugar," she urged, "think about the horrors of youth."

David looked up as Pippin came back. She entered through the courtyard that fronted the house, which was hidden behind its secure airlock and a man-gapple-espaliered outer wall of Lunar bedrock. The service wagon that followed her was filled with layers of thin wide boxes, which David surmised might hold picture frames.

David had to recommend Lunar gravity. It made girls especially walk so nice. Pippin almost floated like a fairy out of his childhood tales. On Earth her full street dress might have flared up on her descent like that of the great icon Marilyn. Here they seemed to put some kind of static whatever on the hem, so it remained sedately where it was supposed to, though it still swished and swayed enticingly.

She had shapely legs. Delicate hands, which she used to help punctuate her meaning when she talked. An expressive mouth, unhampered by too many snake bites.

It was entirely too bad that she was a woman.

"Any trouble?" he asked her as she passed.

"No. Expecting any?"

"No," he said and wondered if he lied. To cover his confusion he added, "Looking good." Encourage the patient when they've done well. Help them establish good habits. He needed to maintain himself as a positive force in her life if he was going to help her conform.

"Thanks."

It was a pleasant morning. He wheeled Mama Evie out so she could enjoy the morning breeze which came every day at 9:21. That breeze had Applegate Organics to thank, for Applegate apple trees supplied much of the oxygenated and ionized air that came with it. David got a kick out of thinking that Loonies not only regularly ate and drank, but breathed Applegate apple products.

The small garden here was lush and colorful. Two bees even paid attention to the flowers. Beyond the garden wall ran one of Luna City's most prominent and picturesque boulevards, bordered with amazingly tall palm, teak and purpleheart trees.

"I'm still not sure what to think about you," Evie told him from within her bandages, "but Jonathan obviously likes you. I suppose you can stay a little longer."

David had taken a chair in the corner so she could have her privacy. Apparently she wasn't in the mood for that. She parked her scooter next to a patio table on which brunch sat. There too Jonathan lay on his back, stretching preternaturally long as she scratched him.

David picked up his apple-spice chai and joined them. "Howya doin', Jonny?" he asked the cat. Jonathan deigned to roll his head in his direction while keeping his eyes closed. David rubbed him on the chin with his knuckles. "You're a good cat. A lazy cat, but a good one."

Evie smiled at that and continued to attend to her feline baby as he stretched his front paws out, encouraging her to his armpits.

"There you go. So, David, you left family on Earth?"

"My father."

"No mother?"

David sipped his chai. It didn't hurt any more to talk about it. "She died about ten years ago. A simple chin-lift, and something went wrong with the anesthesia."

"She died from that?"

"It's rare, but it happens."

"I'm sorry. Your father?"

"Alive and well. He'd been a psychiatrist too, you know. He was my hero. He showed me that what's inside a person often needs healing even more than what's on the outside."

"Hm."

"Even so, he'd been making noises about leaving the profession. He'd been doing it for over twenty years. You know, about the average time for people to switch professions."

"I'm not. I'm in my business to stay."

"Not that many people can stay in one job for a lifetime. Not as long as lifetimes are these days. Anyway, Mom died, and about two years later he handed the keys to everything over to me. 'It's all yours now,' he said, and then he was gone."

"Disappeared?"

"Went back to college with Mom's insurance money, and took up music. He plays cello with the Venice Symphony. Venice, New Florida, that is."

"A musician." Evie considered. "My grandmother Tang once told me she'd thought about playing the Sousaphone professionally when she was a young girl…"

It was the kind of morning to rock in a chair or a swing and tell one's neighbor, "Nice day if it don't rain," before daydreaming with clouds. Of course here there were no clouds or rain, as everything on this upper level was stuck on "pleasantly Summer."

Jonathan rolled over to lie on Mama's lap while she scratched just behind his ears and spoke of days long ago. He and David shared the sense of timeless reverie, and David softly hummed a low note to accompany Jonny's purr. David couldn't remember feeling this relaxed. No sense of busy, busy, busy, no palm screen to remind him of pending appointments, no to-do list, other than to find his body.

Quiet street sounds penetrated the green barrier of tall bushes, bounded by a faux cast iron fence and the closer low wall. A broad tree blocked the bright tunnel lights above them.

This was the life. David pushed away the thought of finding his body for just a little while more. He half-closed his eyes to absorb the sweet morning.

A new psychic presence brought him out of his doze. A face appeared at the gate.

"Sam," Evie whispered, perhaps to herself. "I can't have him seeing me like this." She shakily propped her elbow on the table and raised her hand to cover her bandaged face, as if she were merely leaning on her arm.

"Evie," Sam called. "It's Sam."

David walked over to the gate to release it. Sam gave him a once-over and then seemed to dismiss him, as if David were Evie's home nurse.

From behind her masking hands, Evie asked, "What did you find out?"

"I told you, they were skimping on the humidity. Gave that woman what-for, said I'd report her if she did it again."

"Thank you, Sam. The roses were looking parched, no matter how much we watered them."

"That should do it." Sam stood with his hands in his pockets, scowling around the garden. "Those city engineers shouldn't deliberately try to mess things up. I told her, 'Plants is air, and air is money.'" He shrugged. "She must be just up from Earth or something. Don't know how it goes here. Thinks air grows on vacuum."

Sam squinted at Evie as if seeing behind the gauze. "Well, I can't truthfully say you're looking good because all I can see is bandages," he said in his solemn way. "But if you weren't wearing them, I probably couldn't compliment you because you're probably still pretty swollen and lumpy and bruised. So I'll just say that it's good to see you up and around, Evie. That's something."

She managed a small, if painful, smile. "That it is, especially at my age."

Sam made a rude noise. "Someday I'll have to introduce you to my grandpa. He's still going like a house afire."

David decided that Sam and Evie were of an age. For Sam's grandfather to still be alive, much less active… David registered that as another plus in Luna's positive column.

"You've got everything you need? Your medicine, food, air?"

"Pippin's taking care of me, Sam. And David, here."

That got him another measuring glance from Sam. "So this is the famous David."

"A close friend of Pippin's. And of Jonathan." Evie perked up. "Here, listen to what David taught Jonathan. Say 'Mama,' Jonathan. 'Mama.'"

"Myamya."

Sam's jaw dropped. "Well, I'll be a…" He knelt down to be on eyelevel with the cat. "Always knew he was a smart sonuvagun. Damn." A quick, contrite glance at Evie. "Sorry."

That brought a laugh. "Just because I'm convalescing doesn't mean my ears are made of glass. Come sit down out here a while, won't you? We have time. I'll have Tiffany bring you a drink."

"Thanks. Don't mind if I do." He nodded at David as he joined Evie on the ornate garden set.

19

Over Pippin's protests, David went inside to set up the dining room for a conference. Tiffany didn't seem to be in the mood to help, so he put out water glasses and extra palm screens, as well as a plate of apple tarts. A hot pot of cidercaff sat ready on a sideboard. David tweaked the flower arrangement alongside it until it looked right. Lovely.

"Aunt Evie should be resting," Pippin told him.

"I'm bored," Evie announced as she scootered into the room. "Time for me to be getting back to business." Behind her neck, Jonathan hung on to the headrest, peering about for possible jump-off points.

A great clatter came from the hallway. Sam entered scratching his chin as if his non-existent beard itched. "Damned umbrella stand," he muttered. "Don't know why you keep those things around where people can trip over them."

"It's Grandma Tang's," Evie told him. "We must respect our ancestors."

"That don't mean you have to bring every last piece of furniture they owned up here."

"It looked like rain," she replied with what could have been a straight face. It was hard to tell under all the swelling.

"You just watch what you wish for. I wouldn't put it past those idiot engineers to foul up the ceiling plumbing," Sam growled with a small smile for her benefit.

"Don't tell me you're in on this too, Sam," Pippin protested. "Dr. Jack said Aunt Evie should wait another week."

Evie waved the idea aside. "He says what I pay him to say. This is nothing against the job you've been doing, Pippin, but I just need to have my hands in the business."

"Obsessive," David muttered. Sam gave a soft grunt of agreement.

Evie sniffed. "I heard that. It's all right to be compulsive if it results in something productive. How many hundreds of thousands of people depend on the products from our orchards? Oxygen isn't free. We must be vigilant."

"We grow to serve," Pippin whispered into David's ear. Her eyes twinkled at him.

"I want you here for this," Evie directed Pippin. "I sent you official notice. The other managers are coming. Brock will be here."

That final sentence was delivered with a musical undertone. David wondered what Evie was getting at. Was she trying to set up Brock and Pip? Or was it something else? Somewhere in that rejuvenated, ancient head of hers, Mama Evie was plotting something for her niece.

"I have a jumper car reserved for this afternoon. If you're back on the job that means my time is my own again," Pippin retorted. At Evie's sour expression, she quickly added, "Tape the meeting for me. I'll look it over when I get back. I want to finish two landscapes while the light holds. The sun'll be too high in a couple days." She held up two fingers. "Only two and a half weeks to go."

Before Evie could protest, Pippin ducked out of the room and into her studio.

David chunked a final extra chair into line along the side of the room. "You need me for anything? Take coats? Serve the cidercaff? Sit on someone's lap?"

Evie slid her scooterchair into place under the end of the table. She arranged first one screen, then another, to comfortable viewing distances. "No," she said. "I'll call Tiffany if I need someone seduced." She glanced up long enough to add, "Give me a few weeks and I'll be able to handle that job myself."

David gave the bandaged matriarch a quick grin and waved as he left for the gym.

Pippin went out alone this time, just her and the vast lunar landscape. She kicked the jumper car east, and the plains bounced by underneath her. An hour passed. Gibbous Earth climbed in the sky as she rounded the lunar sphere. Sunrise lay ahead, tipping the distant mountains with a blazing backlit white.

It was difficult to see the surface properly. Not only was the horizon a lot closer than it seemed to her Terran-born eyes, but almost everything was deep black. Sudden juts only appeared when her lights reached them, and by then it would have been too late for anyone driving manually to avoid. Thus she had set the jumpbug's controls on automatic navigation.

She kept on until the sun's disk hovered just above the mountains, casting long shadows and harsh highlights. Earth was high in the western sky. When she adjusted the polarization of the windows, the highlights subdued to bearable levels and subtle cool light softened the shadows, illuminated by the mother world.

Pippin set up. She worked on two canvases simultaneously: one long and rectangular, the other more square and smaller. For the one she painted a panorama. The other became a close-up of an outcropping where the reflected light pooled against a vein of minerals, and then met the cold sunlight with an unexpected sheen of gold. It was even better than she'd imagined.

Every hour or so she'd stop to exercise. She ate dinner late and then took a nap. When she woke, the light hadn't changed. She resumed her work.

She finished first the large one and then the small, rubbing her chin as she wondered if they needed something else. Her fingers shook from exhaustion, but she applied Dry-All to the canvases. Done!

Now she took hundreds of pictures of various parts of the landscape. Close-ups, blown-out highlights to catch subtleties in the shadow, anything that would help her once this light and she had gone in case she changed her mind about the completeness of her work in the next couple days. Plus, they'd be reference for future paintings.

Unwilling to leave this place of magic, she scouted some more until she found another captivating view, and took more pictures there.

Finally she packed up and bounded home. A sensation almost like warm liquid filled her insides, imbuing her with a calm satisfaction that came all too rarely.

Her art was real. It was more than a photograph. It contained her thoughts, her mind, her processing the scene, and even her feelings and expertise as to how she had chosen her colors and values. Despite everything everyone else said, Pippin knew she was a true artist.

Her car lurched sideways. Hard.

It took a moment for the *WHUMP!* to register. She gasped; gave two blinks; attempted to straighten in her seat– Then the safety conditioning every new Loonie had to undergo kicked in. Pippin scrabbled for her vacuum helmet, double-checked her safety harness, and then snapped on the car's exterior floodlights. Holy jesus,

"Emergency," her car told her through her helmet.

what was that? She peered around,

"Make sure your impact belts are fastened and your vacuum suit is completely sealed."

just in time to see it–

"Authorities have been notified. Help is on the way."

bearing down on her again! Another jumper car! It had reared up, its jumper feet poised as if it were a boxer, ready to strike.

She braced herself for impact. Her teeth still rattled from the force of the first one.

"All safety features are now engaged. Please relax and do not remove your belts."

The hell she wasn't going to touch them! The car crashed into her again with two solid wallops, this time from beneath, though "beneath" was now "on top," since her car was rolling. Her brains felt unglued.

The emergency system stopped talking. Maybe that last hit had taken it out. Pippin thumbed the emergency button on the personal com unit inside her vacuum suit.

"We've lost your car transmission," Emergency Services told her immediately as the connection went through. Thank God for them! "Are you injured?"

"No, but my car's upside down. And the other car that hit me– Uff!"

Again came the impact, knocking her sideways from where she'd been. Now the roll didn't stop but picked up speed. "I think I'm rolling into a crater!" She didn't mean to sound hysterical, but here she was!

"We've got your position," Emergency assured her. "Other vehicle?"

"Someone in– hup!– a jumper car is attacking mine," she said. "It's green. I can't figure out the make." Damn, why hadn't she studied jumper car trends? Jumper cars weren't trendy, that's why. "I think it had a white stripe along the side. Could have been a scrape. Couldn't see– whup!– who was inside. Yow! Whoa! Hit something again, but I think that was a rock. The other jumpbug had their interiors off."

She was *not* going to throw up, no matter how many times she turned over! She used to be able to ride rollercoasters in Terran grav conditions, for pete's sake.

"Systems just registered a crack in the car body," Pippin told Emergency. "Whoa, make that a hole." Thank God she'd sealed those canvases, though her *plein vacuum* equipment was probably ruined by now.

"Pressure suit?" the emergency voice asked with audible anxiety.

"Holding fine. I just had it worked on." Thank goodness. If not for finding that nick in it the other day and getting it fixed, she'd be toast. A red button lit by her right hand and she slapped at it. Why else would it blink, but to alert her to hit it?

She felt a lurch, this time a soothing one as the roll slowed and then stopped. "Um, I think some kind of impact bag just deployed," she said.

"Oh, very good. Officers have you on visual. Hold on just a few minutes longer. Don't move. Telemetry says you're hyperventilating. Please adjust your suit; we can't do that from here."

Darn tootin' she wouldn't move. Pippin tried to remember safety procedures in vacuum conditions and set her suit's atmosphere as best as she could. She sat in her web of safety belts and scanned the sky through every window that gave her a good view.

Except for the approaching red lights of the emergency crew, the sky was clear.

There was one redeeming result of the accident: accompanied home from the hospital by a police escort, no Fashion Cop dared to ticket her. No, two redeeming items: though most of her supplies were indeed now dead, her canvases and cameras had survived nicely.

Unfortunately, only one of the photos showed what might possibly have been her assailant in the distance. The police took shots of the jumpbug marks at the scene. Theoretically every jumper car's feet held slightly different patterns, but how close would that come to matching reality?

Third good thing, Pippin corrected herself as she found herself greeted at homecoming: Aunt Evie, David, Sugar, Sam and even Jonathan looked like they were very glad she was alive and in one whole if bruised piece. They babied her and ran to fetch everything they thought could make her comfortable.

"You have any enemies before I showed up?" David asked her when they finally got some privacy.

"You are not leaving," she informed him. For a moment he looked as if he would argue, but then he nodded. That night he ceded the entire bed to her and slept like a guard dog at its foot.

She was suitably attired when they ventured out to the city again, makeup in place and bruises camouflaged.

"Business," she muttered. "First it was apples and now it's art. It's taking up half the time I've got any more. You'd think you could just go online, find a simple caterer, tell them what kind of party you're holding, and that was that. But no. You have to meet in person. Sample their food. Discuss traffic patterns through the gallery." She gave a snort.

"If you don't attend to this, you won't have a show," David said. "You tell me what I need to be doing, and I can help. You can go back home where it's safe."

She turned to him. "You're supposed to be looking for a body," she said.

He nodded as they continued through the busy streets of Upper Luna C. "Too many hours on the puter and I go insane," he assured her. "I need to get out into the fresh air. My daily walk was always on my schedule. Now I just do it 400,000 kilometers from where I used to."

"I don't see how you managed to walk so much on Earth," Pippin said. "I don't remember doing it when I was a native. What, did you wear special shoes? Take a tank of oxygen with you?"

They waited at an intersection as three taxis and two trams trundled by, leaving only a slight electronic hum in their wake. People lined up along the curb waiting for the signal to change.

And catty-corner across the street, David saw a flash of oddly-colored hair. It was off the usual gay platinum shade he usually saw in Vegas, so he noticed it: short strawberry blond hair on top of a Thirties make.

"Shit," he hissed. "Don't look."

Pippin jerked to alertness. "Don't look at what?"

"Hsh! Look natural. I just spotted myself."

It took a beat for it to sink in. "For real this time?"

"For real. He's made me a blond, but I think it's me. Yes. I can feel it. I can feel that he feels that I feel–"

"Let's call the cops." Pippin fished into her purse for her cell.

"Damn! There he goes!" Now David pointed at the figure striding away from the corner. He took note of oncoming traffic and darted across the road, waving for her to stay put.

"David!" she shrieked.

The signals finally changed as David reached the other side. He crashed through the pedestrian crowd, always keeping the reddish head in his sight.

He pushed past a Fifty make, a Seventies make… and then suddenly every man on the street seemed to be a Thirty. Some were low in the range and some high; some had lighter brown hair than dark, and a few were even blonds, but they all resembled the face and body he'd seen in a mirror for so many years.

Where was he? Where was his self?

The traffic pattern grew sparse, then crowded, then thinned, and David drew to a stop. He'd lost himself. Was he really sure it was him?

"David!"

With nothing to aim for, he turned at Pip's call. There she was: a Twenty and blonde like the rest, but he'd be able to spot her in a crowd of a million. It wasn't just the way she got so disheveled particularly on her right side where she was always fiddling with her hair or dress, but the expressions that crossed her face, the gestures she made and the way she moved. In all ways she expressed Pippin Applegate.

He could see her search the crowd for him. Her gaze touched his and slid by, but came back a moment later. The question was plain to read on her face: "Are you David?" before she settled on determining that yes, he was probably the one she sought.

His own body had slipped away. David punched the side of a taxi in frustration just as Pip reached him.

"And were you going to kill yourself to get him?" she demanded.

"He got too much of a head start."

"That's right. We'll never catch him now." She pulled him to the wall of the nearest building, where the sidewalk crowds were thin. "So you catch your breath. Did you get anything from him?" She wiggled her eyebrows.

"Telepathically?" His downcast face took on a more determined, angry look as he gritted his teeth. "No. Just recognition. I should have– I acted like an amateur– Next time–"

She straightened his collar. "Well, you are an amateur when it comes to this. Cut yourself some slack."

"Next time–" he repeated.

"Next time? Luna C's a pretty big place. I doubt if you'll just happen to–" She gave his collar a final jerk to get rid of a fold in the fabric and suddenly stared up into his face. "It wasn't a coincidence, was it?"

"Maybe. Maybe not. At any rate, he knows that I know. He knows that I'm still around. He's got to be furious that he can't access his accounts."

"Maybe you should release them to him. That should cool him off."

David looked off the way that Other-David had fled. "No. I'm not going to buy his ammunition for when he comes after me."

He was in a funk when they got home. Pip used the home office to view the website and e-publicity spam the gallery had set up for her show, but Jonathan was in no mood for seriousness.

As David walked past the entry's antiques display, a paw reached out from behind a blackened wok to grab his trousers. Claws sank in for a moment, and then the paw disappeared into the shadows again.

David proceeded at an easy pace to the parlor but once inside, he whipped around and got down on all fours. He stuck his head out into the hall just long enough to catch a glimpse of the wide-eyed, alert cat staring at him. As he pulled back he could hear the thump-thump of Jonny's tail and imagine it vibrating in anticipation.

David changed his position so the door would hide him. Eventually Jonny crept around the edge of the doorway, looking this way and that.

David jumped out with a howl. Jonny leapt into the air, his tail and back fur standing straight up, and then took off down the hallway, David in hot pursuit.

"What the hell was that?" came a bellow from the back: Mama Evie.

The two boys chased each other. First one would duck into one of the many rooms that opened off the main hall, and when the other would investigate– attack! The chase reversed and it was cat chasing man, then man chasing cat, then…

They both slid along the wonderfully waxed floors– not too much, not too little, with good traction when needed– and knickknacks went flying, though David did manage to save a few.

Jonny made sure David saw him from the entry to the kitchen, and then turned and disappeared beyond the doorjamb. Tiffany shrieked. David plotted a way to make her do likewise as he passed. Jonny should know that David could do the same amount of mayhem as he.

But the cat was still on the run. David rushed past the maid into the studio and spotted Jonny hiding behind that far table where they'd both bitten that awful sculpture guy weeks before.

"Got you now, Jonny-boy!" David gave an evil laugh and stalked slowly, enjoying how Jonny's tail thrashed in anticipation. "Gonna get you. Gonna GET you…"

He gave an overblown lunge toward the cat just to give him room to escape at the final second. Jonny darted between his legs, sending him to roll on the floor as David tried to somersault to regain his balance.

Instead he knocked a canvas off a shelf. He reached out to save it. Pip would kill him if something happened to, well, whatever she did in here. He caught it by the corner, careful to keep his fingers off the front. He'd heard enough tirades about people and their bodily oils that could eat through paintings.

He straightened it to replace it on the shelf and stopped.

It was a lunar landscape. It was…

Eternity, staring him in the face.

The harsh light of Creation itself blazed over those rocks and mountains. How long had this place lain there, exposed to the universe?

He set the canvas back on its shelf and took a step back. Then he stepped forward to examine the sureness of the brushstrokes, the subtle colors that seemed somehow to lie just under that overexposed surface, seeping with stilled life.

Another– there had to be another he could look at. He went over to the canvas that Pip had propped on her main easel. Even unfinished, or perhaps because it was unfinished, it was even more amazing. Look at the matrix of colors and the way she'd layered them to make a landscape that was monotone, yet infinitely not so. And just look at that view, with Earth hanging above the horizon! His heart ached to see his home looking so lonely.

He pulled another canvas from its berth in the racks. And another. And another. Soon he had the studio lined with moonscapes and the occasional interior landscape or portrait– there was Sugar, looking like Doom Incarnate! His mind couldn't quite grasp it all. He wanted to stare at each for long minutes, and some of them for hours.

He'd never been in here before, never as a human. He'd always tried to lure Pip out, away from her work.

She found him there two hours later. He looked dazed but exuberant, concentrated and humble as he communed with a small group of her paintings arced in front of him.

"What the hell have you done to my studio?!" Canvases lay everywhere, stuck upright for viewing.

He turned slowly to her. "You are an artist," he said as if it had never occurred to him before.

20

"Well, duh," she said, taken aback though she wasn't sure at what. Perhaps it was mostly his expression: wonder, surprise… respect. "You knew that."

He vaulted across the table, landing in front of her with such momentum that she quick-stepped back. But he grabbed her by the shoulders and shook her.

"You're an artist! A real artist. You led me on."

"Hey!"

He released her as if she were a live electric wire. "Sorry. It's the Kane in me." But still he stood in front of her, accusation twisting his features. "Why didn't you tell me?"

"What the hell are you talking about? You knew."

She saw something in his eyes– those eyes that could be so cold–"You lied. You lied to me!" she exclaimed. It was betrayal of the deepest sort. Hell, she'd shared her bed with him. Pippin reared back her hand and landed a savage slap against his cheek.

He never even tried to defend himself.

The welt rose almost immediately. He grimaced and raised his hand to cover the wound.

"You lied!" she hissed. There were so many foul names she wanted to call him, but they fought against each other trying to leave her mouth.

"I lied," he said softly, and all the names halted.

Instead, "Why?" came out of her.

He shook his head. "I don't know. After a while it became a habit. I wanted… I needed…" He seemed almost helpless as he looked past her to what she realized was a lineup of her paintings along the wall. "I didn't realize," he whispered as his gaze returned to her face.

She considered slapping him again. Or turning on her heel and stomping out of her own studio. Or throwing him out of the house by his collar. But she had to know.

"Why?"

"I thought… I thought wrong. At first I was confused, there in my new body. And this body can really lie; it's not a good excuse, I know. But this was home and you were home and…"

She held still, seeing it from his point of view though she didn't want to.

"And I got it into my head that I'd pay you back for all the good you'd done for me and for Jonathan."

"Jonathan?"

The cat raised his head a few millimeters at his name and then settled back down to his nap on the worktable.

"He thinks very highly of you, and I can see why. As a person, that is. I was humoring the artist part, trying to get you to, um…"

"To–"

"Trust me." His jaw worked as he studied the floor. "I was going to give you a free makeover when this was all over. Turn you into the perfect executive."

Again Pippin couldn't think of the proper expletives. Instead she turned from him and stalked toward the door.

"Wait!" David called. "I was wrong. I was completely, totally wrong."

How often did you hear a man say that? It struck a chord as deep in Pippin as any of the flattery he'd ever given her.

She stopped but did not face him. "Keep talking," she ordered.

"I, uh… I wasn't really aware, uh, I didn't actually know… I mean, I've never actually been in your studio and looked around before. I've never seen your work."

He couldn't mean that. "You were in here a lot. When you were Jonathan."

"Ah, he didn't actually look at anything. Well, he did, but to him it's just light and dark and color–"

Pippin looked at Jonathan, who was in that phony cat-snooze where she knew he was awake but he didn't want her to know. "Cats can see color?"

"Oh yes. But it was muted. Not quite how we see color, and he's really nearsighted. He didn't know how to look. It took me forever to get him to be able to understand Mama's pictures, to see that they were of her and not just a bunch of colors on screens."

Her brain refused to comprehend it all. "You've been lying to me all along. You can't blame it all on your body."

The urge to lie pressed on him. No, David wouldn't lie. It was this body and its memories that wanted him to do it. He had to work for Pippin's best good.

"I didn't do it with any evil intent. I wanted you happy. At least until you got through this show."

"And then?" She put her fists on her hips.

"Art is dead. It's all been done; there's nothing new to be said. Thinking you were an artist was a waste of your time, especially when you showed such savvy at the office. You'd be better off as an executive. Everyone knows that."

He raised his arms to take in the entire studio. "But they haven't seen this. You are an artist. That is what you are."

The words were sweet but the lying weeks he'd been here lay bitter, tainting the substance of her studio. Pippin picked up a vase of brushes. For a moment she looked at it blankly, then plucked the brushes out with one fist and let loose at David with the other.

Reflexes honed to that of a cat allowed David to catch it– barely. He fumbled with it, unwilling to let it hit any of the paintings or Jonathan, who had reared up.

"Hey! Ulp, ulp," David tried to right the vase as it wanted to keep tipping. He finally hugged it to himself. "I used to be good at this, back when I was a shrink. I was David Lumen. Who am I now? I don't know. What makes me worthier than the next Thirty-make psychiatrist? I don't know. And now I'm not even a Thirty, not even a complete David."

Pippin backed up as David set the vase down and quickly came around to her. "I will tell you what I am," he said with frightening force. "I am your champion."

Suddenly David dropped to his knees. He took Pippin's hands in his. "I will worship you," he told her. "I will adore you chastely, like the knights of long ago. You will be my Guinevere."

Pippin squeaked, "Champion?"

David nodded. "You are the most unique person I have ever met. I could point you out in a city of Twenties. You are kind and true, lovely and gifted. Such a pure love I hold for you. I'll keep it locked in my heart until the time when I get my own body back."

Oh dear. What could she say to that? "Ahhm, okay. Then what?"

"Then I will also love you as a man loves a woman. A goddess."

She squinted at him. "Are you on a testosterone high again?"

"Don't make fun of my feelings!" he pleaded. "I'm telling you the truth. I stand beside you as your champion. I stand before you as your guard. If Ethan Kane comes near you, he will die– my body or no."

"So you're my Lancelot. Didn't everyone in that story die a horrible death?" Pippin retrieved her hand and clasped it in the other over her heart even as she stepped away from this lovely madman. "It's been a long time since they forced me to read the classics."

"We'll make our own story."

"Oh dear, poetry." She rolled her eyes at him but gave him a weak smile.

He swore. "It's this damned body. I feel like crying and spouting poetry and then shooting someone dead."

"Not me?"

Still on his knees, he scuttled across the floor so he could take her hand again. "Never you. I will defend you to the death, my lady."

He looked so damned earnest. "I suppose that will do. You can get your body back soon, right?" That night of passion suddenly seemed as if it had just happened.

"You have been sorely neglected in all areas of your life. I'd guess for a very long time too," he told her. "You ignored your basic needs and locked yourself up for months before I arrived. You were a prisoner. I was lucky to be there when you released yourself."

An uncertain smile rewarded him. "You have a funny way of talking."

"I tell you, it's this body; it's not me. Wait until I'm fully David again, Pip. I will prove myself in all ways to you."

"Oh," she said faintly. "Oh, okay."

"And if Ethan Kane comes near you, I'll kill him dead."

Though he'd warned her a thousand times today, David and Jonathan found Pippin unescorted at one of the company orchards. Where Pippin went, he went. It hadn't been difficult at all to track her down.

Still, it cheered him somewhat that the guard had to call her to get him permission to come in. The guard herself was burly and surprisingly bright blonde. David would have taken her for an out lez, and thus advertising with darker hair.

"I'd appreciate it if you could keep a tight watch on Ms. Applegate for the next few weeks," he confided to the guard as he released the cat. "She may be in danger."

"Danger? Ms. Applegate?"

"She's unwittingly come into contact with some criminal activity. I don't know how far these guys will go if they think she knows anything. The main guy is a Thirty, reddish-blond hair."

The guard frowned. "We should get her a gun."

He patted the slight bulge under his armpit. "I have one. A mondal maser." He didn't mention the three other weapons he had hidden on him.

"Good choice, if you have potential assassins in your area."

"Hopefully it won't come to that."

"You a cop, Mr. Lumen? You look like one."

He lied without missing a beat. "A reformed criminal myself. I hope that'll be enough to keep Pi– Ms. Applegate alive and well. If it should come to that. We're talking worst case. Probably nothing will ever happen."

The guard frowned at the vagueness. "If you say so, sir. Still, I'll spread the word– quietly– to all shifts. There are a limited number of access ports to the orchards, all kept very secure. Pressure problems, you know, as well as preventing inorganics seeping in. The company building is practically wide-open, though. I'll get them word."

"Thank you." Movement through the trees, burgundy red with autumn leaves, caught his eye. "Sam!" he called and waved.

It took only minutes to explain the situation to Sam. "Evie's told me a little about you," Sam said, his eyes narrow on David. "I think she's left a lot out."

"Probably not."

"I'm just simple country folk. I'm not used to telepathic thriller vids."

"You've never struck me as a particularly simple man, Sam. And Jonny likes you."

"Jonny." Sam added a strained chuckle: "Huh," and scratched at the front of his company overalls. They were stained from dirt and mulch, with dark patches that looked like the remains of oil. "I can't get over how much that cat has changed. I just saw him in the top of one of the trees. Never saw anything that could climb like that. Good thing harvest is done here or there'd be hell to pay."

Now the two of them could see Pippin set up on the thick lip of the shade apparatus that covered half the sky above the crater. David wondered what she'd do with it, how she'd incorporate the machinery into the riotous color beneath. Whatever it was, he knew it would be amazing.

"I was hoping you could keep an eye on the house for the next week or so," David told Sam. "Nothing to upset anyone. I just need to expand my search. I've got to find my body before he can make a move."

"I don't see why you don't just call the cops."

"Officer Sugar's working on convincing them that what I say is true. So far–" David grimaced.

"Huh." This time the word held a hint more humor behind it. "I can see where that might be a problem."

"I have some weapons at the house. I can show you how–"

"Got my own gun, Lumen. I helped settle this place. Back in the day, things could get a little wild. Can't have that in pressurized conditions. I haven't forgot how to handle a piece." Sam flexed his hands. They were broad and, despite the availability of any variety of skin conditioners, covered with calluses. These hands were strong and sure, and not even considering the idea of retirement yet. Great hands…

Damn that spark of sexual awareness! There was no room for that here. "Good to have you on the team," David said.

They both turned at the sound of an airlock cycling at the edge of the orchard. David trotted to investigate with Sam close behind. The airlock guard stood at a fair approximation of military attention, looking as alert and spiffed as possible as Evie entered the crater on her scooter chair. For the most part loose clothes covered her from head to toe, and her chin and nose were still bandaged securely in warm colors that complimented her complexion. Her white gloves seemed more formal than medical.

"Mama!" David called, a big grin of welcome on his face.

The corners of Evie's mouth turned down. "Stop calling me that." Still her right cheek quirked as if it might want to smile.

"Sorry. Evie. Ms. Applegate," David said contritely.

Evie rolled her eyes behind her dark sunglasses. "I suppose 'Evie' will do. Sam." Now that mouth indeed relaxed into a smile. "You certainly get around. I don't know what we'd do without you– and you'd better not think about it!"

Sam asked to her health, concerned that she might still be in pain, but she reassured him that everything was taken care of. "You should be home resting," he rebuked her.

"Bored out of my mind. No one interesting to talk to. Nothing interesting to see there." She patted Sam's hand as it lay on the arm of her scooter. "What have you been up to in here?"

There followed specifics of various nutrients and temperature controls for the crater/orchard, and a condensed report of the results of a successful harvest.

All three of them startled as limbs suddenly rustled above them.

"What the–" Evie sputtered, even as Sam muttered, "Crazy cat."

"Jonny!" David called. From the base of the nearest tree he looked up. "Come on down. I'll catch you if you fall."

"Jonathan?" Evie clutched at her chest. "You brought Jonathan here?"

David watched Jonathan make his way down the tree trunk with all the precision and care of a mountain climber. The cat looked this way and that of his choices for footholds for his back feet. "I've got you, buddy," David reassured him. Without looking her way, he told Evie, "Pippin brought him here a few times while you were in hospital. It was a form of efficiency."

"Efficient! Why... The trees– The ground– Jonathan himself– He's never been in a tree. And if he, ah, peed or something on the tree–"

"It would be organic pee," Sam told her. "One cat is not going to destroy a grown tree, much less an orchard."

Jonathan scrabbled down, deliberately avoiding David's too-helpful hands to jump the last few feet and then run to Mama's lap.

"Jonny loves it here," David assured her. "The first time, we went crazy, jumping high in the branches." David bit his lower lip. "He did have a bit of trouble getting down."

The concern on Evie's face showed sharp even as she gently rubbed Jonathan's ears. The cat closed his eyes and leaned to her touch.

"But we got down safely, 100%," David was quick to reassure her. "And if it was his first time, I think he did a damn fine job of it. He's getting better. His mind is lightning quick. Well, as long as it's something he's interested in."

"Did you know they'd brought Jonathan with them when they visited?" Evie asked Sam in sharp accusation.

"I didn't notice David here, Evie, but yes, we knew about Jonathan. He wasn't going to hurt anything. And if he left anything behind, well, we're going to be putting down some acid mulch after harvest anyway. It's been testing a tad alkaline here on this end."

He granted David a brief warning scowl. "It's okay as long as it's just the one cat."

David splayed his hands in surrender. "I wouldn't dream of bringing in any more cats," he said. "Or any other kind of pet. Unless you need some birds in here."

"To eat our crop?" Evie screeched. She shook her finger at David. "Don't you get any ideas." She waited until Sam was chuckling and then asked, "Whose idea was this crazy project, yours or Pippin's?"

Sam immediately sobered. "Ma'am?"

"Don't 'ma'am' me, Sam Greenwood. I see what's going on in Melissa."

"Pretty little crater," Sam said.

"Whose idea were the oranges?"

"That idiot Brock was against it." Sam had turned from Evie so that only David could see the smug expression on his face.

"Brock? Oh hell, you've ruined it for me," Evie sighed. "I suppose I'll have to sign off on the project now."

"Pippin's already done that," Sam murmured to David, but an unladylike grunt came from Evie's direction.

David almost ignored them. Though they were wandering through the orchard, he still kept track of where Pip was. She'd step back a few steps and then forward, the plane of her canvas hiding her from him. How he burned to see that painting! How he yearned to have her explain to him how she'd arrived at whatever she had. What kind of thought processes led to those kinds of paintings? Would she be proud of her work? Would she smile at him?

"I'm just going to check how the painting is coming," David said over his shoulder as he trotted off.

Sam hiked the shoulders of his overall. "If he was straight, I'd say he had the hots for her. What the hell's going on between them, anyway?"

"Damned if I can figure it, Sam. I just hope the police can solve this problem of ours before it gets out of hand."

"David explained it to me," Sam said. "At least, he claimed it was an explanation."

"I've got my own people trying to puzzle it out," Evie said.

"I'll tell you what I can't understand," Sam suddenly blurted. "Why Evie Applegate gets a total rejuv. Like she was afraid of showing her age."

"I'm not afraid of anything, Sam Greenwood. Not even you."

He leered a grin at her. "I think you're afraid of me all right. You're trying to hide behind a pack of admiring young boys. You can do better than that."

"Young boys. I wish Grandma Tang had heard that one. She'd have clobbered you with that cane she used to carry around." Still, a blush came to her cheeks, which contrasted against the classic ivory gauze that outlined her face.

Perhaps it was that that drew Sam's fingers to smooth an edge. "There was nothing wrong with you before, and now it seems to me like you're changing your make again. You're a Twenty, Evie, and don't try to hide it."

Evie sniffed. "Twenties don't age well."

"Oughts look like they're on death's door. A good breeze generator'll blow 'em away."

"Oh, don't tell me you're never going in for another rejuv, Sam."

He scratched his chin, where the slightest trace of whiskers were beginning to show. "I'm thinking that I'll wait for natural rejuv. Reincarnation." He gave her a mocking half-smile. "You believe in that, don't you? Grandma Tang would have. I bet she was a smart old gal."

"But it messes up so many things." They emerged from the orchard to the enviro-display units clustered on the outer perimeter. "Personal accounts. Not only do you lose your family's wealth as well as your family, but it's difficult to establish who you are once you've been born again. And damned hard to figure who you'll be so you can will your money to yourself."

"Ask the Dalai Lama. I'm sure he'll give you some pointers."

"And you have no control over what sex you'll come back as, much less your body type. Why, I could be a Nineties lump of a man. And gay. Look at what David says changing sexual orientation has done to him. I'll have none of that." She snapped her fingers, which didn't work well against her gloves. "Reincarnation screws entirely with the idea of personal control. I'm a woman who likes her control."

"Hadn't noticed."

She heaved a sigh. "Some things never change, Sam. Women have to rejuv. Women age while men grow more distinguished and handsome. Why, just look at you."

"Is that a compliment?"

She made a face at him. "As much as you're going to get from me."

David jogged up to join them as they entered a new, enclosed section of orchard. In its increased warmth odd fruit grew thick on the trees that were noticeably shorter than the others. Two green-overalled workers stepped out of the woods to greet them, taking places on either side of Evie's scooter as they updated her on orchard status.

Evie maneuvered her scooter within an inch of its life. David could only wonder at the skill involved. Here on Luna, though things only weighed a sixth of what they did on Earth, they still retained full mass with full inertia. It was damned difficult bringing something in motion to a stop.

But Evie had that thing pirouetting on the uneven grounds of the orchard.

"She told me they never allowed her to drive back when she was a kid on the home planet," Sam confided to David. "I can see her at sixteen: hell on wheels."

Of course now she was playing her grande dame role, instructing her assistants who now trailed her meekly, their hands clasped behind their backs, as Evie pointed out first this, then that and that among the trees.

David wrinkled his nose. The air in this section made his nose itch, it was so acidic.

"It's the old citrus cross," Sam explained. He almost plucked one of the greenish globes growing on the tree nearest them. It looked a little moldy to David.

"Smells terrible. You're not going to get anyone to eat that."

"It gets worse when it's ripe." Sam patted the tree's trunk. "You know that on Earth they grow citrus berries to make organic plastics, plastics that degrade easily."

"Ah, no, actually," David said as comprehension hit him.

"They do. And this is Applegate Organics' own trademarked Citation Citrus Apple. We've got a few variations in R&D. Extremely high oil production–that's for the plastic, high yield. And in a bind you can actually eat the things and they won't kill you. They'll even stop your scurvy. We make vitamin C and antioxidant supplements out of the plastic byproduct."

"I'm beginning to think that all this apple stuff is a lucrative business, Mr. Greenwood."

That made Sam howl with laughter. Evie looked around and then directed her runabout in their direction.

"He thinks apples could be lucrative," Sam told her, and they shared a grin.

"Now convince my niece, David," she said.

David shook his head. "She's lucrative in and of herself," he said. He turned around suddenly, though no one had called him. "She's getting ready to leave," he told them. "I should accompany her home."

"Very good, David," Evie said.

David nodded meaningfully at Sam before he took off toward the exit.

"Guess I'm on a new work shift," Sam drawled. "I'm taking orders from a new boss for a while, Evie. Hope you don't mind. I'll be dropping by your place when David's not around."

"You don't have to–"

Sam cocked his head, regarding her on her little scooter. "I'll do what I damned well feel I ought to, Evie. If I need to camp out on your doorstep because Loonie cops are too provincial to understand modern mutant-techno-teep terrorists, then–"

"We'll let you come inside, Sam." Evie's voice was warm as was her smile. "We may even feed you if you come by around suppertime."

"You have cruel eyes," Pippin told him as they neared the house.

"I'll have them redone tomorrow," David assured her. "If I decide to keep this body, that is."

"You're considering it?" She couldn't tell if he was serious or not.

The way his face twisted meant he was serious. "I haven't had any damned luck finding myself, have I?"

She tried to joke him out of it as she wrestled with the front door. It was sticking again. "It's very handsome, in a bad boy w–"

"This body is dark and angry– and it leads me to places I don't want to go!" He yanked on the door for her, and it grudgingly gave way before him. With a curse of frustration David shimmied out of Pippin's backpack that he'd insisted on wearing for her. She held her bound canvases out of his way.

"So what we have to do is to get you out of it," she said.

"Oh yeah? Got any great ideas?"

Pippin walked quickly to the back, toward her studio. "Why do I have to think? I have a show I should be working on."

David hung back. "Yeah, you do. Let me figure out my own solutions."

She turned around at that. His stood as if six tons of gravity was pulling on him. "You haven't been looking long," she said.

"Weeks. Luna City isn't that big a place. Hell, Luna isn't that big."

"We could always hang a sign on you saying, 'Come and get me,'" Her nose wrinkled in thought behind its two snakebites. "We need a disguise."

Pippin snapped her fingers. "Got it!" She set her paintings down on a hallway chair and then pulled him into her bedroom.

"Female disguises–" he began, but she was already flicking on her palm screen.

After a moment, it answered, "Pippin?" in Sugar's voice.

"Sugar, don't ask me why I need to know. Just do me a favor. One favor in my entire life."

"I've done you–"

"One favor, Sugar. What's today's bag color?"

It took David a few seconds to understand. Then he knew: the bags that FeePs placed over the heads of the most heinous of fashion criminals– colors were changed every day. Before they'd been rotated, some habitual fashion-breakers wore their bags day after day, just to avoid being reticketed.

"A bag!" David took a physical step back from the very thought. His skin crawled at the idea. Bagged! In his entire life, he'd only gotten two FeeP tickets, and they'd been minor.

"It's not fatal. No one will recognize you if you're bagged," Pippin told him with steel in her voice.

"I can't give you that information," Sugar informed them.

Pippin and Sugar argued a few minutes before Pippin signed off. She opened a dresser drawer. There, neatly arranged so as to gather no wrinkles, was a veritable rainbow of bags.

David swore. "Why the hell did you keep them?"

"Oh heck, most of these aren't even mine," Pippin told him as she sorted through. "I just thought that if times got really rough, there might come a day when– ah, here it is. Magenta with a double-green stripe."

She pulled it over his head before he could protest, and then adjusted it so the eyeholes lined up properly.

Mewling sounds of revulsion and panic came from within.

"You're too neat," she announced as she viewed the result. "Put on that gray sweater of yours. The one from the coldsleep place."

"And wear it in public?" David squawked from within the bag.

"Yes. It makes you look less like a Fifty. And scoonch down your pants so they bag. You don't have a larger size, do you? That would make it look more... awful." She spread her hand against her heart. "Jeez, is this what they see when they see me?"

David ripped off the bag. "I just can't do this." He panted in relief; or had he been hyperventilating? "Not even for my body." Though he did add, "If it were a matter of life or death–"

"David."

The squeak he made was a complicated, multi-layered and eloquent plea to her humanity, but she had none of it. "You'll live," she said. "This is for your own good. How many times have you told your patients that? I know: consider this a command from your Guinevere. Don your bag, varlet."

21

David inched open the door to the clinic, made a visual search of the waiting room, and slipped in. He ducked his head to make himself a smaller target of attention, but he needn't have bothered.

Fifteen Thirty-make men sat in varying degrees of boredom or feigning of same. They studied their palm screens, studied the institutional walls... and studiously avoided looking at the Man with the Bag on His Head.

David was the visible Invisible Man. The elephant in the room about whom no one would speak. His skin curdled at the thought.

But twenty minutes of feeling sorry for himself in his empty corner of the waiting room– men stood on the opposite side rather than take a seat near him– allowed his thoughts to clear enough to focus on this most miserable of missions.

Chances were good that Ethan Kane would come here to alter his appearance. The clues were beginning to come together: the clammy feelings of solitude, the overwhelming need to keep looking over his shoulder... Ethan Kane was looking for a body to hide in permanently. David's would be perfect for him.

Luna's best Thirties specialists operated this clinic. Would Kane remain within his new make, or try to revert to his old self? David guessed he'd stay a Thirty. Changing David's body's appearance further could only help his anonymity.

David studied the others in the waiting room from behind his two dark eyeholes. The men didn't need to look around. They all knew what the others looked like: open, friendly faces, medium builds, dark hair. Thirties were good at interpersonal jobs. They made newsmen you could trust, service people who wouldn't cheat you... psychiatrists to whom you could bare your soul in confidence.

A kid across the room seemed as if he'd shake right out of his chair if anyone came up to him and whispered, "Boo." He was right at the start of his make, though of course the basic body structure was there. He merely needed to be refined, to mature into his type.

If these were Thirties and David's body was a Fifty, then what did that make David? He didn't feel like a Fifties businessman; he felt dark and compressed, shoehorned into something that didn't fit. Was he really like all these others? Wasn't there anything about him that was special?

A thought hit him and he almost chuckled out loud. Pippin would be able to spot it, whatever it was that made David Lumen unique. Why, just look at the way she'd painted Sugar, the perfect, top-of-her-make Sixty. She'd peeled the facade off to reveal the inner truth that David had only guessed at. Now he could spot Sugar in a crowd of 69's. Well, if he had a few minutes to sort.

What was it that set humans apart from each other, that made them individuals instead of bits of a herd? Was it the id, the ego, or super-ego? Was modern thought wrong? Would psychiatry be forced back to the dark ages of Lacanian psychoanalysis? What would happen to organized culture if everyone followed their personal whims?

Patients were called into the inner sanctum and then left. New ones entered the waiting room and took a seat, awaiting their turn. No one asked what the Bagged Man was doing here.

For a while he daydreamed about undergoing surgery to transform Kane's body make. Fifty to Thirty– the results might clash. And he'd still be gay. No, he was stuck with this body the way it was for a while.

What would happen to him when he did find his own body? Barring the mechanics of how the hell he'd get back into it– and by God once it was found, he *would* accomplish that– what would happen to him, the him he'd grown into here on Luna?

Parts of Jonathan's personality would always stay with him. At first David thought there could be no positive from the Kane body, but look what it had brought him: a night with Pip that had linked them indelibly.

But would he be attracted to her as himself? Would those same chemical fireworks that were lust and infatuation happen again? That question seemed distant next to the overriding imperative that David did not want to disappoint Pip. She was so fragile deep in her mind, a treasure to be protected at all cost.

And Ethan Kane's body was the one to protect her as she grew. It held reflexes and buried memories of violence and defense that David Lumen completely lacked.

So it was gay. Under the bag David rubbed his lower lip as he pondered the inner consequences. Gay was a balancing act of yin and yang. Yin was traditionally much more sensitive than the yang, which was brutish. Straight men so often held that fear of the feminine side. He'd seen grown men run pell-mell from any hint of it without rational reason.

Was Ethan Kane the one who could appreciate what Pip did? Was a gay man the only kind of male who could savor the magic she made on her canvases? When he became David Lumen again, would the world coalesce into dullness? Would he lose his insight into art?

Was it merely something in Kane's physical makeup that made him and him alone appreciative of her talent? No one else saw it, though some tolerated it.

"Yeah, she's good," Sugar had confided to him, but Sugar's comment hadn't held any awe. Was she accustomed to it after all these years, or was she just not sensitive enough to notice? Or not schooled enough to realize true worth from the junk that populated the world?

No David Lumen appeared in the waiting room, so after two more hours David went into the bathroom and stripped off the offending bag. He used two fingers to drop the offending item into the recycling bin. He removed the sweater and disposed of it as well, straightened the shirt he'd worn underneath, and adjusted his pants to proper decorum. After he fixed his hair he emerged into the waiting room, unnoticed among all these Thirties. He dropped a card at reception with the reward notice on it and left.

He was so relieved to be free that he stepped into a public vanity booth just outside to re-check that his appearance was inoffensive. Sure enough, his collar was askew. As he patted it down, a Teen-make face appeared in the mirror behind him.

Dougie Chu.

"He's not in there, you know." Dougie's chin stuck out defiantly but his lower lip quivered.

"So where is he?" David tried to peer past Dougie's natural mind barriers. It was tough to do with loners, tougher with angry people, and toughest still with those accustomed to living near telepaths. "Lower levels." David gave a cruel smile. "Living with the rats of society. At least he knows his place." Deeper, deeper.

Anger boiled over the fear on Dougie's face. "Leave him alone! It's damned hard to get out of the business. I mean completely out, no looking back, no fears. Sometimes luck gives you a break. Others shouldn't interfere. He's not hurting you."

"He's got my body," David growled.

"You have his life."

"He gives me back my body; he can get his life back," David offered. "These are my conditions. I've stopped running. Deal, or–"

"Somebody could get hurt. Ethan's the best at what he does."

"And yet I'm still alive."

Dougie's upper lip curled at the realization. "You're a teep. I don't think he's ever gone after a teep before." The jutting chin returned. "Those others with you– they're not teeps. The Applegate bigwig, that young chick–"

David grabbed Dougie's collar, dragging his face toward him. "You don't harm any of mine," David hissed. "The second I even suspect that you're considering it, I'll come after you. You think Kane's going to protect you? I know Kane better than he knows himself. I'm in his body. I can use it and my own skills to do what has to be done."

With an inarticulate shout, Dougie swung at him. David blocked it and punched low. Cold satisfaction oozed through him as he felt the solid impact.

Dougie was good, though. He caught David on the chin and shoulder before David got in another belly blow. Dougie fell to the ground. David drew back his foot to kick Dougie's head in.

This isn't me, it's this body! With more effort than it should have, he steadied the foot, steadied his nerves. He stood there towering over Dougie, his fists almost shaking as he kept them through sheer will at his side.

"You don't know what you're dealing with," Dougie managed to say.

"I know *who* I'm dealing with," David retorted. "And I'm not defenseless any more. Once upon a time, Kane caught me by surprise. Now I've got him inside me as well as myself. We're better than him alone. Get up."

Warily Dougie got to his feet, trying not to stagger. A trickle of blood caught the corner of his mouth.

"Tell him I'm willing to make a peaceable trade, body for body, no double-cross on either side." David ignored his jaw and the shooting pain that centered there. "How can I get in touch?"

"He's watching you. And the others."

Fury iced David's veins. "He touches anyone of my friends and he's dead," he vowed. "I don't care which body he's in at the time. I will blast brain and mind to Kingdom Come. Tell him to stay away from them!"

David planted his feet shoulder-length apart as Dougie lurched back down the street. Damn it anyway; his temper had prevented him from delving deeper into Dougie's mind for information. Passersby who had paused at the fracas now continued their peaceful amble, aiming as far away from David as they could.

Not a one of them was a Thirty.

"Shut up and tilt to the left," Pippin barked.

David aimed his chin toward the main spotlight she had trained on him. "I was stupid," he said.

"Imagine that. Now hold still. I don't want to have to work from a photo." She continued the warm pattern of highlights that ran down David's left cheek and jaw. Beside her, Jonathan lay dangerously near her palette on top of two photos David had printed out for her: his real face, with hair color altered to reflect its present condition, and that of this Dougie Chu fellow that he'd been fighting in public. Jonathan ignored them, his paws tucked under his chest as he watched.

"Lower levels," David ground out. "How many of those are there?"

"Dozens," Pippin replied while concentrating on that cool flow of color just where that lusciously– no, stupidly, but what a great violet it was– bruised jaw curved away from the light. It made the warmth of his highlights vibrate.

"And he knows that I know now. So he won't be there."

"Oh, he'll just trade one lower level for another somewhere else. He doesn't want to risk coming under police surveillance."

She stood back to squint at the portrait. Portraits were always hell. She was a landscaper, but even she knew that she had to switch off now and then. Besides, gallery manager Pamela had the idea to break up groups of landscapes at the gallery with single portraits. She also wanted to alternate exterior landscapes with interior cityscapes. Pippin wasn't sure how that idea would work. Well, they'd see when it came time to hang the gallery. Jesus, only ten more days.

"Stop grumbling," she ordered as David said something to himself. Jonathan reached to grab her brush as she neared the palette. "No. I'm not playing," she said in stern tones she hoped the cat would understand.

Jonathan watched Pippin paint. She studied David closely before each brushstroke and then held out her brush arm straight toward her canvas but not touching it. She pivoted that arm in a large circle, decreasing the radius with each rotation and getting closer until the brush paused, then touched and swooped for a bold stroke. Then she'd start the process again.

"She's painting me," David told the cat.

"D'you think he can understand you now?"

"He does on the simple stuff. And vice versa. This is like those pictures of Mama, Jonny," he said. "Only it's kind of... kind of..." He shrugged his shoulders.

"Still!" Pippin barked.

"Trust me," David said to Jonathan. "I'll show you when it's done. That's the thing about paintings, you have to wait until they're done to see the picture."

Pippin rolled her eyes. Amateurs never understood. Part of the enormity of art was the journey, not merely the end.

"Really," David assured the cat.

Pippin painted through a cat nap and hastily rearranged her palette as Jonathan woke and stretched. "Watch out," she warned. "You'll get paint all over yourself. And you won't like having a bath, will you?"

Jonathan blinked at her and then regarded the painting. Now a definite pattern of lights gave form to the darks and medium tones that had previously filled the space. David gazed out from the canvas.

Jonathan reached out and patted a paw print of orange into the corner.

"Jona– !" Pippin eased the paw off her canvas. Luckily, it was in a corner where background would easily cover any remains after she scraped it off.

Pippin cleaned the pad of Jonathan's paw with a rag. He fought the interference. "Don't touch the canvas," she said and then laughed despite herself. That had been cute, almost as if the cat had wanted to paint too.

She resumed her painting, and Jonathan sulked next to the palette. He swatted at some paper where she'd done initial value studies. Neither Pippin nor David noticed him. David was dozing and Pippin was all concentration on his neckline and the transition from skin to clothing.

Stealthily Jonathan reached out and smushed into the orange again. Then he rubbed it on the paper, leaving a tight arc. A mound of dark color lay conveniently near him, so he chose that one to scrape over the orange. It was a good, large bit of color, so he used that, smearing it in long loops. The orange that was still on his paw showed through here and there.

"David," Pippin called softly, "are you doing this?"

He blinked awake. "Doing what?" At her motion, he got up to examine what Jonny was up to.

Over the base of dark brown, Jonny was putting a couple pats of blue, the blue Pippin had mixed for the local color of David's shirt.

It was a rough capsule-shaped creature with five wobbily appendages, topped with what was definitely a head, crowned by a mass of orange. The blue only appeared on the upper torso.

"It's you," Pippin breathed. "You with orange hair. Does he know that you have red hair in your real body?"

Apparently the cat thought that the masterpiece was finished, for he sat back, looked at David and said, "Mow."

David frowned at the picture. "Two arms and two legs…"

"Well, the fifth could be– I don't remember it being that–"

"He gave me a tail."

Jonathan obviously was proud of his painting. They made sure that he knew that David would keep the original (signed with a blue paw print) protectively framed next to the bed, that Evie would keep a copy of same ditto, and that the entire family and guests could enjoy yet another copy mounted on the wall of the breakfast room.

Every time Jonathan passed it, someone would reach down to pet him and tell him he was a good boy. He guaranteed that because every time he passed it, he hit the frame button so it said, "Mow! Mih-ya-mow," which was his way of saying, "This is my work." Sometimes he stopped and had a conversation with himself until Tiffany ran him out of earshot.

So far he didn't seem inclined to work on Masterpiece #2.

Now David told him, "You stay inside," as he tried to accompany David out the front door.

David gave the cat a gentle push. "I've got to do some things," he told him as he secured the airlock, careful that it shouldn't shut on a yellow tail.

A small, formal envelope lay on the doorstep. Pip must have dropped one of her show announcements. David picked it up.

Wrong size.

He turned it over. No writing other than a scrawled heart, done in what looked like red industrial marker.

Bad omen washed over David. No wires stuck out; he couldn't feel any suspicious lumps. What kind of micro-deviltry did it take to make a letter-bomb?

He tossed it onto the garden's patio. No kablooey; that was good.

Call the cops! one part of him shouted.

To them I'm the boy who cried wolf, the left side of his borrowed brain replied.

He used two ornamental pieces of railing to pick at it while he crouched behind the faux-cast iron table. The improvised chopsticks finally opened the envelope.

No kablooey.

He eased toward the envelope. It lay torn around two pieces of paper. When he saw Pippin's picture on one, he reached automatically to retrieve it.

It was a shot of her and him, walking down a city street. The picture had been taken at eyelevel, from a little behind them as Pippin turned around to say something to him.

The other piece of paper was a printout of the *Luna C Magasite*: the upcoming calendar announcement for Pip's show.

David's heart stopped.

Sugar sauntered into the house much as usual, smiling her Sugar smile and divesting herself of her visored FeeP hat (with trailing lilac ribbon) as she entered. "Hi, David," she said a little too loudly for the benefit of any passersby on the street. "Pippin here?"

"She's in her studio," David lied and closed the door.

"What is all this?" Sugar hissed as soon as the seals snuck tight. "What's so urgent?"

"Pippin's life is in danger. What the hell are the police doing that it's taking so long? I need someone to believe what I have to say so she can get some protection."

Sugar didn't object as he dragged her into the study. Her pleasant demeanor tightened into a frown as he awkwardly pulled on some of Pippin's plastic work gloves and then set the photo in front of her and told her of the mystery envelope.

When he finished, she took the gloves from him and put everything into plastic bags she kept in her utility bag. She linked from her official FeeP com to Civil Police, Luna City HQ.

Lt. Nick Savonarola took her call. "Oh yes. Officer Sugar, the coma man story, and the Applegates," he said with only a hint of condescension. "Unlicensed teeps switching minds. Booga-booga."

"At least realize that it's theoretically possible," David pleaded from Sugar's side. "Evie and Pip believe me. Pip's already been the victim of several attacks and suspicious accidents. If Kane's escalating this war, she needs protection. More protection than I can provide."

"I have new evidence," Sugar reported as matter-of-factly as any cop. "Believe just the threat, Lieutenant. Here's one that was delivered today. Add that to the attacks that are on record and you can't ignore this situation."

David's face was pale and grim. "I'm moving out. I'll hole up somewhere to throw him off-target." To the lieutenant on screen he asked, "Can you get someone to live here for a while? Until you catch him?"

"I can't authorize anything like that on this kind of evidence," Lt. Savonarola sniffed. "Look. I can send an e-query somewhere, ask them if this kind of thing's even possible. I can run some tests on that stuff you got. We don't want terrorists or kidnappers on Luna. I might be able to run a warrant for personal surveillance through, keep track of things that way."

"Mention 'Applegate' and the judge will okay it in a minute," Sugar suggested and the lieutenant nodded.

"We might even be able to spare one man– not 24/7– to keep an eye on Evie Applegate."

"It's Pip that I'm particularly worried about," David said.

"One man," the lieutenant repeated. "And that's it, until I get harder proof."

"Like a dead body?" David's lips drew back in a sneer.

"David, you are not moving out," Sugar ordered. "You'll stay right here. Kane knows Pippin and Evie are your vulnerable spots. If you disappear, he'll go from three targets to just the two." Her right eyebrow raised. "Sorry, but if I have to choose, you're the most expendable."

He surprised her by saying, "I agree."

"Where's Pippin?"

A jerk of his chin indicated *out.* "On the surface."

Sugar tapped her perfect lips. "That's right; she mentioned it. This was her last *plein vacuum* trip except for final touch-ups before the show."

"She'll do her touchups in the studio," David said in a voice that presaged an order.

Sugar nodded. "Glad to see the borrowed body has some sense. Nick?" she asked the lieutenant. "I'd appreciate all the help you could give us on this. Not only are these my friends, but I believe the whole impossible story. Stretch the regs just this once, interdepartmental courtesy. Please?"

The look on the lieutenant's face was sour and not flattering to his ninety-make. "I'll see what I can do, Sugar," he told her.

Sugar closed the com with a sigh. "I should have enjoyed that," she said. "I guess real life isn't as thrilling as make-believe, huh?"

Eight days until the reception. Tito Roland strolled around Pippin's studio with his trademark beret slightly trademark askew. He picked up first this painting, then another, without saying a word. Behind him his uninvited shadow, Ricardo Raj, took the paintings for a sour examination before replacing them on the floor or shelf from which they'd come.

Tito shook his head sometimes, sucking air through his teeth as if he were decompressing. Pippin wanted to throttle him, wishing the sound were truth. *Just twenty seconds of vacuum, Lord,* she silently prayed. *It wouldn't kill him.*

They finished their circuit of her studio. Tito stood with his hands on his hips, giving the room one final evaluating sweep. His upper lip bunched. The lower puckered to begin the squeeing sound, but instead he decided to speak.

"You don't have it here. This stuff isn't commercial. It's artsy-farts."

"Artsy-farts," Raj echoed.

"It's theoretical. Over their heads. Here." Tito picked up the nearest canvas and waved his fingers in front of it like a magician in front of a red hankie.

"It's so reddish gray. You need a bright color shape here, maybe a mauve or gold. They're this season's colors. That way the painting will match someone's decor and they might buy it."

"Add some Terran elements." Raj's head almost rattled from nodding so hard. "People don't relate to vacuum. They want to buy something that reminds them of pressurized conditions. A stream. A herd of cows."

"Cows?!" Pippin blurted before she stopped herself.

"Atmospheric perspective," Raj insisted as he took the painting from Tito. "Make the landscape fade in the distance as if there was a lot of air."

Tito made an approving sound as he wiped his hands lightly against his shirt. Maybe he was wiping off the ambiance of the painting. "Learn to coordinate your colors with a decorator, Pippin. A Terran decorator; they're the leaders in the field." He tapped his fingertip against the canvas. "That's the first thing any true artist has to do."

Pippin wanted to scream at him to get his damned oily fingers off her painting, but she forced herself into a rictus smile. "That's good advice," she managed from between clenched teeth. "Thanks so much."

"Uh oh, cauliflower," Raj singsonged as he spied another picture. Of course he'd zero in on that one watercolor with the blotch. She should have thrown that one out. Shouldn't have given them extra ammunition.

Raj set the reddish-gray painting down. Pippin wanted to snatch it up and hold it to her bosom, protecting the dear thing from his miserable cooties.

"I can't recommend this to the people at *Luna C Magasite,*" Tito told her.

22

"Then don't tell them anything," Pippin snapped. "Let them make up their own minds when they see the show. All the site has to do is post the event, not give it an advance review." Goodness, she'd sounded like Aunt Evie then! Damn, but she'd kill to get great publicity.

She suspected that Tito would accept a bribe. Indignant fury boiled in her like a white fountain, making her entire body tremble. Never, never sell out!

"They should be warned," Tito said.

"Warned? Am I some kind of art terrorist?"

"You're getting upset. I'm trying to be professional. These aren't your babies. They're just sellable—"

"They *are* my babies!" Now she really did snatch that painting. She cuddled it against her. "This is my work. My thoughts, my feelings, my point of view. Not pasteurized, processed pablum. Not dumbed down for anyone."

Tito rolled his eyes. "Oh, it's *art.*"

"Yes. Art. Sometimes I wonder if you know what that is."

"But he's the Heavenly Painter!" Raj gaped at her temerity in the face of Tito's self-marketed title. "You can't talk to him like that. He makes tens of thousands of dollars every quarter off his work."

"Yes, and so does a Terran lumber mill or a manure farm. Don't compare my art to your assembly line formula."

"He won't stand here and be insulted," Raj sniffed.

At her tirade Tito struck a contraposto pose with his lips tightly pursed. The snake bites crossing the bridge of his nose clumped together into a clog of violent purple. "No, I will not," he decided. "Good day, Ms. Applegate."

He turned sharply on the heel of his weighted foot and headed toward the studio entrance. Raj suddenly realized what he was doing and sprinted ahead of him to open the door.

Yet with all his meticulous fussing, Raj still tripped over the cat.

A few minutes later David stuck his head into the studio. "I can feel your anger from out in the street," he told Pippin, who snuffled despite every effort not to. "Don't worry. I made sure they didn't steal anything on their way out. And I managed to clip the little one with the gate."

That brought a hiccup of a smile from her.

"Why the hell did you have guests so early?" he asked as he passed her a cup of cidercaff. "I thought you were supposed to be working. Ah, you *were* working." He pointed at the drying rack on the far side of the studio, loaded with canvases he hadn't seen yet.

"Oh boy, Christmas." He rubbed his hands and trotted across the room.

A tight bubble in Pippin's chest suddenly released, and she relaxed at last. David smiled to sense it. He swore to himself never to allow those two, whoever they were, back into this house. They wouldn't hurt Pippin again.

As usual of late, she had been painting all night. Paint streaked her cheeks, golden hair scraggled every which-way, and the gray sweats she wore looked like she'd found them in one of the dumpsters of Vegas's lower-class districts. He was surprised that she'd greet visitors in such a condition. They must have come as a surprise.

Sleepy fulfillment glazed her eyes, though. David vowed that someday those eyes would hold a different kind of fulfillment– by his doing.

"Get a lot done?" he asked as he righted some canvases in his path.

"Hm. And then *they* came. I asked Tito to come around sometime, but I thought he'd call ahead. He's on the art review staff for *Luna C Magasite*." She took a long, lingering swig of the cidercaff. Her eyes closed in ecstasy and again, David imagined a different set of circumstances.

"Thank you," she said, and David chuckled to himself. Oh yes, she'd be thanking him.

With the drink, color returned to her face. She stood up straighter, scratched herself in various places even David found unappealing– well, maybe it was just his body's opinions– and seemed to regain some semblance of normalcy.

So he turned to the next items of importance. Three paintings lay on the to-be-dried rack. Landscapes. He'd seen sketches lying about the last week that related to these. David propped them up and then stood back to admire them and take them all in. Number two struck him with its dynamism, the difference from Terran landscapes always startling as things didn't fade into the distance. It gave the painting a feeling of completely uncompromising reality.

But the other two… David tried to figure out what it was. They also showed the starkness of the surface. Prominences held the subtle banding that Pippin liked to find. But something…

"So?" Pippin asked softly from behind him. She held her coffee cup in one hand and nodded to the results of her night's work.

At first David began to tell her that they were all beautiful, but he stopped. Pippin was a professional, and deserved his honest criticism. He stopped himself again. Pippin was Pippin and mustn't be hurt.

Being Pippin's champion was sometimes a difficult role.

"I like the middle one very much," he finally decided to say. "It's the best of the group."

That pleased her. She stood with him, admiring her handiwork for a few long moments before she realized that he didn't go on.

"And the others?"

"Well, ah…"

"You don't like them."

"I uh… They're not… Well, they're nice," he hedged.

"Nice."

"Ah, colorful. Yes, the same colors as those big ones you did last week. I really liked those."

"But not these."

He didn't like the way her brows creased at him. "These are nice," he repeated and added, "very nice."

"You don't like them."

Finally he shrugged. "I don't know why. I don't have to like everything you do. Lord knows I adore most of it. These are just, well, I dunno, not to my taste." He added hastily, "Which doesn't mean they won't be to someone else's."

She glared at him. "They'd probably be to your taste if they had a nice blue sky, wouldn't they?"

"I never said that."

"Maybe a little babbling brook running through the valley? Tweety-birds flitting here and there?"

"I never said– I'm perfectly aware of the difference between–" He could almost hear the echoes of others' comments in her mind.

"I'm never letting those oafs in here again. You're exhausted," David said.

"How dare you come in here and judge my work, you– *shrink,* you! How much schooling in art have you had? Do you even know the difference between composition and value?"

"Pippin, calm down. I was not making a broad statement of your–"

"Out!" she screamed at him. She held the hand with the cup straight out to show him the way to the door. The cidercaff sloshed onto the floor, thankfully missing any art. "Out!"

"You're tired," he said as he retreated as gracefully and quickly as he could. "Get some sleep. You'll think better when you've–"

"Out!"

Pippin kept that pointed arm in place until he'd snapped the door shut behind him. Good. Critic gone. Bad critic. She didn't need another one.

Her fear had kept her awake all these past nights and painting. She turned to the paintings she'd finished. The one he'd liked had been the first she'd finished last night. The other two– the one the bastard dared to comment on– had come after hours of her berating herself, doubting herself.

Bad critic, bad!

Wait. That was David.

Catman, teep, wrong-body David.

He usually liked her work. He'd clipped Raj for her.

"Oh, jeez," she muttered and turned back to her paintings.

Was there something wrong with them? He said they used the same colors as the two large pieces from last week. That was perfectly fine; she was exploring a specific palette. Artists did that all the time.

But painting number one had deviated from that, hadn't it?

She hauled last week's large pieces out from the racks and put them next to the two new paintings. Yes, same colors.

Same… everything, almost.

"Damn!" She was repeating herself. Working so hard, she couldn't come up with a creative idea anymore. Maybe she was dry. Maybe she was finished as an artist. Real artists didn't dry up. She wasn't a real artist.

She stared at the paintings for an hour. Tiffany came in with brunch and she let it sit on the worktable behind her as Pippin stared.

"Dammit, pick up a brush," she ordered herself and did so. She sat there for another fifteen minutes, holding it in the air.

"Paint," she ordered again. She rifled through the tubes of paint with her non-brush hand, and chose a tube she hadn't used in a long time. A pthalo-ish purple. With her thumbnail she flicked it open, squirted it onto the palette, swabbed her brush through the pile, and slapped pure tube color onto painting #2. Another swash and painting #3 was also irrevocably changed.

"Okay," she asked herself, "so now what do you do?"

First she laid it under the Seal n Heet, but instead of setting it to "dry," she clicked it down to "smooth," and the brushstrokes on the painting melted away, leaving flat color that was ready to be painted over.

The purple– actually Ultra Dioxazine 4– was an opposing color to one of the secondary colors she'd used in the scene. Now instead of an analogous color scheme, she altered it to split-complementary, a color scheme that used two opposite colors and then added two closely-related colors to one of those complements. She loved split-complementaries anyway. And since the purple was so very jarring, she moved shapes about on the composition to balance it.

Step back. Step forward and thrust. Back to check. Forward for two more brushstrokes. *Dégagement. Glissade.* She parried and riposted for four more hours.

When he returned from a day of scouring more levels of the city, David found her emerging from the bedroom looking pieced together a lot better than she had that morning. Still those dark circles marred her eyes.

She gave him a weak smile. "I owe you a huge apology," she started.

"You were tired. I think you'd been pretty hard on yourself last night."

She nodded. "That doesn't excuse it. You've been so helpful to me, David. So supportive, and I really need that. You keep telling me when I'm doing something wrong. I need to hear that from someone who… Who…"

"Understands?" David asked.

She smiled at him. Eased close to him, put her hand around his waist. "Someone who's David," she told him before she kissed him on the cheek. "Thank you. And I'm very sorry for treating you like that. I mixed you up with two very rude gentlemen I had just seen."

The way she held him triggered memories. "I wish–" David began.

"I know. Soon," She smiled at him again, and then pulled him toward the back of the house. "C'mon," she urged.

David didn't know what he would tell her when he saw these paintings she was so obviously excited to show him. Should he truly be honest? How could he couch his words so she wouldn't take offense? Did he really have the right to–

She had the revised paintings front and center.

"Wow," David said before he could think.

Pippin laughed as she hugged him.

Pamela Ahmad-Smythe looked as if she had been raised in a perfectly pristine plastic bubble. She was a top-make Ought, of course: lean, svelte and ageless, the make every clothing designer kept in mind.

And she was Pippin's hero. This woman was opening her art gallery to her. Granted, Pippin was partially paying for this, but the gallery was topmost-level, and Pamela had scheduled the show to run during two large cruise tours due in from Earth. Wealthy tourists would be swarming through the area looking for distinctly Loonie souvenirs.

Pamela was a fast-talker, a natural-born saleswoman who could charm the most balky potential client. She also loved her publicity. Now she posed again and again for Pippin's photographer and the one from the *Luna C Magasite*, producing a practiced, blinding smile as she wrapped her arm around Pippin's waist.

Pippin was so glad she'd been able to get Sugar's stylist to prep her for this. She'd not only put Pippin into a Shelanda Jones tulip skirt but a Shelanda halter top as well, with a Shelanda twist in her hair.

"Done so soon?" Pamela's disappointment was obvious as the magasite photographer began to pack up his equipment.

But all four turned as two newcomers swung into the glass doors of the gallery. Tito Roland and Raj strode purposefully their way, faces grim.

"This can't be good," Pamela muttered, and Pippin had to agree.

The two came to a stop. Tito took a pouty stance, his hands on his hips, and Raj slapped a readout into Pamela's hand. "This show has been canceled by order of the Luna City Arts Council."

The magasite photographer swung his camera up into filming position.

Pippin peered at it as Pamela did the same. "This is just a petition," Pamela finally decided. "There's nothing legal here."

"We have a judge working on it right now," Tito said. "This show will lower Luna City's cultural index at a time when important tourists come through. We can't have that."

"Your artistic license will have to be revoked," Raj added.

Pippin scowled at the petition and then at them. "You only have six signatures."

Both Tito and Raj looked at her blankly.

Pippin waited for their response and when it didn't come, said, "Petitions are supposed to have hundreds of signatures. Thousands."

"But only a few people work in the Arts Council office," Raj said.

Pamela pointed at the signatures. "Looks like only four, plus you two, Mr. Raj. Mr. Roland."

Tito and Raj both protested loudly as they took the petition back, with Pippin adding some colorful retorts.

Pamela grabbed the petition from Tito. "Has this been released to the press?" she asked him. The camera zoomed in for a close-up, which she then angled for the camera's best view.

"Why would you want–" Tito asked just before his mouth formed an "o."

"Too late." Pamela nodded, her saleswoman's eyes flashing in anticipation. "We'll have two petitions inside at the show, one in favor and one against. We could– we will– invite citizens in to vote before the cruise ships arrive. Maybe some news crews would be interested to see how many people show up to protest?"

Behind his lens the cameraman looked uninterested though he kept filming.

"But what if the vote goes against you?" Tito asked.

Pippin nudged Pamela. "Is there anything that says we have to turn the petitions in to anyone?"

Pamela was too busy considering to notice the question. "Protesting is a difficult job. I think maybe I'll open a cash hors d'oeuvres table center mall, just outside the front entrance. To service the line I expect. Since it's for art, we'll arrange an unusual buffet that only truly worthy citizens can appreciate." She turned toward the camera. "We'll surprise the taste buds of all of Luna City."

"Applegate Organics has a few unusual products in our line," Pippin suggested.

Pamela nodded as the cameraman resumed packing up, the story over. "And since it's art *and* unusual, they won't balk at prices a little higher than normal. Maybe a mead-tasting table as well? People love the chance to get drunk in the name of culture. My cousin Mildred has a string quartet. She's fairly good, cheap, and if I recall, available at peak viewing times."

"Your brilliance leaves me awestruck," Pippin told her. "Have you ever met my Aunt Evie? She'd like you."

"For Evie Applegate, free hors d'oeuvres."

David knew he was the object of mild attention. Other StarBuffs customers sipped their honeyed cidercaff and noshed on deep-fried cinnamon apple rings waiting for the afternoon breeze while he sweated shirtless under his weights. He could pick up a good deal of libidinous thoughts but pushed them away even as he pushed back against the bar.

Weights on Luna were tricky things. Though they didn't weigh as much as they did on Earth, they still had inertia so the machine's movement was much faster than what he remembered from high school and college gym days. The object here was to stop the movement and the mass behind it, and not necessarily lift the weight.

His next machine involved the masses coming at him from either side, and he alternated using his arms and legs to counter it. Once you got the rhythm down, it was simple enough. He paused the machine to increase the mass, but his finger halted just above the touch-screen.

Ethan Kane.

Instantly he resisted the instinct to look around. Don't make himself look vulnerable, as if he was just another victim to be taken at will. Instead he reached out and slammed his mind against that other one.

And he took him by surprise.

Now David did look up. The entire storefront of StarBuffs was windows. There– David spotted the reddish-blond head on the opposite side of the mall.

He swung up out of the saddle of the machine and ran to the doors. The redhead was on the run too.

Let's see what this body can do.

David increased his pace. He wasn't out for a morning powerwalk now; he was running for his very body. And he knew that his true body wasn't up to this kind of treatment.

This borrowed body was no stranger to running, plus David was now used to Lunar gravity and could adapt to his new conditions. He loped low to the ground, taking advantage of quicker touch-downs to kick off again. Keep it low, low, low, tail down, tippy-toe.

He ate up the distance between the two of them. Kane glanced back at him and David could sense if not see the shock at the nearness.

Coward hitman. Didn't like to be caught off-guard. If only David had packed his gun with his gym shorts–

Kane grabbed the edge of a building to pivot himself to a stop, and planted his feet solidly. Then he loosed a mind-blast at David.

The world spun in David's eyes. The ground tilted; he stumbled and caught himself on his hands.

And when he looked up, Kane and his body were gone.

Damn, damn, damn! He'd have to prepare for that next time. How could–

"Very good, citizen," a voice said behind him.

David turned. A female FeeP was ripping off a ticket from her palm pad. She handed it to him.

"Splendid display of athleticism," she said. "It encourages the masses, you know?" Then she turned and went on her way.

David glanced down at the ticket. It was a commendation, good for an invitation to one of the meet-n-greets held periodically at the Luna City Grand.

David grimaced and stuffed it into his pocket. It had better be transferable. He would steal his proper body back soon.

23

Pippin was surprised to discover that Sugar's tastes in which color mat went with which painting was spot-on.

"You should come by every time I get in a framing frenzy," Pippin approved as they both stood back to appreciate the effect.

"I found him!"

They turned as David burst through the studio doors, waving his palm screen. Jonathan galloped in behind him. "Got him on the webcam!" He paused to see Sugar there, but recovered quickly enough to point to the palm screen.

"You two stay here," he ordered. "Here you're safe. Keep the doors locked. Where's Mama? I'm going after him."

"Sam took Aunt Evie to work," Pippin said and David nodded.

"Call him," he told her. "He'll know what to do if it comes to that."

Sugar peered at the palm screen. "You really know his location?" she asked. "We'll call the cops." With a frown she grabbed the screen from him. "This is from yesterday. This doesn't tell you anything. He could be anywhere."

"It narrows the search. He's in Luna C., and he's operating at least in…" he checked the screen, "Belle Rock in the northwest, not GayTown at all. I'm going out there and track him. I'm tired of sitting in front of a computer screen all day. I need to get out."

Pippin dusted the shreds of mat-cutting detritus from her shop apron and joined the two. She looked at the screen. "That's five levels down," she said.

"Just where he'd crawl to," David told her with satisfaction. "I've got him."

"You don't have anything," Sugar said.

Pippin nodded. "This will have to do. You need to go down there and walk around, David. See what you stir up. Sugar, can you get a cop to follow him?"

"Follow him? On this kind of evidence?" She put her hands on her hips, sucked in air through the side of her teeth, and snorted like one of those tough vid cops. "'You wanna waste my time doing what? Lady, I got real crimes to solve,'" she quoted from the famous *Final Night 6*.

"Or not," Pippin muttered.

"I can take care of myself," David declared. "That's what I'll do, go down and flash myself."

Sugar eyed him appreciatively. "Might be worth a look at that," she decided.

"Not that way. Walk around, talk to people. Loudly. Put on a show."

"Flashing would do that. I'd give you a permission slip."

Pippin nudged Sugar into silence. "Don't even joke about it. His testosterone and that body make him crazy. David, you need backup. It's too dangerous alone," she insisted.

That steely look stole into David's eyes, that hardness and darkness that he could sometimes get, springing out of nowhere... or somewhere deep inside himself. "I can take care of myself." He flexed his fingers like cat's claws. "I'll get my guns." A quick glance showed him the fear that flashed in Pippin's face. "I've been training. A lot. Don't worry."

He turned to Jonathan, who had taken a seat on one of the studio's stools. "You guard them, Jonny. Give me a heads-up if anything strange happens."

The cat's ears perked up and he twitched his tail twice.

"I don't want you two coming with me," David insisted as Sugar and Pippin flanked him down the ramps.

"Too bad," Pippin said.

"I am an officer of the law," Sugar reminded him.

"Yes, and if we run into any poorly-dressed drug dealers, you can fine 'em," David muttered.

"I placed top in my sub-class at Police Academy," Sugar insisted. "We're trained to back up the police in case of emergency."

"We are coming with you," Pippin stated in flat tones. She and Sugar were dressed similarly to David: in dark worker jumpsuits that wouldn't draw attention to any of them. Well, perhaps to Sugar, who looked spectacular in hers.

David kept a running soliloquy going, lower than the two of them could hear except for the occasional, "dangerous," "murderer," and such.

Pippin didn't like these levels. They might be illuminated with full-spectrum lights, but they still didn't have the same feeling of openness that the skylit upper levels had.

Homes were darker here, crammed together with little or no space between. Trees were as few as gardens. This was a gray world, a cavern of souls.

For a brief moment the right side of her brain flared to life, sparked by the newness of the images she saw and groups of bright-clad people who contrasted so well against the low-intensity setting. It reminded her of Group of Seven paintings of dull but pulsating Canadian winters. A shaft of light from above caught one building's corner and–

Pippin jerked her gaze away. This was about David. David's future. Even if he didn't fulfill the things with her he'd promised, he still must have that future available to him as his true self.

She smiled at him, but he didn't see. He kept glancing this way and that, searching with what she knew was more than his eyes.

Following the map to the cam position, he pointed them down a street.

"Any sign?" Pippin asked. At least Sugar had her FeeP BuzzBox in her hand, ready for any trouble.

"He's been here, but I can't tell how long ago."

"You can sense that?" she asked, pulling the hood on her jumpsuit closer about her head. Something about this made her hair stand on end.

David nodded absently. "Humans leave a slight presence, a residue wherever they pass through. Imagine how much residue they leave behind in their own bodies."

His left ear twitched and Pippin startled. Then he swung around to that direction. He let out a low growl.

"There, I take it?" Pippin asked.

"Pippin, stay back," Sugar said.

"Don't know what it is," David said in a low, dangerous voice that Pippin had never heard him use before. "You two stay here. I mean it."

He pushed Pippin back roughly, sending her tumbling into Sugar, who caught her. When Pippin stood a step forward, Sugar pulled her back.

"He's the hit man now," Sugar whispered to her. "Let him operate the way he knows."

David faced a dark alleyway between two storefronts, apartments on top, fire escapes between. Recyclables had been stacked along the left wall. Some of them had tumbled at the alley's far end.

He sniffed the air and peered into the shadows, turning his head this way and that. Sugar held Pippin tight, steering her toward the edge of the alley where they'd be out of street traffic and unnoticed.

David crouched and scuttled forward in the long arcs that Lunar grav permitted. He stopped at one recycling can, appeared to take another inner sweep of his surroundings and then crept forward.

At the third toppled can he stopped, looking at something that the women couldn't see. He glanced around himself again, all directions, up and down, and slowly stood up.

"Use your damned BuzzBox," he called down the alley.

Pippin broke away to run to him. She skidded to a stop when she saw–

Dougie Chu. She'd only seen his picture, but it was him, lying on the pavement, moldy recycling strewn over him. He lay face-up, and there was a perfect bullet-sized hole in the middle of his neoTeen-make forehead.

Lieutenant Savonarola sat David down at HQ. He still didn't seem to have a good grasp of the situation.

"You say you killed him, but you didn't?"

David tried to be patient, but his fingers tapped away the seconds on the table, and something in his hips kept jiggling up and down with nervous energy. Police made him nervous. "No, the man who is inhabiting my body killed Dougie."

"So you're possessed." Lt. Savonarola leaned back in his chair, speculating on David. His beefy, Ninety-make frame reminded David of something bad that had happened in the past, something that wouldn't focus for him. Or for Kane's body.

"Not possessed," he said quickly. "Oh, maybe if you go by strict definition… Oh hell, I'm not bipolar, officer. I'm a teep, fully licensed and respected. And the guy who stole my body is an unlicensed teep. I've reported this before."

"Yes, I know." Savonarola glanced for a second at the screens on his desk, then back to David. He leaned forward.

"Then you happen to come upon this body. By accident. This body whom you just happen to know."

David heaved a sigh. "I told you," he said. "I only know– *knew*– Dougie because he thought I was Kane. And then the real Kane apparently caught up with him, because he clearly knew the situation just a few days ago, and he made threats."

"Which you then killed him for. We have tapes of the two of you fighting in public."

"I could have killed him then if I'd wanted, but Dougie– he was my in to Kane. Another clue to where my real body is."

Savonarola leaned back in his chair. "So you're a peacenik. Caught carrying four pieces." He snickered at his own joke.

"Legal pieces. And I bet my mondal maser's signature doesn't match what killed Dougie. Looked like a 10 mm SilentBurst to me, and I thought those were outlawed on Luna."

Savonarola ground his teeth, eased forward and carefully placed both fists on his desk. "They are. And while you're sitting here, we're searching all your haunts to make sure you don't have one hidden away."

"Kane's got it, wherever he is." David slammed his hand down on his chair arms. "Damn it! I'm so close to finding him!"

"But you are Ethan Kane."

"I am in Ethan Kane's body," David repeated for the infinityeth time. "I am Doctor David Lumen! Ask me anything about myself and I can answer you."

"All right," Lt. Savonarola said slowly and precisely. "Dr. Lumen, where is your body?"

Sugar stayed at police HQ. Her call to Pippin came through as soon as she and David got home. On screen, Sugar's eyes sparkled; her face was flushed with excitement.

"I'm temporarily off duty as a FeeP," she confided. "They've got me filling out a million forms about the case down there. I'm supposed to take the next few days tracking Kane through omni-surveillance systems."

Pippin clapped her hands in delight. "Oh, Sugar! You be sure to enjoy it while it lasts."

"Every millisecond," Sugar assured her. Still, her expression turned sour. "I just got the word," she said.

Pippin braced herself for bad news.

"I'm no longer a perfect 69. Shelanda Jones's nose now rules."

"Oh. Oh, Sugar, I'm… sorry, I guess. I like your nose."

Sugar shrugged. "It makes you think, doesn't it? Maybe this is a sign from, well, Shelanda. Maybe it's time to reconsider things."

"By the time you have to have the surgery, Shelanda Jones will be old news," Pippin reassured her friend.

"So whose nose will I have to have then?"

Pippin couldn't answer that.

David had been listening as he riffled Jonathan's fur in his arms. "She's carrying her cop fantasy too far," he observed after Sugar signed off. "She might begin to mistake it for something more serious than it should be. You should warn her about it."

Jonathan began to gnaw at his knuckles. David gave him a playful growl and the cat kicked his forearm as he grappled with his prey. "I don't think she'd listen to me about that kind of thing unless she were seeing me professionally."

"Warn her off?" Pippin clicked off her messages. She erased three from Brock without looking at them. Instead, she made her way back to her studio with David and Jonathan following. Tiffany didn't even notice them violating her kitchen space.

"Warn her off." Pippin snorted in very unladylike fashion.

"I mean it, Pip. You don't know what kind of permanent harm this could do her if it goes on too long."

Pippin stopped sliding the landscape of Pytheas' spring blossoms out of its slot in the storage racks. "Harm? I would think it would do her good. She's always dreamed of being a real cop. Didn't you see how happy she was?"

"But she's a Sixty-Nine FeeP and a damned good one." Jonathan squirmed in David's arms, so he set him down on the floor. "Look how well she's brought you along. There should be more FeePs like her."

"FeePs!" Pippin almost spat the word. "The world would be a better place without them. They get in my way."

"They shouldn't," David was quick to assure her. "You're above them."

She blinked at that and then looked pleased. Then thoughtful. "But why aren't more people, as you say, above them? It seems to me that we waste a lot of time that could be used on important things in worrying about what others think of us."

"We're human." David settled onto a stool so he could more easily access his teaching mode. "As social animals, humans need to be accepted by others."

"Is that all we are, David? Social animals?"

He gave her a calming smile and gestured at the studio. "Some are meant for better things. Higher concepts."

"But not everyone? Is it just me out of twelve billion? What proportion of the population would you say are better than just social animals?"

"Come on, Pip–"

"How many?" Pippin leaned over the worktable toward him. "And who the hell gave someone the right to determine who could achieve their dreams and who had to sit on them, ignore them, and suffer all through their lives?"

"That's why I'm here. To help them so they don't suffer."

She stared him down. "If you didn't know me, if you hadn't had your instant of–" she waved her hands to indicate *enlightenment*–"would you take me on as a client? Would you teach me how to ignore who I am?"

The awful truth of his past plans tore at David. "I would never–" he lied.

"Well, that's good to hear. But how about you, David? Have you made any progress with your body?"

"What do you mean?"

"I mean, are you feeling less gay these days?"

He rolled his eyes. "Oh, that. I–"

"Less homicidal? I've seen you with your guns. Hell, I've seen you playing with Jonathan. You're half-cat. You're gay– even though you once told me that you of all people would be able to counter that– and you're aching to kill this killer."

"I wouldn't– I'd never–"

"Who are you, David Lumen?" she demanded.

He sat there, unable to answer.

"Why is David Lumen, or any other human, able to tell me who I should be if they don't even know what they are or why they are, much less how to control whatever it is that combines to make them them?"

"Society–"

"Screw society," she said with quiet fierceness. "At their core, people are what they are. They're like… trees. No matter how much you prune or graft, the root remains true to itself. An apple tree can't morph into an orange tree. Maybe you could disguise it with plaster and paint so you could fool almost anyone, but the truth would still be that apple tree."

"If we screw society we wind up with bedlam. Twelve billion people– even just Luna's population, which is what?– just a few million– in a pressurized environment– Screw society and you wind up with chaos, and chaos on Luna means death. We are controlled because we don't want to die."

He raised his fist to show her his determination to his mission, his core. "That is who David Lumen is, Pippin. I help people. I am society's policeman. I maintain the balance because it's so precarious. And I am damned lucky because I was born with an ability that helps me do just that."

"Others are born with abilities," Pippin countered. "They might not be so flashy. They might be unfocused and never trained. But what if they were encouraged to find those abilities? What if those secret desires they have are arrows directing them toward those abilities? What if Sugar's best talent was to be a cop, a real police officer? Wouldn't that help society?"

"But Sugar's a Sixty-Nine."

"She wasn't born a Sixty-Nine!" Pippin threw her hands into the air. "Maybe she was born a cop and somehow got on the wrong path. It's close to cop, you've got to admit that."

David gave a sideways nod, unwilling to give ground. "Only legally."

"Well, that's society for you. It hands out artificial labels."

"Look, Pip, if you'd rather I talk to Sugar–"

"Out!" Pippin shouted. "I'm sorry, David, but I can't take this attitude right now. Too many negative vibes. You need to figure yourself out before we have this conversation again. Now get out. Let me work."

Mystified, David scooped up Jonathan and left.

24

She was just tense about the nearness of her show, David decided. Of course she'd snap, and she'd snap at those she trusted most first, for those were the ones who'd forgive her. He certainly did.

She let him into her bed again, but didn't say anything as he warily crawled in. Pippin wasn't a loner at heart, in bed or out in the world. She wasn't the jewel of society, but she had friends enough. If this coming show were a success, she'd have more friends, even hangers-on. Perhaps she'd begin to set societal standards of her own as she became the latest fifteen-minute phenom.

The trouble with phenoms were that they shook things up too fast too often. They'd come from the left and then the right, and you didn't know where to look to spot the next one. All the new fads wore you down as the media buzzed them up and copied them so they blasted at you 24/7. You might not believe whatever it was, but you bought into it for a while at least.

To fit in.

David nestled his chin along the line of Pippin's shoulder. He fit nicely here. It was so strange. As Jonathan he'd also fit with Pippin, and he knew that as himself he'd fit even better.

Pippin was stability. With all her craziness, her blitz of creativity, she knew who she was and what she was doing. She believed in her work, if not always her worth.

Pippin was truth, and in her truth was great beauty.

Pippin was real.

Lying there in his borrowed body, David wondered just how real he was.

He cat-dozed a while, but then dragged himself out of bed. He went to the bathroom and leaned over the sink, staring into the wall mirror. Was this the body he was fated to have? Fate: what a romantic spin to put on hard circumstances. Could he handle the life of a Fifty?

Just because he was in the body of a Fifty, did that make him one as well? Wasn't he truly a Thirty? A straight Thirty at that?

He didn't act like one. As Jonathan jumped up on the vanity to sit within petting distance, David could admit that the cat had taught him a lot. New experiences had been what had shaped David, not being inside Jonathan. Right?

He flexed his hands, splaying his fingers and opposable thumb. These were not cat paws, yet there was now a power within them that was definitely feline at its base.

Look at Jonny. He was a tamed cat, yet David knew that hidden wildness was the motor that ran his life. Jonny only pretended to be tame. He acted that way because Mama would pet him so it felt good, and so he'd get his dinner on time and a clean litter box.

Of course Jonny loved as wildly as he played. Was that because he was domesticated, or did that have its roots in Jonny's ancestors as well? Was it ancestral memory or cell memory?

Had nature or nurture shaped Ethan Kane? David stared at the borrowed, familiar body and its features in the mirror. Was it toilet training, reincarnation, heavenly purpose, body chemicals, astrological sign, or the universal memory field that made humans individuals? Of course humans could be reshaped, whether by behavioral or chemical means or a combination.

But reshaped from what primordial base?

Were we all mass-produced, arriving in only five types per gender? Did only skin color and sexual orientation offer acceptable variances?

There had been a plot once to infect the entire human race with a gene-replacement virus that would have given everyone the same medium-brown skin tone. People had been outraged when the quashed plot was made public. Skin tone was a private but proud affair, something that culture hung upon. And culture helped define individuality.

Sexual orientation was taboo, of course. For millennia gays, lesbians and the entire range of queer-ness had been outcasts. Then the PC movements had taken over and non-straights had been legally granted all the rights that the rest of humanity held. Still, though, the minority liked to stress publicly that they were not straight. Perhaps what they were "gay and proud" of was not their sexuality but rather their uniqueness.

The man in the mirror stared back at him. If he kept this body he shouldn't remain a psychiatrist. Fifties made lousy personal service providers. Yet David still yearned to help humanity and if that wasn't providing a service, what was? How could he be a Fifty and feel (for the most part) like a Thirty? This body's chemicals should be reiterating the Fifty role to him. Every cell in his borrowed brain should be reminding him and reinforcing patterns that were unique to a Fifty.

Unique. Individual.

David.

"Yeow?" Jonathan asked as he raised his chin to David.

He scratched it automatically. "Yeah," he said. "You know exactly who you are, buddy. Now the only question is: who am I?"

David jerked at the stuck painting and cursed under his breath. One final jiggle and it was free.

"Watch it! I almost had it," Sam snapped at him as he crouched upon the rented wagon's storage armature. "Next time, let me work it all the way out of its bindings. That Tekto-Cote ain't armor, you know."

"Sorry," David muttered. The strain of it all was getting to him. Kane's presence seemed nearby, but he knew that odds were it was just his own unease. Still, it could be Kane. The delay in searching for him grated on whatever nerves he had left. Why, this morning even Jonathan had pointedly ignored him after he'd done a half-hearted job of petting him.

The police cuff on David's left arm didn't help. It meant that he was a Person of Interest in the murder of Dougie Chu.

"It also means that you have your own BuzzBox," Pip had pointed out. The bulky white cuff did indeed have a "summon help" button he could use in case of emergency.

"Where does this one go?" he bellowed as he hefted the huge painting inside the gallery. They were unloading from the back alley, and the glimpse of the inner goings-on at an art gallery didn't impress him. They were just making a gigantic mess. Crates, plastic shields and packing littered the floor amid propped-up canvases.

"Over there," Pippin directed, and he leaned the canvas against the short temporary wall before returning to pick up the next one.

They'd managed to fit all of Pippin's show paintings into just one Haul-a-Kart. A mountain of narrow crates made up the bulk of it, paintings that she thought should be spotlit in the show. The rest she'd rigged so they were separated by the thinnest of Tecto-Cotes, all standing up like an electrified deck of cards. Loading had taken four people to accomplish, and he and Sam had trotted beside the long wagon all the way here. Now it was just he and Sam unloading, with Sam handling the fasteners that connected the cushions and paintings.

Most of Pippin's work wasn't nearly as large as the three main pieces that had been such a pain to haul. David maneuvered these more adeptly. He fought down the impatient comments that he longed to mutter– just one would have worked off so much negative energy!– and meekly waited for Pippin and the gallery director to decide which wall needed to be propped up with the particular painting he held.

David steered another crated canvas into the studio. It might not weigh much, but it didn't like to change direction. "I can't believe you're making her wait for your decision," he grumbled.

Evie took a sip of the tea she utilized as unofficial Traffic Coordinator, pointing with her cup to various personnel and locations. "I believe you call this 'tough love,'" she claimed as she followed him. "I specified boundaries for her. I don't want her to think that I'm backing down."

"You always have to win, don't you? Obsessive."

"Yes." She gave an imperious nod to the gallery staff who accepted the crate from David. "I've had to fight all my life. I've had to dare. And lose. Pippin's had it easy."

"In some ways. I don't think you have to maintain a chokehold on her, though. She's yours. You know that. She's absolutely loyal to you."

"And Applegate Orchards."

"No, to you. You just happen to be Applegate Orchards. She's a good orchards assistant, Evie, and she's even good CEO material, despite her being a Twenty."

"I'm a Twenty," Evie declared and then added hastily, "At least, I was." She was walking well, though often she had to rest. Most of her bandages had been removed now that the swellings were down. She'd emerged as an Ought, even more slender, almost boyish, than she'd been, with a hint of hard angles to her joints. Her cheeks had been sculpted even finer than they'd shown in the photographs of her Before. Sometimes David wondered if he would ever recognize Mama in a crowd, but there was something about Mama that was Mama and couldn't be denied.

"Oughts especially aren't CEO material," David declared. "They're put there for show, for sales on high levels where impression is more important than substance." He drummed his fingers on the top of a crate. "Lately I've begun to think about things like that."

"And why is that?" Evie's pinky pointed as she took another sip through pursed lips.

"You're an exception to the rule, Mama Evie. Pippin is an exception too. Do exceptions just run in the Applegate family? Or are there more exceptions out there, just enough conforming to the rule to make it appear to be inviolable?"

"Rules are rules," Evie declared.

"But what if they're false rules made up of insufficient data or false reads? That's one of the strengths of humanity, to be able to identify things with only a few clues as to their nature. But sometimes it serves us wrong. Sometimes it destroys lives."

He gazed at Pippin across the room, almost glowing in excitement and nerves. "Her path lies in another direction."

"Apples are in her blood."

"Let's hope not."

"Her very name–"

"'Applegate' was Grandma Tang's invention, wasn't it? A marketing ploy. Don't make Pip into a mere tool of your company."

"The company has always been good enough for me, young man."

He laughed. "Now I know you're mad. You're not old, Mama Evie, and you never will be. And you, I will believe, do indeed have apple juice and Luna C Mead running through those veins of yours, keeping you so cantankerous. Ease up. Ease up on the people around you and especially on the people who love you."

"Shrinks," Evie muttered as she set her tea down. She busied herself shuffling through labels.

"Yeah. I might stay one when I get my body back. Maybe I'll go into the self-help business. I think I'd make a fine guru. I'll start a place, the Evie Applegate Personal Growth Clinic and Pet Rejuv Center. You like the name?"

She looked at him sideways. "You even stoop to blackmail. I'm impressed."

That garnered a chuckle. "I'll be much too busy with my new guru-dom and with agenting Pippin's career to help out in the orchards. Much. You'll have to start training someone besides Pip to be vice president. How long can you keep dangling that Brock before her? It's too obvious."

She choked.

"He's such a loser. Looks good, though. He's got all the moves down. He'd make a good stand-in for that Steele Gambino."

Evie snapped her fingers. "Is that who it is. I've been trying to place him since we first met."

"And you hire him just to show Pip that unless she signs on the team, Applegate Orchards will fall to some idiot who'll run it into the ground. You've never truly meant for him to take over, Mama Evie."

She stood there stone-faced for a moment before a hint of resignation played across her as a frown. "It was *not* obvious. You're a teep and a psychiatrist; only you'd see that. Just how long have you been here on Luna, David?"

"Long enough to see the obvious. Like Sam Greenwood."

"The orchards couldn't run without him, but Sam's not CEO material, either."

"But he could run things almost all the way up the line. Maybe he would make a good CEO too. Ever trained him in the upper echelons?"

She clucked her tongue as she made a sour face. "He's not family."

"Oh hell, he could be if you'd just loosen up. Why, he even likes Jonathan."

"You're just trying to make an old softie out of me."

"You don't want to let a man like him get away. Once I get my body back I will deny I ever said this, but Sam's a hottie. If you like mature hotties."

Evie chuckled. "He *is* very nice-looking." A faraway look came into her eyes before she snapped back, "You're slacking off. I'll tell Pippin."

David trotted off dutifully.

"How many more, Sam?" he called through the open door to the back alley.

What sounded like a groan answered him. "Didn't get that," David said as he exited and turned toward the wagon. He stopped.

Sam sprawled on the ground, his body twisted as he tried to get up and hold his head at the same time.

"Sam!" David exclaimed as he sprinted toward him. He knelt to help the older man sit.

The slightest trickle of blood oozed from a cut marking the center of what would be a spectacular bruise.

Sam hadn't just fallen. "Did you see him?" David demanded. "Is he still here?"

Sam shook his head, and David hit the button on his cuff. "Are you all right?"

"Hit me from behind. Knocked me down."

"That's it?" David asked. "I mean, that's bad enough, but—"

"I know what you mean." Sam grimaced. "I don't think I have any laser holes in me. Though I've never been shot to know."

"I have," David told him and then wondered: *when?* It was this body that had been shot in the past, not him. It had answered Sam.

Gently he maneuvered Sam to sit on the kart's tailgate, and he managed to find a cloth to hold against the man's forehead. Finally two police arrived on rollies.

"Stop fussing," Sam whispered to David. He took hold of the cloth himself.

David and Sam filled the cops in, thankful that they hadn't come through the gallery to upset the people there. Instead, Pippin stuck her head into the alley.

"What's the holdup?" she asked, though her mouth didn't complete the final syllable as she took in the scene. "Sam? David? Are you okay?" She turned and shouted into the gallery, "Aunt Evie! Come quick!"

"Don't scare her!" Sam scrambled from his seat and his knees buckled. David grabbed him before he could hit the pavement.

"Sam? Sam!" Evie rushed to him, her face white. "What happened?"

They went through another round of telling them the circumstances but one of the investigating officers interrupted.

"Who's this meant for?" he asked, and held a flimsy paper note so they could all read.

It said: "That portrait doesn't look like me."

David's teeth ground together as he let out a growl that originated deep in his chest.

Evie scowled at the note. "That's some sense of humor he has."

"We can be thankful he was in a good mood," David told her.

Pippin looked thoughtful. "Maybe this was part of David coming through," she said. "Maybe he's being influenced by his body as much as you're being influenced by his."

David longed to snatch the note from the cop's hands even as it was being laminated for evidence. "Tell that to Dougie," he muttered.

David prowled the reception. He slunk between murmuring groups who had come to see and be seen, and reconnoitered the line at the bar.

He hunted Ethan Kane.

"For God's sake, either settle down and smile, or leave," Evie commanded him. "You're spoiling this party."

David's gaze returned to Pippin, who stood in front of one group and pointed out some of the aspects of one painting that they'd missed. Her statement, whatever it was, brought an approving murmur and nods all around.

Her hair was pinned up in a cloud of jeweled apple blossom pins. Those blossoms also showed up as a print on her gown, which showed her figure to perfection. Not too frou-frou; not too staid.

She looked gloriously happy.

"Pippin's the only one who matters here," David told Evie.

Evie gave him a starched chuckle. "Everyone here could be of some service to her, even if they don't buy her work tonight. You have to think long-term with potential customers."

David almost licked his suited shoulder to cover his anxiety. Instead he scratched at it, twitched, and eyed the crowd anew.

"I've hired extra guards. Lighten up." Evie patted his back.

"And keep an ear out." Sam Greenwood came up from behind them, startling Evie. David had felt his approach: no harm there.

Sam handed an extra drink to Evie, who took it with a small, considering smile. He held her gaze for a moment, and her smile relaxed.

"Go talk up Pippin to the heathen," Sam hinted to David as he pulled Evie away. "You've lost a future CEO," he told Evie.

"I have not. Pippin's the only choice."

They strolled around the crowds to take in the show along with everyone else. "No," Sam said, "Pippin's not the only one who could do it. CEO of Applegate Orchards– there's got to be three or four people in the universe who could handle that. Time to expand your search, Evie."

"I don't–"

Sam stopped and pulled her into a darkened wall niche near the employees only area. "Face up to the truth. Pippin's out of the race."

Evie looked over Sam's shoulder at the murmuring crowd. "They don't know what to make of it," she said. "There's still a chance–"

"No. Let Pippin be Pippin." He cocked his head at her. "Although you won't even let Evie be Evie."

The new Evie Applegate had dressed to the nines tonight in sparkling gown and snippy elfin hairstyle straight from the day's fashion headlines. Her lipstick was precise, punctuating lips that were not to be kissed so much as ones that were to be heard– and obeyed. She looked fresh from modeling school and ready to pose beside a rotating red sportscar at some design show.

"Don't you like Oughts, Sam?" she asked coquettishly.

"I like Oughts on Oughts. This is going to take some getting used to. I met you as a Twenty. Worked with you when you decided to go Forty on us. Now you look too young and useless to be running a corporation."

That pleased her, to judge from the slight blush that rose on her cheeks. "Useless, hm?" she hummed. Then her eyes brightened. "Oh! There's Jack. He wanted to take me out for coffee later."

"Coffee?" Sam snorted as he spied Evie's ex-husband in the crowd. "Spendthrift."

"He has the money for it. So do I. So do you, Sam."

Sam shook his head. "Don't go out with him, Evie."

"I don't know why I shou–"

Sam pulled her to himself and landed a determined lip-lock upon her.

Her surprise made her draw back. She looked up at him with unaccustomed uncertainty, so he took the time to take gentle hold of her head and kiss her thoroughly. After a moment she leaned into him.

"Let's go get a late dinner," he said. "I know a place." He offered the crook of his elbow to her.

The right side of her mouth crooked up before the left one caught up. "I hope they cater to old-timers," she said. "I haven't had a yeastburger on synthawheat in years."

"They even have carbo-shakes," he told her.

"Anything but apple-flavored, please."

David truly tried to arrange his features into a more pleasant configuration for the event, but strain stretched his muscles taut. He wished he had a tail so he could twitch it and work off some of this energy.

It was like just before a summer storm on Earth, where the lightning hovered as sheer electric potential. Danger spun the air, ready to strike without warning.

He nodded at one small group of chit chatters, and made a large circle around another where the people talked a little too loudly, some syllables slurring already though the evening was still young.

He would go mad before all this was through!

A nearby man in a burgundy night cape let loose a guffaw and David jumped a full six lo-grav inches.

Draped in blue chiffon, Sugar paused by him just long enough to force a glass into David's hand. "Drink!" she ordered, and then was off on the arm of an unpinned Nineties make whose neck betrayed his age, and his suit, his bank account. She pointed at a painting and the man changed course to follow her finger.

David patrolled the gallery, then trotted out to the Applegate Organics apple blossom wine tasting and mead tables just outside in the mall. A line stretched down the street of people waiting to get in, attracted by the publicity buzzing on the newsnets. A police officer stood by the gallery's front door, ostensibly to make sure fire code occupancy maximums were observed.

David studied the people on the dance floor they'd set up between the wine and the gallery, and then made a circuit of the interior again.

His eyes were slits and his hand constantly gravitated to the back of his belt, where– before he'd gotten his cuff– he'd kept his maser. Damn it all! The cuff would get fast response, but the gun would be even quicker. The shocker he wore on his left leg wouldn't be picked up by the cuff's sensors, but it would be useless at anything besides close range.

Nervous, are you? a quiet voice whispered in his mind.

It wasn't his own. He whirled at the glassed doorway to the gallery, his chin jerking this way and that.

Quiet laughter echoed through him and he struck out with hatred and determination. *Touch one of mine and you'll be dead!*

No answer. The presence lifted. Gone.

David slammed the flat of his hand against the doorsill and stifled a curse he'd never spoken before.

"Block-ing," a familiar voice singsonged behind him. Pretentious, prissy but male.

David stepped away to let Tito, with Raj just behind him, saunter into the gallery. They both gave David the merest annoyed glance, dismissing him.

Immediately they discovered the table placed front and center: the vote to close the show or not. Camera crews now trotted to the scene as the fellows stirring up the controversy made their appearance.

"What a bore! I've never seen such trash," Tito announced in a loud voice. His sequined beret seemed to vibrate.

Raj's volume was equally loud. "Where does she come off thinking this is art?" he sniffed, and the camera lenses zoomed in, as did a certain perky vid entertainment anchor.

She interviewed Tito, the renowned "Heavenly Painter" of Luna. He concluded his practiced sound bite with, "Tonight puts a black eye on the Man in the Moon. I've seen kindergartners who could do better than this. Just slap some paint on a canvas, stick a high price on it, and expect people to swallow the swindle!"

With a flourish, he took a pen and signed his name to the "no" column of the tally.

While he was writing and sure that the cameras were on them, Tito added, "We should get a collection going. Send the artist to art school. I hear she's a failure at Applegate Orchards too. I mean, any idiot can grow an apple, right?"

Red flashed before David's eyes. His ears laid back; his teeth bared. He advanced like a warrior. Racial memory provided him with an invisible sword of justice.

"Get out!" he roared. "You pretenders! You fakes! Thinking that you can smear paint by number and formula and fool people who've never been shown what true art is!"

The camera swung to take him in, and the crowd regrouped into a circle to best witness the spectacle. David gestured to Pippin. He didn't notice that her mouth hung open; instead, she was Artist, Pure and True.

"Here is a bonafide genius," David announced.

Luckily Pippin closed her mouth before the camera took her in.

"How many geniuses have remained unsung during their lifetimes because others said they didn't follow the old rules?

"Well, here is a woman– an artist– who breaks the rules that don't apply anymore. Look at her work. Even an idiot–" he gestured at Tito and Raj– "can see it. They're afraid that others will notice. They're afraid tonight's exhibit will demonstrate just how far they've slipped out of fashion." David used his arms to attract the reporters' attention so they swung the camera back from those awful men to him, to where he was pointing.

Across one of the central canvases of the show the surface of Luna lay bleak and commanding. Yet underneath a subtle beauty of color and texture supported the unearthly shapes of the landscape. The mood recalled something basic and familiar to every human. Stardust called to stardust.

"Pippin Applegate has managed to capture the very soul of Luna in her brush. Through her skill she reveals what she sees. Not the pompous illusion that others–" David waved off the threat of Tito and Raj– "would pander to an ignorant audience."

Righteousness lit his face. "Look at these paintings with unbiased eyes. See the truth. Luna stands in all her beauty, without illusion or artifice. She is naked before you!"

Now his arm moved again to point accusation at Tito. "Philistine! Coward! You're afraid because Pippin has changed the direction of art, and you can't adapt to it. You're not only a dinosaur but a fake dinosaur. You've shaped yourself to look like we suppose artists to look like. You may advertise yourself as an artist, but inside, where it counts, where the true heart of every individual decides their own best destiny, you've chosen not art but the safe route of conformity. Remember the people who tried to stifle the Impressionists? I don't. We won't remember you, either."

Members of the crowd began to boo and hiss Tito. Sam Greenwood might have been one of the first to do so, and Evie joined in with a grin. Raj stepped away from his mentor.

"Out!" "Get out!" "Losers!" the people shouted, and the cameras followed the two as they slunk out the door. A cheer went up for David, but he bowed and gestured in Pippin's direction.

How she glowed as she gazed at him! It seemed to take her some moments to realize that now the crowd was cheering for her. She nodded her head in thanks and asked everyone to please go back to what they were doing and to have a pleasant evening.

Five people rushed to David to ask how he wanted payment for the paintings.

25

The next afternoon Evie looked up at the doorbell. "I bet you Brock's come early for the meeting," she said. "Good. I have something to tell him in private. Show him in, dear. I don't think Tiffany heard it."

Pippin skipped as she answered the door. She still hadn't come down from the previous night. News crews had surrounded her, printed business cards and return-programmed cells had been pressed into her hand. She'd received nine blatant propositions. This morning had been a whirlwind of interviews for both Lunar and Terran network tabs. So this was success!

It was even better after wonderful David's wonderful wonderful speech. And to have Sugar, Aunt Evie and Sam supporting her as well… Life didn't get any better than this. Even Brock Monark couldn't spoil today.

She straightened the antique dried apple doll and frying pan on display in the entry– Jonathan had been in one of his world conqueror modes last night– checked her appearance in the hall mirror, and pulled the lock up. It made the familiar chucking *swoosh* as tiny differences in air pressure equalized, and the heavy steel door swung open.

Instead of Brock, there stood a man of medium height. He was dressed in blue overalls and cap and steadied a hand-truck beside him. "I've got an order for a pick-up," he said, and drew a pink screen out of his hip pocket.

He was a mid-make Thirty with reddish-blond hair.

Pippin shoved into the door to shut it, but its mass refused to move fast enough. The man straight-armed it. His expression betrayed the effort it took him to do so, but he squeezed into the entry and pushed the door closed with his back.

"Know who I am, toots, do you? I don't have to introduce myself?"

"I don't know you," Pippin managed to say from within her fear. She tried to remember every pointed or heavy item in the area behind her, something she could grab to fend him off long enough to– "Call the– !" she began to shout.

Ethan Kane clamped his hand over her mouth. "People inside, eh? We don't want you warning them. And police always make crime scenes so very uncomfortable to be around."

Behind her– the umbrella stand. Her fingers closed around the handle nearest her. He wouldn't get past her to harm David or Aunt Evie.

"I've come for the body," Kane said. His voice was low and menacing, the way David's had been when he'd found that dead man.

Kane wrapped one arm around her middle as he reached back to secure the door, freeing her mouth. "What body?" she asked as she stalled for time. "You've got the wrong house." She shifted her fingers for a firmer grip. Kane's fingers slipped down to grip her neck.

"Now then, don't try to pretend with me, darlin'. Remember, I'm a teep. Just like him." His voice held some kind of accent, as if born from the sewers.

"Leave us in peace," Pippin said as she eased the umbrella out of its stand as unobtrusively as she could. That meant that she had to stand in the same place when every muscle told her to run away from him as if he'd been some kind of feral animal.

Create a mental picture in case he could read her. Think of big, burly husbands and their friends running to the rescue. Friends with weapons. Don't think of the um–

"Oh, you'll be peaceful enough once I'm gone," he said. For a split-second he glanced away to check the hallway and she swung at him hard with the umbrella. The stand fell over with a calamitous clatter. She got him full on the left temple.

"Call the cops!" She yelled as she skewered him in the belly. "Aunt Evie, get to the safe room! Tiffany, call the cops!"

She got in two more heavy whacks with the handle before he ripped the umbrella out of her hands.

His cheek bled from an angry red welt. A lump disfigured his forehead, and the mark of the umbrella had seared itself into his neck.

With one motion he hauled her into a hard, locking embrace with his right arm. "You shouldn't have done that," he growled. "Now I'm mad."

He struck her hard with his mind. Pain slashed through her head as though he'd pummeled her very brain. Pippin screamed. She couldn't think. Great black spots obscured her vision.

"Get away from her!"

From far away she heard David's roar, and then she was falling, flung to the floor. She blinked hard and shook her head. Her arms refused to support her as she tried to rise.

David pitched himself in a low, fast arc at Kane. His hands clenched in tearing position, ready to rip to shreds the man who would threaten Pip. His teeth bared to rend flesh. Kane barely had time to assume a guard position before David fell upon him.

Pip was twitching back to consciousness, easing away from the danger but far too slowly. David tightened his stranglehold on Kane. Kane fought back with a kick that couldn't get through because of their tangle. Then he rammed his mind into David's.

David reeled from it. Kane kicked him again, this time connecting hard. David rolled away.

David could feel the umbrella hit Kane's head as if it had struck his own. The man let go a guttural curse. Struggling to open his eyes, David saw Pippin fall again to the floor. This time she was turning white.

Dead white.

She was trying to call his name, but he only heard it in his mind.

Blazing fury fueled him as he lay on to Kane, pummeling him with his fists– and his mind. By God he'd push him out of there where he could never harm Pippin again!

Somewhere nearby Jonathan *hoooled*. David could sense every hair on the cat's yellow body standing on end. Then–

With a rush of air though the room was still, he was *somewhere else.* David sat stunned. He was on this side of the battle. The entry looked different somehow.

And then he saw himself– no, Kane– sitting there also with a look of dumb amazement on his face.

An umbrella slammed him on the forehead. He looked up to see Pippin lift the umbrella stand like a boulder, about to release it.

"Pip–" he croaked and pointed at Kane. "Him."

She paused in confusion long enough for Kane to tackle him. They rolled across the floor, upsetting Pip.

"Call– cops!" David said. Then he remembered. He grabbed Kane by the arm and hit the Buzz Box on his, or Kane's, cuff.

They battered each other physically and mentally as they tumbled across the entry and into the office. Suddenly Kane shrieked. A twelve-pound orange cat attached to his ear by its teeth. Jonathan scrabbled at Kane's neck with his claws.

So Kane took the easy way out– he jumped into David's body.

But David hadn't left it. He knew how to stand his ground now. He held on through sheer strength of will, feeling the empty body across from him reaching out for a mind, any mind…

"PipPIN!" he shouted. He reached out for her mind and stood in front of it to shield her from Kane's barrage. "Never!" he cried. "Never!"

She could not be harmed. Kane fell back into his own body before David's attack, and when he tried to swerve to jump into David's body, David expanded his very self to protect both him and Pippin.

Ethan Kane would not harm any in this household! David erected a mental shield that surrounded Kane and contracted it as if he'd closed his fist around him.

Little man.

Shouts echoed from all around him as the world suddenly blossomed again. He tried to catch his breath. He felt solid. Felt real. But was he himself?

Legs stood in front of him. Uniformed legs. Pip legs. People were babbling until his mind calmed enough to sort it out.

"Which one is it?" a male voice demanded. "Cuff 'em both until we sort it out."

He could feel Kane unsteady in his body and sure enough, Kane and that body sat confusedly across the entry from David.

David looked up. "Lieutenant Savonarola," he managed in a dry voice. "I'm David Lumen. This is the body I was telling you about."

Evie had joined the crowd, Jonathan growling toward Kane at her feet. She held an old-time frying pan in her hand, a kitchen decoration. Pippin looked from David to Kane. David felt blood running down both sides of his face. Kane looked much the same, except that he seemed to be missing part of an ear and a few chunks out of his throat.

"Pip, are you all right?" David asked anxiously, checking her color. He turned to the lieutenant. "She needs medical help."

Something clanged across the room and David jerked around to see that Evie had walloped Kane on the head. That ancient pan must have been heavy.

"It slipped," she told the police without blushing.

"Good… Mama Evie," David managed. "He's an unlicensed teep," David reminded the lieutenant. Ow, it felt like he'd cracked his chin implant on top of everything else. It hurt to talk.

Savonarola nodded. "Sedate him," he ordered. Kane's mind blanked to David's senses as a stunner flashed.

"Oh, good," was all David could find to say. Jonathan jumped on his chest as he sank against the wall. "Good boy, Jonny," he whispered.

Pip knelt next to him. "Are you all right? Are you hurt bad?" She smoothed his hair back from his face, eying what David knew must be significant injuries. He hurt all over, like he'd been buried under a rockslide. "Are you really David?" she asked him softly.

Jonathan purred loudly as Pip checked out David's eyes. Were they bloodshot?

"They're not cruel," she said.

"That's because they're looking at you." David realized something and against all the aches, all the burning sears about his body and his mind and his shattered chin, he gave her a small smile. "I think I'm straight," he said.

"You're…"

"Yep, pretty sure about that." The smile became a wobbly but wolfish grin.

And hers answered his.

Sam arrived along with the ambulances. Members of the Orchard Directors ambled about the patio trying to keep out of various officers' way, but he pushed past and into the house.

"Evie!" he called. "Evie! Are you all right? Pippin?"

Evie looked up from the desk in her office, where an officer had been questioning her. Sam's face was pale, his eyes darting until he saw her. From behind, another policeman grabbed him.

"Oh no, officer, he's family."

"What the hell's going on? Officer Sugar called me—"

"I tried to call you, Sam, but things were too crazy. I asked Sugar to call you when she showed up."

Sam pressed her to his chest, raising his head to Heaven, his eyes closed.

"I'm all right, Sam," she said softly. "Everyone here is." She hugged him tightly.

"Evie! Pippin!" a familiar voice called from the hall.

Sam and Evie both turned to see Officer Sugar dragging Brock toward them by his collar. He sported a beautifully black eye. "A little help, boys?" Sugar asked the two male cops in the area. "FeeP handcuffs aren't heavy-duty like yours."

After a terse exchange of police codes, Sugar trotted back to Pippin's room and emerged wearing plastic gloves, with Pippin's pressure suit in her arms.

"I caught him back there jimmying it," she told the group and showed a small video eye. "I managed a good long taping of him doing it before he noticed me. I think it's not the first time he's done it, either."

"I don't know what she's talking about," Brock sputtered.

"Yeah, you were only in Pippin's room to sniff her underwear, I know," Sugar sneered at him. "I bet if we look hard enough we'll be able to trace a certain jumper car back to you. And maybe even a street scooter that almost ran down Pippin a couple weeks ago."

"She's lying," Brock declared. "Lying! Evie, I—"

"Good work, Officer Sugar," the lieutenant told her as he clapped real cuffs onto the would-be CEO of Applegate Orchards. "You know what to do with the crime scene tape?"

"Sure do, Nick." Sugar beamed at him.

"Brock," Evie said from Sam's arms, "did I remember to tell you that you're fired? We don't allow bad apples in our orchards." She turned to the officer closest to her and said, "As soon as we come back from the hospital, I'll sign whatever needs to be signed to charge him. He tried to murder my niece!"

"Somehow I'm actually surprised," Sam said.

Evie frowned at Brock as the door closed behind him. She said, "Wish I'd had the chance to use that frying pan on him. I would have heated it up first."

At first the investigators who came to the hospital treated David's story as if he were a lunatic. David did not remind them of the meaning of the word and that they were all, technically, Lunatics. Upon doing an ident-check, though, and working with Lieutenant Savonarola and Officer Sugar they began to sort things out.

First they confirmed that he was indeed a teep, plus a respectable psychiatrist who had mysteriously disappeared only to show up as the Coma Man on the Lunar Express. They also coordinated with organized crime investigators to discover that Ethan Kane had been preliminarily identified at a handful of mob hits, with the witnesses dying shortly afterward. Two almost unobtrusive but positive childhood telepathy tests had apparently missed being properly filed. Kane's personal records and accounts held the same signs of using laundered money that *l'Ögre* commonly used.

"He's not going to talk," a burly lieutenant, a 90, told David. "We can put you under witness protection."

"But if you do that I won't be able to see Pippin... I mean, Ms. Applegate, or her family," David protested.

"The law prohibits us from using drugs to make him testify against himself. We can only tranquilize him enough to keep him from doing to someone else what he apparently did to you."

"I'm a private citizen and a teep," David retorted. "I have a special bond with him. You ask him questions and I'll be able to read him. It's time someone brought him down."

So David sat in his wheelchair for three days behind a mirrored wall as they questioned Kane within a millimeter of what was permissible under law. On the second day a squad of six Terran detectives arrived to focus the investigation. They brought disks filled with unsolved murders and disappearances.

Kane knew about many of them, but he wasn't talking.

Only deep in his mind where David insinuated himself did he talk and recall with startling detail. David blabbered on, perked by stims and double-strength cidercaff even as Kane's defenses were lowered by the merest legal whiff of tranks.

They paid special attention when David uncovered the group that had carried out the bombing that had wracked Lisbon three months before. *L'Ogre* had been experimenting with an alliance with terrorists. Now those same terrorists were unveiled in the same way that *l'Ögre* was being dissected.

David breathed a sigh of relief; on Luna those same explosions could have killed tens of thousands.

"You know we can't use this stuff directly in court," Sugar told him on a break from the Police Academy. Her application had been accepted so quickly David wondered if anyone named Applegate had sped it along.

On Terra, hundreds of detectives sprang into action, opening closed files. Questioning old suspects with new questions. Digging in new places. Piecing together cases that would now hold up in court.

"They have no idea it was you," Lieutenant Savonarola told David. "Our records will show that Kane never spilled a word. He'll be put away for life up here for the murder of Dougie Chu and the attempt on the Applegates, and will never have a chance to communicate with anyone on Earth. His Terran lawyer will be too busy trying to save the rest of the organization to even talk with him."

"There's no rejuv for felons, right?" David asked.

"None. You'll outlive him by at least a century." The lieutenant shook his hand. Very gently, around the splint. "You've done two worlds a great service."

David held Pippin close as she admired her new Lunar Cultural Treasure license, the first of its kind.

"Sugar says it's good for at least five years," she told him. "And as long after that as the art-lover tourist ships keep coming in from Earth."

"They'll be coming for a long, long time," he assured her.

"Yours will last just as long." While the courts were still smiling favorably upon him, David had secured a special license for limited personal eccentricity just before returning his hair to its natural (and rather violent) red.

Above them a tree limb swayed. Its burden of ripe apples swung precariously near their heads as Jonathan ran pell-mell, his tail a glorious arch of pure freedom. Pippin clutched David as Jonathan made a daring leap, and he couldn't withhold a wince of pain.

"I'm sorry!" She immediately backed off.

He tried to make light of it. "It's nothing," he said of his taped ribs. "You know, I used to tell some of my patients that they should stop beating themselves up so badly, but now I think that I'm the only one who ever really did that."

Pippin gave him a sly smile and leaned back to him, careful not to touch any of his most sensitive wounds, which she knew well. "So. You'll stop beating yourself up?"

"I will."

"Good. In that case, I'll take care of you."

"No no, I'll take care of *you.*"

"No, I'll take care of *you.*"

They went at it a few more rounds until they both chuckled and faded into a noninjurious but contented hug.

"I want to name the new clinic after Jonathan," David said. "He's the guy who brought us together."

"And you'll use Ethan Kane's accounts to finance it?"

"Cops gave their okay. Mama Evie's lawyer said that up here there's an ancient tradition of 'finders, keepers' that can be invoked despite the law. If the money's going to a good cause, the courts will overlook the fact that it doesn't quite belong to me."

"Ah, Lunatic law," Pippin murmured.

They walked further, loosely trailing Jonathan's path through the trees. Above them, a full Earth shone above the crater's lighting.

"Aunt Evie says she's going to name the first orange hybrid after you. 'David,' with a French accent. She says it'll be more marketable that way." Pippin shook her head. "Don't expect it for a while. The Miranda orchard is starting from pure Terran stock. It'll take time to produce Lunar hybrids."

"By then I think they'll be called 'Samuel' orangapples anyway," David said. "Under all that steel, Mama Evie's got a heart of mush."

"Maybe. And maybe we'll come up with two new hybrids instead of one." She perked up. "New types of trees to paint. New still lifes. I've never been into orange much before– I mean, other than the siennas– but I might be willing to experiment by then."

"We'll all be experimenting by then," David told her. "I mean to fix this society, get everyone back to being what they were supposed to be. Destined to be." Even with his injuries he couldn't stop smiling these days. "You do know that I love you?" he asked.

"I knew that you loved me even when you didn't know," Pippin said.

"But maybe I knew that you knew that–"

She shushed him with a finger to his healing lips. "I know. And I love you too, you big pussycat."

It was difficult to kiss around the hard bandages that covered his broken nose and restructured chin, but by now they knew what angles to attempt their approaches. This time they got it exactly right.

"This is my destiny," David declared softly. "Here, with you, and doing the good work. How often is it that a skilled psychiatrist is faced with a world of Lunatics?"

"Oh, like you aren't as well." She snuggled under his arm sling. "Sometimes I think you're an artist too. That's why you could look at my work and *see,* unlike everyone else."

David placed his unhindered palm upon his heart. "I am a sculptor of souls," he intoned with solemnity that made Pippin break into laughter.

"I like it. It's even better because it's absolutely true."

"Pippin," David asked, "are there any snakes on Luna? Any serpents?"

"Snakes?" She leaned back to try to figure out this new conversational arc from his expression. "Of course not. Well, maybe in a reptile exhibit somewhere, but…"

David crouched and then with a whoop jumped up to pluck a juicy-looking apple from a branch in this, his Garden of Eden. He offered it to Pippin.

"Grow old with me. The best is yet to be," he said, and she accepted with a knowing smile.

An answering yowl echoed through the trees. Beyond them, Jonathan leaped in an arc six times mightier than any Terran cat could hope for, to prowl the forests of Luna.

* * *

When you think of strong women and strange worlds, think Carol A. Strickland.

Although born in a small town in Illinois noted for its Nineteenth Century demonic possession cases, Carol claims that all those voices inside her head are a result of having stories to tell and books to write. Even so, her strange devotion to and study of Wonder Woman would seem to indicate an abby-normal brain.

A one-time comics letterhack and outspoken member of various comics message boards, Carol has found herself the basis for two comic book villains (at times her opinions have not been taken well by the books' creators) (both villains were soundly thrashed) (and both, for some perverse reason, were male) and had one superhero wear her costume design. (Light Lass!)

Carol has also become an award-winning painter. Along with her writing, she exercises this skill in her secondary hours (both of them) as she waits for the lottery to free her 9-to-5 time to more fulfilling pursuits.

Dear Reader,

I hope you had as much fun reading this as I did writing it. I'd appreciate it if you left an honest review, good or bad (hopefully not meh, but that's okay as well) on your favorite book site. Reviews are gold! (And thank you for leaving one!)

Come on over to my website: http://www.CarolAStrickland.com and look around. There's lots to see there, including info on my other books and really, too much ranting information about Wonder Woman. Can I help it if I'm obsessed? Or join me on my Facebook Pro Page (look for Carol A. Strickland), where I'll be holding occasional contests and generally jabbering away. This is something I also do on my blog: http://carolastrickland.blogspot.com, where I'm liable to write TMI by the bucketload.

Now if you don't mind, I'm off to do some *plein air* painting of my own. Where'd I leave that blasted bug spray?

Keep reaching for the stars!

Carol Strick